Lizzy Albright

and the
Attic Window

Ricky Tims *and* Kat Bowser

Publisher
Autumn Rock Publishing. All rights reserved
under International and Pan-American Copyright
Conventions. No part of this publication may be
reproduced, distributed, or transmitted in any
form or by any means, including photocopying,
recording, or other electronic or mechanical
methods, without the prior written permission of
the publisher, except in the case of brief quotations
embedded in critical reviews and certain other
noncommercial uses permitted by copyright law.
For permission requests, contact the publisher.

Editor Jan Mark
Cover Illustration Ricky Tims and Joyce Robinson
Digital Illustrations and Maps Ricky Tims
Graphic Design Joyce Robinson

Acknowledgements
Margaret Boe, of Edinburgh, Scotland, for assisting
with McDoogle's Scottish brogue.

Scott Avery, Sarah Christian, Susan Cusenbary,
Carolyn Martin, Kellan Scott, and Toi Scott, for their
input and guidance.

www.lizzyalbright.com

ISBN 978-1-7352986-0-3
First edition printing, July 2020.
1-2020 ARP

Printed in the USA

"To all those who believe in the unbelievable and reach for the impossible."

—Ricky Tims

"To family and friends for support, encouragement, and inspiration."

—Kat Bowser

CONTENTS

Ricky Tims

Ricky Tims has enjoyed a long and diverse career that coalesced from a variety of creative art forms. He is well-known in the international quilt industry as a TV host, best-selling author, teacher, award-winning quiltmaker, fabric designer, inspirational speaker, and live performance entertainer. He was selected as one of the Thirty Most Distinguished Quilters in the World. The readers of *Quilter's Newsletter Magazine* voted him (in a three-way tie with Alex Anderson and Karey Bresenhan) as the Most Influential Person in the Quilting Industry. The popular national television news show *CBS News Sunday Morning* featured him as one of their profiles.

Ricky, a gifted musician since early childhood, is a pianist, conductor, composer, arranger, music producer, and performing artist. With the publication of this book, he adds novelist to his long list of creative endeavors. Ricky was born and raised in North Texas, but now resides on a remote mountain not far from the small town of La Veta in Southern Colorado.

Kat Bowser

Kat Bowser is a dynamic vocalist and consummate entertainer. Her performances—ranging from her remarkable tributes to Janis Joplin to her intimate piano bar weekends on Fort Lauderdale Beach—have thrilled local music lovers and tourists from around the world. She has toured internationally with recording artists Oleta Adams and Jon Secada, opened for Tony Bennett and other celebrity vocalists, and performed with a who's who of recording artists like Sam Moore, Robben Ford, Russ Taff, Don Felder, Carl Verheyen, and Larry Dunn.

She has been an integral part of the studio scene for years. Kat's voice has appeared on hundreds of records. An LA session guitarist and member of the English rock band Supertramp, Carl Verheyen, says, "I've met many studio singers on the LA session scene, but none quite as versatile as Kat Bowser. Her range is from Janis to Ella and everything in between. But it's when she sings with her own unique voice that her emotional impact is the most powerful!" Kat is a native of Overland Park, Kansas, a suburb of Kansas City, now residing in Fort Lauderdale, Florida.

Ricky and Kat met in the mid-1980s in Waco, Texas, when they were introduced during a joint musical endeavor. A lifelong friendship was born. Over the years, the two have recorded and performed together often. This book is their collaborative effort in the literary realm. It is the result of Kat's vision to create a story that would inspire a new generation of quilters—a story inspired by a quilt, but not necessarily *about* a quilt. While the original idea for Lizzy was to write a book targeted to young children, the idea grew to become an imaginative fantasy novel with diverse appeal that would connect generations. They believe this is only the beginning of the Lizzy Albright journey. Bang!

7

GRANNY'S 1930 SAMPLER

Sampler quilts featured a variety of different quilt blocks. This is the quilt that Lizzy's gandmother, Esther McHale, made during the Great Depresssion.

1 Doves in the Window

2 Dresden Plate

3 Mariner's Compass

4 Jacob's Ladder

5 Old Maid's Puzzle

6 Churn Dash

7 Storm at Sea

8 Postage Stamp

9 LeMoyne Star

10 Snail's Trail

11 Double Pinwheel

12 Square in a Square

13 Robbing Peter to Pay Paul

14 Scottie Dog

15 Double Nine-Patch

16 Sawtooth Star

17 New York Beauty

18 Ohio Star

19 Rail Fence

20 Pickle Dish

21 Puss in the Corner

22 Sunbonnet Sue

23 Friendship Star

24 Kaleidoscope

25 Hunter's Star

26 Bear Paw

27 Spools

28 Pineapple

29 Fifty-Four Forty or Fight

30 Honey Bee

31 Moon Over the Mountain

32 Tumbling Blocks

33 Grandmother's Flower Garden

34 Grandmother's Fan

35 Delectable Mountains

36 Courthouse Steps

37 Dutchman's Puzzle

38 Birds in the Air

39 Double Wedding Ring

40 Log Cabin

41 Broken Dishes

42 Kansas Dugout

9

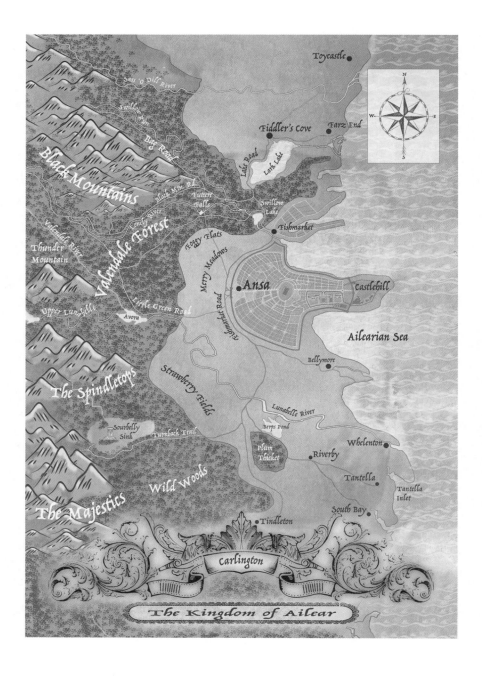

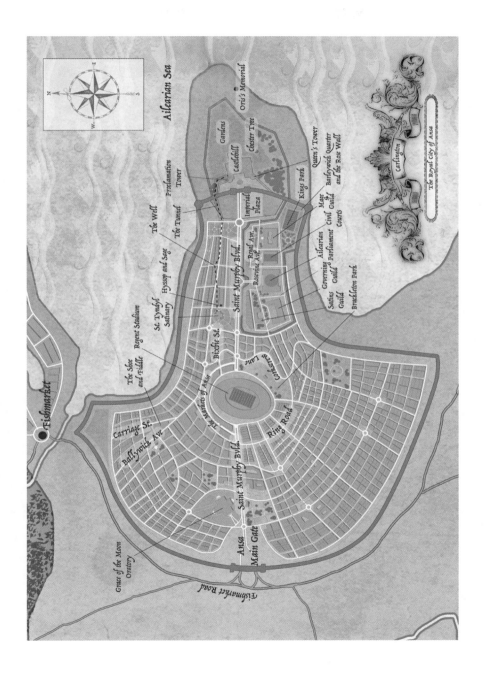

Ailearian Sea

The Royal City of Ansa

Carfington

Orti's Memorial
Gardens
Chester Tree
Castlehill
Proclamation Tower
Queen's Tower
King Park
Bartywick Quarter and the Rose Wall
The Well
The Tunnel
Imperial Plaza
Royal Ave.
Roevine Ave.
Mace
Hyssop and Sage
Saint Murphy Blvd.
Governing Ailearian Guild
Parliament Civil Guild Courts
St. Tymbf Satinary
Sabits Guild
Brackleton Park
Regent Stadium
The Shoe and Fiddle
Bicchie St.
Concerta Lane
The Markets of Ansa
Carriage St.
Bailywick Ave.
Ring Road
Grace of the Moon Oratory
Saint Murphy Blvd.
Ansa Main Gate
Fishmarket Road
Fishmarket

PRELUDE

A Dire Situation

The room erupted in chaos.

"Who would have predicted that she could have gathered such a force? They are indomitable!" shouted Orlin from his perch on the bench.

"So it appears," shouted another council member, "but Ailear is doomed if we don't find a way to stop her."

"And just how do you propose to do that?" demanded one of the other mages.

There were several mages who held the opinion that apprehending the sorceress was the highest priority. They were incensed that the senators had not yet taken any action. Others argued that she should be left alone and that their primary focus was to locate the child.

Baron, the newly elected high mage banged the gavel and stood. Being a bear, his domineering presence commanded the attention of the council members. "Order!" he roared. "We will have order in this chamber immediately!"

The assembly reluctantly obeyed.

"It appears she has only one goal," continued Baron.

"Beyond that, she has never been a serious threat. As mages, we are the only ones who can find the child and bring her back. Is our librarian, Ms. Flutterfield, present?"

"I am, Your Excellency," Gertie replied.

"Would you please approach the bench."

Christmas Eve 1964: Be Careful What You Wish For

Lizzy didn't mind that her birthday was on Christmas Eve. She simply pretended the whole world was decorated in her honor. She loved the sights, sounds, smells, and flavors of the season. Mrs. Albright always made sure that Lizzy received a proper birthday cake and that her birthday gifts and Christmas gifts were kept separate.

Lizzy's tenth birthday began this morning when Mr. and Mrs. Albright woke her with a vibrant rendition of "Happy Birthday."

Lizzy rubbed her eyes, sat up in her canopy bed, and said, "Is it really? I forgot all about it." Of course, she hadn't forgotten about her birthday at all. She had been so excited last night that before bed, her stomach was full of butterflies. She wasn't even asleep when her parents came into her room, even though she pretended to be.

"Do you want to open your gifts now or after we have lunch?" Mrs. Albright asked.

"Hmmm...I'll wait," Lizzy responded. Although she really wanted to open them right away, she chose to delay opening the presents in order to make the birthday part of her day last a little longer. She knew that soon enough the family would be driving to Granny's house for their annual Christmas gathering and her birthday would be overshadowed by the trip.

"I made your favorite chocolate cake. I'm sure Granny will have something for you too! We'll celebrate twice today!"

"A double celebration," Lizzy thought to herself. She decided she would to try to fall asleep on the ride to Granny's and upon waking, she would pretend it was a completely new day making her the only one in the world with a two-day birthday.

Mr. and Mrs. Albright left her room. She heard her father shout down the hallway, "Doug! Allen! Up and at 'em! Times a-wasting!"

Lizzy had begun packing for the trip before she went to bed. She would, of course, be taking Fluffs, a larger-than-life stuffed rabbit that Lizzy's Aunt Rachel had given to her on her second birthday and had been her constant companion ever since. He had extra-long ears, a few patches where his fur had worn thin, and a broken seam along his back that Granny had helped repair. He was also missing an eye. On more than one occasion Lizzy had fashioned an eye-patch for Fluffs and pretended that the two of them were off sailing in a pirate ship looking for deserted islands and hidden treasure. Lizzy picked up Fluffs and wound the little key on his belly. The music box inside began to softly play "Brahms' Lullaby."

She walked over to her bookshelf and began reading the titles on the spines, trying to decide which book to take with her. She considered *Rumpelstiltskin*, *King Arthur and His Knights of the Round Table* and *Charlie and the Chocolate Factory*. She then pulled *The Wonderful Wizard of Oz* from the shelf. She flipped through the pages looking at the illustrations and reflecting.

Since Lizzy was born in Kansas, *The Wizard of Oz* was one of her favorite stories. She never missed the annual presentation of *The Wizard of Oz* on television. Since the movie started at six o'clock, it was a family tradition to have dinner in the living room. Mrs. Albright would make tuna melt sandwiches with mac and cheese served on TV trays. This was one of the few times dinner was allowed in the living room. Mr. Albright was in charge of making popcorn, which he always did about the time Dorothy met Scarecrow in the cornfield.

Even though Lizzy knew the entire story, when the scene in the haunted forest began, she would crawl up next to her dad. The lingering scent of his Old Spice cologne reminded her that she was safe at home, that this was just a story, and that there were no haunted forests in the real world.

Watching *The Wizard of Oz* in 1962 was the most memorable of all. That was the year when the Albrights bought their first color television. They watched with great anticipation for the moment when Dorothy landed in Munchkinland and the dismal black-and-white of the previous scenes turned into magical and vibrant Technicolor.

Lizzy closed the book and put it back on the shelf. "Not this time," she thought to herself. After scanning the bookshelf again, her eye came to rest on a particular favorite.

"*Alice in Wonderland*," Lizzy said out loud. "Yes!"

To Lizzy, Wonderland was more of a real place than a fantasyland. She loved to create makeshift costumes and act out scenes from her books. Once, she used the foil from a used Jiffy Pop popcorn container to make the perfect crown for her role as the Queen of Hearts. She then spent the rest of the day going up to her brothers and saying, "Off with his head!" She removed the book from the shelf and placed it next to Fluffs on the bed. She folded up the well-loved, but not tattered, snuggle quilt that Granny made for her when she started first grade. Granny explained the quilt featured the Rail Fence pattern, but Lizzy never thought it looked much like any fence she had ever seen.

After lunch Mrs. Albright presented the chocolate cake, illuminated with ten red, yellow, and blue candles.

"Make a wish," Mr. Albright said.

"Hang on," said Lizzy. "I'm thinking!" But she wasn't thinking at all. Lizzy was just prolonging her moment in the spotlight. She knew exactly what she would wish for—a new red cloak that she had seen a girl wearing in a television commercial. Over the past several weeks she had mentioned it to her mom several times. This was her wish. Finally, she opened her eyes.

"Blow out the candles," Mrs. Albright instructed.

"All in one breath," Allen reminded Lizzy.

Lizzy easily extinguished the candles.

"Wait for the wishing candle," her oldest brother, Doug, said.

They all watched and waited to see which candle had a wisp of smoke lingering the longest before it was fully extinguished. That was the wishing candle. Doug plucked out the wishing candle, licked the icing off the bottom, and handed it to Lizzy.

"Put this under your pillow tonight so your wish will come true," Doug instructed.

"Here you go, birthday girl!" Mrs. Albright said as she served the first piece to Lizzy. It was a corner piece with extra icing.

"Open ours first, Lizzy," Allen insisted impatiently, pointing at a wrapped gift. "Doug and I went in on it together."

Lizzy could easily tell by the size and shape that it was a new record album.

"Hmmm...I wonder what it could be," Lizzy said jokingly. Everyone laughed. She loved to sing along to records and was thrilled that her brothers thought to give her one for her birthday.

As she peeled back the wrapping paper, she shrieked in delight.

"It's exactly what I wanted! *Beatles '65*!"

Lizzy had the first four albums from the Beatles and this newest release completed her collection.

"I can't wait to play this! Thank you!"

"And here's our gift, Sweetie" Mr. Albright said as he put what looked to be another album in front of her. "Something to counter-balance that rock-and-roll stuff."

She unwrapped the record. "Barbra Streisand! I love her music too. Thanks, Mom and Dad!" Lizzy loved to sing along to her albums, usually drowning out the superstars.

"That's not all, Lizzy," Mr. Albright said. "Here's a string for you to follow."

Whenever a gift was too big or too awkward to wrap, Mr. and Mrs. Albright would hide it somewhere in the house and run a long string from the gift to the kitchen. Following the string made for a fun adventure of anticipation.

"Oh, wow. Now I really don't know what to think," Lizzy said excitedly. She took the end of the string, remembering that last year a new purple Schwinn bike was at the end of the string.

She followed it through the kitchen, into the living room, circled through the family room, until the string ended at the door leading to the basement. Lizzy turned the doorknob and descended the stairs to the finished basement. She saw what appeared to simply be a large wooden cabinet, but Lizzy knew exactly what it was...a new Magnavox stereo record player and radio.

Lizzy stood frozen with her mouth open. "It's wonderful!" she finally said.

She quickly ran over to the stereo and slid open the top, revealing the turntable and radio. The smell of new electronics permeated the air.

"This is for the whole family to use, but we knew that you'd use it the most," Mrs. Albright said with a wink and a smile. "Well, you and Doug."

Lizzy didn't mind that the stereo was more of a family gift. She was just happy to know she could play her new records and sing to her heart's delight.

"Can I play my new records now?" Lizzy asked with excitement.

Mr. Albright looked at his watch. "I 'spose so, but unfortunately there's only time for one of them. There's a winter storm moving in this evening. I want to be sure to get to Cordelia before it hits, so we need to get on the road as soon as possible."

Doug, being in on the secret that the family was getting a new stereo, had followed Lizzy to the basement with her records in hand. "Here! I have a few of my own that I can't wait to hear on this thing, but since it's your birthday, you get first crack at it."

Knowing the boys wouldn't care about listening to Barbra, Lizzy chose to play the Beatles album. When she peered inside, she noticed a small 45 record already on the turntable. She looked closely and read the title.

"'Eight Days a Week'!" she shouted with delight.

"It sure is—and it looks like it's headed to number one on the charts this week. There was an extra copy at the radio station and they all wanted you to have it for your birthday," confessed Mr. Albright.

"Oh my, I'm so happy! Please tell them thank you!"

Lizzy lowered the needle down onto record. The three kids instantly began singing and dancing along to the music. It didn't surprise them when Mr. Albright started singing along with them. Ollie Albright was not only a good singer, but he was also a DJ for a local radio station and was familiar with all the latest pop music. His famous DJ signoff was "This is Ollie Albright, playing all the gold, all the time!" Because of her father's profession, Lizzy was exposed to all kinds of music.

When Lizzy was little, she always listened to her father on the radio. Once she started school, her school hours kept her from listening to his program; so every evening at the dinner table Lizzy would ask her father what songs he played that day. Yesterday they had talked about how popular "Rockin' Around the Christmas Tree" had become.

After "Eight Days a Week" ended, Lizzy changed the switch from 45 to 33 and put on Side One of *Beatles '65*. She sat down close to the front of the Magnavox, closed her eyes, and absorbed every note and word. Soon a dull whirring sound alerted Lizzy that the album had finished playing. She looked around to find that she was the only one left in the basement.

"It's time to pack the car, Lizzy," Mrs. Albright called down the stairs.

"OK, Mom." Lizzy carefully put her records back in their sleeves, turned the power off, and closed the lid. She then skipped up the stairs, humming Beatles songs to herself.

"Go ahead and bring your suitcase to the garage, Lizzy. I think your father is eager to get on the road soon."

Mr. Albright had backed the station wagon to the opened garage door and the family began filing out with suitcases and wrapped Christmas presents.

Allen, being a typically curious thirteen-year-old, inspected each wrapped box before putting it in the car. His sloppy blond hair swooshed around as he held each package to his ear and shook it.

"By the shape and sound of this box, I'd say this is a jigsaw puzzle," Allen proclaimed with certainty.

Lizzy rolled her eyes and began humming to herself to drown out his guesses. Suddenly she remembered she had better act fast. "I call dibs on the very back seat," she announced.

The Albrights' 1960 Chevrolet Kingswood station wagon had a rear seat that faced backwards. Lizzy always asked for this seat. Even with the extra luggage and gifts, she was still small enough to be comfortable making a nest with her snuggle quilt, Fluffs, and a book.

"You don't have to call dibs on that seat, Lizzy," Doug said. "It makes everyone want to puke riding backwards."

In reality, Doug was fairly big for a fifteen-year-old. His stocky build made it difficult for him to fit into the very back seat, but it made him the perfect football candidate at school. Mrs. Albright wouldn't allow Doug to play football after one of his friends was injured. He was secretly happy that he could blame his mom as the reason he left the team. He had started playing electric guitar and had visions of being a rock star. He recently began to pester his parents for permission to let him grow his hair longer.

"I like the very back seat," Allen said defiantly.

"Too late, I called dibs first," Lizzy said, reminding Allen of the rules for calling dibs.

"Then I call dibs for the trip back," said Allen.

"You can't call dibs that far in advance. That's not fair," Lizzy said.

Mr. Albright interrupted the squabbling kids and redirected their attention by pointing toward the sky and saying, "Look up there! Hear that squawking?" As they looked up, they saw geese flying overhead in a V-shaped formation.

He explained, "Those geese are flying south for the winter. You can always tell that it's about to turn really cold when you see them fly in formation headed south." Then Mr. Albright began imitating the geese by prancing about and flapping his arms—making the whole family laugh out loud.

"Do you think they are talking to each other?" Lizzy asked.

"I s'pose they could be. Maybe they're even singing their own version of 'Eight Days A Week'," said Mr. Albright with a wink and a smile.

Seeing the flying geese reminded Lizzy that she had not filled the bird feeders in the backyard. She raced back through the garage and grabbed two old coffee cans to fill with seed and acorns.

"What are you doing?" Mrs. Albright called out to Lizzy. "We have to get on the road before the storm hits."

"The bird feeders, Mom. I'll be quick," Lizzy yelled back.

Lizzy ran to the backyard and began filling the bird feeders that were hanging from three Bartlett pear trees next to the fence. She began talking to the birds even though none were nearby. "Now listen up, birdies, you have to make this food last a whole week, and Mr. Squirrel, here are some acorns for you and your friends so leave the bird feeders alone!"

Lizzy, still humming Beatles tunes to herself, headed back to the house. She brushed the seed from her coat and felt a chill in the air. The sky had begun to turn a dark gray.

Hearing a squawking noise overhead, she looked up and saw one goose all alone. She assumed it had fallen behind the rest of the formation. She called out, "Catch up to your friends, Mr. Goose. You need to fly south to stay warm. If you get lost, you can follow us, we're going south too!"

Lizzy perceived that the bird looked directly at her and imagined that it understood every word she said. In fact, Lizzy always felt that it was much easier to talk to animals than people.

"Okay, I think we're all packed," Mr. Albright said. "Everyone, use the bathroom now. We'll only stop once for a break."

"Don't forget to wash your hands," Mrs. Albright instructed as the kids rushed back into the house.

"I call dibs on where we stop! I choose Whipples," Allen said, still intent on winning a dibs game.

Margaret Albright, who everyone called "Maggie", had long brunette hair that was always neatly teased and pinned into the popular "beehive" look and held in place with a heavy dose of Aqua Net hairspray.

Lizzy's hair, on the other hand, was curly, unruly, and flaming red. Being the only redheaded family member, it had once crossed her mind that she could have been adopted. She quickly dropped that notion after she learned that her McHale lineage was Scottish and the McHales all had intensely red hair.

Lizzy washed her hands and looked into the mirror. She let out a sigh as she studied her freckles and frazzled hair. Dad had given her his brown eyes, but her mom had given Lizzy her freckles. They dotted her nose and cheeks in unmistakable abundance. Lizzy did not like her freckles and learned early on that no amount of soap, water, or scrubbing would wash them off. She made a silly face at herself in the mirror, dried her hands, and ran back to the car.

A Whistle-stop at Whipples

"Are we there yet?" asked Lizzy as she closed the back car door. The station wagon was still parked in the driveway.

"Very funny," Doug said snarkily.

Lizzy thought it would be funny to get a jump-start on the typical travel silliness, but the timing of her joke was off and it didn't elicit the expected result from her brothers. Even so, she had not been ignored. Mrs. Albright, while placing two packets of Juicy Fruit chewing gum and a fresh box of Kleenex in the glove box, replied in a sing-songy lilt, "No, we're not there yet!" Pulling down the sun visor, she looked into the mirror, puckered and pursed her lips, and freshened up her lipstick. "We're off," she said.

"Off like a herd of turtles in a sea of peanut butter!" Mr. Albright said as he pulled out of the driveway.

"I thought it was 'off like a dirty shirt,'" said Lizzy.

"That works too," said Mr. Albright, peering into the rearview mirror. "I should say it works on those occasions when we get going lickety-split. But that wasn't today, now was it?" He clicked on the left blinker and turned onto West 99th Street.

"I like 'off like a herd of turtles in a sea of peanut butter' better," Allen laughed.

Doug replied, "Well, I like 'off like a dirty shirt' the best!"

Lizzy was gazing out through the back window when she spotted a lone goose off in the distance. It seemed to be traveling in the same direction they were. She froze with curiosity. Was this the same goose she had seen earlier? Was he really following them? And that's when she shouted, "Off like a south-bound goose!"

"Good one, Lizzy!" replied Mrs. Albright.

They puttered along, winding their way toward the main highway. Even though it was early afternoon, they each took turns pointing out the various holiday decorations along the way.

Traffic was light and a blanket of quietness fell over the car. The only thing to be heard was the humming of the engine and the gentle whirr of the tires rolling on pavement. They had barely crossed Overland Park's city limits when Lizzy broke the silence.

"Are we there yet?"

She giggled under her breath, knowing that this time the question would get a better reaction.

"Are we there yet? Are we there yet?" Allen repeated. He mimicked Lizzy by using a whining falsetto. Lizzy smiled.

"I'm hot," said Doug.

"I'm cold," replied Allen.

"I'm hungry," added Doug.

"I need to pee," Lizzy giggled.

Everyone laughed.

The station wagon finally reached the main highway, turned left, and headed south. Mr. Albright reached over and switched on the radio just as Burl Ives was beginning to sing "Have a Holly, Jolly Christmas". They all joined in singing along.

The song ended and the radio announcer said in a lively and robust voice, "It's not too late for you to have your own holly, jolly Christmas. The Christmas tree lot located by the Woolworth's department store on the corner of Troost and Linwood has a few trees left for any of you Scrooges out there who just might have a change of heart today. Fresh Scotch pines along with noble and Fraser firs are still available, as well as my personal favorite — the blue spruce! Everything is 75% off until the lot closes at 10 p.m. tonight."

"I want to be Scrooge!" Doug said.

"You can't be Scrooge," exclaimed Lizzy. "You *like* Christmas. Mr. Scrooge hated Christmas. He thought it was a humbug."

"Maybe I do like Christmas, but I still like the idea of being a Scrooge."

Once they began driving through the countryside, they played a couple of short-lived road trip games and intermittently sang along with the Christmas songs on the radio. As usual, it wasn't long before everyone migrated to their own dreamworlds. Mr. and Mrs. Albright softly spoke about some recent PTA issues. Eventually the din of the road hypnotized the kids. Soon daydreams and drowsiness won out over radios and road games. Their eyes shut and their heads nodded.

An hour had passed when Mrs. Albright broke the silence and asked, "Guess where we are?" Nobody answered.

She looked back to see Doug and Allen with their eyes closed. Lizzy was surely laying down as no part of her could be seen. Mrs. Albright reached back and tapped Allen on the knee.

"Are you awake? Guess where we are?" She said more loudly.

Allen opened his eyes and looked out. "Alright! Iola! Are we stopping at Whipples?"

Lizzy popped her head up over the rear seat and chimed in, "Are we?"

The small town of Iola was situated halfway along the Albrights' route from Overland Park to Cordelia and sat at the intersection of two well-traveled state roads. While the Portland Cement Company may have been the town's biggest employer, the most popular place in Iola was Whipples Café. The A-frame building with its iconic red roof was famous for their chicken-fried steak platter and a huge assortment of ice cream, milk shakes, and malts. To Lizzy, reading the list of ice cream toppings was like going through the nail polish colors in the Avon catalog. Even though it was cold outside, everyone in the family ordered an ice cream cone except Lizzy.

"I'll have a banana split with chocolate ice cream, nuts, whipped cream, and two cherries on top!" she ordered excitedly.

"Please put two spoons on that," Mrs. Albright instructed the clerk behind the counter, knowing that Lizzy would not be able to devour a full banana split on her own.

After about twenty minutes, Mr. Albright announced, "Okay, everybody...let's get going."

"But I'm not done with my banana split," Lizzy whined.

"Here, I'll help," Doug said as he grabbed one of the cherries and shoved it into his mouth.

"Mom!" Lizzy cried to her mother.

"Douglas! Apologize to your sister!" Mrs. Albright said firmly.

Doug knew that if their full first names were spoken, it was serious business. When it came to discipline in the Albright home, there was one thing all three kids knew for certain: when their first, middle, *and* last names were used, they were in serious trouble.

"She was taking too long and...." Doug protested.

"Douglas Brian!" Mrs. Albright interrupted with a more serious tone. He realized that he was heading toward the all-three-names scenario and wisely decided to cease his defense.

CHAPTER TWO

"Sorry, Lizzy," Doug begrudgingly said with no further prompting.

"It's okay. I sort of figured you would do that anyway, which is why I ordered two cherries!" Lizzy shrugged it off and finished her banana split.

As they were leaving Whipples Café, Mr. Albright said, "Maggie, I'll call your mother to let her know what time to expect us."

He went to the pay phone located near the entrance and dropped a dime in the slot. "Operator? Yes. I would like to make a call."

Limited Options

A hush of anticipation filled the council chamber as the librarian came forward.

"Ms. Flutterfield...you are a mage practitioner, is that correct?" asked Baron.

"I am, Your Excellency," confirmed Gertie. "It was my choice to not advance any further. I felt I was better suited for the position as the mage guild librarian. I've held that post for more than fifteen years. I feel I made the right choice."

"Would you be willing to relinquish your post and finish training to become a master mage?"

Gertie was taken by surprise. It was not something she had ever considered. "Why are you asking? What purpose would it serve?"

"In order to find the child, we must appoint a master mage that has the ability to fly long distances. Orlin is a master mage, but being an owl, it's not likely that he could successfully make the long journey. You're a goose, so you can more easily manage the trip. You would have to become a master mage. That will take time...and a serious commitment."

Gertie had not comprehended how complicated that it would be to locate the child. "I must be honest with you," she replied. "I don't feel qualified. I know my limitations and I'm afraid I would fail. It would take several years and we only have ten years before Castlehill is lost. May I suggest another option?"

"Yes, what is it?" asked Baron.

"My daughter recently finished secondaries and has already started training as an apprentice mage. She was *primo perfecto* during her last two years of school. She's smart. I'm confident that she could advance quickly if the mages would allow it."

Murmurs rose from the assembly.

"We only have ten years," cautioned Igree. "There's only been one other mage in the history of Ailear who advanced from apprentice to master in such a short time. It would be a risk."

"Perhaps...but appointing me would be a bigger risk," confessed Gertie. "I highly recommend that the council consider my daughter."

After much deliberation, the council voted unanimously to accept Gertie's proposal. The quest to find the princess had begun.

Lizzy
Albright

CHAPTER THREE

The Pride of Cordelia

"Hello?" Granny asked as she picked up the phone receiver. "Oh, hello, Oliver!... Iola? Wonderful! Well, you're making good time!... No, there's no big change in the weather here yet. It's just cold. Okay, we'll see you soon and thanks for calling."

Granny hung up the receiver, walked through the hall, and went back into the kitchen. Nellie, Granny's live-in helper, had just checked on the roast beef and was at the sink peeling sweet potatoes. She hummed along with the radio, as Brenda Lee sang "Rockin' Around the Christmas Tree." She didn't know all the words, but she jumped right in and sang along to "Deck the halls with boughs of holly," which was her favorite part. Nellie was always cheerful.

"They'll be here in about ninety minutes. We better hurry things up, Nellie. We will have to use the quick set method. Would you please hand me the Jell-O molds?" Nellie set up the molds and Granny began to pour the green lime-flavored liquid into them.

McDoogle barked, trotted into the kitchen, and sat down next to Granny. "Well, there you are McDoogle! How was your nap? Did you chase any rabbits? Would you like a cookie?" McDoogle wagged his tail. "Okay, just a minute." She stopped what she was doing, reached into his treat jar, and pulled out a dog biscuit. McDoogle sat up on his haunches. "You're such a good dog!" Granny gave McDoogle the biscuit and patted him on the head. "Wanna go outside?" McDoogle gruffed. Granny opened the back door and McDoogle trotted out, saw a ground squirrel, and bolted after it. He had never caught a squirrel—his short legs were not fast enough— but it didn't stop him from trying.

"Sarah did a great job on McDoogle. He looks so handsome, don't you think, Nellie?"

Sarah owned the Happy Pamper, the only groomer in Cordelia. Being a Scottie, McDoogle didn't require a lot of maintenance, but Granny made certain he had regular appointments and always made sure he looked his best for the holidays.

"Indeed he does," replied Nellie. "I love his new red plaid collar!"

"Oh well, you know me, I just couldn't resist it!"

Scottish terriers had been part of the McHale family for generations. In fact, Granny had never lived a day of her life without one. She felt McDoogle was just about the smartest and best-natured dog she had ever owned.

"Which china set should I put out this year?" asked Nellie. "I believe we've used the Currier & Ives set for the last couple of years."

"We have, and it's still my favorite, so I say we use it again this year." Granny paused a moment in thought. "Let's make it a Christmas Eve tradition. Currier & Ives every Christmas Eve," she said with a smile and a lilt in her voice as though she were breaking some rule of etiquette. This particular set of china had a decorative rim of green holly and red berries alternating with sprigs of mistletoe. Each plate had a different winter scene in the center. It was far more spectacular than the other two sets of Christmas china Granny had inherited.

Nellie entered the dining room and went to the cabinet to retrieve the china, "I bet I know where to place each of these," she giggled to herself.

Each grandchild had a favorite plate. Allen always chose the one with the train stuck in a deep snowdrift. Doug liked the plate with the three-mast clipper navigating through an icy passage. Lizzy's favorite was a snowy scene with a large pine tree near the edge of a pond with red grouse snuggled together for warmth. Lizzy was fond of birds and envious that they could fly and she couldn't.

As Nellie set the table, she stopped and noted the opulent room that was scarcely used any more. The room was wrapped in rich mahogany paneling. Antique paintings hung on the walls. There was a large painting by Edwin Lanseer, a portrait of five various breeds of dogs—including a Scottish terrier—sitting regally in a craggy Scottish landscape. The McHales took pride in their Scottish heritage and many indications of that fact were scattered throughout the family mansion.

The antique Chippendale dining table was a showstopper. Dating back to 1770, it too was made of highly-polished mahogany and could accommodate eighteen. The set exhibited the elegant designs typical of the Rococo style. The front legs of each chair gently tapered downward and transitioned at the bottom where they became the feet of a sharp-clawed animal—like a bear or a tiger—that was clinching an orb.

Hanging from the lofty dining-room ceiling was a crystal chandelier that Malcolm McHale rescued from the Penn-Stroud Hotel in Philadelphia before its demolition. There wasn't a person who walked into the McHales' dining room who didn't comment on the magnificent chandelier.

"What fruit shall I put in the Jell-O?" Granny called out to Nellie, who was by now almost finished setting the dining-room table.

"We have fresh grapes, canned pears, and mixed fruit," Nellie responded. "It's also good just plain," she said with a tad more emphasis. That was Nellie's way of saying she preferred Jell-O without fruit in it, and she knew Doug did too.

"No fruit it is!" Granny confirmed. Nellie smiled.

Nellie tended to the final details of the table setting and then went back to the kitchen where Granny was preparing to make her famous homemade cranberry sauce. While it was certainly popular to buy canned cranberry sauce these days, Granny was not giving in to any notion that canned cranberry sauce could possibly come close to measuring up to her culinary standards.

"Esther, do you think it's time I should put the sweet potatoes in the oven?" Nellie was looking at the kitchen clock and the question was intended to be more of a suggestion.

"Oh goodness, yes!" said Granny. "Look at the time! There should be room on the rack below the roast. I s'pect it's almost done."

Esther was Granny's given name. Her full name was Esther Anne McHale-Winters. She had married Nathaniel Winters in 1924 at the age of twenty-four. As a strong independent suffragette in the 1920s, she chose to break with tradition and hyphenate their two last names to show her independence as well as her solidarity with the other suffragettes.

She also kept her financial independence as a way of protecting the McHale fortune and investments. The Missouri-Kansas-Texas railroad had allowed Malcolm McHale to soar to financial success. His son Lincoln, Granny's father, had invested in oil in 1892. That was the year when the Norman No. 1 well struck it rich, kicking off the Kansas oil boom. Holes were being punched in the ground left and right and gushers were springing up all over the region. Malcolm had provided investment funds and gave his full support to Lincoln, who eventually became one of the most successful oilmen in the country. The McHale Oil Company was legendary and the McHales became pillars of support for the region.

The estate on which the mansion sat had once required the service of dozens of workers. The McHale family was known for being generous and kind to their employees. There were farm hands, house maids, a cook named Mr. Butler, and a butler named Mr. Cook. On any given day, the house bustled with family, friends, and workers. As a young girl, Esther befriended everyone who worked at the estate. When some of them began having children, she would often ask to help care for them. Such was the case with Nellie.

Nellie Butler was the daughter of Joseph Butler, the cook. Granny was only ten years old when Nellie was born, and she immediately took to caring for her. When Nellie turned nineteen, she married and moved to Oklahoma. One year later, Nellie's husband died in an accident, leaving Nellie with no source of income. Although by then Esther and Nathan had married and moved to Kansas City, she pleaded with her parents to allow Nellie to move back to the estate and live with the family as long as she needed. They agreed. Nellie was invited to live there and work alongside her father in the kitchen until he retired. After he left, Nellie took over as the main cook, and she had been there ever since. The McHale mansion was Nellie's home, and Esther and Nellie were more like sisters than anything else.

"Nellie, I do think we have managed it!" said Granny. "I guess I better go put the outside lights on. They'll be so surprised to see the decorations that Marcus put up."

Nellie nodded. "I predict they will be *astonished*! Have you told them about your new Christmas tree?"

"Which one?" Granny chuckled. "There's two they don't know about."

"I guess that's true," said Nellie. "You are full of surprises this year."

"I haven't told them anything. I can't wait to see their faces!"

Granny walked down the hall and turned into the foyer. She stopped at the towering grandfather clock. It had been a gift from her parents on her twenty-first birthday.

"Well, sir, you and I are coming upon another birthday, and guess what? We're both still ticking!" Granny wound the clock, walked past the grand staircase, and switched on the outside lights.

Lizzy Albright

Upstairs, Downstairs

Lizzy, having fallen asleep shortly after leaving Whipples, shot up suddenly in the back seat. The sound of the car rolling on the bumpy brick road alerted her to the fact that they had finally made it to Cordelia. The sky was cloaked in gray clouds, but it wasn't fully dark. She looked excitedly out the windows to take in the town's holiday decorations and began pretending it was day two of her birthday celebration.

Cordelia's holiday decorations were so abundant that it made the tiny town feel much larger that it really was.

"Look at the giant Christmas tree!" Allen said, diverting everyone's attention to the park.

In the middle of Glasford Park was a towering Colorado blue spruce. It had been planted in 1871 when Malcom McHale founded and plotted out the community, naming the town after his wife, Cordelia. Everyone in the car *oohed* and *ahhed* at the beautifully decorated tree—even though they had seen it many times before.

A few windows in town still displayed aluminum Christmas trees even though the fad was fading. Their feathery tinsel-like branches were lit up from below by rotating color wheels. Each wheel had four plastic colored panels—green, blue, red, and yellow—perched on a stand with a light. As the light shone through the rotating panels, the trees would appear to change color. Lizzy thought they were beautiful, but she didn't know anyone who had one.

Mr. Albright turned on Parson Street and noticed several taillights in front of him. He slowed and pulled up in line. As the car crawled forward, they soon were able to see people standing outside the main gate of the McHale estate. The scene was puzzling, but they inched forward and slowly made their way to the entrance.

"Holy schmoley!" "Look at that!" "Wow!" "How did she...?" "It's amazing!" All of these exclamations issued forth at the same time.

They were reacting to Granny's decorations. The traffic jam had been caused by sightseers coming to see the new McHale holiday display. Some cars drove by slowly, while other spectators parked and got out to get a closer look. Some were even taking photos with their Kodak Instamatic cameras.

Mr. Albright slowly turned and went through the gate. With eyes popping and mouths agape, they drove into a fantasyland. A fifteen-foot tall, fully decorated Christmas tree stood in the center of the circular drive in front of the house. It even had a twinkling gold star on top!

The posts on the wraparound front porch were dressed with red and white ribbons and matching red and white lights that transformed them into glowing peppermint sticks. Multicolored lights adorned the eaves and outlined the gables. Guardian nutcrackers flanked each side of the large front door.

As magnificent as all that was, the most amazing sight of all was the display on the lawn. A life-sized scene of Santa's workshop was lit up by at least two dozen floodlights. A number of elves were building toys and wrapping packages. One elf was standing on the shoulders of another elf so that it could reach high enough to hang stockings on the mantle of a freestanding fireplace. Two elves were trying to push a train into a gold box that had a big red bow on top. Three elves were trying to heave Santa's gigantic toy sack up into his sleigh. Santa sat in a chair wearing a red union suit and red velvet trousers held up by black suspenders. He was wearing red socks and his big black boots were sitting on the floor beside the chair. He was looking at a book titled *Naughty and Nice*. Mrs. Claus was standing next to him holding his red jacket and pointing to the mantle clock. It was obvious she was coaxing him to hurry up. Off to the side, nine reindeer were supervising the elves' activities. Rudolf, with his red lightbulb nose, was easy to spot. The whole scene was a snapshot frozen in time.

Granny always had the house decorated with lights, but this year's added attraction had people driving from miles around just to see it! It was by far the most extravagant display ever created in Labette County.

The family parked near the front steps and saw Granny standing on the porch eagerly waiting to greet them. The station wagon doors flew open and the kids rushed to greet her.

As Lizzy began running toward the house, McDoogle ran out and greeted her.

"McDoo!" she exclaimed.

Lizzy knelt to the ground and opened up her arms to embrace the barking dog.

"Hi, McDoo...what?...how?...I'm glad to...calm down...I love you too." Lizzy could barely get a word in as McDoogle excitedly licked her face and made her giggle with delight.

"Happy birthday, Elisabeth," Granny hugged Lizzy and gave her a kiss. "I have a surprise for you that I think you'll like."

Lizzy's eyes lit up. "What is it?"

"It won't be a surprise if I tell you," Granny winked. "So what do you think about the new display?"

"I can't believe it," said Lizzy. "I've never seen anything like it."

After all the hugs and hellos, the kids raced off to see the display up close.

"Watch out for the electric wires!" called Granny.

"How did you manage to do all this?" asked Mrs. Albright.

"I don't know if you saw it, but last year, the *Kansas City Star* published an article with photos about a display that had been put up in Lawrence. I did a bit of snooping around and found the man who did it. His name was Marcus Willowby. He spent all year creating this for me. He's already working on the secret surprise that I will add next year."

"You know you've started something that you can't ever stop, Esther," said Mr. Albright. "But one thing is for sure: it's something people will never forget."

Granny giggled. "Just think of what this will mean to all the children who come to see it. That's what it's for, isn't it? Christmas cheer? And good memories?"

"Indeed it is!" Mr. Albright agreed.

They gave the kids a few more minutes to explore the decorations, and then Granny called out, "Come inside where it's warm!"

As they made their way inside, they all chattered about the new display.

Nellie called out from the parlor, "Y'all come on in here. I've got a fresh batch of hot chocolate ready to warm your bones."

"Nellie!" they exclaimed. They ran to the parlor and gave her warm hugs.

"Please don't tell me how much I've grown!" begged Lizzy. "You always say that."

"Okay," said Nellie. "I promise I won't mention the fact that you must have grown at least two inches since last summer."

Everyone laughed. Nellie was known for having a quick wit.

They gathered in the parlor and drank Nellie's delicious hot chocolate. Granny's decorations were classic and tasteful; the Douglas fir tree was beautifully decorated with traditional multicolored lights, strands of garland, and unique family heirloom ornaments. The whole tree was drenched in tinsel icicles. Doug was excited to see that his favorite bubble lights were strung up and still working.

On the coffee table sat a red, cut-glass bowl with a lid. It usually sat on the kitchen counter, but Granny had moved it to the parlor for this week. Allen was the first to notice it. "Oh boy! I like the butterscotch ones," Allen said, reaching for the lid.

"Good, more caramels for me," Doug laughed, reaching his hand into the bowl.

The candy dish was filled with Brach's candies. Butterscotch, cinnamon, and peppermint discs, along with a variety of toffees and caramels, were always available. Lizzy took two cinnamon disks.

"Where's the ribbon candy?" asked Lizzy.

"Now, don't you worry, Elisabeth. I have a package in the pantry. I just haven't put it out yet."

"Ollie, I think we better go ahead and unload the station wagon," suggested Mrs. Albright.

Mr. Albright nodded in agreement.

"C'mon, you three," said Mrs. Albright. "Time to bring everything in. We don't want to be lugging in suitcases and packages while it's snowing." Mrs. Albright said this more for her own benefit, or rather the benefit of her hairdo, than for anyone else's.

"Awwww," the kids sighed in unison. The cocoa and candy party was interrupted.

Mrs. Albright raised her eyebrows and nodded toward the door.

After grabbing another butterscotch disc, Allen jumped up and headed back outside. Doug and Lizzy followed.

As soon as Lizzy stepped through the door, she heard a familiar honk. She looked across the side lawn where there was a large pond. Next to the pond was a goose, honking and looking right at her.

"Mr. Goose, you followed us!" Lizzy exclaimed.

"What are you talking about?" Allen asked incredulously.

"I saw this goose flying all by itself when I was putting birdseed in the feeders. And I told it to follow us if it got lost."

"It's not the same one, Lizzy," Allen said in his know-it-all tone.

"How do you know? It could be!" Lizzy spiked back.

Allen knew better than to keep up this argument, so he didn't respond. He joined Doug and got busy carrying suitcases and packages inside.

"Now, lookie here, Mr. Goose," Lizzy began, as she slowly stepped toward the large bird. "You need to catch up with your family. A storm is coming and they'll be worried about you." As though it understood every word she said, the goose stood up and expanded its wings. "Go on now! Go south before it starts snowing!"

"Elisabeth Anne!" scolded Mrs. Albright from the porch. "Would you please come help unload."

The goose took a few steps forward, and with one graceful move, it flew away. It circled above the mansion once and then disappeared.

Lizzy had been distracted by the goose. She ran back to the car to help take things inside. The last thing she grabbed was her mother's overnight bag. She knew that it needed to go up to the second floor, to the far back bedroom where her parents always stayed. Because Lizzy frequently visited Granny, she was never scared to explore the old mansion—that is, as long as the lights were on.

She had once overheard other kids in Glasford Park say that the mansion was haunted, so she asked Granny if she had ever seen a ghost.

"I've never seen one. But then again, the McHales are the only ones to have ever lived in this house, so if there are ghosts, they are part of this family." Granny's answer left some question on the matter, but made Lizzy feel like any encounter with a ghost would be a friendly one.

She ascended the main staircase. At the top of the second floor landing, Lizzy stopped and glanced down the hall to another short flight of steps that led up to a door. Behind that door was Lizzy's favorite place in the whole world: the attic. It wasn't like her attic at home. This attic had a wooden floor, and even though it was full of old furniture and boxes of memorabilia, it was organized in a way that made it look as though someone could bring a suitcase and move right in.

Granny was an excellent seamstress and made her own gowns. She stored them in a cedar-lined closet tucked in a corner of the attic. Each gown had a pair of matching satin high heels that Granny had hand-dyed herself.

Lizzy's favorite gown was made from light blue taffeta. It swam around her tiny frame so Granny would pin it up so that it wouldn't drag on the floor. It didn't matter to Lizzy that she looked more like a poorly wound bolt of fabric than the princess she imagined herself to be.

Antique dolls and stuffed animals were piled on tables and lounged in rickety chairs. Lizzy would put the dolls and animals on the seat of an old divan and tell them stories or sing songs. She always included Fluffs in the audience. When she pretended to be a queen, they were her royal subjects.

Sitting beneath the attic window was a cedar chest that held some of Granny's most treasured possessions. Lizzy loved going through the contents of the old chest with Granny. There were jewels and bobbles, hats and gloves, old pictures and letters, and even a fox fur that still had the head on it. Lizzy didn't care much for the fur. She delivered the overnight bag and went back downstairs.

"I smell roast beef," Doug said when he came into the kitchen.

"Indeed you do, and there's sweet potatoes, carrots, and your favorite...lime Jell-O. It's plain this time, no fruit." Granny winked.

Suddenly, Lizzy screamed with delight, "I can't believe it!" She ran in every direction on the main floor shouting, "You've gotta see this! In the solarium! Hurry!" Granny was pleased that Lizzy was the first to find it.

Everyone rushed toward the back of the house to see what Lizzy was so excited about.

"Well, would you look at that!" Mrs. Albright said.

"Groovy!" Doug mumbled under his breath.

Allen stopped in his tracks and just stared. "How does it work?"

Everyone was as still as a statue, standing face-to-face with a six-foot, silver aluminum Christmas tree, complete with a spinning four-color wheel at its base.

"Isn't it fun? Hypnotizing, I would even say. I won it!" Granny said with delight.

"It's so...unlike you," said Mrs. Albright, fumbling for words.

"Oh, phooey! I can be unpredictable sometimes," said Granny, feeling rather proud of herself.

"I did some volunteer work for the annual Cordelia veterans' Christmas dinner. Everyone who volunteered received a raffle ticket to win this tree. At the end of the dinner, my ticket was drawn. I think it's beautiful!"

The entire family couldn't stop staring at it. They soon became mesmerized watching the colors gently shift and change.

"I like when it goes from green to blue," said Lizzy.

Mrs. Albright agreed.

"That's neat, but I keep waiting for when the blue changes to red. I like the purple," added Allen.

They all watched for several minutes, just taking it in and commenting on how peaceful and magical it really was. Finally, Granny said, "Let's eat!"

The table was set for a perfect Christmas Eve dinner. They were all getting situated at the table when the phone rang.

Beehive Beasley Brings Breakfast

Granny put the phone receiver in its cradle and went back to the dining room.

"Pearline is coming over. She says she has a little something to bring by and was going to come tomorrow, but with the bad weather on the way, she wants to come tonight. She'll be here shortly."

"Should I set another place at the table?" asked Nellie.

"No, I don't think she'll be here before we finish dinner."

"It will be great to catch up. I wasn't able to see her the last time I was here," said Mrs. Albright.

Doug nudged Allen and whispered, "Beehive Beasley."

"Or more like 'Buzzing Bee,'" said Allen under his breath.

They both started snickering.

"What was that?" Mrs. Albright asked.

"Nothing," said Doug, scooping up a bite of Jello-O, trying to be evasive.

"You *will* use your manners, Douglas. Do you understand? Pearline is a wonderful friend of mine and I'll not have any of you making fun of her," Mrs. Albright reminded him.

Pearline Beasley and Maggie started first grade together and had been inseparable until they graduated from high school. When Maggie went off to college, Pearline went to beauty school and came back to Cordelia to open her own beauty shop—the Kut-n-Kurl. That's when everyone started calling her Miss Bea on account of her last name and her beehive hairdo. She kept up on all the latest fashion trends featured in magazines such as *Cosmopolitan* and *Mademoiselle*. She was platinum blonde—but not really. She had been blonde for so long nobody knew the natural color of her hair. Her mile-high beehive hairdo swarmed around on the top of her head, making her taller than anyone else in town. Her hips were equally impressive.

Pearline most often wore ruffly, blousy tops made from sheer floral fabrics that wafted and fluttered when she moved about. She thought they made her look dainty—like a butterfly. But "butterfly" was not a word anyone ever used to describe Pearline.

Fortunately, the back doorbell didn't ring until the dinner dishes were being dried and stacked. McDoogle barked. Granny looked out the side window. "Douglas, would you answer that?"

"Hello, Miss Bea," Doug said as he opened the door.

"Douglaz! Douglaz Albright? Goodnezz, graciousz! You're a full grown man! Let me look at you!" She set a casserole dish on the counter next to the door.

"Come here!" She grabbed his face with both hands and gave him a kiss on his forehead. "And you're zshaving!" Pearline said when she felt the soft stubble on his cheeks.

Doug was cringing on the inside and trying very hard not to let it show. He was so relieved when she let go and turned to Lizzy.

"Lizzy, Lizzy, Lizzy!" Pearline took hold of Lizzy's face too, giving her a kiss, and then ran her fingers up through her hair. "Do you know how many people I know who would kill for thiz fabulouz red hair?"

"Thank you, Miss Bea," Lizzy said politely.

Allen, who wanted to avoid the same fate, had quickly grabbed a towel and started drying dishes. But he didn't escape. Pearline still managed to fawn over him too. She made the rounds and greeted everyone with the same effervescence.

"Thank you aaall for allowing me to crazh your partee. I brought thiz egg cazarole for your breakfazt tomorrow. It's called Zouthweztern Zurprize."

"Pearline, you certainly did not need to do that, but thank you very much," said Granny.

While Pearline had many memorable characteristics, it was her unmistakable way of speaking that stood out most. When she was a young girl, she had a rather significant speech impediment. She learned that if she softened each S, it wouldn't whistle, but by doing so, each S sounded more like a Z.

"Pearline, let's go to the solarium and catch up."

"Okay," said Pearline, "but if it ztarts to zleet or znow, I need to leave right away, before the roads get zlick."

"Get ready for this," said Mrs. Albright. "You're not going to believe your eyes." Pearline saw Granny's aluminum tree and squealed.

The evening was winding down. Mr. Albright had his mind set on a project that had been bugging him for a while. He went to the garage to look for tools.

Nellie turned off the kitchen light, "Esther, I think I'll make my way to my room and rest...if that's alright with you. Is there anything else you need?"

"No...thank you for everything. I'll see you in the morning."

Granny took a cup of coffee into the parlor. McDoogle curled up nearby and was soon snoring. The kids had gathered around the Christmas tree and began rearranging the presents. Doug wanted to organize them by size, Allen wanted to group them by name, and

Lizzy wanted to make them pretty by putting similar wrapping papers together. The packages were constantly shuffled and relocated. For the most part, the fussing was minimal, and they were having a good time. Allen picked up a gift that had his name on it and gave it a shake.

"Daaad, Allen is shaking the boxes again," Lizzy complained.

"Stop shaking the presents," her father called out from the foyer. "Some of them could break."

A few minutes later Mr. Albright poked his head through the entrance of the parlor and said, "You guys wanna come check this out? It's not as amazing as Santa's workshop outside, but it's pretty cool."

"What is it?" said Allen.

"Come on, check it out!"

The grand staircase at the front of the house had ornate, hand-carved wooden railings. At the base of the railing was an elaborate pedestal with a marble top. On the pedestal was a bronze statue of a cherub holding a frosted-glass ball.

Back when Mr. McHale converted the dining room chandelier from gas to electric, he also had the pedestal wired and installed a lightbulb inside the frosted globe. It hadn't worked in five or six years and Mr. Albright decided he might as well try to fix it so it could be part of the Christmas celebrations.

"Neato!" cried Doug.

"Dad, you fixed it! Mom, come look!" Lizzy shouted down the hall.

Everyone gathered in the front hall and admired the glowing glass ball.

Granny gave Mr. Albright a hug. "Thank you, Oliver. I had forgotten how special it was."

"My pleasure, Esther. It was easier than I thought, once I got inside."

Pearline walked over and took Mr. Albright by both shoulders. He was worried that she was about to kiss him, but instead, she said, "Ollie, you are a jack of all tradz! Reztoring thiz light haz made my Christmaz! I have zo many memoriez of it from when I waz a girl."

The grandfather clock began to chime eight times.

"Two more hours...no...make that three more hours before bedtime." It was Christmas Eve and Mrs. Albright didn't mind letting them stay up later than usual.

"Look!" cried Allen, pointing to the front window. "It's snowing!"

They all went to look outside. The big flakes were just starting to fall and a little dusting of snow began to cover the driveway and lawn.

"I'm so excited," cried Lizzy. "We're going to have a white Christmas!"

"You were right, Dad," exclaimed Doug

Mr. Albright chuckled. "Wow, how often can I expect to hear that from a fifteen-year old?" They both laughed.

"The znow is falling and that'z my cue," said Pearline. "I better get going. It'z been wahnderful to zee you all. Maybe we can get together again later thiz week, Maggie."

"Let's do! I can come by the Kut-n-Kurl. Let me walk you to the door."

Lizzy announced that she was going to the attic to play. "Do you want to come with me?" she asked Allen.

"Nah, I'm going to finish figuring out what all these presents are."

Lizzy didn't mind playing in the attic alone. It gave her the opportunity to make all of the decisions without fuss or compromise.

"Okay, I'll see ya later!" She said as she headed up the stairs.

"You might just hear reindeer prancing on the roof tonight!" Mr. Albright called out.

Lizzy laughed. "Oh, I hope so!" she called back.

The short flight of stairs leading to the attic door was in between her bedroom and the room Doug and Allen shared. The boys would often hide in the stairwell and jump out, scaring Lizzy as she passed by. But it wasn't the boys who startled her this time.

"McDoo! You scared me!"

McDoogle had followed Lizzy and dashed up the attic stairs ahead of her. She had forgotten how quiet he could be.

"You want to join me, McDoo? You want to be in my play? Okay! I have the perfect part for you."

Lizzy went into the attic and turned on the light. She was milling about inside the cedar closet, browsing through Granny's gowns when she heard footsteps coming up the stairs.

Treasures from the Past

"Lizzy, are you up here?"

"I'm up here...with McDoo!"

Granny and Mrs. Albright climbed the stairs and opened the attic door.

"May we join you?" Granny asked.

"Oh, yes! Perfect timing! You can help. I was just about to reenact the story of "Little Red Riding Hood" because McDoogle is the perfect big bad wolf! Now that you are here, it's even better. Granny, you can be Little Red Riding Hood's grandmother, and Mom, you can be the woodsman who comes to save the day."

"Well, now, that is perfect, isn't it?" said Granny.

"Why?" asked Lizzy.

"Because it's the perfect time for your birthday surprise."

Granny went into the cedar closet and began rifling through the racks.

"Why, here it is!"

She passed the garment bag to Lizzy, who laid it on the old divan. Lizzy tried to open the bag but the zipper was stuck.

"Mom, it won't open."

Mrs. Albright fiddled with the pull as Lizzy squirmed in anticipation. The zipper finally released. Lizzy unzipped the bag and removed a red cloak.

"Wow! It's just what I wished for. How did you know?"

Granny smiled. "A little birdie told me."

"Was this yours?"

"It certainly was! I wore it when I was about your age. I loved it so much that I saved it. Go ahead, try it on."

Her mother wrapped the cloak around Lizzy's shoulders and Granny fastened the clasp at the collar.

"It's perfect!"

Lizzy stood in front of the dressing mirror. She twirled around, watching the cloak flare out and spin. She imagined herself trotting through the forest on an adventure. She glanced down at McDoogle who was sniffing at the hem of the cloak.

"Are you a big bad wolf, McDoo? You first have to find me in the woods." She reached down and scratched McDoogle behind his ears.

Lizzy acted out an abbreviated version of the story and Granny and her mother played along. Near the end, she realized that McDoogle was going to have to eat Granny, so she made up a different ending in which the Big Bad Wolf learned a valuable lesson and became the Big Good Wolf.

She finished her play as she always did by saying, "And they all lived happily ever after!"

Everyone laughed and applauded wildly. McDoogle barked and jumped around with excitement.

"Would you like to look through the cedar chest tonight?" Granny asked. "There's still plenty of time before lights out."

"Mom, is it okay?"

"I think it's a great idea," said Mrs. Albright. "I bet there are many things in this old chest that I haven't seen in a very long time." Mrs. Albright looked at Granny and winked. Granny winked back.

Lizzy took off the cloak and hung it on a hat rack that was near-by. Granny took the key from her dress pocket and unlocked the chest. The creaky top opened and the familiar smell of cedar permeated the room.

Lizzy reached for the jewelry box first. There were so many rings, necklaces, pendants, and bracelets that Lizzy always imagined it to be a pirate's treasure chest. They sifted through yellowing papers, and flipped through the pages of the old family photo album. There were baby shoes that had been dipped in bronze, and military medals that had been awarded to Malcolm McHale for his service as a general in the Civil War. Granny and Mrs. Albright provided commentary on the items, and Lizzy tried to absorb as much as she could. She tried to imagine what it would be like to go back to the times when all these things were new.

Granny lifted out the top tray from the cedar chest and set it aside. They began rummaging through the contents in the main part of the chest. There were two antique dolls, assorted knitted and crocheted items, and the fox fur that gave Lizzy the creeps. At the bottom of the chest were a couple of christening gowns that had been worn by Granny and her sister.

"Well, that's it," said Lizzy, looking at the empty chest. "I don't remember making it all the way to the bottom before."

She ran her hand along the finely finished cedar interior.

"Hey, what's that?" She turned to Granny with a questioning look on her face.

"What? Did we forget something?" asked Granny.

"No, that!" exclaimed Lizzy, pointing to a brass hole in the bottom, near the frontside of the chest.

"Hmm," said Mrs. Albright. "It looks like a keyhole to me. What do you think mother? Does that look like a keyhole to you?"

"I do believe it does!" Granny concurred. "I wonder if there's a key?"

"What about trying the same key?" suggested Lizzy.

"Good idea!" said Mrs. Albright.

Granny handed the key to Lizzy. She put the key in the keyhole and turned it. She heard a series of clicks, and suddenly, the decorative wooden skirt on the front of the chest popped open.

"Oh my! Look! A secret compartment!"

She had read about these in her Nancy Drew books. But now, here she was, staring at a real hidden drawer. Her heart raced with excitement and butterflies fluttered in her stomach.

"Go ahead, open it," said Mrs. Albright.

Lizzy took a deep breath and carefully pulled open the drawer. Her face slowly transitioned from showing anxious anticipation to that of bewilderment and dismay. She was expecting...well, she didn't know what she was expecting, but she wasn't expecting this.

"A pillow?" queried Lizzy. "Why would a pillow be hiding in a secret drawer?"

Granny urged Lizzy to take it out of the drawer and have a closer look, which Lizzy did. She flipped the pillow to one side and then to the other. She then looked inside the pillowcase.

"This doesn't look like a pillow."

She recognized the patchwork of fabric and stitching.

"It's a quilt!" Lizzy said, solving the mystery.

Granny pulled the quilt from the pillowcase. She and Mrs. Albright began opening it up. The more they unfolded it, the bigger Lizzy's eyes got. Once it was fully open, they spread it out over the old divan and it spilled onto the floor.

"It's huge...and beautiful! I've never seen anything like it." Lizzy was happy to see the quilt but she was puzzled as to why it was kept in a secret place—after all, it was just a quilt.

She surveyed the quilt and noticed all the different fabrics. There were plaids, checkerboards, and dots. One fabric had maraschino cherries on it, which made her think of the cherry that Doug stole from her banana split earlier that afternoon. Another design had little sunbursts splashed around on a dotted background. A fabric with small tilted squares reminded her of Allen's pajamas.

She giggled when she found the singing roosters and shrieked with delight when she saw the fabric with the Scottish terrier puppies. The puppies were frolicking around on boxes that had stars painted on their sides.

"McDoo! You're in the quilt!" McDoogle looked at Lizzy, wagged his tail, and gruffed.

"Where did you get the quilt?" Lizzy asked.

"I made it. I made it many years ago."

Granny went on to explain that she had started making quilt blocks because she was worried. It helped take her mind off her troubles.

"Why were you worried?" asked Lizzy.

"It was a bad time for everyone, not just for me. The country's money system failed and caused the Great Depression—it started in 1929."

She explained that the hardships resulting from that financial disaster lasted a very long time, and many wealthy businessmen lost everything they had. Businesses that for years had been successful crumbled and failed.

Granny emphasized that the McHale family had not escaped the crisis. They too had suffered tremendous financial loss, but luckily, her father had managed to survive the ordeal without losing everything. It took him years to recover, and even so, the McHale family fortune never amounted to what it was before the Great Depression.

Granny also told Lizzy about how prices skyrocketed and that people couldn't afford the most basic necessities. The government gave out rations for eggs, sugar, butter, meat, fish, and cheese. Rationing helped to make sure that those who most needed these things got what they needed—but it almost never seemed to be enough.

"So you see, Lizzy, in many ways, this quilt tells that story."

"What do you mean?" asked Lizzy

"During that time, one of the things people needed most was quilts to keep them warm. They couldn't afford to just go out and buy blankets, and they couldn't even afford to purchase fabric to make a quilt. They had to use what they had on hand. In those days, sacks for seeds, flour, and sugar were made out of cloth. Times got so bad that when the sacks were empty, they were washed, and mothers would use the cloth to make clothes for their children. Some companies started printing pretty designs on the sacks, so at least the kids' clothes looked a bit more cheerful. The leftover scraps were used to make quilts."

"That sounds horrible," sighed Lizzy. "It's so sad."

"It was a sad time for sure, and it was during this worrisome period that I spent most of my time making these quilt blocks. I used pieces of fabric that I found at home. This one was from a dress I once wore." She pointed to a colorful fabric with nesting circles.

"Making this quilt kept my mind off of our troubles and gave me something to do. I made many different blocks and I learned all their names."

"They have names?" asked Lizzy?

"Of course they do. Remember the quilt I made for you? It's called Rail Fence. It's an easy block to make. There's a Rail Fence block in this quilt. Can you find it?"

Lizzy scanned the quilt. There was so much to look at.

"There!" Lizzy pointed to the familiar design. 'That's it!"

"It sure is," Granny confirmed. She then pointed to a different block.

"This one is a Dresden Plate. Back in those days, a set of Dresden china was the envy of every bride. But when times got bad, it was much harder to afford a set of china...let alone, expensive Dresden china...so it became popular to make quilts with this design. Look at the wedges coming out from the center, can you see how the block resembles a fancy dinner plate?"

Lizzy nodded when she saw the similarities.

"Since each wedge is a different fabric, making the quilt used up a lot of scraps. Dresden Plate quilts were often given as bridal gifts."

"I never knew all this. I never knew quilts had stories. Can you help me make a Dresden Plate quilt sometime," Lizzy asked.

"Well, of course I can, and your mother can join us."

"That would be wonderful...a family affair," Mrs. Albright beamed.

"What's this block called?" Lizzy said, pointing at a block with jagged triangles.

"That's a Bear Paw Block. The points of the triangles are his claws."

"Oooh," said Lizzy. "That would be a scary quilt to sleep under! Is there a less scary block...like one with a cat?"

Granny laughed, "As a matter of fact there is. It's called Puss in the Corner." Granny found it and pointed it out to Lizzy.

"And what about this one?"

"It's called Moon Over the Mountain"

Lizzy could see exactly why it was called that. A large circle was partially covered by a triangle that pointed up and looked like the peak of a mountain.

Granny pointed out other blocks. "This is a Honey Bee block, and this one is called Old Maid's Puzzle."

Lizzy giggled at that name but couldn't make out anything that resembled an old maid—or a puzzle.

"Look at that one!" said Lizzy excitedly. "It's a Scottie dog! McDoo! Look at you!"

McDoogle, who had been snoozing, wagged his tail and yawned.

"I remember that block, Mom. It always reminded me of Toshie."

"Who was Toshie?" asked Lizzy.

"When I was your age, we had a Scottie named Toshie. Toshie was short for Macintosh. He was notorious for chasing the geese away from the pond outside. Remember that, Mom?"

"Oh Lord, yes, I remember. He would race after those geese and they would scatter to the four winds like marbles dropped on a dance floor. He then pranced back to the house as if he had just saved his castle from an invasion of winged water rats. Those poor geese!"

"I saw a goose at the pond earlier," said Lizzy.

"You did?" queried Granny.

"I did. And I told it to go find its family before the storm, and it took off just like I said. I didn't have to chase it away or anything. It just understood what I said and flew away."

"Well now, I suppose that is one very smart goose! And do you know what?"

"What?" said Lizzy

"There are geese in my quilt. Look at the border!"

Lizzy pulled the quilt closer and grabbed the edge.

"These are called Flying Geese. They are triangles that chase after each other all going in the same direction." Lizzy gently touched the different colored patches in the border and and easily understood why they were called Flying Geese.

Granny pointed out other blocks: the Double Wedding Ring, Courthouse Steps, Snail's Trail, and Robbing Peter to Pay Paul. She couldn't remember the names of all the blocks, but she had made a chart and kept notes. They were in an envelope that was labeled "My Sampler Quilt, 1930." The envelope stayed in the cedar chest, but Lizzy hadn't seen it because she had not bothered to look at any documents or letters.

The quilt had sparked Lizzy's imagination with curiosity and wonderment. She worried about Peter getting robbed. Who was it that needed to pay Paul? She wondered what it would be like to climb up the steps to the courthouse.

Granny asked, "Do you see how each block has a strip of fabric on the left side and another darker strip along the bottom?"

The question brought Lizzy back to reality. "I do," said Lizzy.

"When quilt blocks are sewn together like this, it's called an Attic Window setting. I saw nothing but a jumbled mess when I put my blocks side by side. But then I thought about trying the Attic Window, and it worked like magic!"

Lizzy stepped back and noticed that each quilt block appeared to have been placed inside of a window frame. It made her think about how every window on earth had a different view—and that outside of every window was a world of possibilities. She studied the quilt quietly. She was in awe of Granny's accomplishment.

In that moment, something changed inside of Lizzy. She was a bit wiser and a little bit more grown up. She had a new-found appreciation for her grandmother. She had always just accepted the fact that Granny was rich. But now, she realized that Granny was practical, and very thankful for the things that she had. It now made sense to Lizzy why Granny would volunteer for the veterans' Christmas dinner, and why she would go to such great lengths to put up a Christmas display that would bring happiness to the community. She also made a promise to herself that she would never again think of a quilt as being just a quilt. She now understood why Granny kept her most precious quilt in such a safe place.

"Can I sleep under the quilt tonight, Granny?" Lizzy asked, barely able to contain her excitement over this new discovery.

Granny and Mrs. Albright exchanged glances. "I suppose so, Elisabeth, but you must promise to be extra careful with it."

Lizzy nodded in agreement. "I promise!" she said, wondering how she could ever fall asleep after this much excitement. No amount of reindeer prancing on the roof could make her any more excited.

After everything was put back in the cedar chest, Granny and Mrs. Albright carefully folded the quilt. They shut off the light and descended the attic stairs to Lizzy's room. Mrs. Albright spread the quilt over the bed while Lizzy ran to the bathroom to brush her teeth and change into her nightgown. She came back to her room and crawled under Granny's quilt.

"Good night, Sweetie, and happy birthday once more," Mrs. Albright said as she leaned over and kissed Lizzy on the forehead.

"Sweet dreams, Elisabeth," Granny said as she turned out the light. The two left the room.

The street lamps below were providing just enough light for Lizzy to make out the patterns on the quilt. She quietly said the names of the blocks, touching each one gently.

"Hello, Flying Geese. You'll be warm here for the winter," she said with a giggle.

"Little Scottie Dog, do you know McDoogle? I'll introduce you. I think you will like him."

She began to feel herself getting sleepy. She pulled the quilt up under her chin and closed her eyes. It wasn't long before the sandman came and she was fast asleep.

Snow Globe

Tap, tap, tap.

Lizzy was sleeping peacefully. She was dreaming that she was walking through a beautiful forest when she came upon a red door that was blocking the path in front of her. She rapped on the door, but nobody answered.

Tap, tap, tap.

Tap, tap, tap.

Still nobody answered. She began to feel anxious. She needed to go through to the other side, so she knocked harder.

Tap, tap, tap.

Tap, tap, tap.

The persistent tapping brought Lizzy closer to reality. She became vaguely aware of a tapping noise in her room. Groggily, she opened one eye and looked around the room.

Tap, tap, tap.

Tap, tap, tap.

She looked over to the window and realized that the snow had turned to ice and it was now pelting against the window panes. She pondered briefly, and found it amusing, that noises in the real world could become part of dreams and sounded differently when she was awake.

She closed her eyes and smiled as she imagined the enchanted winter scene that she expected to see outside her window the next

The Attic

morning. Feeling the comfort and warmth of the quilt, she quickly fell back asleep.

Tap, tap, tap.

Tap, tap, tap.

"Gruff, gruff."

McDoogle's gruffing caused Lizzy to stir. She pulled a second pillow over her head to muffle the sound and tried to go back to sleep.

Tap, tap, tap.

"Gruff!"

This gruff was louder and more closely resembled a bark. It was loud enough that Lizzy woke up and looked at McDoogle.

"Gruff!"

"What is it, McDoo?"

Tap, tap, tap...

"Grrrrrrruff!"

The tapping sound was louder than she originally realized. McDoogle was sitting just outside her door, intently focused on something in the hall.

Tap, tap, tap.

"Grrrrrrrrrrrrrr!" This time McDoogle gave a soft, long growl.

Lizzy now realized that the tapping was not being created by an ice storm, and she was too awake and too curious to ignore it. She got out of bed, walked to the door, stood next to McDoogle, and looked down the hall.

Tap, tap, tap.

"What is it, McDoo?" Lizzy whispered.

McDoogle glanced at Lizzy. He slowly approached the opening to the stairway that led to the attic door. He stopped and gruffed again.

Tap, tap, tap.

It seemed to Lizzy that the taps were coming from the attic, but she wasn't sure. The entire situation had Lizzy spooked, and then she remembered the rumors that were spread about ghosts living in the McHale mansion. This thought only made matters worse.

Tap, tap, tap.

McDoogle whined, acted agitated, and then gruffed again.

Lizzy, speaking as quietly as she could, said, "Okay, McDoo, if you will go with me and attack any ghosts, we can find out what this tapping is all about."

McDoogle stretched out his front legs and lowered his chest to the floor. Lizzy perceived his bow to be a sign of affirmation. But then, he shook his head in such a way that she couldn't exactly tell if it was a yes or a no.

Lizzy had to know what was causing the tapping. Being cautious and apprehensive, she tiptoed up the stairs and cracked open the attic door.

Tap, tap, tap. It was louder.

"You were right, McDoo. The sound is coming from the attic."

As she opened the door a little wider, McDoogle squeezed his head through her legs and peeked into the room. He gave a serious, low, rumbling growl.

"Shh. You're going to wake up the whole house!"

Tap, tap, tap.

It finally dawned on Lizzy that her brothers might be up to one of their typical pranks. Right after they had moved into their new house on Juniper Lane, the boys went to her bedroom and tied a clear fishing line to one of her favorite stuffed animals, a large giraffe. Once Lizzy went to bed, they planned on making the giraffe scoot across the floor which would no doubt frighten her. Fortunately, Lizzy saw the line before she went to sleep and realized what they were planning to do.

When the lights went out, she quickly arranged the pillows under the covers to make it look like she was in bed. She grabbed her flashlight, padded lightly across the carpet, positioned herself just behind her bedroom door, and waited patiently.

As soon as the house was quiet, the boys snuck out of their rooms and met in the hall. They took the line and started slowly pulling the giraffe toward the door. When it got to the threshold and nothing had happened, they suspected that they were too late, and that Lizzy must have already fallen asleep. They cautiously peeked their heads through the doorway, and from the glow of the night-light, they could see that Lizzy was asleep in her bed.

"She's out like a light," whispered Doug. "Let's put it back. Then we can hoot like an owl and see if that will wake her up."

"Okay. Go put it back," said Allen.

"No, you go put it back," argued Doug.

"I'm not gonna go put it back. I'm gonna be the owl."

This went on back and forth with neither of them wanting to go into the room. They finally agreed that if they were going to do it, they would have to do it together.

They took hold of the giraffe and slowly and quietly began carrying it back into the bedroom. They shuffled right past Lizzy who was frozen in place and breathing as quietly as she could. As soon as they had passed the doorway and were in the room, she slammed the door, jumped from her hiding place, and shouted, "Gotcha!"—shining the flashlight in their faces at the same time.

The boys almost jumped right out of their skins. They were so startled that they screamed, tripped over each other, and tumbled to the floor. Allen banged his elbow on the footboard of Lizzy's bed, and while scrambling to get back on his feet, he kicked Doug in his crotch, which made him howl. He rolled on the floor in agony. Lizzy laughed so hard her sides hurt. They looked like two floundering, whimpering fools.

"I got you! I got you good!" laughed Lizzy.

The boys' egos were crushed by the fact that their little sister had managed to beat them at their own game. Plus they were embarrassed that they had been so terrified that they actually screamed. Defeated, they left the room. Lizzy was still laughing as they walked down the hall. Mr. and Mrs. Albright had heard the commotion and figured out the gist of what had transpired.

"Maggie, I think I'll just let this one play out on its own...no need for us to intervene." Mr. and Mrs. Albright both laughed and shook their heads.

Lizzy went to sleep that night with a smile on her face. It was a smile of contentment like she had never known before. She had won this round and that was enough satisfaction for now.

Tap, tap, tap.

"I bet this is another one of Doug and Allen's scary pranks," Lizzy whispered to McDoogle.

"Okay, tapping noise, I hear you. I've got my attack dog ready to pounce. You'd best be moving along now."

She purposefully began speaking a little more loudly, partly to convince herself she wasn't scared, and partly to alert her brothers that she was on to them.

The boys rarely went to the attic and did not know it as well as she did. She knew every nook and cranny. The light switch was just inside the door, but since her eyes were already adjusted to the darkness, she decided it would be best to leave the lights off, giving her the better advantage should there be any confrontation. Besides, the street lamps outside provided enough light through the attic window that Lizzy could see nearly everything in the room.

Tap, tap, tap.

McDoogle suddenly darted between Lizzy's legs and bolted toward the attic window. He jumped up on the cedar chest and barked vigorously.

"What is it, McDoo?" Lizzy asked, cautiously walking toward him. She had left the door open in the event she needed a quick escape.

Lizzy looked toward the window and saw the silhouette of something moving. She put aside the notion that her brothers were up to something. They would not be outside on the roof for any reason—especially in this weather. However, Lizzy had not yet ruled out the possibility of it being a ghost.

"I bet it's just a tree branch hitting the window," Lizzy said softly as she continued toward the cedar chest. The silhouette moved again, and then the shape became undeniably clear. There, sitting just outside the window on the overhang of the roof, was a goose.

Tap, tap, tap.

"Oh no!" said Lizzy. "It's my goose. The poor thing didn't find his family. He needs help." McDoogle started jumping up and down, running in circles, and barking.

Tap, tap, tap.

Lizzy needed to get closer to make sure her eyes were not playing tricks on her. She crawled up on top of the cedar chest, cupped her hands around her face, and peered through the window pane. Indeed it was a goose and now they were eye to eye.

Tap, tap, tap.

This time the tapping was so close to her face—and so unexpected—it made her jump.

"McDoo, what can we do? We have to help. Look at all the snow outside. We have to let it in." McDoogle barked in agreement.

Lizzy found the window latch and switched it to the unlocked position. She pulled the handle, but the window wouldn't budge.

"The window is stuck!" cried Lizzy.

"Try again!"

Lizzy gripped the handle as hard as she could and pulled.

"It won't open. It's really stuck!"

"It's not stuck. You just have to open it."

Lizzy took a deep breath, gritted her teeth, and yanked as hard as she could. The window flew open with such ease that she fell backward and toppled off the cedar chest.

A blast of frigid, howling wind shot through the window, sending swirls of snow flying into the room. Lizzy climbed back onto the top of the cedar chest, and the goose stuck its head through the window.

"I told you it wasn't stuck."

Lizzy's eyes nearly popped right out of her head and her jaw almost dropped to the floor. She wasn't sure if she really heard what she *thought* she heard.

Baffled and stunned, she asked, "Did you say something?"

"The window...I told you it wasn't really stuck."

The winter storm's blustery winds forced more snow through the window. Lizzy was astonished that she could understand what the goose said. She was at a total loss for what to say or do. She just sat there, looking at the goose...frozen.

"Gruff! Pardon me, Lass, but maybe ye should be askin' Missus Goose if she's lost or if she's needin' ony assistance." Lizzy instantly looked down to McDoogle, and then around the room to see who said this. She didn't see anyone, so she looked back to the floor where McDoogle was sitting, wagging his tail, and looking directly at her.

"McDoo? Did you just say something?"

"There's a goose peekin' through the windae, Lass. Did ye open the windae and let yer manners go blowin' away on the wind?" chastised McDoogle.

This was unreal. There were now two animals talking to her—and she *understood* both of them. It was a fact she was trying very hard to deny, and it made her think she must be dreaming. But what she couldn't deny was the biting, bitter wind and snow. It was very cold, and *very* real.

"Lizzy, my name is Gretta," said the goose.

Lizzy looked back to the window, too stunned to even acknowledge that the goose knew her name.

"Are you lost? Can I help you?" asked Lizzy.

"No, I'm not at all lost," replied Gretta. "But yes, you most certainly can help me. We are in desperate need of your help!"

A gust of wind swooshed through the window, causing a lamp to crash to the floor.

"You talk people talk?" Lizzy raised her voice in order to be heard above the gale. More snow ushered in through the window.

"Yes, yes, of course! Or maybe you speak animal talk. Whichever it is, is not important right now. But you must come with me, Princess. Time is running out and we desperately need you!"

"Princess?" Lizzy looked around the attic again to see who Gretta might be talking to.

"Are you talking to me?" Lizzy was having to shout above the blasting gusts. "I'm not a princess. What do you mean 'come with you'? How? Why? Who are you?" Lizzy was riddling Gretta with questions.

"I'll explain everything soon, but we must be on our way. The entire kingdom is depending on you and time is of the essence. We've been looking for you for a very long time. Please, come with me. I promise you'll be safe."

The wind was becoming more fierce. The door to the attic slammed shut. Snow was building up on top of the cedar chest and drifting onto the floor. Lizzy's hair was starting to freeze from blowing snow, and the icy wind and sleet were beginning to burn her face. She was so miserable that she felt that she needed to shut the window or she would surely die.

"Please don't shut the window," pleaded Gretta, as if she somehow knew what Lizzy was thinking. "It's cold inside, but it's wonderful out here. Climb out the window! Get on my back! Come with me!" shouted Gretta.

"What do you mean, 'get on your back'? I'm a girl. You're a goose. I'm too big!" The wind blew her words back into her mouth so they couldn't escape.

"Princess! Please hurry! It will all make sense soon!"

"Lass, wud ye go if I were to go wi' ye? I'll be puttin' up me mitts if onyone were to try to bring ye any harm."

The force of the wind blew the other attic window open and brought twice as much snow into the attic. It swirled with such vigor that the room began to look like a snow globe.

McDoogle raced to pull the red cloak from the hat rack where Lizzy had left it. "You might be needin' this to keep ye warm."

She wrapped the cloak around her shoulders and fastened the collar. The cloak warmed her slightly—which calmed her a bit.

"I'll get in trouble! This is crazy!" Lizzy thought.

The force of the wind caused the tails of the cloak to fly up, flap, and flutter. She couldn't stand the wind and ice any longer. Lizzy looked back over her shoulder and saw that the entire attic was now filled with snow. She could only see the very top of the old divan. The cedar chest was completely hidden. A snow drift was pressing up against the door holding it shut.

"I promise you'll be safe. Take a leap of faith, Princess!"

"I'm right behind ye, Lassie!"

Lizzy began to crawl out the attic window. She hoisted herself one leg at a time through the window and sat on the sill.

"Get on my back!" Gretta was shouting, but the wind was roaring so loudly that Lizzy didn't understand her plea.

"What?" asked Lizzy. "I can't hear you."

Lizzy held tight. She could no longer hear nor see. Her hair was whipping in every direction. Pelting ice forced her eyes shut. The wind was now so fierce and loud that it almost blew her back into the attic.

"Jump!" McDoogle barked at Lizzy from behind. "Jump!"

She heard McDoogle, and without thinking, she pushed herself up and leapt blindly out into the storm. Her arms were flailing and she felt herself sliding down the roof.

She screamed.

She was falling.

She kept on screaming.

She kept on falling.

She felt a hint of warmth on her face, and she was finally able to open her eyes.

She wasn't falling—she was flying!

Lizzy found herself nestled into the soft, warm feathers of Gretta's back with McDoogle snuggled under her arm.

"Are you getting warm?" asked Gretta.

"It's amazing, yes. I'm very comfortable, thank you." Lizzy felt tremendous relief. "I've never felt so free in all my life."

As Lizzy looked at the snowy landscape below, she was no longer astonished or bewildered. She was simply filled with wonderment. She felt courageous and confident. She felt hopeful and free. And better than that, she was flying!

"Miss Gretta?" McDoogle called out.

"Yes, Mr. McDoogle?"

"It seems we havenae formally met, but I'm McDoogle, which ye may already ken. And ye're Miss Gretta, which I already ken. It's a pleasure to meet ye."

"It's a pleasure to meet you too, Mr. McDoogle."

"But I do need to tell ye..." said McDoogle.

"What's that?" asked Gretta.

"I'll be keepin' a beady eye on ye. I won't be allowin' ony tomfoolery."

"Alright, Mr. McDoogle. Alright! No tomfoolery."

The sky was clear and filled with twinkling, brilliant stars. Lizzy began to recognize a few of the constellations. The air was brisk and cold—brisk enough that each of them could see their breath, but not so cold that it was uncomfortable.

Lizzy pointed. "There's the Big Dipper! And that one, all by itself, I think it's the North Star. Are we flying north, Gretta?"

"Yes, Princess, we are."

Gretta continued to ascend. The moon was full and bright. Lizzy began to see a swirl of color up ahead.

"Are those the northern lights?" asked Lizzy.

"They most certainly are. Look how they dance in the night sky."

"Wow, I've always wanted to see them. They're beautiful!

As they approached, Lizzy was mesmerized by the dancing wisps of light. The misty hues began to assemble and form a tunnel. Gretta flew directly toward it. When they entered the tunnel, they were enveloped by stars that rotated around the tunnel creating a vortex of light. Lizzy had never seen anything so magical.

Gretta stopped flapping her wings. She was able to rest as the light carried her on. The tunnel slowly narrowed which made them accelerate. As they came to the end of the tunnel, the stars flashed—then vanished. They were floating through an endless void of total darkness.

One by one, Lizzy began to see stars appear. The blackness shimmered and twinkled as more and more stars fell into place. Lizzy looked for the Big Dipper. Even though she didn't find it, everything felt very familiar—like she was home. In her wildest dreams, she never could have imagined what she had just experienced.

Gretta began slowly flapping her wings with a gentle, steady rhythm. After a while, the cool night air, Gretta's soft feathers, and the soothing sound of a gentle breeze lulled Lizzy to sleep.

The Royal Brothers of Ailear

Cedric stood up, walked to the window, and looked down. Thousands of citizens were gathered below. They had been there for days. Their mood was somber as they watched and waited. Only a few people were looking at the tower when Cedric appeared, but within seconds, a murmur rippled through the crowd and everyone looked up.

Eight days ago, their beloved King Eoseph had caught a fever. The news spread quickly throughout all of Ailear that the king was gravely ill. Almost everyone in the kingdom admired King Eoseph. He had made the kingdom more productive and the people had prospered. He ruled with fairness. He had a reputation for being more generous than greedy. To show their love and respect, Ailearians from all across the kingdom had been steadily streaming into the city and gathering outside the walls of Castlehill. They eagerly awaited the reports regarding the king's failing health.

Those who followed the Book of Satins went to the satinaries and left offerings on the altars. Many people lit tightly bound bundles of stargrass and placed them in the smokepots that were attached to the outsides of their homes and businesses. During the past week, the sweet smell of stargrass abundantly and prayerfully floated through the streets of Ansa.

The finest mages and physicians in the kingdom had overseen King Eoseph's care. They all felt he was improving. Just yesterday, when Cedric appeared in the tower window, he had raised one fist into the air, indicating that the king was improving—but not healed. The crowd had cheered wildly when they received the good news. They had hoped for him to raise both fists into the air, indicating that the king had recovered and that there was no more cause for concern, but that had not been the case. While sPeaksees were used throughout the kingdom to distribute and receive messages, the royal family followed the ancient traditions of making announcements from Proclamation Tower when it came to matters of births, marriages, illnesses, and deaths.

Today Cedric appeared in the window earlier than usual. The crowd grew silent and focused their attention toward the tower. Cedric hesitated. He put his hands on the window sill, exhaled, and then unfurled the black banner. It poured out the window and trailed down the side of the tower in the same way his tears poured from his eyes and trailed down his cheeks. He turned and vanished from the window.

As with all previous changes in Ailear's royal leadership, it was the responsibility of the Ailearian Parliament to make the ruling on who would be the king's successor. It was typical for the parliamentary senators and magistrates to select the eldest royal offspring as the new ruler of Ailear. King Eoseph had two sons—twins—Cedric and Gethric. As the eldest child of King Eoseph, Cedric was in that position. Still, the law required that Parliament convene and cast its votes. If for any reason Parliament determined that the next in line was unfit for the crown, it could choose anyone—royalty or not—as the new ruler. Parliament rarely broke from tradition. Likewise, Parliament also held the power to remove a king or queen if deemed necessary.

Cedric was thirty-four years old when he was crowned king of Ailear. His beloved wife, Oris, became queen consort. Gethric was appointed as the chief royal advisor. Gethric's wife, Genevra, Oris's younger sister, served on the royal council. The sisters were thankful that the celestial realm had predestined both of them to fall in love and marry into the royal family. It had allowed them to remain close.

Neither of the twins had ever coveted the position of king, but they grew up knowing what would eventually be expected of them.

Their fates were sealed by the royal bloodline. They sat under the tutelage of the King's Council, which not only oversaw their general studies, but also trained them in all aspects relating to kingship, including finances, protocols, strategies, and negotiations. When the king held court, they were usually in attendance.

The King's Council had commented quietly amongst themselves that Gethric would be a better fit for the throne. Although the twins looked very much alike, their capabilities and demeanors were totally different. Gethric wasn't careless and he rarely made emotional decisions. He was focused, practical, and slow to anger. Cedric, on the other hand, often made hasty choices and jumped to conclusions. His emotions fueled many of his actions.

Whether he liked it or not, Cedric was now king. He would fulfill the role as best he could, even though sorcery was his passion. He would have much preferred to have been appointed high mage than king of Ailear. He was, after all, a master mage, and as such, could be considered for that position. Sorcery had been his life up to this point. The powers of mysticism had sought him out at a very early age.

When the twins were young, they were in the care of Lessa, their day nurse. Many mornings she would take them out to the garden so they could explore the flora and fauna. Gethric loved insects, especially caterpillars and beetles. He had the most fun searching for rolypolies. He was obsessed with watching them curl into tiny balls when he touched them or prodded them with a stick. He would patiently wait for them to uncurl and then watch them float along on their fourteen tiny legs as they continued their journey. Cedric, on the other hand, was interested in the various birds that flittered about. He also liked learning from Lessa about the various plants.

One particular morning when the boys were five, they were out with Lessa in the garden. Cedric came upon two robins hopping about on a bungabella bush. They seemed anxious and chattered with such a fuss that Cedric could not ignore them. He soon discovered their nest lying in the grass. It had been blown out of a tree during the previous night's storm. Two fledgling robins were on the ground nearby. One of the birds seemed a bit wobbly, but was otherwise unharmed. The other fledgling seemed lifeless.

"Come quick! I think it's dead!" cried Cedric, calling out to Lessa and Gethric.

The two ran to where Cedric was kneeling. He had picked up the lifeless bird. His heart was broken for the poor thing and he began to weep.

"We have to help it!" Cedric pleaded.

Lessa looked at the tiny feathered creature as it lay cradled in Cedric's hands. She prodded it gently. At first she was sure there was no life left in the little bird, but then she noticed one of its legs move with a slight twitch. She nudged it again, but there was no additional movement.

"I'm sorry Cedric," she said. "It might not be dead, but it will surely die. We can't save it."

Cedric continued to sob. Tears rolled down his cheeks. As they flowed from his face, they fell onto the little fledgling.

"I want it to live! I don't want it to die! It can't die!" cried Cedric as more tears flowed into his hands.

"You can't die; you must live," he commanded the little robin. Then he raised the bird to his face and gently breathed on it.

Lessa saw the bird twitch.

"C'mon, little bird, wake up!" Cedric was insistent.

The fledgling twitched again, shuddered, and then shook its head. It opened its eyes. Soon it peeped, sat up in Cedric's hands, and opened its beak as wide as possible, begging for a meal. Cedric stopped crying and began cheering. Lessa could hardly believe her eyes. It was clear to her that the bird had been dead, or on the brink of death, and now it was alert and looking perfectly healthy.

Gethric shouted, "You healed it, Cedric. You healed it!"

Cedric put the two fledglings back in their nest and then handed it to Lessa.

"Will you put it back in the tree?"

Lessa took the nest in her beak, spread her large, bronze, iridescent wings, and flew up to a high branch. Her glorious plumage flashed in the morning sun and her crest twinkled like stars. She found a sturdy fork in the tree and positioned the nest so that it was secure. The adult robins flew up to check on their offspring and then flew about in joyful celebration, circling Cedric's head in gratitude.

"It looks like Master Cedric has worked a miracle this morning," she said to the robins. They sang and chirped in agreement.

Lessa leapt off the branch, glided back down, and strutted over to the boys.

"Is it going to be okay?" asked Cedric.

"Thanks to you, it looks as if it will be out of the nest and flying on its own very soon."

Lessa knew she had witnessed something exceptional, but she chose to remain cautious and not jump to conclusions. She decided to wait and not report the story until it was time for them to go back inside. In the meantime, the boys carried on in the garden in search of small wonders. Lessa was delighted when she discovered that the winds had rattled the chester tree enough that it had sprinkled an abundance of fresh, tiny chester nuts onto the ground. Chester nuts were a peafowl favorite. She pecked at the seeds while the boys teased the roly-polies.

Once back inside, Lessa sent the boys to the dining hall for their lunch. She reported the incident with the robins to Garlan, the royal mage, who in turn told the king what had happened. The story was so fantastic that it created doubts regarding its validity. If it were true, the implications regarding Cedric's abilities were astonishing. Lessa and the boys were all interrogated separately, but their accounts of the event were always the same.

Garlan met privately with King Eoseph. "We have no evidence of white magic being able to raise the dead, but white magic *can* heal. If Cedric, at age five, healed that bird with his natural, untrained powers, then he surely must be sent to mage guild for school."

Garlan believed that both boys would likely share the same talent for mysticism and suggested that Gethric be sent to mage guild as well. King Eoseph made an appointment to meet with the mage council to discuss the matter further. After much consideration, it was decided that the twins would not be attending the governing guild, as was traditional for children of the royal family, but they would become students at mage guild.

The following year when the boys started their primaries, they moved into a private dormitory at Mage Guild Hall. Like all other primary students in mage school, they were required to wear the identifying red cloaks of novice mages. Other than having private quarters, the princes were treated no differently than the other students.

Throughout their primary and secondary years, both boys excelled in all their classes. Gethric enjoyed learning spells and potions. He felt that the magic he learned was good and had practical uses.

Cedric tolerated his basic classes, but he loved all of his magusology classes. To him, magic and mysticism was as natural as a leaf quaking in the breeze. He could easily memorize complex spells and recipes. He became adept with his wand and his staff. He quickly became fluent in the archaic language used by sorcerers, and he was always the *primo perfecto* at the end of each school year.

After graduating from their secondaries at age eighteen, both boys went on to train as apprentices of sorcery. They rapidly advanced to become practitioners of sorcery, and by the age of twenty-six, they both had acquired mage status. It only took Cedric two more years to become a master mage. He was only twenty-eight years old, making him the youngest master mage in the history of the guild. Although Gethric continued to practice as a sorcerer, he never received the purple and black cloak of a master mage.

"Let's celebrate," said Gethric. "I'm going to arrange a party!"

"A party?" asked Cedric.

"Yes...indeed...a party!"

The royal family had never done anything as common as having a party. They had banquets, feasts, and festivals. A royal celebration would call for a spectacular display of fireworks. A magnificent feast would take days to prepare, and the finest jesters, acrobats, and musicians would be called upon to entertain those fortunate enough to be on the guest list.

"Do you mean a party as in the type of thing that the city folk do when they celebrate?"

"Yes, exactly," said Gethric. "We must do something out of the ordinary. We never go to the pubs...we aren't allowed. Let's have a party at the Shoe and Fiddle. I hear it's the best pub in Ansa. It will be fantastic to do something so uncharacteristic. We will never forget it!"

Cedric raised an eyebrow. "Are you drunk?"

Cedric knew his brother. The idea of having a party was totally uncharacteristic. It tossed tradition aside. It was unpredictable, carefree, and a folly.

"No, I'm not drunk. I've really thought this over. You have achieved something amazing and wonderful, spectacular—even historic! The mage guild will organize a banquet in your honor, you already know that. Let *me* organize something that is just as amazing and unprecedented. And what's more unprecedented than two royal brothers secretly having a party at the Shoe and Fiddle?"

Cedric smiled. "You're right! You're absolutely right. Your logic... as annoying and irritating as it can be...is your guiding light. Let's do it!"

Gethric put both hands on Cedric's shoulders and pulled him close. "Leave everything to me!"

Barleywick, Biggleston, and Beards

The mage guild was in recess for three weeks, so Gethric scheduled Cedric's party for Freeday night and took care of all the arrangements. The royal guards would not be in uniform, and they were instructed not to drink more than one pint of ale each. Spirits were strictly forbidden. They were offered double pay for doing the job and keeping the event a secret. Gethric also threatened that they would be discharged from their positions if they muttered a peep about the party to anyone.

He met privately with Brandt, a senior guard and someone he considered a close friend. Gethric offered Brandt a bonus of two-thousand krotes, but there were conditions. Brandt would refrain from drinking any ales or spirits. He would keep his eye on the other guards to make sure they upheld their end of the deal. Finally, Brandt was instructed to bathe and brush his coat.

"I mean this as a friend," Gethric had told Brandt. "Just because you *are* a bear, doesn't mean you have to smell bad. Your brother attends mage council meetings with no offensive odor. Can you please, on this occasion, try to do the same?" Brandt promised he would.

Gethric sent Fergus, his dresser, out to buy appropriate clothes for the occasion. He too would get a bonus for keeping the secret. The dresser returned with several boxes and bags filled with selections that he felt were neither too fancy nor too casual.

"I hope you like these," said Fergus. "I went shopping, just as you asked me to. These are..." He put his hand to his forehead and paused.

Fergus was not only Gethric's personal dresser; he was also the royal tailor. Yesterday, when Gethric asked him to go shopping for clothes, he became so wispy-headed that he had to pour himself a glass of water and sit down. Fergus made clothes, he didn't *shop* for clothes. Gethric asked Fergus to please not be offended and explained that for their safety, they had to look like every other person out on the town.

"I can make you *plain* outfits if that's what you want," Fergus had argued.

"Two outfits? By Freeday afternoon?"

As Fergus shook his head in disbelief, his ginger coiffure jounced about as if it were a fox trying to escape from a trap. His mind raced around searching for a solution other than shopping at regular clothiers. He repeatedly plucked at his bow tie, and then he began tapping on his oversized red-framed eyeglasses. He stood up and walked to the window, fanning himself with his hand, and trying to usher in some fresh air. He couldn't think of a way to make it happen. Just acquiring the right fabrics would take two days, leaving no time to actually make the garments. So he relinquished his argument, took it as a challenge, and went shopping.

Fergus took a breath and started once again to describe his purchases. "These are common-made by Jerome and Sons, from the Skidoo Emporium," he said—nearly choking on the word *Skidoo*.

Fergus untied the boxes with dramatic flair and whisked out each item, adding full commentary about each one.

"Two fashionable, three-quarter length, dandy jackets with lightly flared tails! One is made from an Oxford blue twill and features a leather waist-strap, with decorative bronze clasps. The other is made with cattail brown tweed and has leather epaulets accented with a cascade of brass chains."

Gethric nodded his approval.

"Two pair of charcoal, corduroy, Pedelton breeches, with double-button drop fronts, right and left flanking pockets, and fashionable leather lacings, running the entire length of each side, and woven through bronze eyelets."

"They're perfect!" said Gethric.

Fergus continued showing Gethric the other items: linen shirts, argyle socks, and two pair of two-toned Broxfords, with buckles—one pair was brown and tan and the other pair was black and cream.

Fergus had purchased two hats. One was a multiblue leather-paneled top hat, and the other was a brown bowler. It had a leather band that was secured by a metal clasp.

Fergus pointed out that the styles for both outfits were similar, but that one was primarily a dusty blue ensemble with tea rose complements, and the other one was primarily wheat toast brown with amber accents. He also pointed out that the clothes were fairly common and that they could possibly come upon other Ansarians wearing the same garments.

"You'll blend right in with the crowd," said Fergus, doing his best to not show his disdain over that idea.

"This is exactly what I needed!" said Gethric. "Thank you."

Getting to the Shoe and Fiddle posed another problem but also provided another opportunity for Gethric to do something uncharacteristic and surprise Cedric. He would have their regular driver take them to mage hall, where they would pick up their BMC triwheel motorbies and drive themselves to the party. Gethric was so excited that he spent the entire morning doing nothing but washing and polishing both of their motorbies.

Being princes, they were restricted from being in public without an entourage—it simply wasn't safe. They did, however, have total freedom to move around anywhere within the Rose Wall that surrounded Barleywick Quarter. The wall got its name from the rose-colored granite that was quarried for its construction. Copper-domed senate chambers, a resplendent courthouse, government offices, and the three prestigious Rose Vine colleges, were all located inside the Rose Wall.

The same granite had been used to build the regal and stately buildings for the satins guild, the governing guild, and the mage guild. Roses skirted along the entire perimeter of the Rose Wall—both inside and outside—for all to enjoy. When rose season was at its peak, Barleywick Quarter was not only a magnificent sight to behold, but the sweet scent of roses permeated the air.

Also located within the quarter was Kings Park, a large recreational area that was used for sports, picnics, or to just relax. There were several private houses lining Regal Avenue. One of the houses was owned by the royal family. Cedric and Gethric were there more than they were at Castlehill. The Rose Wall separated the quarter from the rest of the city and could only be accessed via the four entry gates that were guarded twenty-four eight.

Barleywick Quarter was large enough that driving was sometimes more practical than walking, but not so large that transportation was required. Jaunting about on their BMCs inside the perimeter of the Rose Wall was a good distraction when they needed a break from the tedium of their studies. They had recently traded their old ones for the newest model.

Each year Biggleston Motor Company came out with only one new triwheel motorbie. They all featured two large rear wheels, one small front wheel, and an overhead canopy. They came with a choice of handlebars or a steering wheel. The engine was contained in a bulbous compartment that hung below the main frame and looked like the abdomen of a bloated spider. From year to year, BMC made slight changes to the contours of the vehicle. Other than a few slight improvements, the vehicles didn't change much.

The dramatic changes came from the add-ons that kept rolling out each year. Nobody ever bought a BMC and left it plain. The practicality of having transportation was one thing, but Ailearians were prone to individuality, and the options for customizing a basic motorbie were endless. Ailearians wanted to look bang. They especially wanted to look bang when tooling through the streets in their motorbies. Making your motorbie look bang was easy. Some businesses in Ansa sold nothing but motorbie accessories. There were so many options that no two motorbies looked alike.

Gethric added a dorsal fin to the canopy, an ooga horn on the handle, and a twirly-gig on the front fender. His choice of add-ons were stylish, but reserved. Cedric had an ooga horn and a twirly-gig, but he also added a sphere scope. The scope was inside a pair of goggles that dangled down from the canopy and allowed him to see in any direction without having to turn his head. He also installed pop-up rotator blades above the canopy that he could deploy at the press of a button. They used a lot of extra fuel, but enabled him to fly short distances. Finally, he had attached a back-facing bumper seat that would accommodate an additional passenger when necessary.

Gethric suggested they get haircuts and beard trims. Both of them had allowed their beards to lengthen naturally, which was common among sorcerers, but not required. A variety of beard styles were becoming fashionable.

They sent for the owner of the The Groomed Goat because he seemed to have the best reputation for keeping up with the newest trends and styles. The barber was escorted to the castle carrying his satchel of supplies, which, of course, had to be examined by the guards. There was no concern for his combs, brushes, shampoos, or oils, but his scissors and single-blade razors were lethal weapons. A sentinel was stationed in the room to keep an eye on the barber.

Brock, the footman, entered the room, raised up on his hind legs, clicked his hooves twice, and said, "Presenting Carlson Wetherby, a certified barber in the city of A-a-a-ansa, and the proprietor of The Groomed Goat." He then stepped back and motioned for the barber to enter the room. As Carlson walked forward, Brock looked himself over. He thought himself to be a fairly well-groomed goat, with a fairly well-groomed beard. He raised an eyebrow, shrugged, hrummphed, and left the room.

Carlson showed no signs of nervousness. He was perfectly comfortable in the presence of the royal princes. The brothers went to him and extended their hands.

"Your Highnesses—at your service! As a matter of curiosity, may I ask if you can list the three days in the week that start with the letter *T*?"

The brothers were actually caught off guard by the question.

"Excuse me?" asked Gethric, confused—but chuckling.

"Can you name the three days in the week that start with the letter *T*?"

"Hmm," said Gethric, with a blank face.

"Ah, it's a riddle!" said Cedric. "Let me see. There's Sunday, Moonday, Treesday, Windsday, Earthday, Kingday, Freeday, and Satinsday. There's only one day that starts with a *T*, and the other seven don't." Cedric looked to Gethric. "Do *you* have it figured out?"

Gethric, who loved a good riddle, shuffled through the days of the week in his head again, but couldn't come up with the answer.

"Here's a hint," said Carlson. "Think about today."

"Today is Earthday," replied Cedric, "...the fifth day of the week."

"Indeed it is!" confirmed Carlson.

"But Earthday starts with an *E*."

"Indeed it does," replied Carlson.

Cedric scratched his head.

"Aha!" said Gethric, laughing loudly. "Treesday, Today...and Tomorrow!"

"You got it!" said Carlson.

"Bravo!" added Cedric. "I must remember that one."

Gethric gestured to the chairs and they all sat down.

"I understand that you are looking to update those beards. Take a look at this portfolio," said Carlson.

Carlson pulled two data disks from his coat pocket and passed them to his clients. Gethric inserted one disk into the slot on his goggles and pulled them over his eyes. Cedric inserted the other disk into the side of his monocle and popped it into place. They both fingered the small dials on their devices and flipped through the pictures. The Ally Cat with its extremely wide handlebar mustache was a style that was common and very dapper. Newer styles like the Double-Trouble, the Savant, the Duck Tail, the Hatchet, and the Boudreaux were very popular. Neither of the men had predicted there would be so many styles from which to choose.

While they were scrolling through the images, Carlson suggested that each man select a different haircut and a different beard style so that they would be easier to differentiate and have more individualistic appearances. After much deliberation, Cedric ended up choosing the flamboyant Prince Valiant, and Gethric—as Cedric had predicted—chose the stylish, but more reserved, Boudreaux.

CHAPTER TEN

Angels in Disguise

On Freeday afternoon, the brothers were driven to Mage Guild Hall. Howart, their driver, dropped them off and was excused for the night. Howart assumed that the princes would be attending an evening meeting at guild hall, and that they would be staying at the royal house in Barleywick Quarter. Gethric didn't think that Howart needed to be in on his secret. The fewer folks that knew about it, the better chance he had of having a successful party.

The stars were just coming out and the temperature was perfect.

"You look fantastic!" said Cedric, tugging on the lapels of his dandy jacket.

"So do you, brother!" Gethric was bursting with excitement. "It will be a night to remember! Are you ready for this?"

"I am. I most certainly am!"

"Here, let's do a selfie." Gethric took out his sPeaksee, flipped the lens around to the front side, and positioned them in the view box.

"Say *Fizzbie*!"

"Fizzbie!" they said in unison. They quickly reviewed the selfie.

"It's great," said Cedric. "We look so bang. Send it to me, okay?"

"Sure thing!" Gethric swiped and tapped on the view box.

"There, you should have it now."

"Bang!" said Cedric. "Are you ready?"

"I couldn't be more ready!"

They hopped on their motorbies, adjusted their goggles, slung riding scarves around their necks, and pulled on their driving gloves. They dialed in their ignition codes and started the engines. Gethric took the lead and they puttered toward the main gate, which exited onto Saint Murphy Blvd.

They stopped at the gate barrier, looked inside the guardhouse, and waved to Henry, who was the guard on duty. Henry waved back, but wasn't sure who he was waving at. Since the twins had new haircuts, new beard styles, and were wearing goggles, it would be hard for anyone to recognize them. Their motorbies had never left Barleywick Quarter so Henry didn't know their vehicles either. He started to get up and question them, but before he did, Gethric had pulled off his glove, reached over, placed his ID ring under the scanner, and the barrier arm raised. Henry sat back down and continued playing Frog Launch on his GameWorld Pod.

Gethric's heart raced as he turned on to Saint Murphy Blvd. His adrenaline flowed and his senses were heightened. The soft rumble of wheels on cobblestones sent shivers that rippled from his heels up to his head. Soon he motioned for Cedric to pull up beside him.

"This feels amazing—like I'm free!" Gethric's joy was contagious.

"I know what you mean!" shouted Cedric. "Woo-hoo!"

Gethric breathed in the Ansa air as if it were from a new world. Although he had traveled these streets as a passenger in the royal shuttlebie countless times, this was the first time he had done it on his own without security.

"Watch this!" shouted Cedric. He pulled the glove from his left hand, pointed to Gethric's front wheel, and snapped his fingers. "Spark! Alamah!"

The front wheel hub of Gethric's BMC started shooting a spectacular fountain of sparks which looked very much like the spray from a welder's torch. The brothers both sounded their ooga horns and whistled. The sparks didn't last more than a minute, but a few onlookers who were walking along the sidewalks clapped and shouted their approval. Ansarians liked a show, especially on Freeday night. And although the sparks were short-lived, those who had witnessed them were thrilled.

Cedric knew that using magic to create a frivolous public display would have met with disapproval by the mage guild. But this night was already full of plans that would be frowned upon by lots of people if they knew about them. It felt as if they had leapt through a threshold and were falling headfirst into a sea of new experiences. It wasn't a night for either one of them to care about what others might think.

Gethric called out to his brother, "That was fun. Now it's my turn. Get ready."

Pulling his wand from his coat pocket, Gethric pointed it toward Cedric's motorbie, and said, "Calliope! Alamah!"

Gethric's spell forced air through Cedric's ooga horn and it suddenly began playing "The Pickle Dish" reel. The ooga's wheezing honk made the tune sound as if it were being performed by an asthmatic duck playing a kazoot, which made them roar with laughter. A young couple on the sidewalk began dancing to the music, while others clapped along in rhythm as the brothers passed by.

They turned off the boulevard onto Corkscrew Lane. Its twisting, winding turns were home to the most trendy shops—and they were open late. It was chock-full of taverns, restaurants, traffle shops, creamy-ice parlors, and gaming arcades. The main cineplex was located halfway down Corkscrew Lane where it crossed Bixbie Street.

The lane wasn't nearly as wide as the boulevard. The two vehicles no longer fit side by side, so Cedric fell in behind Gethric. Gethric's engine began to sputter and cough. His BMC rattled and hiccuped until the engine failed. Gethric veered to the curb and came to a stop.

Cedric called out, "What's the matter?"

"I don't know. It just seemed like it was gasping for a breath and then stopped."

Cedric shut off his motorbie, got off, and went up to Gethric, who was now standing with his hands in his pockets, staring at the vehicle.

"It's very odd. I've never had a problem before."

"Pull the fuel infuser and try starting it again. See what happens."

"Nice wheels!" A voice had come from somewhere across the lane. The phrase was commonly used sarcastically—especially when someone's motorbie had broken down. Gethric looked over to see who had said it. There were a dozen or so folks walking on the sidewalk. He didn't catch anyone's eye, so the comment remained anonymous.

"Thank you!" Gethric shouted with the same sarcasm to whoever it was. He climbed back into the seat just as a horn began honking from behind.

"I'm working on it!" Gethric shouted.

Cedric went to move his vehicle out of the way. Gethric pulled the infuser knob, dialed in his code, and pressed the ignition button. The BMC hacked and convulsed, but the engine didn't start. Traffic was stopped behind them and more horns were honking. Those that could catch a break from the oncoming vehicles peeled out of line and went around. Cedric was able to move *his* motorbie so that about half of it was up on the sidewalk.

"Let's see if we can push yours up onto the sidewalk too, and get it out of the way," Cedric suggested.

Gethric put his motorbie in neutral. They pushed, but it didn't budge. The curb was the problem. They weren't strong enough to get the back wheel up and onto the sidewalk by themselves. Finally, a rather beefy fellow noticed what they trying to do and came over to help.

"I'll push; you pull," said the bull.

The bull sauntered over behind the motorbie, got in position, and said, "On the count of three…One, two, three!"

All at once, the bull pushed, and Cedric and Gethric pulled. It worked. They were able to get the BMC out of the way and traffic began to flow. Vehicles went by, honking, whistling, and waving. One motorbie driver zipped by and called out, "Nice wheels!" which embarrased Gethric.

Gethric turned to the bull. "Thank you, sir. What do we owe you?"

"Think nothing of it. Have a great night!" The bull walked over to where two ostriches had been waiting for him. Cedric could smell their cloud of perfume from where he stood. Gethric noticed their pearl necklaces. "Affluent," he thought.

"Let's go, ladies. Time's a-wastin'!" The ladies giggled and they pranced along—one on each side of the bull. As they walked away, Gethric heard one of the ladies ask, "Where are you taking us tonight?"

The bull replied, "My favorite pub in all of Ansa—The China Closet."

"Now what?" asked Gethric. "What magic can we do to fix my motorbie?" It was a rhetorical question. Sorcerers could do all kinds of things with the natural elements—earth, wind, fire, and water— but their powers were greatly limited when it came to mechanical and electronic devices. For all the knowledge they had acquired to become mages, neither of them were mechanically inclined. This was the first time they had realized that they could really use a friend who belonged to the mechanic guild.

Although they both knew it would be futile, they still crawled underneath the BMC to see if there was anything that they might be able to see and repair. Gethric turned the latch, which allowed him to drop the side panel, and looked inside the belly. It was dark and he couldn't see much.

"Light! Alamah!" Cedric snapped his fingers and turned his hand in a such a way that he was holding a small aura of light.

"Does this help? Can you see anything?" Cedric asked.

"That's much better, thanks," said Gethric. "I don't see anything out of order."

"What seems to be the problem?" It was a female voice.

Gethric thought it was someone else trying to ridicule him. He kept on poking and prodding wires, but he didn't ignore her.

"Oh...nothing. I've had a little breakdown...not sure what it is. I'm sure it's nothing," muttered Gethric, half disregarding the voice and half hoping to find the problem.

"Would you like for *me* to take a look?" asked the voice. Cedric was tucked under the backside of the BMC, holding the light for Gethric, who continued prodding at connectors and cables he knew nothing about.

"I suppose you could look if you wanted to. That's what I'm doing—taking a look." Gethric was becoming annoyed by the lady's persistence. He tried not to sound perturbed, but he didn't hide it very well.

"My sister's really good with BMCs. I bet she can fix it," a new female voice said.

They hadn't realized there were *two* females standing there watching them. They suddenly felt very self-conscience and very inept. Neither one of them moved.

They heard the clicks of footsteps move closer to the side of the vehicle. Gethric turned his head in that direction. He blinked, shook his head, and blinked again. He focused on two pair of very lovely legs that were backlit by the glow of the street lamps and shimmered from the running lights of the vehicles passing by. They were wearing peep-toe pumps with five-inch spool heels. His demeanor changed from being annoyed and irritated to being spellbound and intrigued.

"Mind if I take off your seat?" asked the first voice.

Gethric stammered slowly, "Ahm...no...ga-go ahead."

Cedric popped his head up from behind the belly of the motorbie and slowly peered around the side. He saw the profiles of two women leaning into the BMC, apparently fiddling with the seat. The canopy cast a shadow from the street lamps, so he really could only see them from their waists down.

"Gethric!" Cedric whispered. "Get up!"

Gethric closed the side panel, latched it back in place, and slowly pulled himself out from under the motorbie. He stood up and dusted himself off.

"Here it is!" the first voice exclaimed. "The fuel connector. Let me just..."

Neither Gethric nor Cedric realized their mouths were gaping open.

"There, that should do it...for now."

They heard the click of the seat being set back into place. The ladies stepped back and turned around. Their faces came into the light.

"Angels," thought Cedric.

"A-are you sure you f-fixed it?" asked Gethric, who seemed to have suddenly forgotten how to talk.

"Hop on and see if it starts. Be sure to pull the infuser knob," she instructed. "It will need a bit of priming."

Gethric hopped up into the seat, pulled the infuser knob, dialed in the code, and pressed the ignition button. The motorbie coughed and then started right up.

"What in the world did you do?" asked Gethric.

"It was your fuel line. It has a twist-on connector that goes onto the injector just under the seat," she explained.

Gethric shut off the engine and hopped down.

"I'm guessing it was probably already loose and vibrated off," her sister added. "Luckily this model's connector has a safety device so that if it comes off, fuel doesn't spout out. That's why you didn't see anything."

The first sister inspected her hands. Gethric noticed her checking them and realized they had probably gotten dirty. "Here," he said, reaching inside his coat pocket. "Use my handkerchief."

"Thank you...but look...they're perfect!" She held up both hands and showed him the fronts and backs. "You keep it amazingly clean."

"I spent all morning yesterday cleaning, polishing, and rubbing all the nooks and crannies, even under the seat."

"It's possible that you accidentally loosened the connecter while you were cleaning it. Like Oris said, if it got loose, these cobblestones could rattle it right off, so be careful when cleaning under the seat."

"Well, um..., yes, I *will* be more careful." Gethric was reaching for words, but finally remembered to say, "Thank you."

"How do you know about all this?" asked Cedric. He didn't mean for the question to be sexist, but it probably came out that way. He was simply amazed that these two beautiful young ladies, out on the town, had come by at *just* the right time and knew exactly what to do.

"I have one, and the same thing happened to me," replied the first sister. "Just lucky, I guess."

"Lucky for me!" exclaimed Gethric, removing his hat and extending his hand. "My name is Ge..."

It almost slipped out. He couldn't just blurt out his real name. He was in public. He had become so lost in the moment that he had almost forgotten where he was—or rather, where he wasn't supposed to be.

He cleared his throat, "Ahem...excuse me. My name is Gelbert, at your service."

"At your *service*? A man with *fancy* manners. I like that." Her response included a twinge of flirtatiousness. "I'm Genevra."

Her hair was golden and warm like wheat ready for harvest. The soft curls were pulled back from her face and secured with a blue enameled clasp. Her eyes were shimmering sapphires that sparkled in the city lights. She was wearing a flowing, cobalt blue dress with a waterfall hem and a well-fitted, intricately embroidered brocade bodice. Gethric thought she was radiant in every way. He reached out and took her hand. He bowed low and kissed it.

"And I'm Cerrol," added Cedric, also kissing her hand.

Genevra introduced her sister, Oris, and the brothers each bowed and kissed her hand too.

Cedric noticed that Oris let her bronze hair fall about her shoulders so that it flowed in waves and covered the top of her emerald green lace dress. Oris and Cedric locked eyes. Her brown eyes penetrated his with such intensity that his stomach sank and his heart raced. It felt as if she had entered his soul and was attempting to discover all of his secrets. He was the first to glance away.

"It's a pleasure to meet you both," said Gethric.

"Indeed, you are visions from heaven and angels sent to help us in our time of distress," added Cedric.

"You two look a lot alike. You must be brothers," Genevra suggested.

Gethric, who for the past few minutes had felt weak-kneed and brain dead from this unexpected, rapturous encounter, was starting to get his wits back.

"You're very perceptive—indeed we are—and we are having a party at the Shoe and Fiddle if you would like to come," said Gethric, trying to steer the subject in a different direction.

Oris and Genevra looked at each other with questioning expressions. Genevra smiled and looked back to Gethric.

"Thanks, but we already have a commitment at the Snail's Trail," said Genevra. "It's just there." She pointed across the street to the sign hanging above the entrance of a tavern that was a few doors farther down the lane. A motorbie honked as it passed by and the driver whistled.

"Damn! We've got to get our motorbies off the sidewalk."

Gethric had forgotten they were still partially blocking traffic. "Maybe we'll see you later," said Gethric. He had said it as a comment, but he meant it as a question.

"Maybe!" said Genevra.

They turned and walked away.

Gethric and Cedric hopped on their motorbies. By the time they got off the sidewalk and back into traffic, they noticed that the sisters had stopped at a flower vendor on the corner. Across on the opposite corner, a street jester dressed in a dragon costume was blowing fire. They steered their motorbies back into the lane and started on their way. Cedric watched Oris pick up a bundle of yellow roses. As they passed by the flower stand, they sounded their oogas and waved. Oris and Genevra waved back.

Gethric called out, "Maybe we'll see you later?" This time he made sure it was a question.

"Maybe!" The two replied in unison.

The Shoe and Fiddle

Brandt was starting to panic. The king would have his hide if he let anything bad happen to his sons. He had three pair of guards stationed in strategic locations throughout the pub, but it wouldn't matter how carefully he had prepared if something happened to the brothers *before* they arrived. He had warned them about making the drive without security, but they had insisted on it. Now Brandt was biting his claws with worry and felt like he needed a drink. He sauntered over to the bar.

"What'll it be?" asked the barman.

Brandt hesitated. He could foresee what was coming and had to think about it. "Oh, hell," he thought. "Who cares."

"Gimme a lemon Fizzbie, with no ice," he said with a defeated sigh.

The barman laughed out loud. "A lemon Fizzbie? For a big guy like you? I pictured you as a Hammer Down sort of guy."

The barman was spot on with his perception. Brandt was definitely a Hammer Down sort of guy. In fact, he was a *triple* Hammer Down sort of guy, and he needed *two* triples before he would even begin to crack a smile. Brandt lived with a perpetually grumpy face—except for when the effects of Hammer Down kicked in. Then he was all smiles.

"It's a satins thing," he grumped.

Brandt was about as far removed from being a follower of the Book of Satins as anyone could be, but he knew that it was respected. If someone said they were changing a certain behavior for religious reasons, people generally left them without any hassle or additional questions.

"Excuse me?" asked the barman.

"The Fizzbie...it's a satins thing. I did something I shouldn't have done, and now I have to lay off ales and spirits for a while...you know... to get back into the good graces. It's Freeday...and I just needed to get out," explained Brandt.

"It smells to me like you're here to get a date," said the barman.

Brandt had kept his promise to Gethric and bathed. But he had also made an appointment at The Groomed Goat for a brushing earlier that afternoon. The groomer had offered a fragrance spray for an additional fifty krotes. It seemed like it was a good bargain, so Brandt accepted. It was evident to everyone within a twenty-five foot radius that the attendant had been extra generous with the spray.

"*There* you go," said the barman, winking and nodding to a table of five lovely, unescorted damsels who had just walked in and sat at a table across the room. "You better move fast."

Brandt responded with a sly grin that gave the barman the impression he was interested in them. He turned so he was facing in their direction. But it wasn't the ladies he was watching—he was staring at the door. There was still no sign of Cedric and Gethric.

The Shoe and Fiddle was one of the larger pubs in the city. It sat on a wedge where Carriage St., at a very acute angle, converged into Ballywick Ave. It was a triangular building with a prominent four-story facade. Anyone coming down Ballywick Ave., heading toward the intersection, was forced to veer left, staying on Ballywick, or veer right, going onto Carriage St. If they didn't, they would drive right into the front door of the Shoe and Fiddle.

The pub radiated with warmth. The aged, wood-paneled walls were laden with old photographs and paintings, which created an air of nostalgia. Stained glass fixtures dotted the copperplate ceiling. There was a stage along one side of a large dance floor, which was located in the center of the lower level. The dance floor was made from Valendale white oak, which was laid out in a herringbone pattern. The floor was surrounded by two levels of balconies. Tables lined the balconies so that visitors had a good view of the dance floor below.

The centerpiece of the Shoe and Fiddle was undoubtedly the legendary bar, which Jacob, the head barman, kept in immaculate condition. It wrapped around the far end of the pub in a semicircle. It was made from Valendale *red* oak, which had a deep, reddish-brown color and dramatic woodgrain. The back of the bar had ornate, hand-carved columns that separated large, mirrored sections. There were five tiers of glass shelves and hundreds of ales, wines, and spirits from which to choose. Jacob, and some of the other shorter barmen, had to use a rolling ladder to reach the top two tiers where the most expensive libations were kept.

The musicians at the Shoe and Fiddle were the best in the kingdom. There was a drummer, a guitera player, a bass player, a fiddler, a keyboardist, and a piper. The sound cones on the stage were made using the most sophisticated resonators available. The music could easily be heard above the crowd.

Brandt was attempting to enjoy the music, sipping his Fizzbie, when Cedric and Gethric finally came in. He heaved a huge sigh of relief. He nodded to them after making eye contact, and they nodded back. He had questions, but those would have to wait. They were obviously okay.

The brothers stood in the doorway and scanned the room. They spotted their friends in a nook and headed in their direction. As they passed Brandt, the air suddenly thickened with the heavy scent of sandalwood and talcum. Gethric whiffed the air and glanced sideways, cutting his eye to the bear. Brandt made a slight "Yes, it's me" expression, which sent Gethric and Cedric away laughing and fanning their noses. Brandt had reserved the alcove in advance. It was raised two steps higher than the main floor and surrounded by a half wall that kept them separated from the main crowd—giving the guards a better opportunity to watch over them.

Shortly after arriving, Gethric had made sure that everyone in their group knew that he and Cedric each had a *nom de guerre* for the evening, and he urged them to be extra careful not to let their real names slip out. The ale was flowing freely and the party was in full swing.

Brandt had casually managed to infiltrate their group so he could be as close to the brothers as possible. None of their friends knew that Brandt was their chief bodyguard. Within a few minutes, he had managed to gather bits and pieces of what had transpired on Corkscrew Lane, and he stitched the story together as best he could.

Within an hour the pub had filled to capacity. People were carefree, laughing, bantering, dancing, and drinking. Gethric had experienced many banquets and festivals during the course of his twenty-eight years, but none of them had ever come close to giving him the glorious sensations he was experiencing now. The patrons seemed carefree and appeared to be living life with abandon.

Gethric knew this would never be *his* life, but he was glad to know how it felt. He was so happy to be there—that is, until he realized that he didn't *want* to be there. He *wanted* to find a way to move the party to the Snail's Trail to see if he and Cedric could possibly get better acquainted with Genevra and Oris. The image of Genevra in his rear-view mirror, as he drove away, had consumed his thoughts for the past few hours. Cedric had made a similar comment about Oris, and had mentioned that he wished there were some way to go find them. As frustrating as it was, Gethric had to accept the fact that the guards and his friends were already situated here, and he knew it would be next to impossible to change venues.

"Here's to the birthday boy!" shouted David, one of the mage guild fellows. "Everyone! Raise a glass!" He looked around to make sure they had and then bellowed, "To Cerrol!"

"To Cerrol!" the group shouted together. They downed their ales, emptied their glasses, and began singing a rousing round of "Hip and Hooray for the Jolly Good Chap." Cedric was a little embarrassed about being the center of attention, but he thanked everyone for coming to the party. He gave a special thanks to Gethric for arranging it.

The dance floor seemed like a trampoline bouncing to the beat of the music. Everyone applauded and cheered for the band when the song came to an end. The leader whistled, and then shouted to the crowd, "May I have your attention, please?" The room quieted and folks turned their attention to the stage.

The drummer began playing a gentle but persistent boom, boom, boom, boom, on his thunder drum.

"Ladies and gentlemen," the leader shouted, "we have a *surprise* for you." As soon as he said the word *surprise*, the room cheered and everyone immediately began reaching for their sPeaksees.

The Shoe and Fiddle was known for impromptu publicity stunts. Those lucky enough to be in the pub when it happened would take pictos and cinebits and start sending them to their friends. The news of the event would ripple throughout all of Ailear in a matter of minutes. The leader paused again, purposefully teasing the crowd and creating an air of anticipation in the room. The boom, boom, boom, boom continued.

"Someone you know and love...Someone you've heard right here on this stage before...is recording their first album with Carlet Records..." The crowd cheered with excitement. The drumming got louder.

Brandt leaned over to Gethric and said, "I hope it's Ringmaster. I saw him perform here a few weeks ago. He's great."

The leader continued, "They are here to give us a late night preview of one of the songs that will be on their new album. Are you ready?" The crowed roared with excitement even though they didn't have a clue as to who was about to perform. The drummer doubled the thunder drums and the thickness of the beat intensified.

"Let's give a huge...Shoe and Fiddle welcome...to...Ice Angels!"

The band started a cyclical progression of chords over the top of the thunder drums. The crowd started pumping their fists in the air and bobbing their heads to the beat.

"I don't know Ice Angels," Brandt shouted to both Cedric and Gethric, "but I like the name. I guess they're new."

A guitera solo began to sail above the other instruments as three performers appeared on stage. Their entrance had been choreographed in such a way that, as they entered, they would freeze in different positions every eight beats. The lighting was set so that they appeared as silhouettes. The intro escalated into a frenzy until all at once, the music stopped, the musicians froze, and the room went dark. What remained were three blazing spotlights shining down onto a trio of females, posed like marble statues, with a pillar of smoke shooting up from behind each of them.

The crowd cheered wildly and pointed their sPeaksees at the stage, trying to capture as much as possible. The pause ended, and the band resumed playing the same vigorous, driving beat, and the trio began to sing.

I don't know you and you don't know me
But baby, baby my soul can see
You've put a magic spell on me
Now I'm yours for all eternity,
And I like it. I like it.

The dance floor began to flood with patrons who were filtering in from the sides and coming down from the upper levels. The crowd was clamoring to get closer to the stage.

"Cedric, look! It's them!" shouted Gethric.

Cedric was watching and immediately knew who *them* was. "You've got to be kidding me! Really?" he replied, "We've got to get closer."

Gethric turned to Brandt and shouted right in his ear, "It's them!"

"Who?" asked Brandt.

"The mechanics. The sisters who fixed the motorbie." Gethric turned back to Cedric, but his brother had already bolted into the crowd.

"Wait!" shouted Gethric.

Gethric ran after him. Brandt immediately realized that this situation could turn dangerous very quickly. He glanced around to the other guards. They had been alert, and all six of them were trying to move into the crowd in order to get closer to brothers. The dance floor was like a teaming swarm of bees, and the brothers were soon lost in the crowd.

Change Is in the Air

"Did that really just happen?" asked Oris, as she leaned over and sniffed a cluster of red roses.

"Talk about perfect timing!" replied Genevra quietly. "And those names...'Cerrol' and 'Gelbert'?"

"I know!" laughed Oris.

Genevra took a breath. "All things considered, I think we managed that situation pretty well."

They heard a crowd cheer and glanced across the lane. They saw a group of people gathered around a jester who was wearing a dragon costume and spewing impressive flames into the air.

"Maybe *you* managed okay, but *my* heart is still pounding," said Oris, picking up a bundle of yellow roses. "I don't know how you stayed so calm. Do you think she will like these...the yellow ones?"

"I think yellow will be better than red," offered Genevra, "but let's get a spray of angel's breath to add to it."

Ooga horns blared and they turned to look. Cedric and Gethric were waving at them and wearing smiles so big, they could have been seen from the moon.

Gethric called to them, "Maybe we'll see you later?"

"Maybe!" they shouted in unison.

The sisters stepped into the crosswalk. "There's no *maybe* about it," said Genevra. "I can't wait to tell Miona." They chuckled and hurried across to the other side.

Miona waved them over. She had managed to snag a bistro table near the back corner of the Snail's Trail. Sitting on the table was a pitcher of rummyritas and two extra glasses that had sat waiting patiently for them to arrive. The atmosphere at the Snail's Trail was always cozy and comfortable. The crowd was subdued—on purpose—and it was quiet enough in the tavern to actually carry on a conversation. The tavern's quartet played a mixture of gentle broomba and relaxing jass. The entire room was bathed in soothing blue light.

Miona was a student at satins guild along with Genevra and Oris. They had been friends since they started primaries. They chose satins, or rather their parents chose satins for them, not for any religious reasons, but because it was the best place for anyone pursuing the liberal arts. They weren't interested in governing, and they weren't inclined to magic. They didn't mind sitting through the required courses on the Book of Satins, but it was their music classes that they anticipated the most. The best music tutors in the kingdom were at the satins guild. During secondaries they sang a lot of three-part satins music, but when they started college, they started writing their own beatpop songs and sought out opportunities to sing in various pubs and taverns.

As Oris and Genevra arrived at the table, Miona snapped her head and jutted her jaw. Her auburn hair whipped around her shoulders.

"And just where have *you* been?" she teased.

Oris whispered out loud, "Sorry we're late. You are not going to believe what just happened." The sisters were giddy.

"What happened?" asked Miona.

"First things first," said Oris, setting the small vase of yellow roses and angel's breath on the table. She slid them over to Miona.

"What are these for?" She closed her eyes and smelled the bouquet.

"For putting up with the two of us for starters...and for making sure we didn't sign the recording contract without reading all the details," explained Oris.

"Your father would have made sure of that," added Miona while pouring rummyritas into the empty glasses.

"Maybe...but you were being the sensible one...so thank you," said Genevra. They raised their glasses.

"I didn't do anything, but you're welcome. Cheers!"

"Cheers!" they said.

Miona smelled the flowers again. "So tell me...what happened?"

Oris and Genevra both shivered with excitement.

"Do *you* want to tell her?" asked Oris.

"No...you can," offered Genevra.

"But you were the one who..."

"Just *tell* me!" insisted Miona.

They all three leaned in and Genevra whispered, "We just met Cedric and Gethric—face to face!"

Miona shouted, "You what?" Her response reverberated through the tavern. Disapproving heads turned in her direction.

"Shh," said Genevra.

Miona looked to a group who were seated at a table nearby and mouthed the word *sorry*.

"It just now happened, outside the tavern, on Corkscrew! They were on motorbies and one broke down."

"They? The twins? On motorbies? The Royal Princes of Ailear?" Miona was instantly full of questions.

"And...the most handsome and most available men in the kingdom!" added Oris.

"Yes...*they*...Cedric and Gethric—in the flesh!" said Genevra.

"And guess what?" added Oris.

"What?"

"They will be there tonight—at the Shoe and Fiddle when we perform!"

Miona squealed. Once again heads turned to look at her; this time the stares came with audible grumbles.

"You invited them?" asked Miona.

"No, they are having a party there. We didn't tell them anything," explained Oris.

"Tell me the whole story. I want to know every little detail!" Miona insisted.

"Do you remember us telling you that they came into Mo-Bo's to customize their new motorbies a few weeks ago?"

Miona nodded.

On weekends, Oris and Genevra worked at Mo-Bo's Add Ons. It was a small weekend job. Their studies at the satins guild took priority during the week. Their job had been arranged by their father as part of his plan to acquaint them with the various aspects of the family business.

Their father was Bolger Orin Biggleston, the owner of Biggleston Motor Company. The company had been founded by their grandfather, and their father had inherited it. He was grooming Oris and Genevra to take over BMC at some point in the future.

Orin Biggleston wanted his daughters to know the company from the inside out. Both of them had worked on the assembly line in the factory. They knew the official name of everything that was used to build a Biggleston motorbie. The accounting department was challenging, but they managed to learn the gist of what was required. They spent weeks in the service department at Alvar's Motorbie Dealership learning to troubleshoot and make repairs to the vehicles.

They were moved onto the showroom in order to experience the nuances of sales strategies, and how friendly public interaction added to the bottom line. They had recently been moved to Mo-Bo's Add-Ons to learn about all the various accessories that were available for the customization of BMC motorbies.

After Cedric and Gethric bought their new motorbies, they immediately made a private appointment at Mo-Bo's for the customization. Oris and Genevra had been permitted to stay. As observers, they would learn the protocols of interacting with the royal family. They watched from the upper offices overlooking the main showroom floor. They felt like queens, sitting in the royal boxes of an arena, watching a game of chess being played with real players. Each time an add-on was chosen, it was taken to the assembly room to be installed. When the customization was finished, the brothers' motorbies were brought into the showroom and revealed.

The entire experience had lasted nearly three hours. By the time the motorbies were finished, the sisters felt as if they had come to know the princes. They hadn't, of course, but they had become very acquainted with their new motorbies.

"We wouldn't have recognized them without their motorbies," said Genevra. "They have new haircuts and new beard styles. Their beards are bang as firecrackers."

"...and *you* fixed their motorbie!" chuckled Miona. "I bet they were flabbergasted."

"I'm pretty sure they were," confirmed Oris. "Can you imagine how flabbergasted they will be when they see the Ice Angels and put two and two together!"

"Honestly, I can't!" said Miona. They laughed and finished their rummyritas.

"Look at the time. We better get going," said Miona. "I don't want to be rushed getting dressed for the show."

"Is anyone nervous?" asked Genevra.

Oris replied, "I wasn't until you asked."

§ § § § §

The audience at the Shoe and Fiddle went wild over the Ice Angels' performance. Pictos and cinebits were flying across the kingdom and the crowd begged for more. A man wearing a black leather jacket wormed his way through the teeming mass. The crowd, still focused on the stage, was oblivious to his bumps and nudges. He was moving in the direction of Cedric and Gethric who had managed to reunite several feet away from the stage during the performance.

The man in black was almost to them. The twins were not aware of him until he was nearly upon them. He reached inside his jacket. Instantly, two royal guards tackled him. The commotion cause the crowd to part slightly and they pinned him to the floor. The cheering continued. Most people were oblivious.

"Get off me, you dungballs!" cursed the man. "What's *wrong* with you?" He fought against their grip. "We're royal guards!" one of the two shouted. "Stay where you are."

"Royal guards, my ass! Where's your uniform? Let me go! There's no use for royal guards in a pub."

"There is when there's royalty here," said the guard.

Cedric and Gethric watched the guards subdue their attacker. They were stunned by the sudden realization of how quickly things can change in the real world.

The guards got the man to his feet and instructed Cedric and Gethric to follow. They headed in the direction of a door on the left side of the stage with a sign that read "Backstage Entrance."

"You oafs! Let me go!" The attacker continued to wrestle against them.

With the excited crowd still cheering, the Ice Angels began making their exit on the opposite side of the stage from where the ruckus was occurring. Brandt skirted the main cluster of people and headed in the direction of the left backstage door. Inside the dressing room hallway, the guards began to search the man in black.

"Where's your weapon? Did you toss it?"

Brandt arrived just as the man said, "I don't have a weapon, you idiots! I'm the manager for the Ice Angels."

"Yeah, yeah, and I'm Princess Pinochle," said the guard. "What were you reaching for?" He patted the man's jacket but didn't feel anything like a weapon.

"It's a note!" said the man. "I was sent to give it to that guy," pointing to Gethric.

"What note? Who sent you?"

"The note in my jacket pocket! It's from Genevra, the blonde Ice Angel."

The guard reached inside the man's jacket pocket, found a folded piece of paper, and pulled it out. He looked at it and raised his eyebrows.

"Now *you're* the one who's after the wrong guy, buddy. This is addressed to someone named Gelbert," said the guard.

"Let me have it," said Brandt, snatching it out of the guard's hand.

Brandt looked at the note and then looked to Gethric.

"Is there anyone here named Gelbert?" he asked, waiting for Gethric to fess up.

Gethric shook his head. "Please ease up on the fellow. It's not a mistake. I'm Gelbert."

The guards let go of the manager and he brushed himself off. They stood there, bewildered. Brandt handed the note to Gethric.

"But..." One of the guards started to speak.

Brandt raised his paw and the guard stopped instantly. There were no more questions. Gethric opened the note and read it to himself.

> *Dear Gelbert and Cerrol,*
>
> *We hope that you will accept this invitation to visit with us backstage after our performance. If you choose to accept, Marlow, our manager, will escort you.*
> *Yours,*
>
> *Genevra and Oris*

The door on the opposite end of the hallway opened and three very excited young ladies rushed in.

"I could get used to this," said Miona. All three ladies were bubbling with energy.

"Did you see how the crowd was..." Genevera interrupted herself as soon as she saw Gethric. She recognized the folded piece of paper in his hand.

Gethric looked at Brandt. "May we please we have a moment? My brother and I would like to have a word with these ladies." Brandt and the other guards stepped back.

He then asked Genevra, "Is there a place where we can talk privately?" She pointed to the dressing room door.

"Brandt, if you would be so kind as to keep watch, I would be very grateful." Brandt nodded.

"Do you mind, Miona? For just a minute?" said Oris.

Miona barely shook her head. She was entranced at seeing the royal brothers.

"N-no, I'm f-fine. Use the dressing room...it's...okay."

Cedric opened the dressing room door and ushered Oris and Genevra inside.

"That was absolutely fantas..."

"Wait," said Genevra, slightly raising her hand and interrupting Gethric.

"Your Highness..." she said to Gethric, "and your Highness," she said, nodding to Cedric. Both ladies bowed appropriately.

"You know?" asked Cedric in disbelief.

"We *knew*!" said Oris. "We knew when we offered to fix your motorbie. We knew you would be here so Genevra sent our manager to deliver the note. She pointed you out to him when you were in the alcove."

"But how?"

Genevra and Oris spent the next few minute explaining things and answering the brothers' questions. The twins were astounded to learn that the ladies were Bigglestons. They appreciated them for respecting their privacy and not blowing their cover on Corkscrew Lane. None of them could believe the numerous coincidences that had led them to this moment. The conversation was comfortable and the room was filled with laughter. Gethric rarely broke eye contact with Genevra, and Oris kept looking into Cedric's soul.

"So you *are* angels after all," Cedric said, smiling.

"Apparently," said Oris. "Ice Angels."

Gethric thanked them for the concert and the pleasant surprise. Although Cedric wasn't really ready to say farewell, he knew it was best to follow Gethric's lead and restrain himself from being overly enthusiastic. Tonight's party had come to an end and it was time to say goodbye.

"Maybe we'll see you again?" asked Gethric.

"Maybe," they said in unison.

§ § § § §

On the day King Eoseph died, the kingdom of Ailear grieved the loss of one of its most beloved rulers in history. Cedric had gone to the tower window and unfurled the black banner. It had flowed down the side of the tower in the same way his tears flowed down his cheeks. He turned and went back into the room. Cedric embraced his brother and they cried. Deep sorrow swept through the entire kingdom, but nobody grieved King Eoseph's death more than Cedric and Gethric, and their wives, Oris and Genevra.

Lizzy Albright

A Bumpy Landing

Lizzy felt a soft mist brushing her face and slowly opened her eyes. She realized she must have fallen asleep. As she regained awareness, she realized that she had not been dreaming and was indeed flying through the air on the back of a goose with McDoogle snuggled up next to her. Although it was no longer dark, Lizzy couldn't see anything other than the goose and McDoogle. It was as if they were floating through a heavy purple fog.

"Purple?" she mused.

She straightened up, took a deep breath, and then noticed that the purple mist was slowly changing to blue. Surely her eyes were playing tricks on her. She shut her eyes tight and then opened them wide, hoping to bring something, anything, into focus. This time when she opened her eyes, the mist was green.

Gretta felt Lizzy shift on her feathery back and asked, "Did you have a good rest?"

"Um, I think so," Lizzy said, gazing into the haze of ever-changing color. "How long have I been asleep?"

"Most of the night," said Gretta. "I was just about to wake you. We are almost there."

"It's aboot time," yawned McDoogle as he stretched out his legs. "I'll no' be wantin' onything to do with ony tomfoolery."

Lizzy scratched McDoogle's head. "It's alright, McDoo. I'm sure it will all make sense soon enough."

"Ach, no soon enough for me, Lass," McDoogle huffed.

"Gretta, why is it so foggy and why is everything so..." She was just about to say "yellow" when she was suddenly bathed in orange. "Um, colorful?" Lizzy asked slowly.

"It's foggy because we are passing down through a rainbow cloud. Isn't it beautiful?"

As confused as Lizzy was, she agreed. "What's a rainbow cloud?"

"Sometimes after a soft morning rain the rising sun makes a rainbow. When the rainbow passes through a cloud, it makes a rainbow cloud and we are just now passing through it."

"Wow!" exclaimed Lizzy, "I didn't know you could be inside of a rainbow."

Gretta finally dropped below the cloud and Lizzy saw a magnificent sun-drenched landscape. There was a range of snowcapped mountains in the distance on her left and she could see a large sparkling sea off to the right. There were rivers, forests, lakes, and hills. Below, she saw a patchwork of farms with fields that were outlined with fences made from stacked stones.

Now Lizzy could see how the rainbow ascended, passed through the cloud, and then reached down and touched the horizon on the other side. The rainbow reminded her of stories that she had been told about leprechauns and their treasures. Of course, she knew that leprechauns were little, make-believe, magical creatures, but if she could fly on a goose through a rainbow cloud, it might just be possible to find a pot of gold.

Hillsides were dotted with little puffs of white that Lizzy determined to be sheep. She looked more closely, hoping to find a black sheep, but she didn't spot one. She found a road and followed it into the distance.

"Wow!" said Lizzy. "Look at that!"

Up ahead was a city perched on a finger of land that rose upward and jutted out into the sea. The towering cliffs below the city were being violently battered by crashing waves.

"Is that where we are going?" asked Lizzy.

"That, my dear, is Ansa, the royal city of our beloved Ailear. Our destination is just on the other side of the city."

Lizzy whispered to herself, "Ansa. Ailear." Though these names were unfamiliar, she thought they were beautiful. She slowly and deliberately repeated them again, "Ann-suh. All-air."

"If Ansa is a city, is Ailear a state, like Kansas?"

"Kansas?" replied McDoogle. "Ah, Lass, I'm fearful to tell ye, but I don't think we're in Kansas ony mair."

Gretta chuckled. "Ailear is our kingdom...our country. Everything you see around you is part of Ailear!"

"I've never heard of Ailear. Is it part of Europe?" Lizzy queried.

Gretta hesitated, "Ailear is not part of anything. Ailear is...well, Ailear is *here*."

Lizzy's face contorted into a confused expression. Even though she wasn't sure about where *here* was, she decided to hold off on more questions until later.

"We are getting close to the city. It will be best if you hide as best you can, Princess. Tuck yourself back under my feathers."

Lizzy did as she was told, but she situated herself so that she could still see the sights below. She pulled her cloak close. Though they were flying high over the city, there was still plenty to see.

Ansa filled the entire surface of the peninsula. Stone buildings with red clay roofs lined the cobblestone streets. Chimneys were puffing up columns of delicate smoke that dissipated and vanished. Every now and then Lizzy thought she caught a whiff of freshly baked bread wafting up from below.

"Do you smell the traffles?" asked Gretta.

"Whattles?" asked Lizzy.

Gretta laughed. "Traffles! Traffles are yummy. You'll be having one soon enough!"

"Aye, ma stomach is knockin' on ma backbone. I sure hope we'll be eatin' pretty soon!" McDoogle chimed in.

"Indeed, you will, Mr. McDoogle. Indeed, you will!" replied Gretta.

People—or what Lizzy perceived to be people—were scurrying about through the city. Lizzy expected to see cars, but there weren't any. Instead, there were vehicles of some sort that didn't look like anything she had ever seen before. From her vantage point high above the city, she couldn't make out the finer details, but they looked fun to ride.

Most of the larger streets in Ansa flowed toward the center where a series of buildings wrapped around a large, circular area. Inside the hub was a large open-air structure with terraced seating that Lizzy suspected was a sports stadium or amphitheater. She wondered if the Beatles had ever given a concert there.

The largest buildings in the city were situated in an area that was surrounded by a stone wall. One building had a copper-top dome that age and exposure had coated with a green patina. Another building had an expanse of steps that led up to a row of columns supporting its elaborate pediment.

The tip of the peninsula was cut off from the rest of the city by a large wall that spanned the entire escarpment. The wall had an enormous main gate with two guard towers. Large, faded, yellow and black banners hung from the towers. Spaced along the rampart, tattered flags fluttered in the breeze. Lizzy assumed that yellow and black must be important colors.

Inside the main gate was a smaller courtyard lined with several small buildings, stables, and sheds. Lizzy noticed a few people and animals, but they weren't moving. She determined that they must be statues. There were other statues on the fortress wall. This interior courtyard lay at the foot of a majestic castle that triumphantly sat on top of the cliffs at the very end of the escarpment. There was a very large garden behind the castle. It was surrounded by an open area that went right to the edge of the cliffs.

"It's like a fairy tale," said Lizzy.

"It *is* beautiful, isn't it?" replied Gretta.

"I hope we are going there. I want to see it!"

"We are, but not today."

Soon Ansa was behind them and Gretta was flying over a forest. They were so close to the tops of the trees that Lizzy felt as if she could reach out and touch them. The trees abruptly stopped and they were instantly flying over a large lake. Gretta swooped down and was skimming over the surface of the water. It appeared to Lizzy that Gretta was headed to a large, grassy bank just up ahead.

"We're almost there. Prepare to land," Gretta called back to the two passengers.

"How do I prepare to....oh, my, oh, ouch!" Lizzy exclaimed.

Gretta was very good at landing on water, but when attempting a ground landing, the result was more like a skipping rock than a smooth glider. She hit the ground with a thud, bounced, and then became airborne again.

McDoogle fell out of Lizzy's arms and tumbled to the ground, "Michty me! Hing on, Lass," he called to Lizzy, chasing after the two.

Several bounces later, Gretta finally got her feet on the ground. Her momentum kept her running several paces beyond the distance she had calculated. She crashed into the tweetle reeds on the edge of a lake. Lizzy tumbled off of Gretta's back and rolled right into the shallow, murky water. Stunned and soaked, she sat upright. Several geese were racing toward her shouting a cacophony of indecipherable exclamations.

"Are you alright, Princess?" a plump, older-looking goose wearing glasses called out.

"I think so," Lizzy said cautiously. She tried to comprehend that she was conversing with yet another goose—except this one was normal size, unlike Gretta who was...

Lizzy looked at Gretta, who was now back to being the size of a normal goose. "What's happening?" Lizzy thought.

McDoogle leapt into the water and paddled over to Lizzy. "C'mon, Lass, let's git ye oot of this mingin loch. Ye're drookit through and through!"

Although he could tell Lizzy was managing just fine on her own, he felt it was his duty to protect her. He thought his heroic actions would at least prove to the geese just how much he intended to keep her safe at all costs.

The old goose turned to the two younger geese and said, "Molly, help the princess out of the lake. Gabby, get a fire going—and be quick about it. We must get her dried and warm."

Lizzy stood up and was removing her now very heavy, waterlogged cloak. Molly went to assist Lizzy, but Gabby, having not heard a word, stood frozen—transfixed on Lizzy. She was staring at a girl who, up until now, she knew only as a myth. And yet here she was, standing right before her very eyes.

"Gabby!" the old goose shouted abruptly.

Gabby was jolted from her trance. "Yes, ma'am?"

"Get a fire started. Hurry!" she repeated.

"Oh, goodness yes, of course. Right away!" As Gabby waddled away, her heart raced with joy and she began to sing:

The princess is here!
She's just as they said.
With freckles and curly red hair on her head.

"Let me help you, Princess!" The young goose went to help Lizzy out of the lake. Lizzy grabbed her extended wing and came on shore.

"I'm Molly," the goose said with a rather shy, but giggly grin, and then she bowed deeply.

"Thank you, Molly."

Lizzy wasn't sure why Molly was bowing, but she thought it must be some kind of customary greeting. Without thinking, Lizzy awkwardly bowed back. "Pleased to meet you, Molly."

"I dinnae ken hoo a goose can be so haunless," said McDoogle, vigorously shaking off his coat.

"Calm down, McDoo. I'm okay. Would you mind helping gather sticks for the fire?"

"Aye, Lass! I'll fetch ye sticks."

McDoogle, who happened to be very good at fetching sticks, scampered away.

Lizzy looked at Molly. "I'm so sorry about McDoo. He'll calm down soon enough. He means well."

"No need to apologize, Princess. He's your guardian. I wouldn't expect him to do anything less."

Fiddler's Cove

Lizzy had never thought of McDoogle as a guardian, but then it dawned on her that he had always been protective of her.

"Follow me, Princess. Let's get you out of that wet tunic," said the older goose with glasses.

"I'll take your cloak," said Gretta, who had been plucking bits of reeds, twigs, and grass from her feathers.

Lizzy followed the three geese down a trail that more resembled a tunnel than a path. The passage led through a dense thicket of brush and was covered by a canopy of tangled vines. Lizzy was barefooted, but the ground was soft. She was glad there were no stickers like the ones she often stepped on when playing barefoot in Glasford Park. A voice not too far away was singing:

> *The princess is here,*
> *The timing is right,*
> *The curse will be broken by Midwinter's Night!*

The little procession soon came to a clearing that wrapped around the sides of a narrow inlet that flowed in from the lake. The stargrass and tweetle reeds were trimmed short and kept well maintained.

Inside the clearing were four of the tiniest, happiest-looking houses that Lizzy had ever seen. Each house faced the water and was painted in the most wonderful colors—each one different from the other. The siding was made from wooden planks that were painted in two different colors that alternated to create cheerful horizontal stripes. Straw thatching adorned each roof and a little black smokestack nested on top. Window boxes were bursting with fragrant blossoms. Valendale oak trees stood nearby and their craggy branches drooped over the housetops. Lizzy thought they looked like the spindly arms of an old witch who was about to reach down and pluck the little houses right out of the ground.

All four houses were perched on poles. Each house had a colorful door, with a small basket sitting beside it and a bundle of twigs tied with brightly colored ribbons hanging over the lintel. There were wooden ramps that extended from each porch to the ground.

"Come, come, Princess!" said Gabby with a lilt, waddling down the ramp to meet her. "Welcome to Fiddler's Cove!" Lizzy presumed her to be the source of the singing she had just heard.

"Let's get you inside so you can dry off and warm up." The goose gestured for Lizzy to follow. Lizzy started up the ramp, but then she suddenly stopped.

"What's wrong, Princess?" asked Gabby.

Lizzy was looking at a goose-sized house with a bright red goose-sized door. She was far too big, or rather the house was far too small, for her to go inside.

"Well, um, I don't think I can fit through the door."

"Don't be silly. Of course you can," said Gabby, giving Molly a wink.

Molly sneezed.

Just as Lizzy turned to say *gesundheit*, there was a loud pop that made her jump. Lizzy saw one of Molly's tail feathers shoot up like a rocket and burst into a cloud of purple sparkles that floated down over the entire area.

"Oh dear, excuse me," said Molly.

"What was that? Are you alright?" asked Lizzy.

"It's nothing, nothing at all. Excuse me." Molly chuckled, passing off the incident as if it were a common occurrence.

Gretta called out, "That sort of thing happens when Molly gets excited. It's noisy, but it's harmless. C'mon now, let's get on inside."

Lizzy shrugged, turned, and continued walking up the ramp.

"Are ye okay, Lass? Whut was that noise?" McDoogle had heard the explosion, dropped the sticks he had collected, and ran to check on Lizzy.

"One of Molly's feathers exploded, Mr. McDoogle," said Gretta, trying to put his mind at ease. "There's nothing to worry about. It was loud, but everything's just fine."

McDoogle huffed. "I dinnae ken whut all the ruckus is aboot, but I've already telt ye, I'll no' be puttin' up with ony tomfoolery!"

He turned to Lizzy. "Are ye sure yer alright, missy?"

"I'm fine. Really, I am!"

"Alright then!" McDoogle turned and trotted off to reclaim the sticks he had left behind.

Gabby opened the door and she and Lizzy went into the house.

"First things first, Princess. Here's a dry tunic that I hope will fit you. You can change in that room over there," Gabby said, pointing to a door. "We'll be in the parlor when you're ready. The traffles are almost done."

Lizzy sniffed the air and recognized the scent. It was the same sweet, toasty smell she had experienced while flying over Ansa. Her belly rumbled. She hadn't realized how hungry she was. She also hadn't paid attention to how cold she had been until she felt the warmth of the fire in the fireplace. She took the folded bundle and went to change.

One by one the other three geese made their way inside.

Lizzy
Albright

Toadschrooms, Traffles, and Tea

Lizzy looked in the dressing mirror. Her hair was a mess. She looked for a brush but couldn't find one. The white tunic fit perfectly and she was glad to be dry. This new gown was a lot like her own nightgown, except that it didn't have embroidered roses and lace along the hem at the bottom.

Lizzy returned to the parlor and all four geese stood up at once.

"Come stand by the fire...and here's a pair of shoes. You'll be needing them. My name is Gabby," she said, bowing to Lizzy.

Lizzy bowed back. "I'm Lizzy, and I'm very pleased to meet you!"

"Oh goodness," cried Gretta. "With all the commotion, I didn't give proper introductions. I'm so sorry, Princess!" Gretta took a deep breath, shook her tail feathers, and announced, "Everyone, this is Lizzy Albright."

Up until now, none of them knew her name, except for Gretta, who only learned it when she overheard Lizzy's mother scolding her for not helping with the suitcases and packages when they were unloading the station wagon. The only thing they had known was that the princess had been located. Many bundles of stargrass had been burned with the hope that she would arrive before it was too late.

The geese were flustered, and they didn't know what to do, so they all began nodding, bowing, curtsying, and smiling. Their exclamations mingled together.

"What a beautiful name."

"Such lovely red hair."

"You're Royal Highness."

"I'm so glad you're here."

"I wish I had your freckles."

"This is the best day in the history of Ailear."

All at once they stopped—and stood there staring at her. They weren't sure what to do next. They had never been in the presence of a princess.

"Lizzy Albright!" Molly finally said, breaking the silence.

"My full name is Elisabeth Anne Albright," she replied. She didn't know why she gave them her full name, but the situation felt awkward and it was the first thing that came to mind. "But everyone just calls me Lizzy."

"You've already met my youngest sister, Molly," said Gretta.

Lizzy nodded to Molly. "Thank you so much for helping me out of the lake."

"Oh, I'm so glad you were not injured," said Molly. She then began spilling all of her thoughts at once. "I saw Gretta coming across the lake...and you were on her back...and I was so excited that I was about to burst. I was jumping up and down. Mother told me to calm down, but I just couldn't calm down. I was so excited. My stomach had butterflies twirling all around, and I thought, "The princess is finally here!" and you are here...and I've never seen a princess before, and then...well...you were tumbling into the lake, and I..."

"Molly!" Gretta interrupted.

"Oh, I'm sorry, Princess," said Molly, trying to catch her breath. "I try not to prattle on. I'm just so excited to meet you. It's such an honor. I was so worried that you might not know how to swim. Do you know what I mean when I say I had butterflies twirling..."

"Molly! Please!" Gretta interrupted her again. "You know what happens when you get overly excited."

Lizzy giggled. "Yes, Molly, I know what you mean about stomach butterflies."

Molly took another breath, bowed, and sat down.

"And this is Gabby, my older sister," said Gretta.

Gabby nodded, bowed, and said, "At your service, Princess."

"Thank you for the dry clothes," said Lizzy, bowing in return.

"We have been anticipating your arrival, and I knew you would be needing a few things. If you need anything else, please ask. I'll be happy to provide it if I can. I'm at your service," said Gabby.

"Thank you," said Lizzy.

Gretta walked toward Lizzy, extended her wing, and ushered her over to the last goose. "Lizzy, this is Gertie...Gertie Flutterfield, our mother."

Lizzy and Gertie bowed to each other.

"We are *all* at your service, Princess. We are so thankful you came to help us." Gertie's voice was soft and instantly made Lizzy feel safe. Gertie raised up, looked over the top of her glasses, and smiled at Lizzy.

"Ms. Flutterfield, I'm so hap..."

"Please...call me Gertie."

"Okay, thank you! Well, Mrs. Flutterfield...I mean, Ms. Gertie, I'm happy to meet you. I'm happy to meet *all* of you, but I'm still very confused about what help you need. I'm not a princess, and I can't begin to imagine what services you would require. I understand there's a..."

Tap, tap, tap. Lizzy was interrupted. "Hullo? Onybody home?" It was McDoogle. "Hullo?" He knocked at the door again.

Gretta greeted him. "Come in, come in, Mr. McDoogle. You're just in time for traffles."

"I kin hardly wait," said McDoogle. "I'm famished!"

She noticed a small bundle of sticks lying at his feet. "We can add these to the fire," said Gretta.

"I've another wee pile of sticks tucked under the porch if you be needin' ony mair. They're all plenty dry and kin be used right away."

"Perfect, Mr. McDoogle, and thank you!" said Gretta. McDoogle trotted inside. Gretta shut the door and introduced McDoogle to the others.

The tray full of traffles was steaming when Gabby brought it into the parlor. A toasty, rich aroma filled the room.

"They are best when hot," exclaimed Gabby, "but they last for days and are very good cold too. They are full of nourishment and will keep your belly full for hours."

Lizzy looked at the tray. The traffles were flat and round, a bit bigger than a donut, except there wasn't a hole in the middle. Lizzy took a bite and was surprised to find they were filled on the inside with a sweet and delicious paste.

"These are fab," said Lizzy. "What's inside?"

"These have the traditional bumbleberry and toadschroom mince," said Gabby.

Lizzy stopped eating and swallowed hard. "Berries and toads?" she asked, feeling her stomach begin to churn.

"Toad *schrooms*," Gabby clarified.

"What are toadschrooms?" asked Lizzy.

"Anything we harvest by picking it up off the ground is considered a schroom. Toadschrooms come from the nuts that fall from the bungabella bush. You can't pick them directly from the bush. The nuts must fall off on their own or they will harden and rot. The bungabella nuts lie on the moist ground and begin to swell. When they are ripe, the shells snap open, causing them to hop off the ground. It's fun to watch the bungabella nuts when they start hopping and spitting out their toadschrooms. So there you have it. They're not *toads*," chuckled Gabby. "They just *hop* like a toad, and that's what gives them their name."

Lizzy's stomach calmed down. "And what about the bumble...?"

"Bumble*berries*!" clarified Gabby. "The bumbleberries come from the bumbleberry tree. They grow abundantly throughout all of Ailear, and we use the berries for lots of things, including the filling we put inside traffles."

Lizzy was on her third traffle, in midbite, when she froze. She looked around the parlor. She glanced at the door of the room where she had changed. She knew that Gabby had come from a kitchen, but all this time she hadn't really paid attention to any of this. This house was spacious. Why hadn't she noticed it before? She chewed slowly and then swallowed. She glanced at Gretta and then looked at each goose one at a time.

"What is it?" said Gretta.

"Something's going on here and I really don't understand it."

"What?" asked Gertie.

"Well, I was outside on the ramp. No...wait!...Let me start over.

"It started in the attic, and Gretta was just a regular-sized goose... knocking at the window. But then without thinking anything about it, like it was perfectly normal, I was sitting on her back and flying through the sky. Then, I get here...and she's a normal-size goose again. It doesn't make any sense. Next, I see your little houses, and I think they are charming, but I realized there's no way *I* can fit inside. But then somehow...I'm inside...sitting here...having traffles...with all of you...and there are so many rooms inside this house. I know they couldn't possibly all fit inside the house that I saw when I was looking at it from the outside. And I'm extra confused because I'm just now realizing it."

Lizzy stopped. Her eyes widened. She slapped both hands on the top of her head, and then threw them up into the air.

"Now I understand! I get it!" she exclaimed.

"You get what?" asked Gretta.

"It finally makes perfect sense. I'm dreaming! And I'm dreaming of everything I love. I'm from Kansas. Dorothy was from Kansas. She's bonked on the head and lands in Oz, but the whole Oz thing is just a dream. And Dorothy has her little dog, Toto, that goes with her to Oz...and I have McDoo. And I was reading *Alice in Wonderland* in the car, and Alice gets big and gets small...so I must be the one who's getting big or getting small...so whatever works, works...because it's all a dream...and I'm ready to wake up now, because I'm not a princess, and I don't have any clue what I can do to help you. It's been really fun, and I wish you all a happily ever after. But I'm going to wake up now. One...two...three..."

Lizzy slammed her eyes shut and crossed her arms tight across her chest. She imagined her bedroom at Granny's house. She envisioned the wallpaper in the room. She could see a gentle snow falling outside the bedroom window. She remembered that she was sleeping under Granny's old quilt. She listed the names of some of the quilt blocks that she remembered and quietly said them out loud—"Bear

Paw, Jacob's Ladder, Pickle Dish, and Snail's Trail." She recalled two fabrics in particular. One featured a singing rooster and the other had frolicking Scottish terriers. She was back. She was no longer dreaming. It was time to wake up and open her eyes.

When she did, she found herself sitting in a parlor with four geese and McDoogle staring at her.

"Are ye okay, Lass?" asked McDoogle.

"Would you like another traffle?" asked Gabby.

You've got to be kidding me! You're still here?"

"Of course, we are still here. Why would we leave?" asked Gretta.

"Who's Dorothy?" asked Molly.

"Where's Oz?" asked Gertie.

"Oh, never mind," sighed Lizzy. "If I'm not in a dream, then why are these crazy things happening?"

"What things?" asked Gretta.

"Like...how can I be inside a house that is far bigger inside than it is outside? How can I walk through a door that is too small for me?"

"There are a lot of things that happen to us that cannot be explained. I don't have the answer for everything, but I do know this: if you think you *can* do something, then you can do it. If you think you *can't* do something, then most likely you can't. Does that make sense?"

"I'm not sure," Lizzy replied.

"Well, for instance, when you looked at Gabby's front door, you perceived it to be too small and decided you couldn't go in. You couldn't go in because you *believed* you couldn't go in. But when you were distracted by the explosion of Molly's feather, you stopped thinking about what you *couldn't* do and just walked inside. Things are not always as they seem, Princess."

"Apparently!" sighed Lizzy. "But I'm going to stick with the notion that I'm dreaming until I'm proved wrong. Since it seems that I can't leave this dream, can someone please tell me why I am here and what I'm supposed to do?"

Gretta went over and sat beside Lizzy.

"I need to let you know that there are some things I can tell you, and there are other things that I'm not allowed to tell you. But I promise you *will* learn everything in time. For now, I'm just asking you to trust me."

"Okay, I *do* trust you, but please," pleaded Lizzy, "tell me what you can."

Gretta began to explain. "Ten years ago a horrible thing happened in our kingdom."

"Whut horrible thing?" McDoogle interrupted.

"Mr. McDoogle," Gretta said softly, "if you'll just be patient, please." Patience was not one of McDoogle's virtues, but he did have manners. He reluctantly curled up on a rug.

"The tragedy revolves around an incident that happened to the royal family, who are in a terrible situation at this very moment. Many of us have been working very hard to help them. As unbelievable as it may sound, it also involves you, because you *are* the royal princess of Ailear."

"But I'm *not* a princess," insisted Lizzy.

"I know it's not easy for you to believe, so I don't expect you to believe it right now. I'm sure you will soon. May I ask you some questions?"

"Okay," replied Lizzy.

"How old are you?"

"Ten," said Lizzy "My birthday was yesterday...on Christmas Eve."

"Exactly, and the royal princess of Ailear was born ten years ago too...on Midwinter's Eve, the same day you were born. Midwinter Day is our most celebrated feast day."

Lizzy raised her eyebrows. "Lots of people are born on Christmas Eve," she submitted.

"That's true," said Gretta. "The next question may seem silly, but...what color is your hair?"

Lizzy grabbed a handful of hair and looked at it. "Red," she answered—and then frowned.

"Why are you frowning?"

"Because that question has always confused me. I don't know why it's called red. My red crayons are not this color at all. Some people call it ginger...but I think it looks more orange...and I don't like it because it's curly...and it's always tangled." That reminded her to ask, "Gabby, do you have a brush?"

"I'll see what I can find, Princess," replied Gabby.

Gretta said, "Our princess is supposed to have ginger hair too, and she would surely have curly locks that would tangle, just like yours."

"Lots of people have red, curly hair," argued Lizzy, and then she remembered that she was the only one in her class with red hair.

"That's true," said Gretta. "Tell me...where do you live?"

"I live in Overland Park, Kansas, on Juniper Lane."

Gretta continued. "When the royal child of Ailear was born, she was in immediate danger. She *had* to be protected."

"Protected from what?" asked Lizzy.

"That's a part of the story I'm not allowed to share with you, but you will have your answer very soon."

"Okay," Lizzy sighed, "but what does that have to do with me?"

"Well, the baby was put in the care of a royal servant, a goose, named Gracella. She swore to protect the infant, and she was instructed to take the child to Overland to find a family that would keep it safe. She left with the baby and flew through the Tunnel of Stars to Overland."

Lizzy's mind flashed back to when she was very young. She was a little girl, in the car, with her father, when he pointed to a big building with lots of windows and asked, "Do you see that big front door?" She had nodded *yes*. "That's where we got you when the goose brought you to us."

She remembered telling her dad that he was being silly because *storks* delivered babies, and he had replied, "Stork...goose...I can't remember for sure...but I *think* it was a goose." Every time they drove past St. Luke's Hospital, she remembered that story, even after she learned that babies were born and not delivered by storks *or* geese.

Lizzy didn't reply to Gretta. Instead, she became quiet and was lost in thought. She was reminding herself about how she was the only one in her family with red hair, which had once made her wonder if she had been adopted.

"Princess, I'm sorry. I can't tell you much more, but the favor I'm asking is that you please come with me. I will take you to the Valendale Forest where you will meet someone who can explain what has happened and why we need your help."

Lizzy thought about it for a moment, and then she remembered—until someone could prove to her that she's not having a dream, then she will believe that she is having a dream—and as long as the dream doesn't get too scary, then she might as well find out what happens.

Lizzy looked at Gretta. "I will go with you! And so will McDoogle!" she said confidently.

McDoogle, who was starting to doze, heard his name and popped his head up. "Aye Lass, let's go home."

Lizzy laughed, "No, McDoogle, I didn't say we were going *home*. I just told Gretta I was going to stay in this dream, and that you will be staying with me."

Lizzy was now bubbling with excitement. "Miss Gretta, what's next?"

All of the geese were smiling and breathing sighs of relief. "We need to take a little journey into the woods, although we won't be flying," said Gretta. "And then, I'll take you to Ansa."

"Perfect!" said Lizzy. "Are you ready, McDoogle?"

"Aye, ready. I'm always ready...as long as there's no tomfoolery."

Molly was so overjoyed with Lizzy's decision that she lost control and accidentally set off one of her feathers, which hit the ceiling, exploded, and showered the room with purple sparkles.

Lizzy
Albright

CHAPTER FIFTEEN

Identified Flying Objects

T hey topped a gentle rise and the road stretched out in front of them, drifting slowly down until it disappeared into a sprawling thicket of trees. "That's Valendale Forest...just there...up ahead," said Gretta.

Lizzy looked at the road as it needled its way through the meadows and disappeared into a thick forest of trees. "Let's stop for a moment. We can rest our legs and have a traffle, shall we?" suggested Gretta.

"Aye, I could use a wee bit of food in me tummy," added McDoogle.

Lizzy admitted that she was hungry as well, so Gretta led them off the road to a spot by the lake that was out of sight and hidden under the shade of several very large bumbleberry trees. They each took a bag from the inside pockets of their cloaks and pulled out a traffle. As Lizzy sat quietly eating her lunch, she examined her surroundings more closely. She was fascinated by the various unfamiliar flowers whose heads danced and pattled in the breeze.

The lake sparkled with twinkling flashes that reminded Lizzy of the holiday lights at Crowne Plaza. It made her wonder if the days were the same here as they were back at home. She hadn't noticed any decorations at Fiddler's Cove, but Gretta had said something about Midwinter's Eve and that it was their biggest feast day. If that were the case, they surely would have decorated.

"Do you put up decorations to celebrate Midwinterfest?" asked Lizzy.

"We do!" replied Gretta. "Did you notice the baskets on our porches, and the bundles of twigs above our lintels?" Lizzy nodded. "The twigs and baskets are our most important Midwinterfest tradition."

"What are the twigs for?" asked Lizzy.

"Ah-ha," said Gretta. "Now that is a question. The bundle of twigs is called a twigsicle. Every child in Ailear wants a visit from Mr. Boots. They make wishes and write them on bright, colorful ribbons. Then they tie their wishes to the bundles of twigs to make twigsicles. The twigsicles are then hung above the lintels of their front doors, so that when Mr. Boots comes along on Midwinter's Eve, he can read their wishes and make them come true. Some children these days use huge ribbons that dangle down in front of the door to make sure that Mr. Boots won't miss them."

"In a way, Mr. Boots is like our Santa Claus," Lizzy noted.

"Is Santa Claus that man in the display that was on the front lawn by the pond?" asked Gretta.

"Yes, except that we put our wishes in letters and send them to the North Pole, or we sit in Santa's lap and tell him what we want," explained Lizzy. "Does Mr. Boots have a big, white beard and wear a red suit?" she asked.

Gretta chuckled, "No, he doesn't wear a red suit, but he does have a beard. He has a very long, black beard that comes to his waist and big, black, bushy eyebrows. He's three feet tall. He wears a brown coat that goes down to the ground, tall black boots that come up to his knees, and a top hat that reaches to the clouds."

"Reaches to the clouds?" puzzled Lizzy.

"It's just a saying everyone here uses to describe Mr. Boots's hat. It just means it's a tall hat."

"I think I would like him," said Lizzy. She was very interested in what Gretta was telling her, and she wanted to know more. "And what about the baskets?"

"The baskets are for friendship, and that's what we call them—friendship baskets. They are placed on the porches eight days before Midwinterfest and are filled with all sorts of fun things. Sometimes they are silly treats, and sometimes they are useful items. During this time, people come and take something *from* the basket—but they also put something *in* the basket. The exchanges are always anonymous, and it's considered bad luck to look in your own basket before Midwinter's morning. At dawn on Midwinter's Day, the basket is brought inside and the friendship gifts are shared with everyone in the house."

"I think that's a wonderful tradition. Maybe I can get that started at home," said Lizzy, taking another bite from her traffle.

Lizzy deduced that if the baskets were still on the porches at Fiddler's Cove, then it must not yet be Midwinter's Day.

"So what day is it now? I mean...when is Midwinterfest?" asked Lizzy.

"Today is Kingday. It's two days until Satinsday, which is Midwinter's Eve, so this year...Midwinter's Day falls on Sunday." Gretta went on to explain the days of the week in Ailear.

"Eight days in a week? That's so fab! Now I *know* I'm dreaming."

"What are you talking about?" asked Gretta.

Lizzy told Gretta all about the Beatles, and how she thought they were the coolest band ever, and that "Eight Days a Week" was the number one hit. She attempted to memorize the names of Ailear's days but quickly decided to do that another time.

McDoogle's keen ears alerted him, and he looked up. "Wud that be them up there, fleein' to the city?"

Gretta and Lizzy looked to the sky. "Yes, Mr. McDoogle, Gertie and Molly are on their way to Ansa. They'll still get there in time for their meeting."

"Ma humblest apologies for me being the cause of oor delayed departure," said McDoogle.

"Think nothing of it," said Gretta. "It didn't take very long for us to make your cloak."

§ § § § §

Earlier that morning, as they had prepared to leave Fiddler's Cove, Gabby finished drying Lizzy's cloak. She bundled it up and put it in a shoulder satchel. She then filled small sacks full of traffles for them to take on their journey. She laid two new leaf cloaks near the front door. Gretta and Lizzy would be needing them.

Molly fashioned a primitive hairbrush for Lizzy made from tweetle reeds. Lizzy was delighted with it, and she spent most of her time trying to untangle the mop that had formed on top of her head during the overnight flight. Gretta and Gertie worked on making a small leaf cloak for McDoogle.

As Lizzy brushed her hair, she watched the two geese masterfully craft the cloak. She also inquired as to why the leaf cloaks were necessary.

"We need them for protection. There will be times when we may need to hide. The leaf cloaks will camouflage us while we are on the road, especially from above. The cloaks are not our only protection. I have a couple of other options up my wings, should we need them. I must protect you by whatever means possible."

"Aye, and I'll be lookin' efter yer protection too, Lass," said McDoogle, reminding Gretta of his duties.

As they were about to leave, Gretta told Lizzy that Molly and Gertie would be flying to Ansa, that Gabby would be staying at Fiddler's Cove to oversee things there, and that she would be taking them to Valendale Forest to a place that was called Deep Glen.

Lizzy had casually replied, "That sounds like a spooky place, but I bet it will be fun. Will there be flying monkeys?"

Gretta cocked her head at Lizzy and queried, "Flying monkeys?"

Lizzy shook her head, "Never mind," and continued brushing her hair.

It was past midmorning when they finally left Fiddler's Cove and started down the trail. The sun warmed the earth and the scent of jumping jacks filled the air. Each side of the trail was covered in pumpkin-colored blossoms. Lizzy had never seen jumping jacks before, but then again, she had rarely traveled very far from Overland Park. Three years ago the Albright family took a vacation to Disneyland and followed Route 66. Lizzy didn't remember seeing anything that looked like jumping jacks on that trip.

Soon the trail ended and emptied onto Lake Road—the main foot road leading to Ansa. Foot roads were reserved for people traveling on foot, but new laws had been passed that allowed bibies and tribies on the road. The change had been a great annoyance to Gretta.

"Now that they've allowed the bibies and tribies, I assure you that it won't be long before fancy motorbies will be scuttling all up and down this road," Gretta grumped. "Just be careful and stay alert. We can't risk an accident."

Two travelers on bibies went by. The seats were much higher than Lizzy imagined, but other than that, she thought that they looked like bicycles, only bigger. She decided that she wanted one, but changed her mind when she saw the tribies with two people sitting side by side. They looked to be a lot more fun.

After a while, Lizzy finally asked a question that had been on her mind. She wasn't even sure if she should ask, but she did anyway. "Why aren't we flying?"

Gretta stopped and looked at Lizzy. "I can't fly you anymore, Princess. Flying you here was a dangerous risk, but it was the only way to get you here. From now on, neither you, nor I, nor McDoogle can draw any attention to ourselves."

Lizzy was beginning to understand that Gretta was very serious about her safety. Although she didn't feel that she was in any danger, she intended to do what she was asked. There was nothing else to do but to wait and see what happens. As far as walking, she didn't mind it, but she was sad to know she wouldn't be flying with Gretta again.

§ § § § §

The lunch break had been a much appreciated respite for everyone. The early afternoon sun beamed down its warmth. There wasn't a whisper of a breeze. It was peaceful and silent.

McDoogle suddenly raised his ears. He was hearing a soft distant whirring noise that caught his attention. He finally spotted something up in the sky, far away.

"Whut's that?" asked McDoogle. "Me eyes must be playin' tricks."

Lizzy and Gretta scanned the skies and finally saw it too. There was some sort of flying machine zipping along, but it was too far away for Lizzy to tell what it really looked like.

"Maybe it's a UFO," exclaimed Lizzy. "Last spring there was one in New Mexico, in Soroc...in...I can't remember the name of the place, but they said it was real...and we talked about it a lot at school."

"What's a UFO?" asked Gretta.

"It stands for Unidentified Flying Object. Visitors from outer space—Martians! I would freak out if that was a UFO!"

"Well, you can calm down because there's nothing unidentified about it. It's a motorbie," said Gretta.

"You mentioned motorbie earlier. What's a motorbie?" asked Lizzy.

"They are motorized vehicles. You'll see lots of them when we get to Ansa. Some people fit them with rotators so that they can hover and fly—but they can't fly for very long. That one won't be up there much longer," explained Gretta.

Lizzy looked again, and sure enough, it was already gone. "You mean to tell me that people living here drive cars that fly?"

"Well, I guess the answer is yes...but not a lot of people have the ones that fly."

Lizzy was no longer interested in a tribie. Now she wanted a motorbie and was imagining what it would be like to fly one.

"I guess we had better get back on the road," Gretta hinted. "We still have a ways to go."

Gretta suggested they fill their water flasks here since it would be a while before they came to fresh water again. They were putting their flasks back in their leaf cloak pockets when Gretta suddenly froze and said, "Shh!" She was listening intently and looking to the sky in the direction of the forest. McDoogle's ears perked up as well.

"Whut's that awful ruckus?" inquired McDoogle.

A black cloud was swirling above the forest. The undulating mass darkened an entire section of the sky. It was tracking a course high above Lake Road and it was heading directly toward them.

"The grackles!" Gretta shouted in a whisper. "Hide now! Under your cloaks...hurry...get on the ground!"

Lizzy saw the swarming mass rushing their way. She and McDoogle both did as they were instructed and dove to the ground, huddled in a ball, and pulled their cloaks tightly around themselves. Off in the distance they could hear the high-pitched chattering that was coming from thousands of birds. The horrific noise sounded like the squeaking shrills of a tortured soul, and it kept getting louder.

"Don't move!" said Gretta, as quietly as she could.

Lizzy wasn't exactly sure why they were having to hide. She had seen large flocks of birds before and didn't understand why Gretta was so concerned. Still, something in Gretta's voice indicated that the situation was serious, and Lizzy realized she needed to heed the warning. Deep down she knew it was best for her to stay out of sight.

The mass of birds was directly above them. Lizzy could actually feel her leaf cloak moving from the wind that was generated by their aggressive, flapping wings. It seemed like an eternity, but the chattering finally ebbed and finally faded away.

"Don't move," Gretta whispered again.

Gretta was listening for any hint of a grackle that might be lingering behind.

"Mr. McDoogle, do *you* hear anything?" Gretta had begun to appreciate McDoogle's ears.

"Naw, Ms. Gretta, I dinna hear a thing."

Gretta poked her head out and scanned the skies.

"Okay. They're gone." She expelled a tremendous sigh of relief.

Lizzy and McDoogle crawled out from under their cloaks, stood up, and brushed themselves off. "What was that?" asked Lizzy.

"That, my dear Princess, was trouble."

Butterfly Surprise

They made it to the edge of Valendale Forest and had no more alarming incidents with grackles or anything otherwise. Lizzy's legs were tired, and McDoogle's tongue was drooping. The sun had fallen below the treetops, and Gretta suspected that it was less than an hour before sunset. The forest would be getting dark very soon, and they still had a ways to go before they reached Deep Glen.

Gretta warned, "There's no option for stopping anywhere in the forest. It won't be safe. And we mustn't utter a peep unless it is absolutely necessary."

Until now, Lizzy hadn't realized how daunting and ominous the forest really was. The small groups of bumbleberry trees elsewhere on the landscape offered friendly bits of shade, but seeing them in a huddled mass made them look like an impenetrable fortress wall. She stopped at the entrance to the forest and McDoogle sat down beside her.

"What is it?" asked Gretta.

"It's the forest," said Lizzy. "I'm not so sure that I want to go inside now."

"Are you feeling afraid?" Gretta asked calmly.

"Hmmm," she replied. She didn't want to admit that she was afraid. "I'm just unsure at the moment, that's all," added Lizzy.

"Indeed, listen to the lass," urged McDoogle. "There's uncertainty in her voice. Pay attention to the uncertainty. Caution is the better part of valor."

"Is it the darkness you are worried about?" Gretta asked.

"I think maybe, yes, the darkness. I've never been in a dark forest before—not even in a dream."

"That's richt! We've...ahem...er...I mean...*she's* never been in a dark forest afore. Maybe we should be rethinkin' the plan," McDoogle cautioned.

"We will be safer in the forest than we are here in the open. And the safest place of all is where we are going. We must get to Deep Glen; someone is expecting us soon."

"Do you have a flashlight?" asked Lizzy.

Gretta hesitated to answer. She wasn't sure if what she was thinking was smart or foolish, but if Lizzy wasn't going into the forest otherwise, she felt her idea was the only solution.

"I have something like a flashlight that we can use, if that will make you feel better."

"It will," said Lizzy.

"A wee bit better," added McDoogle. "And I must say, Miss Gretta, that I'm very impressed, very impressed indeed. 'Be prepared,' the Girl Scout motto. There's no doot in my mind that you were a good Girl Scout. Top o' the class."

Gretta didn't fully understand what McDoogle was rambling on about, but she got the gist of it. "Thank you, Mr. McDoogle."

Gretta turned to Lizzy. "If it's alright with you, I won't use the light until we are inside the forest."

"Okay," said Lizzy.

Within a few minutes they were well inside the towering trees. It was still partially light outside, but the forest was much darker inside, and it was immensely darker than Lizzy had feared. She heard rustles, chatters, chirps, and crunching noises that sent chills down her spine.

"Gretta, please...if we are going any farther, we must use your flashlight."

"Miss Gretta, be assured, we are brave travelers...very brave indeed. We won't be disappointin' ye. And we'll be walkin' right through that dark forest with ye...but a light will no doot be a blessed comfort to the lass."

Gretta smiled. It was obvious to her that a light would be a comfort to McDoogle as well. She stopped, closed her eyes, and took a deep breath. She didn't move.

"Are you okay?" asked Lizzy

Gretta didn't answer. Instead she spread her wings, clicked her webbed feet, and said, "Light! Alamah!" She opened her eyes and a ball of light flashed outward like a miniature, exploding sun.

There wasn't a noise, but the flash startled Lizzy and McDoogle to the extent that they jumped back and nearly fell over each other. They watched in amazement as the light closed in on itself and became a small radiant orb floating above Gretta's head.

"Holy smokes!" exclaimed Lizzy. Her heart was fluttering from fright. Lizzy noticed that the ball of light illuminated the area much better than any flashlight she had ever seen. It pierced the darkness in every direction.

"How did you do that?" Lizzy asked with astonishment.

"It's something I learned how to do," replied Gretta. It was a poor answer, but it was the only answer she felt she could give at the time.

"But that's not possible! You can't just tap your toes and turn on a light—much less one that floats above your head."

"Everything is possible," replied Gretta, "including going inside a tiny house at Fiddler's Cove and flying on the back of a goose through the Tunnel of Stars. Remember, Princess, things are not always as they seem."

Lizzy didn't respond. She was absolutely gobsmacked by the floating orb that was levitating above Gretta's head. McDoogle was speechless too.

Gretta chuckled softly, "Thank you for remembering not to utter a peep. Now, let's get going, shall we?"

The road pushed forward through a tunnel of towering trees whose trunks reached heavenward and whose branches twisted and tangled above their heads like a vaulted cathedral ceiling. Lizzy had wondered if the forest road would be difficult to follow, but it was well defined and that eased her mind.

Just when Lizzy felt somewhat comfortable, Gretta veered off and went through a slit of trees that took them onto a narrow footpath. It was not nearly as wide as the main road and the vines and bushes that seeped into the path kept grabbing at Lizzy's arms and hair. She felt as if they were purposefully trying to scare her like the ghouls did last Halloween when she went through the haunted house in the old Biddle Mansion basement.

The silence had heightened Lizzy's awareness. She could hear their own pattering footsteps. The crack of a twig became an explosion, and the wind that rushed through the leaves sounded like the roar of ocean waves. Although she was surrounded by light, the path ahead of them perpetually vanished into darkness.

Lizzy thought she saw little flashes of light dancing in the darkness up ahead. "What's that?" Lizzy whispered. Her soft voice penetrated the silence and sent a thundering echo out into the darkness.

Gretta looked at Lizzy with a questioning and chastising expression.

"I'm sorry," she mouthed. "But...look!" Lizzy pointed ahead and was frustrated when she saw nothing but blackness.

She pursed her lips. "I promise they were there! Tiny floating lights, like fireflies. They've disappeared," she said as quietly as she could.

"Get close to me," said Gretta. "Mr. McDoogle, you as well. I don't want either of you to bolt into the darkness. You don't need to be afraid, but it's about to get very dark."

Gretta extinguished the light and they were instantly plunged into total darkness. Lizzy stood clinging to Gretta, while McDoogle leaned into her side and shivered. Then tiny floating lights began to appear in the distance.

"There," whispered Lizzy. "That's what I saw."

McDoogle growled.

"It's okay, Mr. McDoogle, don't be afraid; everything's okay. These are our friends. We can all breathe easier now."

Lizzy didn't understand what Gretta meant by friends—the only thing she saw were floating lights. They were mesmerizing as they danced and drifted like dandelion seeds dispersed on a gentle breeze. They continued to appear from nowhere and assembled on the path just ahead.

Each fleck gently pulsated and shimmered like a minuscule star surrounded by a hazy, glowing bubble. The tiny orbs emitted a delicate blue light. Then, in one gentle maneuver, they all drifted in a different direction and the blue shifted to pink. They reminded Lizzy of ballerinas who moved in unison across a stage and then floated back to the other side. As if on cue, the orbs scattered in every direction and became multicolored twinkles—rising, falling, twirling, and drifting. Then they reassembled and shifted their color to green. The cluster of lights eventually grew to extend several feet on both sides of the path and reached well into the distance in front of them. The forest was transformed into a glowing fantasy land.

The orbs in the distance began to separate and an opening slowly rippled forward. A creature unlike anything Lizzy had ever seen was approaching them.

"Hullo, Gretta!"

"Hello, Igree," replied Gretta. "And hello to *all* of you," she added, addressing the small orbs of light. The lights shimmered and twinkled in response.

Lizzy was once again stunned and perplexed. McDoogle took a step sideways and peeked out from behind Gretta.

"Lizzy, this is Igree, one of my very good friends, and all of these lights you see are our friends as well. They are will-o'-the-wisps. They can understand what you say, but they can't speak."

She then turned to Igree and announced, "This is our princess, Lizzy Albright!"

"Lizzy Albright!" Igree bowed deeply. "I'm forever your humble servant and honored to be in your presence."

"Hello...Igree." She had hesitated because she was still trying to comprehend what she was looking at.

"Pickled peaches," said Igree, "she's the perfect portrait of her mother, don't you think?" Gretta nodded in agreement.

McDoogle came out from behind Gretta and sniffed in Igree's direction. Lizzy had never seen, dreamed, or imagined anything like him before.

Igree was taller than Gretta, but shorter than Lizzy. His lower body was like a small kangaroo with reddish-brown fur, but his upper body looked like a large bat. He had black, leathery wings that he would occasionally stretch out and then tuck back in place. He carried a small satchel that was strapped over his shoulder and he was wearing a pair of goggles.

Igree produced a small cup and spit an entire mouthful of dark, grayish-green slimy liquid into the cup, which made Lizzy recoil in disgust.

"This is for you," Igree said, enthusiastically offering the cup to Lizzy.

She didn't know what to do, so she didn't do anything.

"It's okay, Lizzy. Take the cup."

Lizzy apprehensively took the cup but kept it at arms length.

"What am I supposed to do? Drink it?"

"No, no, goodness no, don't drink it," said Igree. "Close your eyes...quick!" Lizzy did.

"Name a flower you saw today. Quick, quick!"

"Jumping jacks," she said instantly.

"Open your eyes!"

The cup she was holding was now filled with a fragrant bouquet of jumping jacks. Lizzy inhaled the wonderful scent. "Oh my, they're beautiful!" she said.

"Now blow on them," insisted Igree.

Lizzy blew on the flowers and their petals began to quiver. One by one, the jumping jacks morphed into a dozen butterflies that lit out of the cup and began fluttering about. Lizzy watched with delight as they danced about her head.

"It's my gift to you, Princess," said Igree.

"A gift?" inquired Lizzy.

"The butterflies will never be very far away from you. When they sense you are in danger, they will flutter about and change from this beautiful blue to a fiery red."

She thanked him for the gift and secretly hoped that she would never see fiery red butterflies.

"Be assured, Lass, that if there's any danger aboot, I'll be makin' sure ye know aboot it," said McDoogle, not wanting his role as her protector to be forgotten.

Lizzy bent down and hugged McDoogle, scratching his head and reassuring him that she was counting on him at all times.

"Let's be on our way," said Igree. "We only have a short distance to go. The will-o'-the-wisps will light our way."

"It will be wise to continue quietly," Gretta added, "but don't worry. If we were to be noticed, nothing in its right mind would want to confront a cloud of will-o'-the-wisps."

Igree led the way. The little band was enveloped by the will-o'-the-wisps' colorful, floating ballet, while a kaleidoscope of blue butterflies fluttered about. For the first time since entering the forest, Lizzy felt comfortable. Instead of trying to avoid the vines and bushes, she reached out and caressed them gently. She no longer saw them as the hideous and ghastly fingers of a ghoul that was attempting to snatch her and drag her into darkness. Instead, she envisioned the encroaching vegetation as being the hands of an adoring public who were clamoring to touch the princess as she processed along the way.

CHAPTER SEVENTEEN

Deep Glen

The location of Deep Glen was a secret and Igree was determined to keep it that way. He made several unpredictable turns and navigated through dense undergrowth assuring that his guests wouldn't be able to find their way in or out without a guide.

The glen was a large circular depression. The sides were steep and dangerous. The air in the glen was thick with moisture that fed a rich assortment of flora ranging from massive bumbleberry trees at its upper rim to giant tree ferns at the bottom. The atmosphere sustained delicate mosses, rock-hugging lichens, and a plethora of different mushrooms—some of which were tasty, some that were used in potions, some that were hallucinogenic, and some that would bring death in a matter of seconds. Even on a bright day, the glen was fairly dark. Only a few shafts of natural light were able to seep down through the vegetation to nourish the moss-carpeted floor.

It was accessed via a sloping ledge that clung to the craggy cliff walls. The trail spiraled its way down over a series of steps and ramps until it reached the bottom. The path had sections that were perpetually slick from the wet, moss-covered surface. Ropes had been attached to the walls, which made the path somewhat easier to manage. Lizzy used them, and even though she was being very careful, she still slipped a couple of times, which gave her a fright. McDoogle hugged the wall as close as possible but the descent still rattled his nerves. It was dark, so the light from the will-o'-the-wisps helped immensely as they cautiously make the trek to the bottom.

A trickling waterfall flowed down the side, splashing onto several narrow, rocky terraces. It delivered a small but steady stream of clear, fresh water to the floor of the glen where it fed Hollow Bottom Pool. The pool remained at a constant level at all times. It never emptied and never overflowed—even in a heavy rain. The few who knew about the pool said it was so deep that it filled the belly of Ailear.

Igree led the group along a stone path around the pool as the will-o'-the-wisps floated about the glen. The lowest level extended under the cantilevered cliff wall. Fitted into this space was a door with two windows on each side. "We are here. Welcome to my home," said Igree.

He waved his hand and said, "Open! Alamah!" The door obeyed. He then flicked his fingers through the doorway and said, "Light! Alamah!" and the lamps inside magically flickered on. This was now the second time that Lizzy had seen the "Light! Alamah!" trick and she wondered if it was something she might be able to learn. Lizzy was expecting a shelter of some kind and had imagined a cave, but Igree's house was nothing like she had predicted.

"You can hang your cloaks there," Igree said, pointing to a coat rack. "Princess, have a seat wherever you like and rest your legs." Lizzy chose an overstuffed arm chair because it looked as if it had the softest cushion.

"Tea first," said Igree, and he hopped away into another room.

"Igree is known for his hospitality. You won't want for anything while you are here," said Gretta.

The parlor was spacious. The walls were made of plaster and big wooden support beams were exposed in several places. The ceiling was vaulted. Large rugs with beautiful woven patterns adorned the highly polished wooden floor. Lizzy noticed that most of the furnishings in Igree's house appeared to be very old.

In a flash, Igree popped back into the parlor pushing a tea tray. The spout on the kettle was whistling and steaming. Lizzy was surprised that he was back so quickly. She was certain there hadn't been enough time for him to boil water.

Igree had his own ritual for brewing and serving tea. He prepared the cups, spooned loose tea into a strainer, lowered the strainer into the kettle of hot water, rang a bell, and then tapped the spoon on the side of a cup while waiting for the tea to brew. Igree amused Lizzy. McDoogle, who had never had tea in his life, curiously sniffed the air. At first he wasn't sure he was interested in having tea, but then he decided to at least give it a try.

"Everyone, drink. I'll have my own cup soon enough. Food, food, food...that's what we need."

"Is there anything I can do to help?" asked Gretta.

"Nothing at all," replied Igree. "It will be ready in a snap."

As Lizzy sipped her tea, she was intrigued by several framed photos on the wall. One picture in particular drew Lizzy's attention. It featured three young ladies in a playful pose with mischievous expressions. They were dressed in outfits that Lizzy thought must be costumes of some sort. The photo was printed in black and white, but it had faded with age. The words "Ice Angels" were printed along the bottom. There were three autographs, but none of them were legible.

The most prominent photo in the parlor was a color portrait of a group wearing purple and black cloaks. They were standing behind a magnificent wooden desk. Igree was in the middle. To his left was a large black bear and on his right, perched on a stand, was a raven. Flanking the trio was a thin, older woman who was wearing round, rose-colored glasses. She had long silver hair that fell over her shoulders and flowed to her waist. She wore a red stone pendant that had an irregular notch at the bottom. The last figure was a man with a long beard wearing a leather top hat. He had a monocle positioned over his left eye. In the background on the wall were two crests. One was yellow and black with a crown in the center. The other was purple and black and featured a mortar and pestle. Lizzy studied the portrait as she finished her tea.

Igree invited them into the dining room where the table was spread with several savory dishes. On the sideboard was a chocolate layer cake and a tray filled with a variety of petits fours that immediately caught Lizzy's eye. They all took a seat. McDoogle felt very important for being invited to sit on a chair at the table next to Lizzy.

"Oh, wait, my apologies," said Igree. He left the room and came back with a crystal vase which he placed on the table. "We don't seem to have a bouquet."

"Flowers! Alamah!" He snapped his fingers and a fountain of golden jumping jacks appeared in the vase. "Now we can eat!"

During dinner Lizzy learned that Igree was one hundred sixty-three years old—which she could hardly believe.

"Nobody lives to be *that* old," she argued.

He told her that *he* did and that he planned to live at least another hundred sixty-three more.

Lizzy told Igree and Gretta about Whipples Cafe and that she was a big fan of their banana splits. She told him that she thought the Beatles were the best band ever. She shared her enjoyment for singing and acting out stories in Granny's attic. She finally got around to asking a question that had been bothering her.

"Why are you wearing your goggles inside your house?" she asked.

Igree didn't miss a beat. "Because I'm blind as a bat without them." He laughed out loud.

Lizzy thought he might be teasing, but she didn't want to say so. "Are you really blind?" asked Lizzy.

"Yes, Princess, I am, but I do just fine with these goggles. Do you think they look good on me?"

She told him that they were better than cool, and then she taught him the word *groovy*. She kept wanting to ask why he was part kangaroo and part bat, but she decided not to. She didn't want to pry any further and embarrass herself—or him.

They had dessert in the parlor. Lizzy had a piece of chocolate cake and three petits fours. McDoogle had been told, on multiple occasions, that he wasn't allowed to have chocolate "because it would kill him." So he ate one vanilla and one peach petit four even though he really wanted to eat them all.

Gretta told Igree about the flock of grackles that swarmed over Lake Road earlier. Igree shook his head and frowned. Lizzy was only partially paying attention to their conversation. Her eyelids were getting very heavy.

"Then it's certain," said Igree. "Somehow she's found out that the princess has arrived. We will have to be extra cautious in how we proceed."

"Who is *she*?" mumbled Lizzy groggily.

Igree could see that Lizzy was exhausted. He pulled up a tuffet and sat down in front of Lizzy. "*She* is someone who did something very bad...and I will tell you all about it...but you and Mr. McDoogle have had a very long day. You both need a good rest. There's a very comfortable bed waiting for you. We'll talk about it in the morning. Is that okay?"

Lizzy was trying to nod *yes*, but when her chin nodded down, it didn't come back up. She fell asleep in the chair. Igree carried Lizzy to her bedroom. He put a cushion next to Lizzy's bed and McDoogle happily curled up on it. Gretta decided to sleep outside by Hollow Bottom Pool. Igree went to his room, picked up his sPeaksee, sent a message, and went to bed.

That night Lizzy dreamed that Pearline Beasley was in the Kut-n-Kurl with one of her customers who wanted a new beehive hairdo, but no matter how hard she tried, the lady's hair kept falling down around her shoulders. She was trying to say "This is not working," but the only thing that came out was "Thiz iz, thiz iz, thiz iz." Pearline started buzzing so much that she turned into a bee and began flying around, trying to find somebody who could help do the lady's hair.

She flew into Granny's attic and found Fluffs sitting on the divan, wearing a pirate's eye patch, and eating a banana split with two cherries on top. He was being very stubborn when Pearline asked for his help, so when he wasn't looking, Pearline took one of his cherries. When Fluffs saw that the cherry had been stolen, he got so angry that he put Pearline in a jar. He then went and laid down under the aluminum Christmas tree, turned on the color wheel, and watched the colors change from red, to blue, to yellow, to green.

Queen Bea

"No!" Beatrice screamed. "No, no, no, no, noooo!"

Euna heard the shrieks and ran up the stairs as fast as she could. There was a loud crash. She burst into the room and found Beatrice pacing back and forth holding a blood-stained cloth. Behind her, through the open door to the bathroom, Euna saw shards of broken mirror scattered on the floor.

Beatrice showed Euna the cloth and then banged her fists on the wall. Beatrice's rage subsided and morphed into uncontrollable sobs. Euna tried to console her. Beatrice's wailing caused her to begin heaving and gasping for air. Her eyes went dark and she collapsed. Euna caught her by the waist and redirected her so that she fell onto the bed. Euna remained calm. This was not the first time that her queen had flown into a rage, but it was the first time she had shattered a mirror.

Euna reached into her skirt pocket where she kept a vial of smelling salts and waved the powerful ammonia under Beatrice's nose. She opened her eyes and began to cry softly.

"Why, Euna, why?" she finally managed to ask.

"I don't know, Your Majesty. I just don't know." Euna felt helpless. There wasn't an answer to her question.

Euna went into the bathroom, navigated the broken glass, and brought back a cool washcloth. She folded it and placed it on Beatrice's forehead.

"Maybe next month," Euna said. "Let's hope."

Beatrice spent the next few days under a cloud of depression. She had yet to produce an heir. She was thirty-six years old and consumed with worry that time was running out. Her twelve years of marriage to Alford had been fruitless and she was overwhelmingly desperate to have a baby.

§ § § § §

The queen sat by her window, observing the world outside of Castlehill. She became fixated on a few, innocent puffs of white clouds floating above the city. She watched them drift and dissipate, then rebuild and assemble.

"Rainclouds," she thought. "They will produce rain."

She pointed her index finger to the sky and stirred it in the air—willing the clouds to move. The wisps danced and swirled at her whim. This obedience pleased her, but it also angered her.

"You *will* rain! You *will* produce!"

She swirled her entire hand and the clouds swelled and blackened. Angry venom slowly began spewing from her soul. Within minutes, turbulent clouds had sprawled over the city and grew to great heights. They obscured the sun and the tempest began boiling in the sky.

Beatrice blew as hard as she could and violent gusts of wind whipped through the city. She poked her finger into the eye of the storm and lightning spiked the ground. She let out a scream and a deafening thunderclap rattled windows and shook the earth. She planted both feet firmly on the floor, took a deep breath, thrust both hands at the billowing storm, and screamed, "Raaaaain!"

At her command, the clouds burst, releasing their bounty. An ocean of water fell from the sky. Those who were caught in the deluge scrambled to safety. Every street in Ansa quickly became a rushing river violently seeking to escape its imprisonment from behind the city walls.

As quickly as it came, it was over. Beatrice slumped into her chair. "It rained," she said. "A raincloud is supposed to rain."

§ § § § §

Beatrice woke up drenched in sweat. She recounted the dream in her mind. She looked at Alford who, in the predawn darkness, appeared to be sleeping soundly. She rinsed off at the sink. As she held the soap, she noticed the familiar scar in her palm, rubbed it, and gasped. "Of course," she exclaimed, "the dream...Calixta!" There were still at least two hours before dawn. It was the first time in weeks that she had felt truly hopeful and excited. She rushed down the stairs to Euna's door and knocked.

"Euna, wake up!"

She didn't wait for Euna to let her in. She opened the door and ran over to her bed. Euna had been in a deep sleep and was trying to bring herself into the waking world.

"Wake up, Euna. I need you. I need you to go find Calixta and tell her to meet me."

"But..."

"Are you awake? Do you understand me? I need you to find Calixta. I must see her," repeated Beatrice.

"But nobody has been able to..."

"You have my permission to take anyone with you that you need. Go wake up Nelson or Jamison, or both, but I want you to be gone by dawn."

"But Calixta hasn't been allowed to..."

"*I'm* allowing it. *I'm* the queen," shouted Beatrice. "I say what is and what is not allowed." The queen took a moment to calm herself. "She will have the answer, Euna. I *know* she will. She can help me."

Beatrice moved toward the desk. "I saw it rain, Euna...And I *need* it to rain. Calixta can make it rain."

Euna didn't have a clue as to what Beatrice was referring to, but knowing her obsession, it would surely have something to do with a baby. Regardless of the reason, Euna was extremely apprehensive about Beatrice getting involved with Calixta.

Calixta was legendary throughout all of Ailear as being a bitter and poisonous person. She was known as an outcast—but in reality, she had cast herself out. Those who had been around her when she was in her youth knew bits and pieces of her story. There were very few who knew the entire truth about her.

She had been tried in the mage guild court and had been charged and convicted for "suspicion in the use of dark arts." It was not a civil trial, but the verdict stripped her of all titles, and she was excommunicated from the guild. The trial didn't prove that she had actually *used* the forbidden dark arts, but according to "The Accepted Laws," a conviction of suspicion was enough to disallow any future association with the guild.

The very name, Calixta, carried a mystique that was both feared and respected—meaning she was left alone. Wild stories about her were told in the pubs. Some said she left in anger because she was banned from Castlehill. Others said she had lost her mind when she mismeasured the amount of bitterschroom powder for a potion she had made and had drunk. They said the overdose twisted her mind and that she could no longer function in society.

Children commonly used her name when telling scary stories. Parents disciplined their children by telling them that if they misbehaved, Calixta would come and take them away. As to her whereabouts, those who ventured into the darkest part of Valendale Forest said she lived on a rocky island in a swampy lake, and that it was impossible to reach her house because it was protected by her minions. She was the most notorious person in all of Ailear.

Euna didn't think it would be too difficult to locate Calixta. She did, however, expect Calixta to turn her away. She wanted to talk Beatrice out of her decision, but Euna could tell that anything she might suggest otherwise was not going to change the queen's mind.

Beatrice sat at the desk. "I need to write a note." She took a sheet of paper, grabbed a pen, and began writing.

> *Dear Calixta,*
>
> *I know it's been a very long time, but may I see you? Will you please set aside your animosity? I want to be on friendly terms, and I promise I will make it worth your while. Meet me at ten o'clock, Satinsday morning, by the old well. You know which one. I will treasure the opportunity to see you.*
>
> *Yours,*
> *Bea*

She dripped melted wax on the envelope, used her insignia ring to seal it, and gave it to Euna.

Euna looked at the note in her hands; her feet were frozen in place.

"Go on...please...Euna. I've had a vision, and I need you to get this note to Calixta immediately."

Euna was hesitant—not because she was afraid of Calixta, and not because she didn't know *where* to start; she just didn't *want* to start. In Euna's mind, everything about this situation was heading toward disaster. Still, she had been ordered to deliver the note, and therefore she would.

Euna awoke Nelson *and* Jamison, the two chamber guards who lived in the castle, and asked for their help. As Queen Beatrice's personal sentinels, they were often sent off on unscheduled missions because a particular whim or fancy popped into her head. Euna could trust them to handle any situation and knew they would be invaluable.

"What is she up to now?" asked Nelson, "Has she lost her mind?"

"Perhaps," said Euna. "But we don't have any other choice. At least we'd better try. Can you and Jamison be ready in an hour?"

"I think so," said Nelson. "We'll meet in the courtyard. I'll have Jamison get the motorbies ready."

After Euna left, Nelson pulled out his sPeaksee and called the guards at the main gate. "We'll need a tribie *and* a bibie...that's right... just the two. We'll be there in about an hour."

Jamison brought two motorbies to the courtyard and unlocked the rotator blades. "Flying will be quicker," said Jamison. "Let me take the lead." Nelson gave a thumbs up.

"Goggles on," said Jamison.

Jamison maneuvered his motorbie several feet into the air and hovered while waiting for Nelson to catch up. It was still dark when they lifted out of the courtyard and flew over the main fortress wall. They followed Saint Murphy Blvd. from Castlehill to the main gate at the far end of Ansa.

The guards had the bibie and tribie waiting for them when they arrived. Euna was grateful that Jamison had requested a tribie. It meant she would be a passenger and not required to pedal. She was starting to feel her age, even if she wasn't ready to admit it. Nelson, on the other hand, was young, strong, and very capable.

They had just left the main gate when the pink morning sun peeked over the horizon and sent ripples of light across the sea. Before turning south on Fishmarket Road, they stopped and ate traffles, praising Corvis for their provisions. Euna hadn't wanted to wake Corvis, but the kitchen was Corvis's domain and they needed sustenance for the journey. Corvis had packed several traffles and canteens of fresh water. She proudly added a sack of fresh chester nuts to the basket that she had recently harvested from the garden. When chester nuts were in season, peafowl had them with every meal—including snack time. Corvis was no exception. She had learned the best way to store chester nuts from her grandmother, Lessa. When properly stored, chester nuts could last until the next crop produced.

It was midmorning when they came to the path that veered off to their right. The sign read "Turnback Trail."

"This is it. Who wants to turn back?" asked Jamison.

"I would if I could," said Euna.

Nelson chuckled, "Me too! I've always wondered if the name was meant as a warning or a description. I think it's meant to be a description, but most folks take it as a warning."

It wasn't long before Turnback Trail disappeared into the forest. Fallen logs occasionally blocked the trail and they had to lift their vehicles over them. Soon the trail became too cumbersome for them to traverse on wheels, so they hid their rides nearby and continued on foot.

The humidity thickened and the ground below their feet became soft and boggy. Every now and then they would catch a glimpse of a body of water peeking through the trees.

"What is that smell?" asked Euna.

"It's Sourbelly Sink," said Jamison, "that stagnant, scum-covered lake you see off to the right."

"It's awful," added Nelson. "I hope it's not toxic and that the fumes don't kill us."

Sourbelly Sink was one of the many lakes located within Valendale Forest. While other lakes in the forest were idyllic destinations, Sourbelly Sink was the one place to avoid. Its repulsive stench and surface scum were only two of the many reasons why Calixta had chosen it. It was fed by a freshwater stream, but nothing ever escaped. The water seeped into the ground as fast as it flowed in from the stream. The forest delivered a steady flow of decay, debris, carcasses, and minerals into the lake. It was essentially a cesspool. Gaseous fumes bubbled and popped on the surface. At night, the vapors emitted a green and purple phosphorescent glow. The sight was eerie and beautiful at the same time.

Onion trees thrived in the swampy shallows. Their thick, bulbous bases rose eight to ten feet out of the water before tapering up to thin trunks, giving the impression of large onions. Their main trunks branched out into a canopy with spindly boughs. The onion trees didn't produce an abundance of leaves, but they were laden with spiderweb moss. All the trees around Sourbelly Sink dripped with the stringy, pale green parasite. It flourished on the moist, acrid air. It was enchanting to look at from a distance, but passersby who grazed it quickly learned that it left a sticky resin on their skin and clothes that was difficult to remove.

They continued on the soggy path until they came to a small cut in the trees that went toward the lake.

"This is it," said Jamison, pointing to the path. "I've never been any further than this."

"Then whatever lies ahead, we will discover it together. Let's go deliver this note," Euna said begrudgingly.

Their new path lay along the center of a long narrow peninsula that jutted into the lake. The swamp closed in until it was only a few feet away on either side of them. The finger of land became so narrow that they were forced to walk single file. The path ended at the edge of the water where they were faced with a stretch of stepping stones that barely broke the surface of the oily swamp.

Beyond the stones was a craggy island with a large, protruding rock formation, The rugged outcropping had steep, fern-covered walls that jutted abruptly skyward. The island was protected on all sides by the murky, bubbling water. The only apparent way to access the island was by crossing the channel using the stepping stones.

A path on the island led to a set of steps that had been carved into the sloping sides of the outcrop. They spiraled upward around the rocky face until they reached the top. Situated at the summit was a round stone tower. It was far from impressive. The tower was plain and unadorned. It was no more than fifteen feet wide and not twice that tall. There was an arched doorway and tall, narrow slits that served as windows.

"So this is it," said Euna flatly. She was both surprised and disappointed. As she gazed upon the tower, it began to sink in that this was Calixta's domain, and therefore it would be wise to proceed with caution.

"This may be one of those times when it's best not to judge a book by its cover," she said. "Who wants to go first?"

CHAPTER NINETEEN

Sourbelly Sink

Jamison volunteered to take the lead. About a dozen stones were positioned between him and the island. They were large enough and flat enough that anyone would feel confident using them to cross the channel, but there was no way to tell how deep the water was. The dark and murky water bubbled with gas. Decaying reeds lay rotting on the surface. Jamison thought the best course of action was to take it slow and easy. He didn't have any desire to fall into the oily sludge.

He aimed for the first stone and took a long stride. As soon as his foot touched it, a cacophony of ear-piercing whistles, screeches, and squeals suddenly erupted from above. They hadn't noticed the birds until now. Perched in the highest branches of the onion trees were thousands of grackles. Their sleek, black, iridescent bodies gleamed in the sun, giving them a purplish sheen. Their pendulous tails fluttered in the breeze. They had long, pointed beaks that could easily spear a shellfish, break open a crust beetle, or gouge out an eye—which they had been known to do. They had black, penetrating eyes that could see small details from lengthy distances with amazing clarity, and they had an uncanny ability to locate whatever they were seeking.

Grackles were known to be mean and indomitable. They stole eggs from other birds' nests, tortured small animals, and never showed a hint of hesitation when encountering a venomous snake. A single angry grackle was a terrible menace. Tens of thousands of them could conquer an army. Once they set their mind on a task, they were tenacious and wouldn't stop until they reached their goal. Calixta had taken control of this flock by placing them under a spell of servitude.

Sourbelly Sink

Whatever she commanded them to do, they did, and they did it with full resolve.

Jamison was so startled by the sudden outbreak of screeching grackles that he nearly lost his balance. He managed to regain control and jumped back on onto the land. When Jamison retreated to the path, the squeals subsided. The noise became a low murmur as the grackles gibbered and clacked.

"They're watching us," Euna said with confidence. "These grackles must be her guards, or her eyes—or both. That was only a warning." Euna was right.

"Maybe it was a coincidence," suggested Nelson.

"Do you think I should try again?" asked Jamison.

"Step back. Let me try," offered Nelson.

He slipped to the front and focused on the first stone. At the same time, a large bubble formed several yards away. It burped and broke the scum-covered surface.

"Did you see that?" asked Euna

"See what?" he asked.

Nelson looked to where Euna was pointing and saw the remains of thick ripples, dissipating as they expanded across the surface of the lake. Then it hit them—a stench so sickening that they all grabbed their noses and covered their mouths. It was too late for Nelson. His stomach churned and he doubled over, vomiting into the lake. He heaved two more times before he finally began to recover. Within a few minutes the hideous odor had wafted away.

"Come back and sit down," said Jamison. "I'll go."

Jamison once again hopped onto the first stepping stone. As he did, the treetops exploded with the same annoying ruckus. This time the grackles launched from their perches and the treetops teemed with seething, angry birds. Jamison advanced to the next stone which caused the grackle's agitation to intensify.

As Jamison advanced to the third stone Euna noticed a disturbance on the surface of the lake. It was coming from the same place that the bubble had burst. Nelson saw it too. A large, tubular-shaped hump broke the surface, skimmed through the slime, and then slithered downward until it was submerged again.

"Jamison! There's something under the water!" Euna shouted.

"On your right," Nelson called. "Look to your right!"

Jamison heard their voices but wasn't able to make out what they were saying due to the shrilling pandemonium.

"I'm okay," he shouted. "I'm going on." They couldn't hear him either.

The entire flock had assembled into a swirling vortex. The sight caused Jamison to panic and he began leaping from stone to stone. He had managed to hop to several more stones before the grackles set upon him. He tried to defend himself against the attack but his efforts were useless. Euna and Nelson watched in horror as he toppled into the murky lake.

As soon as he was in the water, the birds stopped their attack, formed a tight formation, and soared upward. Their mass darkened the sky and cast a cloudy shadow over the swamp. They flew heavenward, morphing from one triumphant formation to the next. They had stopped shrieking.

Jamison flailed in the rancid water and finally managed to grab one of the stones. He was coming to his senses when he heard his name being called. Nelson and Euna were both shouting frantically.

"Get out, Jamison, get out!"

"Swim to the shore!"

"It's a swamp dragon. Hurry!"

Jamison wiped slimy scum off his eyes and got his bearings.

"It's coming directly at you...come this way."

Jamison saw a spiny, gray hump moving through the water, its undulating mass slithering through the mire. The creature's massive, fang-mouthed head lurched out of the depths. Its nostrils exploded with a force so strong that water spewed to where Nelson and Euna were standing. Its red eyes blazed with fiery rage, and a foamy slime oozed from its jowls. The dragon released a gurgling roar as it launched itself into the air, completely breeching the surface, dove into lake, and disappeared. The creature's movement created turbulent ripples on the surface as it headed in Jamison's direction.

Jamison began swimming toward the shore as fast as he could. Euna and Nelson watched in disbelief, helplessly screaming for him to hurry. Jamison knew that the swamp dragon would be on him in an instant and he would be devoured in seconds.

Jamison almost gave up, but in his panic, he felt his foot touch bottom. He hadn't realized the water was this shallow. He began running to the shore, fighting his way through the decaying muck. Euna and Nelson pulled him on shore just before the swamp dragon was upon him. They scrambled to get a safe distance away from the lake.

The swamp dragon thrashed in the shallows and snorted out another repulsive spray, drenching them, and causing them to retreat further down the path.

"Jamison, you're bleeding!" Euna held his chin, turning his face to one side and then the other, checking his wounds. The grackles had managed to slice his face in several places. His hands were also bleeding from trying to fend them off. Euna used Nelson's knife to cut off the lower part of her tunic. She compressed the wounds to stop the bleeding and cleaned them the best she could with water from her canteen. She knew Jamison would be fine, but he was going to hurt for a few days.

"What now?" asked Nelson.

"I have a note to deliver," insisted Euna. "Nelson, I want you to stay here with Jamison. Do not follow me...promise?"

Nelson agreed to stay, but tried also tried to persuade Euna to not go back on her own. She vowed that she would not attempt crossing on the stepping stones and swore to avoid anything that might be dangerous or foolish.

The lake had become eerily quiet by the time Euna arrived back at the shore. The grackles were quietly roosting and there was no sign of the swamp dragon. The only thing she heard was the dull plopping of thick gaseous burbles.

"Calixta!" Euna called out. "I'm here with a note from Queen Beatrice!" Her voice reverberated across the lake and lingered in the distance. There was no response, but she hadn't expected one.

Euna examined the island. It was bleak and repulsive, like a hideous, crusty scab, festering on the lake. At first glance, the tower gave the appearance that it had long been abandoned. Spiderweb moss dangled from rocks that protruded from the wall. Partway up, pricklevine had taken a foothold in the cracks. It snaked its way up the tower where it became a thorny, lacy crown encircling the rim. Euna knew that pricklevine would have taken over the entire tower if it had been left alone. Someone was removing pricklevine from around the bottom of the tower. It most certainly had not been abandoned.

"Calixta!" Euna called out again. Still nothing.

Euna sat down and tried to think of anything else she could do. She thought about leaving the note in a place where Calixta would find it, but she was afraid it might end up in the lake. She pulled her knees close to her chest, made a pillow with her arms, and rested her head. She stayed this way for a long time, considering various options, and nearly dozed off.

A gravelly squawk broke the silence. Euna looked up and saw a magnificent raven circling the tower. It gracefully spiraled upward and then glided across to the edge of the lake where it flew around the entire perimeter before returning to the tower. It perched on the thick, woody pricklevine trunk and cawed again.

Euna called out to the raven, waving the note for him to see. "I have a note for Calixta."

The raven extended its wings, launched from the tower, and glided directly toward her. She wasn't sure if it was planning to attack, but she decided to stand her ground. The raven glided down and softly landed in front of her.

"Give me the note," commanded the raven. He was direct and to the point, but his tone wasn't forceful or threatening.

"The note is for Calixta," replied Euna.

"She will not see you. She instructed me to bring the note to her."

"Who are you? What's your name?" demanded Euna. She was not about to tell the queen that she had given the note to an anonymous raven.

"My name is Omen. I serve Calixta."

Euna studied him for a moment. She was willing to give the note to a courier, but she was apprehensive about doing so without some form of proof.

"I'm Euna. I'm the queen's chamber nurse," she said reaching into her pocket. "I'll only give this note to you if you allow me to take a picto of you holding it. I want proof that I gave it to you."

Omen didn't want his picture taken, but he knew that they both were only doing what they had been commanded to do. Calixta wanted the note. If having his picture taken was a requirement, then he would allow it.

"Very well," said Omen. "I agree."

When Euna handed Omen the note, she didn't let go right away. She looked into his eyes and perceived an emptiness that caused her to feel pity for him. She also noticed an undercurrent of gentleness that she admired. She finally let go and took the picto of Omen holding the note. Calixta's tower was seen in the background. She thanked him. Omen took the note to the tower and Euna rejoined Jamison and Nelson.

CHAPTER TWENTY

A Meeting at the Well

Many Ailearians fasted on Satinsday, but Beatrice was not one of them. Her breakfast remained untouched because she was too excited to eat. She paced the floor and watched the clock.

The previous morning, Freeday, Beatrice had put on an uncharacteristic display of contrition and holy reverence. She told Euna that she was going to make some changes in her life and intended to spend more time reading the Book of Satins.

"If I'm more supportive of the Book of Satins, the spirits will surely notice and show me favor. From now on, I will be an open vessel, ready and waiting for their divine intervention."

Euna saw through the ruse, but she didn't know exactly what Beatrice was up to. She wouldn't have flipped a switch and become a follower of the Book of Satins overnight.

"I'll need you to attend satinary tomorrow," she told Euna.

Euna gave Beatrice a questioning glance.

"Yes, at ten o'clock. I need you to be at the satinary and give an offering on my behalf. I also need you to light a stargrass pot and say a prayer."

Euna had no problem doing what Beatrice told her to do. She made *lists* of the things she was told to do, and she did them whether she *wanted* to or not. Euna had the feeling that she was being used for some purpose, but she couldn't figure out what it was. She suspected it had something to do with Calixta. The queen's demeanor had improved significantly after she had returned from delivering the note.

The Well

That night Beatrice couldn't sleep. Her mind raced like a rabbit, while the hours flowed like sludge. She wondered how Calixta might have changed and what she would be wearing. In her mind, she played out multiple scenarios of how she would react when she saw her. She auditioned various phrases trying to decide what she should say first.

Finally, the glow of dawn appeared. Beatrice got out of bed and went about her usual routine. Alford got dressed and said he would stop to see Corvis for a warm traffle and tea before heading off to an all-day Snippits tournament. Euna entered Beatrice's room and set the breakfast on a side table.

"I want you to tell me all about the satins service when you return," urged Beatrice. "And here's some krotes. Please put them in the charity basket for me."

"As you wish, Your Highness."

Euna took the envelope and left the room.

"And don't forget the stargrass pot," Beatrice called down the hall.

Euna turned around and slightly bowed, "Yes, Your Grace."

From her window, Beatrice saw Euna join Jamison on the motorbie and watched as they went out the gate and down Saint Murphy Bvld. Everyone had left. She was finally free to sneak away without anyone knowing. She put on her cloak and quietly left.

Beatrice entered the tunnel and was greeted with a rush of dank, cool air. She reached for the switch and flipped it, but the lights didn't come on. She jiggled the switch several times, but nothing happened. It didn't deter her in the least. She held out her hand and said, "Light! Alamah!" After a sudden burst, a soft ball of light glowed in her hand. She didn't want to carry it, so she sat it on her shoulder.

The tunnel burrowed its way under the streets of Ansa. It had been secretly built long ago to give the royal family an escape route should one be required. It connected the castle complex to Saint Tyndall's Satinary. Only the royal family, the secret guards, and the priest who served at satinary knew that Saint Tyndall's housed the secret exit from the tunnel. The tunnel could serve in other ways too. It could provide sanctuary and protection. The masons had lined the walls of the entire tunnel with large, quarried stones. Numerous alcoves could store food or weapons, and if necessary, could be used as sleeping areas. A well had been dug so that fresh water would be available in case the tunnel was used as a shelter for any length of time.

It was the source of many memories for Beatrice. Once, when she and Calixta were still in their primaries, they decided to venture into the tunnel on their own. They had been forbidden to use the tunnel unless they were accompanied by an adult. They had wanted to share a forever secret and the tunnel figured into their plans. After weeks of plotting and scheming, they settled on the idea of carving their initials into stone because that was something that would last forever.

They made three rules for their secret. First, it had to be done in a scary place that required them to be courageous. Next, there had to be the risk of being caught. And finally, the initials had to be carved where they could never be discovered. Everyone knew that if a secret was ever revealed, it was no longer a secret. A dark corner in one of the tunnel's alcoves met all the criteria.

Beatrice looked at her palm and touched the scar. She reflected on the night she was injured—the night they snuck away to carve their initials.

"It's really dark in there," said Calixta, peering into the opening.

"Let's make our own lights. We both know how...Light! Alamah!" she exclaimed, and a glowing ball of light appeared in her hand.

"Now, you do it," coaxed Beatrice.

Calixta made her light and they began timidly making their way through the tunnel. They had never been in the tunnel alone and it was much more frightening than they had expected. There was a splash. Calixta hadn't been paying attention and stepped in a puddle.

"Damn!" she cursed, uttering a word that was just as forbidden as the tunnel.

"What's the matter?" asked Beatrice.

"Now I have a squishy shoe," she complained.

Drips from the ceiling hit the floor and plinked. Their reverberations lingered for several seconds. Other mysterious creaks and cracks made their insides quiver and caused them to huddle close to each other.

"I don't like it here," admitted Calixta. "There might be a ghost."

"You're not supposed to like it here. Rule number one: it has to be scary! And if there's a ghost...well...I don't know, but I don't think there's any ghosts. So come on," Beatrice insisted. Calixta was shivering with fright, but she was trying not to show it. She was surprised that Beatrice seemed to have nerves of steel.

Suddenly Beatrice screamed and her shriek shot through the tunnel. She began flailing the air and slapping at her face and hair.

"Get it off of me!"

"What?" asked Calixta.

"A spider! I ran into a web. Do you see it?"

She was certain that a poisonous, eight-legged beast had gotten tangled in her hair. Calixta looked, but she couldn't find a spider.

"Are you sure you don't see it?" whimpered Beatrice.

Calixta looked again but didn't see anything. The spiderweb had destroyed Beatrice's fortitude. She fought back tears and tried to regain her composure. During the commotion her light had gone out, so she had to make another one.

"Do you want to go on?" asked Calixta.

"We have to," said Beatrice.

The girls proceeded and managed to avoid any more puddles and spiderwebs. They were afraid that they might encounter a ghost or a monster, but they were even more worried about being caught by a guard—or even worse, their fathers.

The girls arrived at the alcove that surrounded the well, which was located about midway through the tunnel. The alcove went back several feet from the main corridor and had a vaulted ceiling. They had chosen this particular alcove because the well would always be a landmark to help them remember where they had put their initials. The well had a pipe coming out of the ground with a hand pump and a spout. The spout emptied into a round granite basin that was about four feet across.

"This is it," said Beatrice. "Let's carve them on one of the stones on the back wall, but down low, so nobody will ever see it."

Calixta agreed. Beatrice walked forward, pointed to a stone, and suggested they use it as their target. Calixta liked her choice and they both stepped back, pulling out their wands.

"Do you remember the words for the rune-writing spell?" asked Calixta.

"Of course I do. We just had it as one of our final exams."

"Just our first and last initials, right?"

"Yes...just our two initials."

They pointed their wands at the stone and said the words simultaneously.

Flaming fingers, fire alone
Carving runes into this stone
Chisel hard and cut them deep
There they will forever keep

They never knew which one of them got the last line wrong, but the mistake caused the spell to go horribly wrong. Their wands shot fiery arcs into the stone, but instead of carving their initials, the wall exploded—knocking them back several feet and extinguishing their lights.

In total blackness they scrambled to get up. Beatrice slipped on a slick stone and fell. She instinctively reached out to catch her fall and her hand hit the sharp edge of a rock, peeling back part of her fleshy palm.

"Ouch! Ouch! Ouch!" cried Beatrice, obviously in pain.

"What happened?"

"It's my hand...I've cut my hand."

Calixta quickly summoned another light. She saw the cut and knew it required immediate attention. They fled the tunnel as quickly as possible.

Calixta found a dolthea plant and broke off one of the stems. She let the dolthea milk drip onto the wound, which stung and brought tears to Beatrice's eyes.

"Blow on it," she insisted. "It burns!"

Calixta did and it helped to take some of the sting away. She then took a large castola leaf and compressed it against the wound.

"Keep this tightly pressed against your palm, and then wrap it with a cloth when you get back to your room," Calixta instructed.

"What are you going to tell your parents? They must never know where we were."

"I think I should tell them something close to the truth. It's obvious that I fell. I'm pretty good at acting."

"Okay, I'll come see you tomorrow."

Early the next morning Beatrice removed her bandage and pretended to have an accident in the garden. She burst forth with convincing cries and wails, and then she fabricated a story about falling on the footpath. Her parents believed her; the girls' secret remained safe. Twenty-seven years had passed since the incident in the tunnel, and for twenty-seven years, the scar never let her forget.

Beatrice came to the familiar bend in the tunnel and went to the alcove, hoping that Calixta would be there, but she wasn't. She sat on the edge of the basin, pumped the well, and drew up fresh water. She caught a handful and took a drink. In the back of the alcove she found the jagged, moss-covered depression where the stone had exploded. She realized that they really did share a secret—it just hadn't turned out as they had planned.

Beatrice waited. Her mind drifted to some of her own secrets, and how very thankful she was that her secrets remained safe. A few more moments passed. "If I were Calixta, I probably wouldn't come either," she thought. She had been so hopeful, but she was beginning to feel lost and helpless.

A gust of cold wind pushed past her, taking her by surprise. She supposed that the door at one end or the other had opened—creating the breeze. A spark of hope glimmered once again. She peered down the tunnel, but it was empty. She heard a small splash and looked at the basin. A mist had materialized and was swirling just above the surface of the water.

"What do you want from me?" a voice asked.

Beatrice recognized Calixta's voice, but she couldn't find her. She looked up and down the corridor, but it was empty.

"I have no desire to be here," said Calixta. "You asked me to come... and here I am. Tell me...after all this time...what do you want?"

The voice was coming from the alcove. Beatrice peered into the basin and saw Calixta's face reflected in the water.

"Calixta...where are you? "

Beatrice looked all around the alcove searching for the source of the reflection. She tried to touch Calixta's face in the water, but when her hand broke the mirrored surface, the face distorted into ripples. Beatrice was surprised at how much Calixta had changed. Her eyes were empty and cold, and her cheeks were thin. Her long, brown hair looked the same, except for a few streaks of silver that were starting to appear.

"I know what you want," Calixta said with assurance. "You want a child. You are desperate to insure that the rule of Ailear does not pass to a new house." Calixta's voice was dull and matter of fact.

"I wonder who it would be...the new ruler of Ailear. Do you have any suspicions?"

"I'm not sure, Calixta," replied Beatrice. "I didn't ask for any of this. None of this is my fault."

"And you need me to help. Am I right?" asked Calixta.

Beatrice wanted to engage in conversation. She wanted to recollect *and* reconnect. But yes, more than all of that, she wanted Calixta's help.

"I thought maybe...we could just talk," said Beatrice.

"There's nothing for us to talk about, except for me to give you an answer to the question you have yet to ask. So I'll talk, and you will listen. When I am finished, you can tell me if I've missed anything."

Beatrice remained silent as she gazed into the pool.

"You want me to make a potion that will insure that you will have a child. You already know that what you are asking is against the law, because you also know that this type of potion can only be created with forbidden ingredients, and for me to make the potion would require that I practice the dark arts.

"You believe that I am the logical choice, because you believe the suspicions that are associated with my name. You have concluded that if I risk this, you will remain unblemished and innocent, while I, on the other hand, could be convicted and sent into exile.

"You are asking me to do you a favor, but I'm suggesting that we negotiate, and come to an agreement. I will *not* do you a favor...I do not *owe* you a favor...as a matter of fact, I don't owe you anything."

Beatrice interrupted, "What kind of an agree..."

"I'm...not...finished!" Calixta exclaimed. "You've been so self-absorbed and so self-centered that you haven't even considered the fact that someone besides you might want a child too. Well, here's a surprise. *I* do. I want an heir—so to speak—to teach, and train, and carry on after me. But I'm not so desperate that I can't wait a while. So let's negotiate our agreement. I'm sorry for using the word negotiate, because in reality, I'm giving you an ultimatum. There's no wiggle room; there's no room for negotiation.

"I will make your potion, and you will have a daughter. She will be the delight of your life. She will have the most lovely and envious ginger hair. I will add strawberry seeds to insure that her face will be adorned with the most adorable freckles. She will be the most beautiful and most beloved princess Ailear has ever known.

She has been your dream—your obsession—and *I* will make your dream come true.

"But now, my dear Bea, I must tell you that this *favor*—the favor that I don't owe you—comes with a price. You will pay me by promising to give me your first grandchild. Your sweet, precious princess gets to have no say in the matter. If you want a child, then you will give me a child. That, Your Highness, will be our arrangement, and you will promise it in blood."

Beatrice's heart raced; she struggled to catch her breath. The mist vanished and the pool turned black. Calixta was gone. The sounds in the tunnel seemed to have been sucked into a vacuum. The air froze around her. Suddenly, her light vanished, plunging her into darkness.

"Did I miss anything?"

Beatrice jumped with fright and nearly fell over. She was too overwhelmed to answer. There was a bright flash, and then a glowing light appeared. It was coming from an orb that was levitating over the outstretched hand of a beautiful woman. Her face was warm and radiant. Her brown hair was streaked with silver strands that fell down over her shoulders. Beatrice began to weep. Calixta went to her and handed her the light.

"My raven will come to your window next Satinsday. Give him your answer. But do not ever send for me again, unless you intend to swear an oath in blood."

The Blood Promise

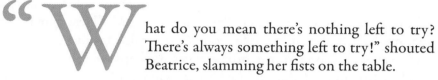

"What do you mean there's nothing left to try? There's always something left to try!" shouted Beatrice, slamming her fists on the table.

Gorva was jolted by Beatrice's response. She hadn't meant to anger or insult the queen; she was just being truthful. She had exhausted every option she could think of to help her. Nobody in the kingdom knew more about the medicinal properties of plants and herbs than Gorva. She had opened the Hyssop and Sage when she was young and had tended the apothecary her entire life. Nobody really knew how old she was, but people believed her to be about eighty years old. She was by far the most well-known and most respected healer in all of Ailear.

Beatrice had been secretly coming to see Gorva once a month for the past year. Euna disguised Beatrice in the vestments of a satins prioress and escorted her through the tunnel. Euna then left Beatrice at the hidden door that opened into the Saint Tyndall's Satinary. A prioress leaving a satinary wouldn't arouse suspicion. All Beatrice had to do was cut across a narrow lane and take just a few steps before entering the back door of Gorva's apothecary. The convenient proximity of the satinary to the Hyssop and Sage made her visits easy to manage.

Beatrice had rejected Calixta's proposal. She knew the seriousness of making a blood promise with Calixta. It was a seal that, if broken, would bring about grave consequences. She wasn't willing to play a game of pawns with her own grandchild, if she ever had one. Having exhausted all other options, she decided see if Gorva could help. But now, another year had escaped with no results and her frustration had caused her to lash out at Gorva.

Beatrice calmed herself and let out a long sigh. "I'm sorry, Gorva. Please forgive me. I know you have done everything you know to do. If you can think of anything else, will you contact me?"

Gorva looked at Beatrice over the top of her rose-colored glasses. Her voice was raspy. "I'll be here if you need me, and if I learn anything that might help, I promise to let you know. I will continue to consult with Ravol and some of the other mages. Perhaps we can discover a combination of medicine and magic that will work."

Beatrice took Gorva's thin, bony hand, kissed it— stroked her long, silver hair, and said goodbye. She left the apothecary through the back door. She wouldn't be coming back unless Gorva called for her.

As she went on her way, an idea stirred in her mind that she had suppressed many times before. It quickly began worming its way to the forefront of her thoughts. She knew that if she made the agreement with Calixta and had a child, it would be years before a grandchild would arrive. Surely that was enough time for her to find a way to circumvent the agreement. In the meantime, Calixta might seal her own fate and be exiled for using the dark arts. Maybe she would just leave—or die. If none of these things were to happen, then Beatrice would have to come up with a plan to keep the baby out of Calixta's hands. She vowed to herself that she would give her own life before letting Calixta have her grandchild.

Beatrice was beyond desperate. She planned to get what she wanted and deal with the consequences later. She would justify her betrayal with the argument that she had exhausted all other options before going back to Calixta as her last resort.

Calixta had made the assumption that Beatrice would eventually accept her terms. After their meeting at the well, Omen had visited every month and perched near Beatrice's window. She watched him with great interest, but never called for him.

It had almost been a month since Omen had last visited. She expected that it would only be a matter of days until he returned again. She kept a watchful eye for his arrival. It was Windsday. She had just finished a royal council meeting and was taking a stroll in the garden when she heard the familiar, gravely caw.

She went back to her room and called out from her window. "What is your name?"

Omen flew to the tower and perched on the sill. "I'm Omen. I serve Calixta."

"Very well then. Will you please tell Calixta that I wish to meet her at the well on Satinsday morning. Tell her I accept her terms."

"I will tell her," replied Omen. "Is there anything else?"

"No," said Beatrice. "Calixta will know what to bring."

Beatrice wanted to have a conversation with Omen. He was a regal specimen, but something about him made her pity him. After observing him for a year, she had become curious to know more about him—but he took flight and was gone before she could ask any questions. She watched as he soared over Ansa. She wondered if she would ever see him again, and she wasn't really sure why she cared.

Beatrice's demeanor had changed greatly after her final meeting with Gorva—and Euna noticed the difference. Beatrice was no longer bursting with emotions. She wasn't ecstatic nor was she depressed. She had been anxious for so long that she was emotionally exhausted. She went about the next few days tending to her queenly responsibilities and resting whenever she could.

On Satinsday, Euna went to satinary to say prayers and make an offering on Beatrice's behalf. She had been doing this every week during the past year. When Euna left, Beatrice donned her cloak and slipped away to meet Calixta at the well.

"Here I am," said Beatrice. "You have your wish."

"And you'll have yours too," replied Calixta.

"Then let's get on with it," Beatrice said flatly. She had no desire for chit chat.

Calixta took a knife from her satchel. "Hold out your thumb," she instructed.

Calixta drew the blade across her own thumb first. She then pulled it across Beatrice's thumb, and they pressed them together. They looked into each other's eyes and spoke the vow.

> *I swear this bond from head to heel,*
> *And with my blood this promise seal.*
> *May plagues and curses fall on me,*
> *If e're unfaithful I should be.*

Blood dripped onto the stone floor as they held their thumbs locked together. Calixta looked into Beatrice's eyes as if she were trying to capture her thoughts. Beatrice remained stoic, void of emotion. Calixta let go, reached into her pocket, and produced a vial.

As soon as Beatrice saw the vial she felt her heart pounding in her chest. She gritted her teeth and slowly drew a breath, trying not to let any hint of emotion or anxiety show. Being an accomplice, she would be just as guilty of using dark arts as if she had brewed the potion herself. She didn't care to know who or what had been sacrificed. Calixta opened the vial.

"Hold this until I tell you to drink it," instructed Calixta, handing the small, blue bottle to Beatrice. "I'm going to put one hand on your stomach and the other on your back. When you drink, swallow it all... do you understand me?" Beatrice nodded. "Now, close your eyes, and keep them closed until I tell you to open them."

Beatrice did as she was instructed. Calixta held her torso and said,

Fra mamah levith valina,
Fertileh ormal ven. Alamah!
Cromethel crevith em mortale,
Vitale, vitale ven. Alamah!

"Now drink," Calixta demanded. "Keep your eyes closed."

The potion burned but Beatrice swallowed. She didn't open her eyes.

"What do you see? Hurry, tell me what you see?" shouted Calixta, taking her hands off Beatrice.

"A child, a girl," Beatrice said. Tears began to seep through her eyelids.

"Open your eyes," said Calixta.

The tunnel was pitch black when Beatrice opened her eyes —yet in the darkness, standing in front of her, was the vision of a young girl. She had long, curly, ginger hair and freckles on her nose. She was wearing a white shift. The red cloak of a novice mage was draped around her shoulders. Beatrice was entranced, but the vision slowly faded away.

"Calixta?" Beatrice called out. There was no answer.

Beatrice summoned a light and looked around, but Calixta was gone.

The Unwelcomed Guest

When Corinna was born, Beatrice had insisted that the celebration last for weeks. But it was nothing compared to what was transpiring prior to Corinna's marriage to Bartlett. Ever since the wedding announcement, the entire kingdom had buzzed with excitement. When the day of the wedding finally arrived, the city overflowed with excited Ailearians.

"Face each other and join your right hands," instructed the priest quietly. He then lifted a length of red silk above his head and addressed the congregation.

"This cloth represents a promise bound in blood," said the priest. He wrapped the silk around their wrists three times. It poured from their hands and reached to the floor where it pooled at their feet.

The priest continued, "It is a symbol that binds their vows and seals the promises they have sworn to each other. May the star of love, the moon of health, and the sun of prosperity serve you faithfully, until the day of transformation, when you shall leave this mundane, temporal world, and become a glorious and eternal light in the vast and great celestial sea." The priest instructed them to release their hands and the red silk fell into a puddle on the floor.

From a pedestal, he picked up two golden bands and held them up for the congregation to see. "The rings!" he exclaimed. He handed the rings to the couple, who exchanged them in silence.

"The matrimonial kiss will express to this beloved assembly your undying love and commitment to each other." The couple kissed. Quiet rumblings of delight filtered through the approving congregation.

"The marriage of Sir Bartlett, of the house of Thayer, and Princess Corinna, from the royal house of Carlington, is now sealed. May the Book of Satins guide them henceforth and forevermore."

Antiphonal trumpets began a fanfare that echoed through the voluminous Grace of the Moon Oratory. It was the largest satinary in Ailear. It was designated as an oratory because it was home to the high priest of satins. The towering architectural wonder, with its imposing edifice, stood facing the main gates to Ansa.

The royal wedding procession made its way through the nave and exited onto the main steps. The couple was ushered into the carriage that was waiting to take them along the processional route from the oratory to Castlehill where a grand royal reception had been planned. The evening would conclude with an unprecedented display of fireworks.

The entire city was adorned with yellow and black flags, banners, and bunting. Tens of thousands of Ailearians lined the Saint Murphy Blvd. Bartlett's popularity had attracted a following of adoring young ladies, but most Ailearians were clamoring along the boulevard hoping to catch a glimpse of Corinna. She was known throughout the kingdom as the "Darling of Ailear." Expectant mothers prayed for the spirits to bless them with a ginger-haired child. For the past nineteen years, the name Corinna was the most popular name for a girl.

The festival hall at Castlehill was soon teeming with the royal guests. Although Corvis was getting on in years, she had insisted on overseeing the wedding feast. It had taken her staff days to prepare. The decorations had been designed by a new, popular Ailearian artist. Corinna's favorite band, The Saddle Dogs, pumped their musical energy into the room.

Beatrice and Alford stood at the railing on the second level that overlooked the hall and reveled in the celebration. Corinna and

Bartlett were seated on a dais, enjoying their guests. The sun had set and soon the throng would move outside to watch the fireworks.

"Do you like the music?" Alford shouted to Beatrice.

"What?" quipped Beatrice. "I can't hear you."

Alford laughed. "I know what you mean. It's too loud—and monotonous. We are beginning to show our age."

"Speak for yourself," she said, slapping Alford's arm. "I'm *only* fifty-seven. Maybe I like this music after all," she teased.

Corinna and Bartlett had moved to the dance floor and it had emptied, leaving them to dance alone. Their guests cheered for them and were sharing a steady stream of pictos and cinebits from their sPeaksees. The kingdom was thrilled with every morsel of news that was pushed their way.

"She's a beautiful bride, isn't she?" Beatrice asked.

"She is," Alford agreed, "and she's witty, and smart, and insightful. And she's certainly more mature at nineteen than either of us were at her..."

Alford stopped abruptly. The crowd was pointing to an illumination that was swirling like a cloud and filtering in through the main entrance. The luminescence began gathering itself above the dance floor.

It began to organize into a sphere several feet above the dance floor. The murmuring crowd stepped back. The band stopped playing and the room grew tense. At first it was small, but it grew to be several feet in diameter. The iridescent energy coalesced into a tangible, yet untouchable, globe. A woman's face appeared and swam around the surface. The room became silent and the woman spoke:

A little flower, a meadowlark,
Grew from a secret in the dark,
When bloody drops fell to the ground,
And promised words from lips were bound.

One drank the cup to quench her thirst,
And from the clouds, the rain did burst.
One watched it rain for several years.
In time, her sunshine will appear.

And when it does, there is a debt
That must be paid, so don't forget.
A meadowlark has but one voice.
Someone here has but one choice.

The face disappeared and the gaseous mass began dissipating into dozens of stringy wisps, moving like eels in every direction, seeking an exit at any open door or window. Slowly, murmurs rose from the crowd followed by hushed conversations. The voice had been deliberate and emphatic. Everyone understood the words that had been said, but nobody knew what they meant—nobody except Beatrice.

Beatrice's heart dropped into her stomach. She had not seen or communicated with Calixta since she drank the potion at the well. Before Corinna was born, her thoughts were consumed with ways to break her blood promise. But as time went on, she had become complacent and focused her attentions on Corinna. In the months leading up to the wedding, the promise had niggled at her, but she had ignored it, hoping the agreement would simply fade away.

Queen Beatrice addressed the crowd. "What royal celebration would be complete without a magical surprise?" she asked with animated enthusiasm. "Let's toast! Raise your glasses to the one voice of marriage, the one choice of an eternal bond!"

Everyone followed Queen Beatrice's lead. They cheered and drank. There were still many who were puzzled by the message and its meaning, but the incident appeared to be over. Beatrice's quick thinking and enthusiastic demeanor had managed to restore the joyous celebration. The Saddle Dogs resumed playing and the dance floor filled once again. Soon magnificent fireworks rocketed skyward and burst over Castlehill, showering the night sky with a variety of spectacular sparkles and booms.

CHAPTER TWENTY-THREE

Confessions and Confrontations

Twigsicles were adorned with colorful ribbons and friendship baskets decorated the porches throughout all of Ailear. In addition to the usual wishes for toys and games, this year's twigsicles were laden with extra ribbons asking Mr. Boots to make certain the royal baby was a boy—or a girl—depending on who had written the wish. Many children had been led to believe that Mr. Boots had something to do with the outcome. The baby was the subject of discussions on street corners, around the dinner table, and in the pubs. It seemed everyone had their own suggestion for a name. Bets were being wagered as to actual day and time that the Castlehill bell would ring announcing the birth.

Bakers in the central market couldn't keep up with the demand for baby cake traffles. Confectioners were making chocolate souvenir coins to commemorate the occasion. Near the market entrance, two towering glass tubes had been constructed as a fundraiser for the Grace of the Moon Orphanage. One tube was supported by a pink frame and had a sign that read "It's a girl!" The other tube was supported with a blue frame and was labeled with "It's a boy!" Visitors would climb the steps to a platform where they could drop a krote into the tube of their choice. On some days the pink tube had more krotes, and on other days the blue tube was in the lead.

The likelihood that Corinna would give birth during the week of Midwinterfest added an element of excitement throughout the kingdom. Some predicted that the birth would happen on Midwinter's Day, while others were hoping the birth would take place on Midwinter's Eve. There was a prophecy in the Book of Satins that foretold a king arriving on Midwinter's Eve under the rising of a full moon.

And on the eve of the glorious feast day, the moon in its fullness will rise.

It will usher the arrival of a king who will possess the light, and at whose command all darkness shall flee.

Hardened hearts will sing again, and the celestial queen will shower her grace o'er all the land.

Then shall it be that the Forever Tree will burst forth with such a perpetual radiance that the eyes of those who gaze upon her shining leaves will be opened to the truth: that good expels evil, that light repels darkness, and that love dispels hate.

— II Moon Tome Chapter Eight, Verses 3-6

Shortly after sunset on Midwinter's Eve, just as the full moon broke above the horizon across the sea, the bell at Castlehill began to ring. Many Ailearians had camped outside the castle in order to obtain the best vantage point to witness the announcement. When the bell rang, hundreds of Ansans rushed to the Imperial Plaza to hear the news. The crowd cheered and celebrated as they awaited Queen Beatrice's appearance. Their excitement was further enhanced by the chatter that was spreading about the prophetic king being born under a full moon on Midwinter's Eve. Even those who didn't follow the Book of Satins were astonished and celebrated with joyful amazement.

The bell continued to ring for almost an hour while the moon slowly rose into position behind the tower. Amidst the continued cheers and clapping, there were groups who were drumming, singing, and dancing.

Queen Beatrice appeared in the window of the tower and was met with cheers from below. She gazed over the throng. They filled the plaza and filtered through the streets as far as she could see. She, of course, had not been the one standing in the window to announce her own daughter's birth, so she took a bit of extra time, basking in the moment. She then raised both arms into the air and gestured with two tight fists, indicating that the mother and child were healthy, strong, and doing well. Cheers once again rose to the heavens. She then reached to the window sill and unfurled the banner. Thousands of pictos captured the historic moment. Queen Beatrice stood in the tower window, a pink banner flowed down the tower wall, a looming full moon illuminated the night sky, and a lone raven soared in circles around the tower.

The celebration around Castlehill continued through the night, but since it was Midwinter's Eve, most of the crowd dispersed and shifted their attentions to their own Midwinterfest activities. By dawn the moon had trekked across the sky and was nestling into a position over the mountains where it would soon disappear. As the kingdom came to life, doors were opening and friendship baskets were being brought inside. Children had learned that the new royal baby was a girl, and if they had wished for a boy, their disappointment was quickly replaced by excitement when they saw the other wishes Mr. Boots was able to fulfill.

After the birth, Gracella, Corinna's nursemaid, had administered an elixir for pain. She brewed a strong tea from sleeping herbs which allowed Corinna to sleep soundly for hours. Beatrice watched over Corinna during the night while Gracella flew off on a mission. The goose had just returned, so Beatrice left Corinna in her care. Whether she liked it or not, it was time to face the inevitable. The queen went to her room to steady her nerves.

The morning was already well-advanced when Corinna stirred and opened her eyes.

"There you are, Princess," Gracella said softly, stroking Corinna's ginger curls with her wing. "You slept a long time."

"The baby?" asked Corinna.

"Safe," said Gracella softly. "Everything has gone just as planned."

Corinna began to cry. She was angry at her mother. Her life would forever be changed—*all* their lives would forever be changed because of her mother's selfish decision.

"There now, Princess," comforted Gracella. "Try not to cry. I have faith that what you have chosen to do is the best thing you can do, as hard as it may seem."

"I keep second-guessing everything. I wish I had known sooner," replied Corinna. "Maybe there was something else that we could have done that would have been easier than this."

Numerous times Corinna had questioned her mother about the mysterious message at the wedding feast, but each time Beatrice had refused to give a direct answer—avoiding both the truth and a confrontation. It wasn't until Corinna was expecting a child that Beatrice finally revealed her secret. Corinna was horrified when she heard the terms of the agreement. Beatrice promised Corinna that no matter what, the child would never be delivered into Calixta's hands.

Last night, after Beatrice had unfurled the banner, her blood froze when she saw Omen circling about the tower.

"Why are you here?" asked Beatrice, knowing full well that Calixta had sent him.

"She sent me to remind you that a promise made in blood is a promise that cannot be broken. She has made preparations and she is coming to collect the debt that you owe her."

"When is she coming?"

"Tomorrow. Midwinter's Day, before noon." Omen's outstretched wings glimmered in the moonlight as he continued soaring about the tower.

"Where am I supposed to meet her?" asked Beatrice.

"She will find you," replied Omen. He didn't say anything else. He flew toward the moon, out of her sight, where he was eventually eclipsed by the blackness of the night.

After Beatrice left Corinna in the hands of Gracella, she had thought about doubling the guards, but she knew trying to avoid Calixta was pointless. Calixta would be persistent, so she decided to get it over with. She paced her room, wondering if she should stay there or go somewhere else. She became too impatient to stay, so she went down to the tunnel and called out, but there was no answer. She went out to the garden and sat on a bench by the old chester tree. She gathered a few nuts for Corvis and tucked them into her pocket. She thought about the plan that had already been set in motion. It gave her courage and fortitude. She thought about going up to the fortress wall to walk along the rampart, but then realized that it didn't matter where she was. If Calixta wanted to see her, she would find her. Beatrice decided to wander along the footpath that circuited along the cliffs behind Castlehill. She stopped at the memorial stone that Cedric had installed. It was the spot where they found Oris's body after the accident. Beatrice rarely went out this far. The marker caused a flood of memories and emotions to well up inside of her.

"Well, Queen Bea, or is it...'Grandmama'? You know why I'm here." It was Calixta. Her voice was hollow and callous. She was dressed in red and held a staff that she cradled at her neck. Her hair was now almost completely gray. Beatrice was both surprised and impressed at how stealthily Calixta had appeared.

"Please don't, Calixta. I've known you forever, and I know you have compassion. You can't hold me to this promise. Please, I beg you!"

Calixta stood up and spiked her staff onto the ground. "Bring me the baby! I really don't have time for your whimpering and groveling."

"But you can't ask a mother to give up her child. It's heartless."

"But I'm not asking a mother to give up her child—*you* are. *You* are the one who decided the fate of your grandchild. *You* are the one who was willing to drown your daughter in grief. *You* are the one who is heartless. *You* made the agreement with full awareness that this day would eventually arrive, and you agreed to the terms. I am here to collect the debt that *you...owe...me.*"

Beatrice was silent. She had hoped Calixta would reconsider. But it was obvious that Calixta was not going to absolve her from her part of the agreement. Beatrice felt she was left with no other choice. Her plan would have to move forward.

"You can't have the baby," Beatrice said firmly.

Calixta's face reddened with seething disbelief.

"Surely you must know that you cannot hide that child from me. So, bring me the baby," Calixta demanded.

"You can't have the baby," Beatrice repeated. "She's been taken away."

"What do you mean, *she's been taken away?*"

"I mean just that," said Beatrice firmly. "She's gone...gone from Ansa...gone from Ailear...she's gone from this celestial realm."

"Do you mean to tell me she's dead? I don't believe it!" snapped Calixta.

"Oh no, she's not dead. No, she's very much alive. But she's gone from your grasp, gone from this world. She was carried to a place of safekeeping far beyond the Tunnel of Stars. You will never get your hands on that child as long as you live!"

"You're lying!" shouted Calixta. "There's nobody within your reach that could travel that far. That feat would require the powers of a master mage, and one with wings at that...and there's no such thing!"

"Or so you think," Beatrice snubbed. "Do you think I would have casually selected a nursemaid for Corinna? You've been so far removed for so many years that you wouldn't know that Gracella was the first goose to become a master mage, and that she has been in our service since Corinna was born. She is a master mage. She has wings. She is most certainly capable of taking our beloved princess through the Tunnel of Stars and beyond your reach—and she did!"

Calixta's blood boiled with anger. She extended her arm and gripped the air with her hand. Beatrice's neck constricted and she felt Calixta's grasp. As Calixta raised her arm, Beatrice levitated above the ground, prying at her neck, trying to break free from the invisible chokehold. Calixta spoke:

> *I swear this bond from head to heel,*
> *And with my blood this promise seal.*
> *May plagues and curses fall on me,*
> *If e're unfaithful I should be.*

She let go of Beatrice, who fell to the ground gasping for air. Calixta stood over Beatrice and pressed the butt end of her staff on her forehead.

"Are any of those words familiar to you? Surely you haven't forgotten them. Did you give any thought as to what would befall the precious house of Carlington when you crossed the bridge of betrayal and broke your bond? I assure you, this will be your final betrayal. Upon you and your house I will set forth the most hideous curse imaginable. Mark my words...try to flee...run and hide...but you will not escape it. I will use the curse to make sure the child is returned to me. You may think you have beat me, but you have only won a battle. I will win the war!"

Beatrice was paralyzed with fright. She felt Calixta's staff lift away from her forehead, but she flinched too late as it came back down. Her head buzzed from the blow. She saw the branches of a nearby bumble-berry tree gently swaying in the breeze as the sky dimmed and faded to black.

Lizzy
Albright

CHAPTER TWENTY-FOUR

Plagues and Curses

A thick, black cloud was boiling in the distance just above the treetops of Valendale.

"What do you think that is?" the guard asked. "It's not a fire—or at least I don't think it is."

The station mate focused his telescope and took a closer look.

"It's birds," he said, "one helluva lot of birds."

They monitored the swarm with great curiosity and were fascinated at how dense and organized the birds were. The churning mass was so far away, and moved so slowly, that it almost appeared to be stationary. It eventually reached the edge of the forest, where it changed formation. The bottom descended to the ground, stirring up dust, while the top rose high into the air. The birds flew in circles, creating a vortex, which made them look more like a cyclone than a flock of grackles.

"Have you ever seen anything like it?" asked the guard.

"No, never," said the mate. "I've seen them swarm before, but nothing like this." He paused to listen. "Do you hear that shrill noise? It must be them."

"It's very odd. Do you think there's any reason to be alarmed?"

"I'm not sure. But we better report this to the sergeant and see what he thinks."

Beatrice had put the civic guards on high alert. For the past two weeks they had been ordered to double check the credentials of everyone entering the city to make sure Calixta wouldn't slip past them. She had tripled the number of guards at Castlehill and had stationed a small army to protect the tunnel's entrance that was hidden in the vaulted crypt beneath Saint Tyndall's.

The grackles reached Fishmarket Road and began a steady progression in the direction of Ansa. Some travelers on the road made U-turns and sped off in the opposite direction. Other drivers didn't act fast enough and were abandoning their motorbies and fleeing into the meadows for safety. The swarm moved with a slow but relentless determination as if it were motivated by some sinister force.

The alarms were sounded and an emergency alert was sent throughout Ansa and the surrounding area. Ansans read the warnings on their sPeaksees, but instead of taking cover, they climbed onto rooftops to see for themselves what a cyclone of grackles looked like.

The royal council was in assembly when it was interrupted with the news. Queen Beatrice knew immediately that it was Calixta. She hurried to the nearest tower window to see for herself the horror that was approaching the city. There was no time to waste, so she didn't stay to watch the advancing menace. She found Nelson and Jamison in the main corridor.

"This is it," sighed Beatrice. "Nelson, find Euna and Gracella and tell them to act fast. You all know what to do. Jamison, you stay with me. I need to see the captain."

An army of soldiers had been dispatched to Ansa's main entrance. The guards shut and locked the gate. A motorbie jam clogged the road near the entry point, making it impossible for the drivers to untangle the mess. They had no choice but to run away or look for a place to hide. As the grackles advanced, their screeching chatter escalated. Those who had clamored to the rooftops began to realize the seriousness of the situation, and their amusement slowly morphed into fear. They scrambled down and began to seek shelter indoors.

In a matter of minutes the swarm would arrive at the walls. The commanders were baffled as to what they could do, and they argued about what course of action to take. Their weapons might dispatch a few birds, but nothing would be able to stop them from advancing into the city. There was no precedent for defending against an onslaught of grackles, so they felt absolutely paralyzed.

Beatrice and Jamison found Burris in the courtyard near the main castle gate. As captain of the guards, he was personally overseeing that all precautions had been taken. He double checked that the portcullis was lowered and that his guards were at their posts.

"That's Calixta," Beatrice informed Burris.

"What do you mean, *that's Calixta*?"

"She's been assembling an army of grackles for years. I didn't realize she had acquired so many. But I assure you, those birds are moving under her command. Jamison has personally experienced the kind of damage these birds can do. What you see is not a warning. They're here to attack!"

"Why would she attack Ansa?"

"She's not coming to attack Ansa. She's coming to attack me."

Burris knew enough of Castlehill's history to know there was a rift between Calixta and the queen. Burris was Brandt's son. Brandt had served both Cedric and Gethric during the troublesome times. On numerous occasions his father had given him firsthand accounts of what had transpired. Burris had not yet been born when Cedric had been forced to abdicate the throne. But from what he knew, he suspected that the situation would have been hard for both Calixta and Beatrice. Calixta had suffered because of it. Burris had no knowledge of recent events and could only speculate that Calixta was coming to avenge her father.

"Do either of you have any suggestions?" Burris asked. He had already positioned every available guard along the rampart, but he had yet to think of an effective way to defend Castlehill against the grackles.

"She's after me, not you...and not the citizens of Ansa," emphasized Beatrice. "I'm doubtful that she would cause serious harm to anyone except those who would try to protect me. If I try to hide, the grackles will wreak havoc until they find me. If you fight them, they will fight back, and there will be far too many unnecessary casualties. If the grackles kill me, then the battle will be over, and hundreds of lives could be spared. The baby is safe and that's all that matters. I've come to tell you not to fight. I'm going to the tower to face whatever fate she has in store for me."

Jamison bristled and said, "Over my dead body, Your Majesty. I will not let any harm come to you without putting up a fight."

"It *will* be over your dead body if you try to protect me. So don't!" Beatrice commanded.

The grackles easily breached the city walls and began aggressively rounding up those who had not taken cover. They began herding them down Saint Murphy Blvd. in the direction of the castle. If anyone tried to stop or hide, they would peck and stab at them until they started moving again. As long as they were advancing, the grackles left them alone.

Burris had taken a position on the rampart next to the guard tower. Jamison, still insistent about fighting the grackles, followed Beatrice up to the tower. Everyone else in the castle knew what they were supposed to do.

The swarm had managed to push more than a thousand terrified citizens into Imperial Plaza in front of Castlehill, confining them there as more grackles moved on to the fortress wall. The pitch and volume of their horrendous screeching was almost incapacitating. The guards who were trapped inside the swarm cowered but tried not to panic. They kept expecting to be violently battered, scratched, and stabbed, but the grackles did no such thing. The birds continued advancing past the wall until they had enveloped all of Castlehill. They were so dense that Beatrice could barely see the guards on the wall, but she could tell that no one was being attacked—including herself.

Then, as if on command, the grackles near the center of the vortex began to rise, swirling skyward. They formed a dome over the entire castle complex so that it was completely contained within a cage made of swarming birds. In the outer courtyard, a separate, tightly formed nucleus of grackles drifted up from the ground and ascended until it reached the very top of the fortress wall. The birds dispersed, revealing a figure standing above the gate, dressed in red. It was Calixta. Her cloak was filthy, torn, and shredded. Most of the hair on the right side of her head was gone. Her face had fresh, visible wounds that had been stitched back together. There was a bruised, sunken depression in the place of her right eye which had been sewn shut. She was a hideous sight to behold. In her right hand she held a staff that had a raven's claw on top. The sight of it was repulsive. Everyone knew that the dark arts required the mutilation of a living creature—or even worse, murder. This staff represented one or the other, and she was brandishing it for everyone to see.

Burris looked to Beatrice, who shook her head, reminding him that the guards should not take any aggressive action toward Calixta. Beatrice felt desperate to come up with a solution, but she was helpless knowing that there was nothing she could do.

Calixta looked across the courtyard to Beatrice who was in the tower window. She raised the Ravenclaw Staff into the air and the grackles ceased their screeching. Calixta then turned away from Beatrice and addressed those who were being held captive in Imperial Plaza. Her voice was raspy, but still resonated with strength and confidence. Some of the onlookers began secretly recording cinebits.

"Good citizens of Ailear, how lucky you are. You get to have a front row seat. You get to be eyewitnesses; you will be able to give firsthand accounts of my visit here to Castlehill. Please, use your devices! Capture this moment so that there won't be any confusion or mistake when you tell the story of today's events to your family and friends."

Several sPeaksees were brought out of hiding as citizens began documenting the event by taking pictos and recording cinebits. The crowd was silent as death. They wanted to hear every word.

"Everyone loves a good story," Calixta continued. "Do you know my story? Oh, please forgive me, of course you don't. You couldn't possibly know the secrets that have been hidden for years inside the walls of your precious Castlehill. But I bet you like secrets, so let me tell you a story *and* a secret."

Calixta began to recount the highlights of events they had read or been told, but for the first time they heard *her* side of the story. She listed a chain of events that led Beatrice to the throne and reminded them that *she*, not Beatrice, was the rightful queen. She spoke of betrayal and deception.

She then mentioned that Beatrice so desperately wanted an heir that she essentially begged her to create a fertility potion that would guarantee her a child. She included details about the elixir, such as the use of strawberry seeds that assured the child would have freckles. She carelessly listed other forbidden ingredients, essentially confessing publicly that she had used black magic to create the potion. She informed them that their precious "Darling of Ailear" was the result. She also reminded them that Beatrice was an accomplice in the matter. She told them about their agreement and that Beatrice had sworn her promise under an oath of blood.

"'May *plagues* and *curses* fall on me, If e're unfaithful I should be.' *That* is what she agreed to. *That* is the deal we made. Your queen has betrayed me. She had Gracella take the baby out of my reach to a place beyond the Tunnel of Stars. The child, *my* reward for a lifetime of misery, has been stolen from me...and now, because of the broken blood promise, Castlehill will pay the price."

As Calixta raised the Ravenclaw Staff, panic swept through the crowd. Most everyone wanted to run, but they were still captives inside the grackles' cage.

"It's true!" shouted Beatrice, her voice silencing the crowd. "It's true that the princess was taken to a safe place." Beatrice had left the tower and was now standing on the rampart near the main guard tower, not far from Burris, and much closer to the crowd.

"How nice that you've left your hive to greet your loyal, royal subjects," Calixta fumed.

"No matter what you have planned, Calixta, you will never lay a hand on that child."

"Mother, get back!" A voice called from the tower window. Calixta had assumed that Corinna would be in the castle and she was pleased with that confirmation. She looked to the tower just as Bartlett was pulling her back inside.

"You think I will never lay a hand on her? We'll see about that! That's your plan, not mine. And it's nice to know that you have gathered your whole family together for this occasion."

Calixta pulled a golden orb from her robe. It began emitting an array of colorful arcs. She placed it on the top of the staff. The raven claw grabbed the orb and clutched it tightly. She raised the staff with both hands and began chanting.

Dwellen a Carlington
An ara castila vara
Ve ara vasha. Ve ara vasha.
Ver dermisa an ver sangrati
Lan darnsor
An ve curna ti granatita
Alamah! Alamah!

Ve am visio, no ve am vociliea
Ve lan bahah an ve lan ohshah.
Alamah! Alamah!

Im solion am vasha destranta.
Be mi im tonse im fentosum authoriznia
An transtum ti babitor o Corinna.
Urgentorum luna dun
Supra montanus tenta entersun av babitor.
Ravin pedtron cradiltun luminor vitor
An solion babitor am disambilora et.
Alamah! Alamah!

Calixta then launched the staff into the air. It sailed upward, arched, and then began its descent. Onlookers scrambled to get out of its way. As it spiked into the ground in the plaza, the crowd rippled away as if a rock had been tossed into a pond.

Beatrice suddenly noticed that she could barely move. She tried to reach out, but her arm slowed and stayed in place. She was paralyzed. She could see Burris—he was staring right at her—but he wasn't moving. She tried to look to the castle window, but her head wouldn't turn. Her eyes wouldn't do what she was telling them to do. She tried to scream, but the only thing that came out was a muffled "mmm."

Everyone within Castlehill was paralyzed and turned pale and ashen, their skin hardened and cracked. Their eyes glazed over and turned dark. They were tormented by the transformation, but their mouths were sealed, so all they could do was moan. The crowd watched in absolute terror as living beings morphed into stone statues.

"If you want your royalty to survive, then find the child and bring her to me. I possess the only copy that can reverse this curse, and I've made certain that the princess is the only one who can read the spell and restore Castlehill. You have until the end of her tenth birthday. If by that time the princess has not yet arrived, then these groaning stones will become a permanent reminder of broken promises, betrayal, and lies."

Calixta called to her grackles. They scattered in every direction and released the crowd. Several of them enveloped Calixta and lowered her to the ground. She left the city just as she arrived—on foot—surrounded by dense, black cloud of grackles.

When the crowd realized that the ordeal was over and they were safe, some of them collapsed—emotionally spent. Others walked around in a daze, not sure what to do. Some tended to minor wounds that the grackles had inflicted. Small clusters held each other—crying. Others looked at Castlehill in disbelief. Their queen, Burris, and several guards were visible from below. They wondered what the situation was like beyond the wall and couldn't imagine the number of those inside Castlehill who were affected by Calixta's curse.

"Are you okay?" Gertie asked Gretta.

"I am...I'm just...I don't know what to think," replied Gretta.

Gertie and Gretta were in shock from the experience. They remained silent as they ambled along with the crowd and made their way to Mage Guild Hall—they had no desire or energy to fly. They stopped next to the Rose Wall and waited until they saw that Calixta and the grackles had left Ansa before turning into the gate at Barley-wick Quarter.

Gretta broke the silence first. "Where would she have learned that spell, Mother? It's the most horrible thing imaginable."

"I don't know, but it must have been in the guild library vaults. All of the forbidden tomes and scrolls are kept there."

"But the vaults are secured and protected. How could she have possibly gained access?" Gertie just shook her head. She didn't have an answer.

As Gertie and Gretta approached the guild hall, they saw several mages gathered on the steps. As they moved closer they perceived something serious was wrong. Igree was slumped over, sitting on the steps, with a look of grief and dismay.

"What is it?" Gertie asked one of the mages. "What's the matter?"

"It's Ravol," she replied, almost unable to speak. "The high mage has been murdered. He's been missing for two days. Igree just found him near the library vault. There were signs of an altercation, and one of his claws had been amputated."

The Portrait in the Parlor

Lizzy woke up but didn't open her eyes. She pulled the covers up under her chin and felt the softness of the quilt. She was still wondering who robbed Peter to pay Paul and whether one of the bees in the Honey Bee block was a queen bee. That made her remember her dream—where Pearline Beasley turned into a bee, and Fluffs got mad at her and put her in a jar.

It suddenly dawned on Lizzy that it was Christmas morning. She turned to see the snow outside the bedroom window, but there wasn't any snow—there wasn't a window—she wasn't at Granny's. She then realized she was still dreaming. She was at Deep Glen, somewhere in a forest far away from home. She looked around the room. Igree had left soft lights burning and their gentle glow illuminated the comfortable furnishings. Lizzy stretched and yawned. She was amused that her dream seemed so real. She supposed that was okay. So far it was turning out to be one of the best dreams she had ever had, and having McDoogle with her made it even better. Some things had been a little scary, but it wasn't a nightmare.

McDoogle heard her stir and raised up on the side of the bed. "Good morning, Lass!" he said with a vigorously waggling tail.

"Why, good morning, McDoo! Did you have a good sleep? Did you have any dreams about Pearline Beazzzley?" Lizzy buzzed.

"I had nae sich dreams, but I'm presuming by yer inquisitiveness that ye did."

"I did," Lizzy giggled. "Pearline Beasley was a bee. She stole a cherry and made Fluffs mad. Do you think dreams mean anything?"

"I dinna ken aboot the meanin' o' dreams, but it sure sounds as if ye had a wild yin." McDoogle sniffed the air. "Ach, something smells good. Shall we check it oot?"

Igree had made a fresh batch of traffles and was already in the midst of his tea ritual when Lizzy and McDoogle made their way to the dining room.

"They're piping hot; help yourself." Igree set the platter on the table. "Now don't you for one minute let Gretta try to convince you that Gabby's traffles are better than mine. Her traffles are very good, but mine are the best." Igree lowered his voice and added, "I have a secret ingredient. I've never told a soul what it is—so don't ask."

"What is it?" asked Lizzy.

"Now, now, I just told you it's a secret," replied Igree. He set the tea on the table, leaned into Lizzy's ear, and then whispered, "It's cinnamon."

Gretta appeared in the doorway. "Good morning, Princess...Mr. McDoogle...has Igree been prattling on about his traffles? He thinks his are the best because he adds cinnamon."

Lizzy tried not to laugh. She swallowed fast to avoid spitting out her sip of tea.

"Igree's traffles are very good, but you won't find them to be quite as tasty as Gabby's."

Igree took a small, framed certificate off the wall and showed it to Lizzy. "My traffles won first prize at the Starfest Bake-off," boasted Igree.

Gretta helped herself to a traffle. "Congratulations, Igree, when was that? Eighty-two years ago...or something thereabouts?"

Igree looked at the date on the certificate and did the math. "Seventy-two," clarified Igree.

Lizzy was delighted as she watched the two of them banter back and forth over traffles. She learned it was an ongoing tradition in Ailear to brag about your traffles whether they had ever won prizes or not. Igree and Gretta both agreed that it was very difficult to find a bad traffle unless it had been accidentally overbaked or burnt.

After breakfast they moved to the parlor. Lizzy sat in her favorite chair. Igree pulled up a stool and sat down in front of her.

"I'm grateful for your patience, Princess," said Igree. "I know you have felt anxious and have been eager to know why we so desperately need your help."

Lizzy nodded.

"Well then, I need to tell you a story about two girls and a broken promise."

Igree began the delicate task of telling Lizzy about Beatrice and Calixta. Lizzy had plenty of questions, which Igree answered the best he could. He spoke fondly of Gracella and how she had flown the baby to safety through the Tunnel of Stars. He explained that such a thing could only be done by a master mage.

"What's a mage?" asked Lizzy.

"A mage? Well, a mage is someone who has studied and performs some form of magic. Magicians, witches, warlocks, sorcerers, sorceresses, wizards, and enchanters—are all mages. A master mage has trained a long time and has the ability to use the most powerful magic. It's very difficult to become a master mage...and it usually takes a long time."

"And Gracella? She was the one who took me...I mean who took the princess, through the Tunnel of Stars?"

"Yes, she did," Igree confirmed.

Lizzy looked curiously at Gretta. "If master mages are the only ones who can fly through the Tunnel of Stars, that means you must be a master mage too."

Gretta smiled softly. "I am. I worked very hard to become a master mage just so that I could go find you."

"Why didn't Gracella come find me?" Lizzy asked.

Igree paused as he considered how best to proceed. He cautiously began telling her the story of how Calixta and the grackles had entered Ansa and placed the groaning stone curse on everyone at Castlehill. Gracella had been turned into a groaning stone too. When Igree finished, they all sat in silence for a few minutes.

Lizzy looked at Gretta and was the first to speak. "And you were there? You saw the curse when it happened?"

Gretta nodded.

Lizzy couldn't imagine what it would have felt like to witness such a horrible thing. Although she had been impatient to know why Gretta had brought her to Ailear, now that she knew the whole story, she was apprehensive and anxious. If what Igree said was true, Calixta had managed to fix it so that the only one who could reverse the curse was the true princess, which insured that the child would be delivered into Calixta's hands.

"Are you going to take me to Calixta?"

McDoogle barked, "By Jove, they will no be takin' ye to that witch!" He jumped up into Lizzy's lap.

"No, no, no...we will not do anything of the sort," said Igree. He leaned in closer to Lizzy. "My dear Princess, at this very moment, you are the most important and most precious person in the entire kingdom of Ailear. We want Castlehill to be restored, but we will not give you to Calixta in order for that to happen. Our goal is to keep you safe. The mage council believes it is possible to reverse the curse and defeat Calixta, but it can't be done without you."

Lizzy remembered the swarm of grackles that had flown over Lake Road yesterday and now realized why Gretta had been so cautious and protective.

"What do I have to do?" asked Lizzy.

"Well," said Igree, "first we need to get you to Ansa to meet with the council. Baron, the high mage, will explain the plan. Then you will have to decide if you are willing to help."

"Are you and Gretta on the council?" Lizzy asked.

"We are," replied Igree.

Gretta stood up and motioned for Lizzy to follow. She went over to the old portrait that Lizzy had studied the night before.

"This was taken many years ago when Igree was the high mage."

"Igree was the high mage?"

"Indeed he was," replied Gretta. "Igree was a wonderful high mage. He was high mage longer than anyone in the history of the kingdom. These are officers who were once on his council."

Lizzy puzzled, "The bear and the raven are mages too?"

"Not only mages, but *master mages*, and they were loved and respected by everyone in the kingdom. Igree is the only one in this picture who is still with us. The others have transitioned to the celestial realm. Igree won't tell you, but..." Gretta leaned into Lizzy and whispered, "he's the most powerful wizard in all of Ailear."

Lizzy's eyes got big and her jaw dropped. "You're a wizard?"

Igree shrugged, blew her a kiss, then snapped his fingers. A rainbow of sparkling stars began floating down over her, which made her laugh.

"The bear is Burton," Gretta continued. "He served as high mage after Igree. His son Baron is the high mage now."

"But he's a bear. Bears are mean and scary."

"Maybe where you come from, but Baron? Why, he's as gentle as a summer breeze. I think you will like him a lot."

Lizzy wasn't convinced. Bears had big teeth, big paws, and big claws, but since so many things were different here, she decided to wait and see for herself.

"Who's the woman?" asked Lizzy.

"That's Gorva. She was a gifted healer...but she was also a wonderful mage. She eventually chose medicine over magic and ran an apothecary called the Hyssop and Sage. It's still there, but it has new owners. Most people say she lived to be over one-hundred years old. She was working in her shop on the day that she died."

Lizzy studied Gorva's long, silver hair and once again admired the pendant she was wearing.

Gretta drew Lizzy's attention to the raven. "That's Ravol. He was migh mage after Burton and served for twenty-two years."

Gretta knew this was a sensitive matter. For the sake of both Lizzy *and* Igree, she didn't say any more. Lizzy didn't need to know how Ravol had died—at least not yet.

"And who's the man with the beard?"

"That's Cedric," replied Igree. "He was one of the most brilliant master mages in the history of the kingdom. He was born to be a mage, and there's no doubt that he would have become high mage, but his father was the king, and when his father died, Cedric became king and...well..." Igree looked at Gretta who shook her head.

"Well what?" asked Lizzy.

"Well..." Igree searched for the words. "Well...his wife died unexpectedly. His grief sent him into a place of darkness, the kind of darkness that comes from deep despair. He never recovered from it."

"He must have loved her very much," Lizzy suggested.

Igree pointed to the autographed photo of the Ice Angels. "He did," said Igree. "That was her...his wife, the one in the middle."

Lizzy admired her beauty. "What was her name?"

"Oris—her name was Oris. He was so distraught over losing her that he did some things he shouldn't have done. The choices he made are what ultimately led us to the situation we are in. But he's gone now, and what is done is done. And speaking of done, if you will agree to help us, we should make our way to Ansa. We don't have much time. Will you meet with the mage council? We must reverse the curse before the moon sets tomorrow night or it will be too late for everyone at Castlehill."

Lizzy was quiet for a moment as she pondered her situation. She thought about what she had been told and was surprised that her imagination could create such a fantasy. She still felt safe, McDoogle was with her, and she liked Gretta and Igree. She assumed at some point she would wake up, and it would be Christmas. She also had a small argument with herself over the fact that this all seemed very real. Cracks in her dream theory were starting to show.

"I will go if you promise that when it's over, I can go home."

"I promise," said Igree.

CHAPTER TWENTY-SIX

Mystery in the Mist

L izzy was surprised at how different the forest looked during the daylight. The forest's canopy was so far above her head it looked like green clouds. The breeze blowing through their tall branches created whooshes that reminded Lizzy of the ocean waves she heard when her family visited a beach during their California vacation.

Igree took the lead. He followed various narrow paths that seemed to twist and wind in every direction. Every now and then he would veer off onto tracks that were barely visible and have to work his way back to trails that were more clearly defined. McDoogle had secretly determined to memorize their route, but even *his* nose became confused, and he lost his bearings as they meandered their way through Valendale.

Their hooded leaf cloaks disguised them against a backdrop of lush green vegetation and also kept them dry as they brushed against the plants that were dripping with dew. They continued to travel with minimal conversation. The fewer the eyes that noticed them, the safer they would be. Lizzy's blue butterflies fluttered about and were never far away. They remained blue, reassuring Lizzy that she was not in any danger.

The forest up ahead was cloaked in fog. Lizzy preferred it when she could easily see everything around her. As the fog closed in she began to feel uneasy, but she didn't say anything about it. Eventually their path emptied onto a main road.

"This is Bag Road," said Igree. "It's the main road from here to Ansa. The journey will be easier—except it will be foggy for a while.

Bag Road crosses the Foggy Flats. The fog from that area rolls up into Valendale. This area is almost always shrouded in fog."

"I don't like the fog," Lizzy announced. "I would prefer it go away."

"It might let up a bit," said Igree. "You never know. But it won't take us long before we get to the Merry Meadows, and you should be able to see all the way to Ansa."

"I hear rushing water," noted McDoogle. "We must be near a bùrn."

"It's Future Falls," replied Gretta. "We're almost to the bridge that crosses the Lonely River. The waterfall is off to the right."

Lizzy was amused. "Future Falls? That's a funny name."

"I think so too," admitted Gretta, "but there are those who believe that you can see your future in the mist."

Lizzy was intrigued. If she knew her future, it might help her to know what to do after she met with the mage council and whether or not she would wake up back at Granny's house in Cordelia, Kansas.

They stopped along Bag Road long enough for a few bites of traffle and refreshing drinks from their canteens. They then began a slow descent that skirted down the side of a cliff. Gretta was right; the bridge at Lonely River had not been very far away, but it hadn't been visible through the fog. The waterfall flowed out from the rocky shelf that they had just descended. Lonely River was not large, but large enough that Future Falls produced an impressive flow. Lizzy had never seen a large waterfall before so she asked if they could stop so she could admire it.

"Have you ever seen *your* future?" Lizzy was gazing at the waterfall so neither Igree nor Gretta knew which one of them she was asking.

Gretta chose to answer first. "Maybe I have…once…I saw something."

"Like what?" asked Lizzy.

"It was when I was in mage school. I saw..." Gretta stepped back and caught her breath.

Lizzy was surprised at Gretta's reaction. "What is it? What's the matter?"

Gretta looked at Lizzy. She was speechless. "I..."

"What?" asked Lizzy.

"I...I just now remembered. It feels like a distant memory, but now it's all so real. I had forgotten about it...but it just came back."

Gretta squatted down to steady her nerves. "I saw myself tapping on the attic window—at the mansion. That's all there was to it. But I have no doubt that was your attic window that I saw in my vision."

Gretta was lost in thought as she tried to comprehend her revelation.

"But that's good, isn't it?" asked Lizzy. "It wasn't anything bad."

"I know, but I really didn't believe that the waterfall could show the future. It was a few years ago when I saw it. I just brushed it off as being my own imagination."

"Maybe there are still mysteries far beyond our understanding," suggested Igree. "I've certainly heard stories from plenty of others who were convinced that a vision of some sort came to them after looking into the mist of Future Falls."

"Has the waterfall ever shown you anything about your future?" Lizzy asked Igree.

"I'm blind, remember? I see differently than most, so I don't see the mist and the waterfall in the same way you do. So, no, to answer your questions, I've not seen any prediction of my future in the waterfall."

Lizzy and McDoogle were both intrigued by the falls. They stared at it for a long while, not saying a word. The fog added to the magical atmosphere that enveloped them. There were wisps that floated and danced about. The fog would thicken into a veil, almost obscuring the waterfall, but then dissipate, forming delicate swirls. The waterfall was tiered, so it splashed on various levels and created a dance of water drops and sprays that was hypnotic to watch.

Suddenly, McDoogle yipped and jumped back. He shivered, shook, and sat down.

"Are you okay McDoo—did you see something?"

"Aye, Lass, I was lettin' me imagination rin awa'."

"What? What did you imagine? What did you see?" asked Lizzy.

McDoogle didn't want to answer the question. What he imagined seemed preposterous, and he didn't want to embarrass himself.

"Silliness is a'. Nothin' but a wee bit o' silliness," shrugged McDoogle.

"But you must tell me." Lizzy turned to Gretta and Igree. "Shouldn't he tell us?"

"It's nothin', Lass. It's no ma fortune. But if ye must know...ach...if ye must know...I imagined masel fleein' through the sky on the back of a big black bird. Then somehow, I fell aff. It startled me, and I yipped. I didn't want to imagine hittin' the grund."

"That's awful," exclaimed Lizzy.

"It's just imagination, Lass, not a prediction o' the future. I dinna have ony intention of ever fleein' on a bird again unless it's on the back of Miss Gretta, fleein' us home. For me to do onything else would be tomfoolery. And I'm no havin' onything to do wi' tomfoolery."

"Alright then, but just to be clear, you are not to get on any bird other than Gretta. Do you understand?"

"Aye, Lass, I understand. And ye don't need to be tellin' me twice. So whut aboot yersel? Did ye see onything?"

Gretta and Igree were extremely interested in Lizzy's answer to McDoogle's question.

"I'm not sure. Not really...at least nothing that seemed out of the ordinary."

"But you saw something?" asked Gretta.

"All I saw was Granny's attic. It was no different than it aways is. I just wanted to see the snow outside, so I climbed onto the cedar chest and tried to look out the window. There was ice on the window panes outside, so I couldn't see anything very well. The window was stuck but I finally managed to open it. It was nothing unusual...not really."

"And did you see the snow?" asked Gretta.

"I did," admitted Lizzy, but it was all that she was willing to admit. "It didn't feel like the future, it just seemed familiar...like something I've already done, something from the past."

Igree's voice was soft and kind. "I suppose you are homesick, and for that I'm sure sorry. Let's get this situation sorted out."

He was, of course, referring to the situation with Calixta and the curse. He was beginning to understand how Lizzy felt about her predicament—something none of the mages had really taken into account. He felt sorry for her and sorry that they had put her in this position. She had a family here who needed her, but to Lizzy, her family was somewhere far away— somewhere beyond the Tunnel of Stars.

Lizzy collected her satchel and was slinging it over her shoulder when they heard the loud croaking caw of a raven. It was not very far away.

"Duck down! Hide!" Igree instructed.

A heavy bank of fog had closed in, which greatly reduced visibility, but it also helped cloak them from being seen. They could hear the raven flying overhead, but it was completely obscured by the mist. They huddled under their cloaks, held their breath, and waited. After a few minutes the caws faded into the distance.

"Do you think he spotted us?" asked Gretta.

"It's hard to say," replied Igree.

"It wasn't a grackle, was it?" asked Lizzy.

"No, not a grackle," assured Gretta.

"So what's the matter then?"

Igree had hoped to avoid telling Lizzy a few things that might add additional concern or cause her to be worried or afraid, but this was something she had to know.

"Calixta has a servant—a raven. His name is Omen. He serves her and reports to her. He tells her everything he sees and hears. We can't be sure the raven we heard was Omen, but if it was, and if he saw us..."

"If he saw us...whut?" interjected McDoogle.

"If he saw us and reports us to Calixta, it could be dangerous for everyone. We had better be moving to Ansa as fast as possible. We can't take any chances." Igree's strong legs were already bounding along at a much faster pace than before. The others were doing their best to keep up.

"How much farther is it?" asked Lizzy.

"We're not that far away," said Igree. "We will be out of Valendale soon. The fog in Foggy Flats will keep us well hidden, but after that we will be completely exposed as we cross the Merry Meadows. There won't be any trees to hide under. We must trust our leaf cloaks to keep us hidden. There will be a motorbie waiting for us once we reach Fishmarket Road."

Lizzy and McDoogle didn't know anything about distances or places. They didn't know how far it was across the Merry Meadows, and they didn't know the location of Fishmarket Road. They had no choice but to trust Igree and push forward. Igree didn't seem to be in a panic, but he was certainly on high alert for their safety.

The fog was so dense that they could only see a few feet in any direction. Igree slowed his pace and urged everyone to stay close so they could see each other—he didn't want anyone lost in the fog. It wasn't long before Lizzy noticed a change in the atmosphere. The ambient sounds around them changed, and she no longer saw trees near the road.

Igree indicated for everyone to stop. "We are out of Valendale," he said quietly. "It won't be long before we will escape the fog. I think it would be best for Gretta to make a reconnaissance flight and alert us to anything that seems out of the ordinary. I fear it would be unwise to start across the Merry Meadows without having some measure of reassurance that we are in the clear."

"I was thinking the same thing," said Gretta, "and I'll only alert you if I see anything that would be cause for alarm."

"Look for Milton. If you see him, tell him not to worry—we are on our way. He knows where to meet us."

Gretta ran into the fog and disappeared. Lizzy heard her wings flutter and fade. Then there was silence.

Saint Murphy Boulevard

Molly stretched out her wings and shivered with excitement. She had spent a day and a half worrying about Lizzy's safety, but she was overcome with joy when Gretta called and reported that Milton had successfully collected them at the rendezvous point. Molly's anxiety shifted to giddy delight when she learned they were finally safe inside the gates of Ansa. Her stomach twittered with anticipation as she paced about, waiting for Lizzy's arrival. She wanted the best possible vantage point to see the motorbie when it came through the gates of Barleywick Quarter, so she positioned herself on the highest step at the entrance to Mage Guild Hall. No matter how hard she tried, she could not stand still. She hopped back and forth from one foot to the other as if she were standing in a hot iron skillet.

"Molly, calm yourself!" said Gertie. "We can't afford to have you creating a commotion by accidentally setting off one of your feathers."

Molly knew she would never become a master mage, but she had her gifts. She had concentrated specifically on distraction tactics in mage school. She had developed the exploding feather spell on her own, but it had a minor flaw. She could conjure the distraction on command, but sometimes, if she was overexcited, startled, or panicking, a feather would shoot into the air on its own where it would explode into a shower of sparkly dust. It would happen with no advance warning.

"Look!" Molly began to ramble. "As the stars twinkle and shine, I think I see the motorbie. What do you think, Mother? Is that them? I think it's them, but I can't quite tell. Is that Milton's motorbie? The red one...behind the blue one?"

"Molly! You *must* calm down. Have patience."

Molly's wishful thinking turned to disappointment when she realized it wasn't them. But it didn't squelch her anticipation or enthusiasm. She continued pacing and watching for Lizzy to arrive.

§ § § § §

Gretta had reunited with the group at the main gate and learned that there had been no unusual events or difficulties crossing the Merry Meadows. She had planned to fly and meet them at Mage Guild Hall, but Lizzy had begged her to not leave again, so Gretta sat next to Lizzy in the rear-facing seat on the motorbie. Igree was riding up front opposite Milton. McDoogle had managed to squeeze in between them. They were not yet to the first roundabout when Milton realized that the traffic on Saint Murphy Blvd. was unusually slow.

Lizzy had marveled at seeing Ansa from above but had not realized it would look so different from the ground. She was amused to see buildings with skewed sides and houses with walls that leaned outwards. Pipes—which Lizzy presumed to be plumbing of some sort—climbed up the sides of structures and were so plentiful at times that it reminded her of the ivy that climbed up houses in the old neighborhoods back home. The tiles on the rooftops were rusty-orange, but the stones and bricks used for walls displayed an array of colors ranging from shadowy charcoal to creamy taupe. Riding backward meant she saw everything as it was moving away, but she was used to that and told Gretta that it felt like she was riding in her favorite seat in her family's station wagon.

Lizzy pointed to an imposing edifice that had three twisting spires pushing skyward and a cascade of stone steps flowing down from the gargantuan, ornately carved doors. One spire had a sun on the top; another had a star. The tallest spire dwarfed the other two and had a crescent moon adorning the apex. Lizzy had never seen anything like it in her life.

"What is that?" asked Lizzy.

"That's Grace of the Moon Oratory. It's the largest satinary in the kingdom."

She explained to Lizzy that those who followed the Book of Satins sought wisdom and guidance from the celestial realm and they assembled each week in various satinaries throughout the kingdom. Lizzy related the satinaries to churches and cathedrals and finally understood where Satinsday got its name. She was full of questions and Gretta happily answered them. It was obvious that the conversation was helping to keep Lizzy's mind away from the topics that were weighing heavily on her mind.

While Gretta was keeping Lizzy preoccupied, Milton was becoming more and more annoyed with the traffic situation.

"I've never known it to bog up like this," said Milton.

"There must be something happening at the stadium," said Igree, making a guess as to the cause for their delay.

"Perhaps, but I haven't seen any notices—and it's the eve before Midwinter's Eve. What could possibly be happening at the stadium now?"

Igree remained optimistic. "Well, at least it's not a standstill."

Although Igree knew that they were all much safer in the city, being confined in traffic was somewhat of a concern. Gretta had become aware of the long line of motorbies that had piled up behind them and called out to Milton.

"Is something wrong up ahead?"

"Something...but we can't determine what it is."

Gretta felt a twinge of concern, but she didn't want Lizzy to notice. So she kept Lizzy engaged in conversation.

"It's nice to see you in your red cloak, Princess! You look like the perfect novice mage."

"What do you mean?" asked Lizzy.

"All novice mages are required to wear red cloaks. The girls wear white tunics, and the boys wear white breeches and shirts. You can easily spot a young mage, even from a distance. I'm sure you will see them; you'll fit right in. And your butterflies make you look perfectly magical."

Gretta's comments made Lizzy pause and think. The fact that she had her own red cloak only added to her confusion. She still didn't believe she was the princess, and she couldn't comprehend being responsible for breaking the curse and restoring the kingdom. But so many pieces fit together, it made her wonder. She was eager to learn what the council would have to say, and she still wondered what she would be required to do.

She almost smacked herself when she remembered this was all a dream. If they wanted her to be a princess, then she could be a princess. If they wanted her to break a curse, then surely she could do that as well.

As they slowly made their way down the boulevard, Lizzy noticed the decorations. Friendship baskets were perched on porches and twigsicles adorned every door. The ribbons glistened in the late afternoon sun. A gentle breeze caused them to flutter and sway.

"There sure are a lot of ribbons on the twigsicles," noted Lizzy.

Gretta nodded. "To be honest, I think there is an abundance of wish ribbons this year because everyone is aware that tomorrow is the last day that Castlehill can be restored. The young ones especially are hoping for Mr. Boots to help. I feel most citizens have lost hope and given up."

"Well then, we will just have to restore the kingdom *and* their hope! How about that?" Lizzy said the words easily, but she was still unsure if she could do whatever it was that she was expected to do. Gretta was encouraged by Lizzy's reply.

"Indeed," Gretta smiled. "How about we do just that?"

They were now moving at such a slow pace that those who were walking on the sidewalk were moving faster than those in vehicles.

A voice in the crowd said, "See? There's four up there...and five of them are squeezed in behind that sign."

Igree and Gretta saw a small group looking upward, pointing to the tops of buildings. Hidden in the shadows were grackles. Upon closer inspection, Igree located more grackles hiding in corbels and awnings, behind shutters, tucked in behind pipes, and nestled inconspicuously in the trees that lined the boulevard. It became apparent that there were thousands of grackles silently lurking in the most unexpected places. Igree presumed that the grackles had filtered into Ansa during the night with such stealth that nobody had noticed their arrival. They had remained so quiet and well hidden that they were only just now being discovered.

A few citizens were rushing down the street in the direction of the stadium. Others looked at their sPeaksees and then took off in the same direction, weaving through the traffic and bringing it to a stand still. Milton looked at Igree and shook his head, silently communicating that they weren't going any farther. They had stopped just short of Ring Road, which was the roundabout nearest the stadium.

Igree's sPeaksee chimed. He immediately forwarded the message to his goggles so that he could read it. It was a mass message that was being sent to every device in the land. His heart sank as he read the words:

I'm in Brackleton Park...with news! Calixta.

The message contained a picto that popped up showing Calixta and several grackles. The caption read, "Come see me." She was wearing a sly, confident grin and a patch over her eye.

Igree knew he needed to stay calm, and he didn't want to alarm Lizzy, but they had to get her to Mage Guild Hall where she would be safe. They could walk from here. But doing so would require that they take Ring Road, which would force them deeper into the gathering crowd. They would have to walk right by Brackelton Park, which seemed risky, but any other route would take much longer. If Gretta *flew* Lizzy to the hall, Calixta would surely see them. If she sent her swarm of grackles after them, Gretta would likely be killed, and Lizzy would certainly be captured. As he was trying to think of what would be the best course of action, Igree reached into his satchel, pulled out a black stone pendant, and slipped it around his neck.

"I think it's best if we walk from here," suggested Igree, trying to sound cheerful. "There's a road block, and it appears it will be a while before it is sorted out. Milton can stay with the BMC. It's just a few blocks to the guild hall." They all hopped out of the motorbie.

"Wud those be Calixta's grackles perching in the nooks and crannies?" McDoogle's tone indicated that he demanded a straight answer.

"They most likely are," admitted Igree, "but whatever they are up to, at least for the moment, they are biding their time."

He didn't want either McDoogle or Lizzy to know that Calixta was responsible for the traffic jam. Gretta was making her own assumptions, and they were correct. Lizzy scanned the buildings and felt very uneasy as she discovered more and more grackles tucked in the oddest places. Gretta shot a concerned glance to Igree.

Igree suggested, "Perhaps it would be smart for you to fly to the guild hall and let the council know we are having to walk the rest of the way—and that we will be there soon."

Igree knew that the mages would have received the same message that he did, and would have already ascertained their predicament, but he also felt Gretta could be more useful conferring with the council.

"Lizzy, if you don't mind staying with me, I think it is important for Gretta to go on ahead."

"Are we in danger?" Lizzy asked bluntly.

"Not at the moment. Look at your butterflies—they are blue, so no, you are not in any danger. But if those are Calixta's grackles, and I suspect they are, we need to blend in and move along with the crowd. I don't want to raise any suspicion."

Lizzy didn't want Gretta to leave, but she also felt it was important to trust Igree's suggestion.

"You'll be safe, Princess. Igree will look after you."

Lizzy stepped forward and gave Gretta a hug. "Promise me that you'll be safe too."

"I promise on every star in the night sky, Princess...I promise."

Gretta ran a few paces and then lifted above the crowd. Lizzy and McDoogle followed Igree down Ring Road. Lizzy watched as Gretta flew off into the distance. The last bit of the setting sun kissed her wings. The trio shuffled along and were soon swallowed up in the flowing multitude.

239

Brackleton Park

Chaos ensued as hordes of Ansans clamored through the streets, dodging abandoned motorbies and shoving their way toward Brackleton Park. They coveted the opportunity to be firsthand recipients of whatever news Calixta was planning to share. Her mysterious message had worked like a charm and drew her intended crowd like a magnet. She watched the migration from a platform that served as a permanent stage for outdoor performances. As usual, she was dressed in red. Her hair had turned completely white, and she wore a red patch over her eye. Her face was scarred. She flung her full-length cloak over her shoulder and strutted about, basking in the attention. Omen arrived and sat on her shoulder. A few dozen grackles were there for her security. If the crowd got too close to the stage, the grackles would push them back. The park filled to capacity and the surrounding streets and alleys were completely clogged.

Igree kept Lizzy and McDoogle on the perimeter of the crowd by skimming close to the buildings. They had stayed on Ring Road but had become stuck opposite Brackleton Park. This section of the street was elevated. Under normal circumstances, anyone from the sidewalk could see all the way down into the park, but Igree couldn't see over the top of the crowd. Lizzy and McDoogle both felt trapped, and they were fearful that if the crowd lost control, they could be trampled—or even worse, killed. They had no idea where they were, or where they were supposed to go. The approaching darkness of night only added to their concerns.

"What's going on?" asked Lizzy. "I'm scared."

Igree did not want to add to Lizzy's concern, but he had to tell her. "I'm sorry, Princess, but it appears that Calixta is responsible for this mess and is planning to make an announcement."

Just then, Calixta shouted, "Light! Alamah!" She jabbed her staff down onto the platform. A bolt of energy shot upward from the top of her staff with a flash that was almost blinding. The crowd reacted with awe but did not panic. The explosion absorbed into itself and diminished until it became a large, illuminated sphere, levitating above the crowd.

At that same instant, the grackles lit from their hiding places and soared into the sky above Ansa. They began organizing themselves, circling around the sphere and creating a massive, rotating canopy over the entire assembly. The density of the crowd and the protection of the grackles assured Calixta that she would remain safe and in full control of the situation.

Lizzy was frightened by the commotion and instinctively looked at her butterflies. She found them fluttering over the crowd, but they had not turned red, which helped to ease her mind. McDoogle's low vantage point prohibited him from seeing much of anything at all. He felt uncomfortable and helpless. Igree could not see Calixta, but he could easily see the sphere of light and the grackles. Igree's goggles alerted him to movement in the sky, and he noticed the raven. He was certain that it was Omen. The raven was soaring ominously above the crowd as if in search of a prize.

Calixta shouted, "Silence!"

She raised her staff into the air. A hush rippled through the crowd like a wave radiating from a pebble tossed into a pond. Calixta waited for absolute silence before speaking.

"Citizens of Ailear, as you know, tomorrow is the end for the stones who groan inside Castlehill—that is, unless the child that was stolen from me comes forward."

Murmurs rose from the crowd. Calixta paused until they were quiet again. She then held up an envelope for all to see.

"These words..." Calixta shook the envelope. "These words...and the rightful heir...are the only two things that can restore Castlehill and bring back your precious queen. I've seen your pathetic display of hopelessness and heard your sickening voices of despair. So let me... the *evil enchantress*...the *frightful witch that comes for your children*.... the *one-eyed monster from Sourbelly Sink*...let *me* be the one to restore your last thread of hope."

The crowd stirred, mumbled, and once again fell silent.

"I hold in my hand one-half of what is required, but someone in this crowd holds the other half. The young princess of Ailear *has* returned, and she is being protected by someone among you at this very moment."

A rumble of questioning disbelief rose from the multitude. Omen soared in a sweeping circle over the crowd and then flew straight toward the area where Igree, Lizzy, and McDoogle were trapped.

Igree wasn't prepared for this situation and struggled with what to do. He knew that if he used a spell to deflect Omen's advance, it would expose them and make them vulnerable to being discovered by Calixta. The butterflies turned red, which terrified Lizzy. Igree instructed her to get behind him. She grabbed McDoogle and they both ducked to the ground. Igree was waiting until the very last second before taking any action. As Omen flew closer, it became obvious that Igree was his target—even though others who were nearby were bracing for an attack too.

Suddenly, Omen shot upward, made a giant loop in the sky, circled back, and then set a course in the opposite direction. He made the same sort of maneuver, targeting the other side of the crowd. He made two more threatening demonstrations in separate areas before returning to his soaring flight path around Calixta. Igree let out a huge sigh of relief.

Lizzy was still crouched down when she tugged on Igree's satchel. "I'm really scared," she admitted.

"It's going to be okay, Princess," Igree said, attempting to comfort her, and at the same time, not knowing if he could. "I'm going to make sure nothing happens to you. Look! Your butterflies are blue. We need to get to the guild hall. Let's try to squeeze our way through the crowd."

McDoogle, who was unnerved, but also trying to be brave and protective, said, "I'll get ye through this crowd, Lass. I'll be bitin' the heels of onyone who won't move oot o' oor way."

As they nudged and squeezed their way along Ring Road, Calixta continued with her message.

"The child was returned yesterday morning by a goose who traveled through the Tunnel of Stars. Look for a girl and a goose. The girl will most likely have ginger hair...like her mother."

Lizzy froze in place. She couldn't believe what she was hearing.

"Or...she might be with the old high mage, Igree. You surely won't have forgotten him, the deformity of nature who is half kangaroo and half bat."

Igree felt his pendant to make sure it was in place. It was. He would be safe for now.

"Find the child and bring her to Imperial Plaza. If you want your royal family back, it's the only choice there is."

With this many eyes roaming through Ansa, Calixta was certain that someone would spot the princess. She presumed that they would covet the notoriety that would come by being the citizen who helped to restore Castlehill.

Lizzy panicked. "Igree, they will surely see you...and then they will know it's me!"

"It's okay, Princess; only you and McDoogle can recognize me. My black pendant is powerful magic. It cloaks me with a spell of deception. No one can identify me unless I allow it."

Lizzy was surprised that a pendant could do such a thing, but she also noticed how people looked at Igree when he nudged past them. None of them seemed to identify him as a creature with bat wings and kangaroo legs. So she accepted his explanation. They had managed to make it to the intersection at Corkscrew Lane and were now only a short stretch from the western gate of Barleywick Quarter.

In one final outburst, Calixta screamed, "What are you waiting for? Find her! Now!"

She spiked her staff onto the platform and the illuminated sphere exploded, sending a cascade of sparks showering the area. The grackles swarmed down toward the crowd, which started a mass panic. To avoid being trampled, Lizzy fled with the crowd, zigzagging in and out of bodies.

"Lassie, where are ye?"

Lizzy heard McDoogle and called back, "I'm here; I'm over here," but she couldn't stop running. McDoogle dodged scrambling feet and kept moving in the direction of the flow. He looked through a tangle of legs that were all running for safety, but he couldn't see her—and she didn't find him.

In an instant, Igree had lost both Lizzy and McDoogle. He too was doing all he could to avoid injury. He managed to stop and spread his wings.

"Away! Alamah!" he said, and the crowd, without realizing it, began flowing around him, giving him the opportunity to stop and look for any sign of Lizzy or McDoogle. He didn't see either of them. He called out, but there was no answer. He looked for butterflies, but there were none to be found. His heart sank as he stood, frozen in place, with outstretched wings.

He closed his blind eyes and called out, "Mother of Stars…Father of Moons…what have I done?"

McDoogle sniffed the air for any scent of Lizzy, but he wasn't successful. His nose scoured the ground, but that didn't help. The crowd had dispersed enough that he no longer felt he was in danger, so he trotted into a nearby alley to catch his breath and to collect his thoughts. He looked around, lost, worried, and feeling sick. He whispered, "Lassie, where are ye?"

Lizzy ran with the crowd for as long as she could. She was out of breath when she tripped and fell. She tucked herself into a ball and covered her head. She felt the rush of the crowd pushing past her. She felt a sharp pain and shrieked in agony. It was her ankle. Someone had stepped on it. She tried to sit up but she was knocked back down. She held her ankle and shivered with fright. A pair of hands came from behind and grabbed her by the shoulders.

Lizzy
Albright

Back Alley Blues

McDoogle found himself alone and dazed from the experience. He was trying to clear his mind and was searching for answers as he wandered along the cobblestones of the dimly lit alley. There were several rear entrances to shops and eateries. Each one had a set of short steps leading up to a door. He stopped at one particular entrance that had an overhead light throwing a fiery glow onto the brick walls and casting harsh, angular shadows onto the ground. The light emitted the soft buzz of an electrical current. Painted next to the door, on the bricks, was a notice. Although the paint was faded and some of it had completely eroded away, McDoogle was able to make out that it had once read "The Groomed Goat—Ring for Deliveries." He saw a wire dangling from a hole next to the door and assumed that it must have once connected to a doorbell.

Dejected, he sat down on the bottom step.

"Why so glum?" A voice cut through the darkness from above.

McDoogle instantly perked up, but he didn't see anything. He then heard the soft rustling of wings.

"Wha's there?" asked McDoogle.

The rustling stopped and McDoogle saw a raven alight on top of a tattered awning across the way. The light reflected off his sleek feathers, creating a blue, green, and purple iridescence. His black eyes glinted with a yellow spark. McDoogle had not realized until now just how large he was.

"I ken who ye are," said McDoogle.

"Oh, do you?"

"Indeed, I certainly do. Ye're the bird that serves the witch. Ye're Omen." McDoogle said his name with a biting growl.

"Well, then, you must know why I'm here." Omen's voice was soft and calm—almost hypnotic.

"No, I dinna ken why ye're here, but I most surely ken whut ye're up to." The hair on McDoogle's back was starting to bristle.

"I'm not sure you do, but I know you *think* you do. I'm doing what *has* to be done."

"Ye're after ma precious Lassie, and ye canna have her. Ye think she's the princess, and ye've come to take her to the witch. Mark my words...I will not *let* that witch have her!" McDoogle shouted.

"Well, where is she now?" asked Omen. "How is it that you are keeping her from Calixta?"

Omen's comment stung. McDoogle became so frustrated with himself that a boiling anger grew inside and he stopped thinking rationally.

"Dinna ye worry aboot that. She's safe!"

"Oh? And so that's why you are wandering around in an alley... alone...feeling sorry for yourself."

McDoogle's anger exploded. "I *don't* have her. I've *lost* her! It's ma *job* to protect her, and I've failed. I rode wi' her on the goose, through that blasted Tunnel of Stars, just to make sure she wud be safe. I was promised that there wudna be ony tomfoolery, and that's *all* it has been! And now she's lost and in danger." McDoogle sank back onto the step. He felt useless.

"Thank you for your help. You've confirmed what I came here to know. But regarding your tomfoolery, may I remind you that not everything is as it seems. You *do* look lost...May I suggest that you turn right at the corner and then go straight until you reach the gate? You'll find Barleywick Quarter. I have no doubt that someone is looking for you. I must be on my way. I have a job to do."

McDoogle suspected Omen's directions were a trick of some kind, but he couldn't muster a reply. He had already said too much, and he knew it. Omen took off and soared between the buildings. A cool breeze rushed through the alleyway causing the porch light to flicker and go out. The electrical humming stopped.

CHAPTER THIRTY

The Hyssop and Sage

Lizzy tried to escape, but the stranger reached under her arms, picked her up, and began to run. She screamed and demanded to be released, but her pleas were ineffective. She found herself dangling in the air—higher than she would have expected—being carried away.

The panic began to subside and the exodus from the park became more orderly, but Lizzy's personal panic was at its peak. She was petrified. Then she noticed her butterflies—they were blue—which confused her, because she felt certain that she was in danger and being taken to Calixta. The stranger gently put her down next to the fence that surrounded the gardens at Saint Tyndall's Satinary.

"I'm sorry if I frightened you. You were in a bad situation and could have been trampled to death. I hope you are all right."

Lizzy was frozen and her mouth was agape. Her eyes scanned her rescuer. She had seen bears at the Kansas City Zoo, but she had no idea they were this big up close. The bear reached out to brush Lizzy's hair from her face. Lizzy winced with uncertainty, but the bear's paw was so gentle, her fears melted and she relaxed.

"So...are you all right?" asked the bear calmly.

Lizzy finally managed to speak. "I am...mostly. My ankle hurts." The bear gingerly lifted Lizzy's foot and looked at it.

"My name is Violet. Does this hurt?" She pressed lightly, checking for broken bones.

"Ahh! Yes, it hurts a little. I'm..." Lizzy wasn't sure if she should say her name. "I'm Elisabeth...with an S," she replied.

"I don't think it's broken, but you need to have it looked at." Violet gently massaged Lizzy's ankle between her paws. "Are you enjoying mage school, Elisabeth?"

The question caught Lizzy by surprise. "Excuse me?"

"Your tunic...and cloak...and these beautiful butterflies. I was wondering if you enjoyed going to school."

She looked at her tunic, which had been sparkling white, but now it was smudged with dirt in several places. "Oh yes, I really love it."

Lizzy suddenly realized that she was going to have to pretend to be a novice mage. She hoped that whatever she said would be believable and that she would not be caught in a lie.

"I'm glad you do. I had the best time going to satins school when I was growing up, but those days are in the past. Get up. Let's see if you can walk on it."

Violet helped Lizzy to her feet. She managed to take a few steps, but it was painful.

"The Hyssop and Sage is the closest apothecary...and it's certainly the best one. Do you know Aloris?"

"Aloris?"

"The healer, the woman who runs the Hyssop and Sage."

Lizzy had never heard of Aloris, but she remembered being told about the Hyssop and Sage. She recalled the photo of Gorva in the portrait in Igree's parlor. Lizzy imagined that Aloris would look the same—tall and thin, with long, silver hair. She also imagined her wearing the same rose-colored glasses and a pendant around her neck.

"Oh...yes...I know who you mean. I've heard she's an amazing healer, but I don't know her," said Lizzy, trying to be convincing.

"Well, then, it's about time you do. Hop on my back. You certainly can't walk on that ankle right now."

Never in her wildest dreams—and this was by far the wildest dream she had ever had—did Lizzy imagine that she would be riding piggyback on the back of a bear.

It was after business hours, but even so, all of the establishments had shuttered and locked their doors early when they saw the size of the crowd gathering in Brackleton Park. For their own safety, they didn't reopen.

Violet was well-acquainted with Aloris and decided to use the back entrance across from Saint Tyndall's since it was the door to the apothecary's living quarters. Aloris had used caution when opening the door, but as soon as she saw Violet and the child, she quickly let them in and reset the lock. Lizzy's butterflies fluttered over to the gardens by Saint Tyndall's.

"I'm sorry to bother you, Aloris," said Violet, "but you were close by. It's her ankle. She fell...I think she was stepped on."

"In the stampede? You poor child, how did you get caught in that mess? I'm surprised you weren't killed. Are you hurting anywhere else?"

"No," said Lizzy. "It's just my ankle." Violet introduced the two. Aloris took Lizzy's cloak and hung it on the wall next to the steps that led down to the basement. She then guided Lizzy to a chair so that she could examine her injury.

Aloris wore a long skirt and a short button-down waistcoat with a leather collar. A beaded belt was tied around her waist with extra-long straps that almost reached the floor. Large golden hoops hung from her pierced ears, and a dozen different bracelets jangled on her wrists. Lizzy noted that Aloris and Gorva had several similarities. Aloris was younger, but she was tall and thin. Her hair was very long and straight—but it was deep auburn and not silver. A pair of round glasses sat on her nose, but they were not rose-colored. The most peculiar similarity was the pendant that Aloris wore around her neck. It looked exactly like the one in the portrait. It was red, and it had the same notch at the bottom. Lizzy was certain that it was the same one. As Aloris examined Lizzy's ankle, she began voicing her opinion to Violet on the matter of Calixta's dramatic announcement.

"I found Kreg and Keltan and made them come inside before things got out of hand. I knew there would be trouble. I won't be surprised if we find out tomorrow that someone was killed. Marten, on the other hand, insisted on going out to see what she was up to. I'll not have any part of it. She's done enough harm and needs to be dealt with."

"Did I hear someone mention my name?" A tall man appeared in the doorway and leaned against the frame. He had long, brown hair that was pulled back with a leather barrette, and a full, well-groomed beard. He had a strong, muscular build and a rugged appearance, but Lizzy quickly got the impression that he was kind, easy-going, and confident. Two boys stood next to him and peered through the door at Lizzy.

"You most certainly did," Aloris jabbed back.

Lizzy sensed the undercurrent of tension between Aloris and Marten, but she found herself more interested in the boys. For all of the unusual characters she had encountered in Ailear, she would not have predicted that two, regular-looking boys would suddenly appear. The sight of them made her miss her brothers. She missed their bossiness and teasing. She missed giving them a hard time. She also missed their help and protection. They had always come to her rescue when she was in trouble, and when she really needed their assistance or guidance, they never let her down. She even missed their pranks. But now, they were so far away, they felt more like a memory than a reality.

She thought about Doug and the banana split, and she decided that the next time they were at Whipples, she would happily offer him one of the cherries. Lizzy wondered if Doug and Allen were snug in their beds—dreaming of Christmas.

Marten stepped into the room. "Hello, Violet! As you can see, my beautiful wife is upset with me. But for the record, I kept my distance, and I left before she sent the crowd into a panic." He walked over, kissed Aloris on the top of her head, and knelt in front of Lizzy. "And what do we have here, an injured mage?"

"She was trampled," said Aloris. "She's lucky it's not serious. Her name is Elisabeth...with an S."

"What a beautiful name! Boys...come meet Elisabeth."

Without hesitation, the boys did as they were told. They were fascinated by the ginger-haired novice who had unexpectedly appeared as they were getting ready for dinner. Kreg, in particular, was curious to know what she had seen and experienced at the park.

"This tall one is Kreg. He's the oldest; he just turned ten two weeks ago." Kreg smiled at Lizzy. "And this one..." Marten pulled the younger boy close, "...this one is Keltan. He will be nine next month."

"Hi," said Lizzy, feeling shy. She wasn't sure what else she should say.

Kreg, realizing that Lizzy might be feeling awkward, tried to break the ice.

"Do you play Caves and Towers?"

Lizzy's face went blank. She had no idea what he was talking about. She assumed it was a game of some sort. But the only thing that came to mind was Chutes and Ladders, which she had sometimes played with her family, but didn't like very much. She couldn't answer his question, so she just stared.

Kreg produced a small electronic device that reminded Lizzy of her transistor radio, only it was much thinner. He held it so that the glass display was facing her. "Look! I've made it to level forty-three."

Lizzy was staring at the smallest TV she had ever seen. The screen played a movie. It was in color, and she heard pulsating music that reminded her of the Beatles. A series of words swooped across the screen that read "Kreg of Molgahoria, Level 43, Xiphos Sword Master." Lizzy could tell that Kreg was proud of his accomplishment, even though she didn't know what it was.

"That's amazing…congratulations!"

Hoping to avoid additional questions, she added, "I hope I get to play it…but I've had a lot going on lately, and just haven't been able to yet."

"Well, you should get it. It's really bang," urged Kreg. "They keep adding new modules. Just load it into your sPeaksee."

Once again, Lizzy's insides sank. She didn't know what a sPeaksee was and didn't have a clue what it meant to load it.

Aloris finished the examination. "It's not broken. I'll make a poultice and wrap it up. You'll be feeling like new in no time."

"Is there anything I can do to help?" asked Violet.

"Nothing I can think of. We'll call the mage guild and see if someone can come get her. Elisabeth, is there someone you want us to call?"

"Ahm…," Lizzy said, acting like she was thinking very hard—which she was. She almost suggested Gretta or Igree, but then she remembered that Calixta had told everyone about them and didn't want to raise suspicion.

"Baron!" she practically shouted the name. "The high mage. He's the bear…or…you could contact any of the other mages."

Lizzy was relieved that she was able to recall a name other than Igree or Gretta. It made her feel proud—and hopeful. She assumed that if they contacted anyone at the mage guild, someone would come.

Aloris cut her eyes to Violet and chuckled, "Yes, he's the bear all right. Violet, do you know him?"

"No, not really. We are distant cousins, but our paths have never crossed."

"Maybe someday they will. We'll try to give him a call. You don't need to stay if you need to get going. Don't worry about Elisabeth; she's in good hands."

"I'll leave her with you then, okay?"

"That's fine. Thank you for getting her to safety."

Violet and Lizzy said their goodbyes. Lizzy was sad to see her go. She had always been told not to judge a book by its cover, and that thought came to mind as Violet blew her a kiss and closed the door.

Marten used his sPeaksee to make the call, but he got a series of beeps followed by an artificial voice that said, "That number is occupied; try again later." He took a walking stick from the closet and handed it to Lizzy. It was taller than she was.

"This should help; give it a try. We'll set an extra place at the table. Can you make it to the kitchen?"

Lizzy used the stick, and she was surprised at how much it helped and how easily she managed. The poultice wrapped around her ankle was already working. She thought that the poultice smelled wonderful and had learned that it contained horsemint, dolthea oil, winterbite pollen, and ground phladelia roots, all wrapped in castola leaves and secured with gauze cloth.

Lizzy was able to determine that sPeaksees were the electronic devices that Marten and Kreg were using. To her, they seemed to be the Ailearian version of the telephone—except they didn't look anything like her pink princess phone at home, with a light-up rotary dial and a curly cord that she was constantly untangling. It also became apparent that the sPeaksee did more than just make a call.

Marten tried to get through to the mage guild several times during dinner, but he kept getting the same message. Lizzy was concerned that they couldn't contact anyone—not that she felt that she was in danger, but she was eager to get back to Gretta and Igree. More importantly, she was worried about McDoogle and wanted to be reunited with him. She trusted that he was somewhere safe, but she couldn't stop herself from worrying.

After dinner, Marten tried to call again. This time, someone answered.

A Breakdown in Communications

As soon as Igree saw the panic begin to subside, he sent a message to the council:

The princess has been lost in the chaos. McDoogle too. I hope they are together, but I suspect they are not. I am going to look for them. Send as many as you can. We must find them.

Igree rushed back to the location where they had been when mass panic started. He felt certain that the rush of the crowd had forced Lizzy to the left—onto Corkscrew Lane—instead of going forward along Ring Road. If that were the case, she could be anywhere. As he turned the corner, his sPeaksee chimed. He forwarded the message to his goggles so he could read it.

Message undeliverable. Try again?

"Yes, try again!" he shouted.

In various locations along Corkscrew Lane there were individuals being tended to who had obviously been hurt in the stampede. He checked to make sure that the princess was not among them before moving along. His sPeaksee chimed again.

Message undeliverable. Try again?

"What's going on?" he said to himself.

The functionality of sPeaksees was extremely dependable. This communication failure was disconcerting and very rare. As he sent the message the third time, he realized the desperate predicament he was in. Several minutes had gone by, and still nobody but himself knew that the princess and McDoogle were missing. There needed to be an all-out search. He was stuck between the choice of finding her on his own or going to get help. At the risk of her falling into the wrong hands, he decided that a search party would be more effective, so he abandoned his effort to find her and reversed his course. He began racing to Barleywick Quarter as fast as he could. It was all uphill. He wished he could hitch a ride, but the street was still clogged with motorbies even though an effort was underway to get traffic flowing. Igree was gasping for air when he reached the west gate and met the guard.

"Sam, I...need to call...Baron...it's urgent."

"I'm sorry, sir, but communications are overloaded. I think everyone was trying to send messages and call at the same time. It must have jammed the system. We've not been able to get any calls out—but I'll try." Sam attempted to connect to Mage Guild Hall, but the call failed.

Igree tried his sPeaksee, but his call failed too. Igree knew that Sam would not be permitted to abandon the gate and drive him the rest of the way, so he took a few deep breaths, and pushed on. As he approached the satins guild, he saw a young student who was about to climb onto his double-seat tribie, and he called out. The student waited and Igree ran his way.

"Can you just...give me a lift...down to Mage Guild Hall? It's urgent...very urgent."

"Yes sir, of course. Hop on."

Igree thanked him and literally hopped on.

Earlier that afternoon, every high-ranking mage in the kingdom had filled the council chamber. The room buzzed with excitement.

They were ecstatic and eagerly waiting for the princess to arrive. Rumblings of concern broke out when they received Calixta's mass message. But when Gretta arrived alone and told them that Igree and the princess had been forced to continue on foot, the mood in the chamber turned to worry and concern.

Then sickening disbelief washed over the room when they watched the cinebit of Calixta's announcement. Their spirits spiraled further downward when they learned of the mayhem that had ensued in Brackleton Park. They felt certain that, after all this time, their efforts and their plans to restore Castlehill were on the brink of total failure. They felt guilty when one of the mages mentioned that an innocent child might now be delivered into Calixta's hands—and if that were to happen, it would be their fault.

When the communication system failed, they sank further into despair. Minutes rolled by as they sat in silence. Baron mentally flipped through pages of possibilities and probable outcomes, trying to decide how best he could redirect their course of action. Then Igree burst through the chamber doors.

"She's lost...gone...I don't know where. The dog is missing too. The rush of the crowd just swallowed them and in an instant they were carried away. We have to find her. Corkscrew...I think she went down Corkscrew."

The chamber erupted as everyone began debating about what they should do. The room rattled with arguments and tempers flared. Baron persistently banged the gavel until order was finally restored.

"Keep calm, and let wisdom prevail," said Baron. "We cannot start our own mass pandemonium. If all the mages in Ailear are seen rushing through the streets, then we will only confirm Calixta's suspicions. It's dark outside, making it even harder for us to locate her. The only mage we have that flies at night is Orlin, and I recommend that he be the first one who goes in search of her. One is better than none, and if an owl is spotted flying around, no one would think twice about it."

Orlin instantly agreed to Baron's suggestion. "I'm on my way."

Igree gave Orlin a brief description of Lizzy and reminded him of the general vicinity where he suspected she might have gone.

There was divided opinion about Baron's decision to not immediately send more of them out to search for the princess, but they all knew that this entire mission held the highest level of secrecy, and it was fully contained within the council of mages. If any hint of their plan escaped and found its way to Calixta, it would be disastrous. Igree sided with Baron. Although his initial message had requested a search party, he saw Baron's point—they had to remain secretive. Baron's advice was received with great respect. He was the voice of reason and was able to keep the fires of hope burning within the council.

§ § § § §

"Excuse me there, Laddie, but I'm lookin' for Mage Guild Hall. Can ye point me in the right direction?" The directions that Omen had given McDoogle were accurate and took him directly to Barleywick Quarter.

"You're close to the right place. May I see your credentials?" asked Sam.

McDoogle cocked his head. "I'm afeard I dinna hae ony credentials for ye. Do ye ken Igree? I was wi' him when the panic took place... an' we got separated."

"I know Igree, but I can't let you in without proper credentials... unless you have an authorized document requesting a visitor's pass, or you are with someone who has their card."

McDoogle slumped. He was weary and extremely discouraged—and worried sick about Lizzy. He seemed stuck once again and was at a loss for what to do.

"Ma name's McDoogle. Can ye make a call and see if onyone wud come for me?"

"The system's down," replied Sam. "I can't get a call to go through."

McDoogle sighed. "How long since ye last tried?"

"Just a minute or so ago."

"Well...wud ye please try again?" McDoogle was trying not to sound as if he were pleading or desperate, but in truth, he was. He didn't know what else to do, so he just stood there and stared at the guard. His weary eyes spoke for him.

Sam shrugged, "Sure, I'll give it a try, but it won't go through."

He attempted to make the connection to the mage guild. Sam was surprised to hear the familiar beeps.

"Hello!" said Sam.

McDoogle instantly perked up.

"Yes. Well, what d'ya know...it's working. It's Sam at the west gate. I have a black dog here; his name is...hold on...What's your name again?"

"McDoogle."

"Oh yeah, McDoogle. His name is McDoogle."

The news of McDoogle's arrival was celebrated in the council chambers with applause, whistles, and shouts of joy. It was the first bit of good news they had had in hours. Gretta volunteered to meet McDoogle at the gate.

"Is Lizzy here?" McDoogle asked.

Gretta shook her head. "No, I'm sorry. There's been no word."

McDoogle sank. "We have to *find* her...I have to find her."

Gretta escorted him to Mage Guild Hall. He received a standing ovation and graciously acknowledged their appreciation, but inside he was worried sick.

Gretta introduced McDoogle to Baron. The terrier was dwarfed by the bear. He noticed his thick black fur and the size of his claws. McDoogle was glad Baron was an ally. He would be a difficult foe to fend off. While Baron was sharing with McDoogle the best options for finding Lizzy, the main chamber sPeaksee chimed again. Baron took the call.

"That was Marten. She's with Marten and Aloris at the Hyssop and Sage. She's safe!" roared Baron.

Marten's call flooded the room with overwhelming relief. Shouts, cheers, and whistles erupted. Molly was so thrilled that she leapt up onto her desk and twirled in circles. One of her feathers shot up, hit the ceiling, and exploded—showering the entire chamber in glittery purple sparkles. The last time that had happened in the council chamber she was reprimanded. This time, everyone cheered and danced.

Omen had lingered in the darkness watching the scene unfold. Perched on one of the finials that lined the top of the Rose Wall, he had a direct line of sight into the window of the council chamber. He grinned when he saw Gretta lead McDoogle up the steps to Mage Guild Hall. He observed how they treated McDoogle like a hero when he came into the chamber. He witnessed the second celebration and Molly's exploding feather. He had seen enough. He shot into night sky and thought to himself as he soared above the city, "Fools! It's a bit premature for a celebration. This isn't over...yet."

The Hangout

"Good news, Elisabeth," said Marten, tucking his sPeaksee back into his pocket. "Someone will be here for you in just a few minutes."

Lizzy was glad to hear the news, but she was also a bit apprehensive and wondered who that *someone* might be—so she asked. "Do you know who is coming?"

"I'm not sure. I spoke with Baron. Surely he will send somebody you know. I thought it was a bit odd that he was the one who answered, but then I realized that the mage council must be in session. I think they are scrambling because tomorrow is the..."

"Marten," Aloris interrupted, "could I borrow you for a minute?" She gave him the most stern look and motioned with her eyes as if to say...*now...immediately*! She had stopped him from mentioning the Midwinter's Eve deadline. She didn't want the curse to be discussed in front of the children.

Marten knew that look. It meant that whatever conversation was about to take place would require privacy. He suggested to the boys that they show Lizzy their hangout downstairs.

"Do you want to see it, Elisabeth?" asked Kreg. "It's a really bang place."

"Sure," said Lizzy. She was curious to know if it was more of a family room or a playroom, and she wondered if they had anything like her new Magnavox stereo.

Lizzy used the walking stick and followed Kreg and Keltan downstairs. She quickly discovered that their *hangout* was nothing like what she had expected. It was a large, open room with a smooth stone floor and rough stone masonry walls. It reminded her of Granny's root cellar, except this room was much bigger. There was a table with two ladder-back chairs and a chest of drawers. There was a workbench with chunks of wood neatly stacked to one side. Smaller logs were tucked in a bin. On the workbench Lizzy saw a set of tools.

"What are these for?" Lizzy asked.

"It's my hobby. I use them to make carvings," replied Kreg.

"He's really good at it, and he's teaching me too," Keltan added.

On the wall opposite of the workbench were shelves displaying numerous carved figurines. Kreg selected his most recent piece and carefully handed it to Lizzy. Attached to a lichen-covered rock were five beautiful and intricately hand-crafted geese made of wood. He had carved them in such a way that they appeared to be in flight, with one goose in the lead and the other four following in their typical *V* forma-tion. Kreg had cleverly arranged them so that, even though they looked like separate geese, in reality, they overlapped and touched in places. The entire carving was made from one piece of wood. Only one goose was touching the base for support. Lizzy was impressed.

"You made this?"

"I did. It's a bang hobby. Believe it or not, I don't *always* play Caves and Towers."

Lizzy took a quick mental note that Kreg had said the word bang again, and interpreted it to mean *cool* or *groovy*, but she decided not to use it until she knew for sure. She studied the carving of the geese and admired the realistic details. They reminded her of the Flying Geese in Granny's quilt—and that made her think that if *she* decided to take up a hobby, it might as well be quilting.

"It's really amazing," said Lizzy. "I've never known anyone who carves. I suppose singing is my hobby...*and* performing. I want to be a professional singer or actress someday."

Lizzy handed the delicate carving back to Kreg. She noticed a larger-than-life poster on the wall, which had not been visible when she first came into the room because it was tucked into a small alcove next to the stairs. Her mouth dropped and her eyes popped wide open.

"The Ice Angels? Where did you get an old poster of the Ice Angels?" The poster filled the wall from floor to ceiling and was slightly wider than a regular door. It was behind glass in a thick wooden frame, and it was mounted to the wall. Other than the fact that it was slightly faded, it was in perfect condition.

"Mom and Dad have a huge collection of Ice Angels memorabilia," said Kreg. "We have *all* of their recordings. This poster is really rare. Some collectors would give anything for it. There were only twenty printed... and this one is the only one that was signed by all three of them. They all died over fifty years ago...but their music is classic. "I Like It" is still the number one song of all time. Sorry...I only know all this because my mom and dad talk about the Ice Angels a lot."

Lizzy knew the name Oris, but she didn't know the names of the other two. She tried to imagine what being an Ice Angel would have been like.

"Do you like their music?" asked Keltan.

It was a question that Lizzy needed to avoid. She didn't know their music and didn't need to show her ignorance on something that might be a popular topic. She escaped having to answer because Kreg changed the subject.

"What did you see in Brackleton Park?"

The question caught Lizzy by surprise. She wondered what purpose Kreg had for asking. She had relaxed once she arrived at the Hyssop and Sage, but Kreg's question caused her to feel uneasy. Her insides began to swirl with fear, but she didn't want it to show.

"I didn't see much of anything really. I wasn't actually in the park; I was on Ring Road. I couldn't see over the crowd. I could barely hear what she was saying."

"So you didn't see her?" asked Kreg.

"No, not at all. I saw the grackles, and the light...and her raven tried to scare everyone. I didn't like being trapped. I hope I'm never caught in a crowd like that again."

"So you didn't see what she looks like?" asked Keltan.

"No, I didn't."

Keltan pulled out his sPeaksee, fiddled with it, and said, "Here's one of the cinebits. It is the first time any of us have seen what she looks like."

Kreg added, "He means, what she looks like now. You can find plenty of pictures of her when she was younger."

Lizzy's heart raced as the movie started to play and Calixta began to speak.

Citizens of Ailear, as you know, tomorrow is the end for the stones who groan inside Castlehill—that is, unless the child that was stolen from me comes forward.

Lizzy's head was spinning. *She* was the child, and she didn't want to come forward. Seeing Calixta on the screen terrified her.

"Why is her face scarred and why is she wearing an eye patch?" asked Lizzy.

"You know why," said Kreg.

Lizzy had to think fast because she *didn't* know why.

"Yes...but tell me the story that *you* were told."

"It's the story that we are *all* told. Were you asleep in royal history class? She *killed* Ravol, the high mage. She killed him to get his claw to make the Ravenclaw Staff that turned everyone in Castlehill into groaning stones. He plucked her eye out and clawed her face while he was defending himself, but she still managed to kill him. The old high mage, Igree, was the one who found him."

Lizzy's mind raced to the portrait in Igree's parlor and she saw the large raven that was perched on the stand, draped in a purple and black cloak. She couldn't help but wonder how all of this had happened and what had started it all. She knew that everyone in the portrait, at one time, must have been like a family. She couldn't imagine what it must have felt like for Igree to find his friend—murdered.

"Oh yeah, I knew that part. I thought you were talking about something different."

Kreg raised his eyebrows and gave Lizzy a strange look, but he didn't press the matter.

"Do you want to see them?" asked Kreg.

"See who?" asked Lizzy.

"The groaning stones. We can take you to see them. If we hurry, we'll be back before your ride gets here."

Lizzy thought the idea was absurd, but she had a strange desire to see them anyway. She wondered if they would be horrifying, or if they might give her a better understanding of everything she had been told.

"I'm sorry, but I'm not going outside again...not tonight...not until they come and get me."

"But we don't *have* to go outside," said Kreg. "We will use the tunnel. It's abandoned now. It's been abandoned for years. The statues can't hurt you. They can't move."

"What tunnel? And what if we get caught?"

"There's a tunnel that goes to Castlehill. We won't be seen. The castle is abandoned too...so nobody will ever know."

"We've never been caught," said Keltan. "We'll go and come right back."

Kreg removed a loose stone that fitted into the wall and collected a key from the compartment behind it. He reached behind the poster and found the lock. The entire poster was actually a door which swung open, revealing a dark passageway.

"We found it by accident. I'm sure we are not supposed to know this is here, which is why the poster is hiding the entrance. It's amazing. Do you want to go?"

Lizzy's insides were swarming with mixed emotions. Her head was telling her one thing, but her heart was telling her another.

"Okay," said Lizzy. "I'll do it."

"It's cold in the tunnel," said Kreg. "I'll sneak up and grab your cloak."

At the top of the stairs, he overheard his mother say, "...if that is true, then an innocent child is in danger. Can you please try to find out more in the morning?"

Kreg wasn't sure what they were talking about. He snatched the cloak and tiptoed back down the stairs.

"It's dark in there," said Lizzy. "Are you taking a light?"

"We usually do, but you can make a light, right? Isn't light one of the first things novice mages learn to conjure?"

Lizzy knew this was the end. She could no longer keep up the ruse. She knew the words *Light! Alamah!*—but she didn't have any magical powers. She would be exposed as a fraud. She thought of how far she had come and the crazy, unbelievable, and impossible things that she had experienced since she first saw Gretta in the attic window. Gretta had guided her and reassured her, but Gretta wasn't here. Then, out of the blue, she recalled what Gretta had told her at Fiddler's Cove.

If you think you can do something, then you can do it. If you think you can't do something, then most likely you can't.

Lizzy regained her confidence. If this was a real dream, then she could be a real novice mage. The only thing keeping her from it was her own disbelief.

"Yes, of course. I'll be happy to make a light."

She put on her cloak and grabbed her walking stick. They all walked a few steps into the passageway and quietly closed the door behind them. Lizzy took a deep breath and mustered all the confidence that she had.

"Light! Alamah!"

A flash of light burst forth and then contained itself into a beautiful luminescent orb resting on the top of her walking stick. She wanted to scream with excitement, but she managed not to. She was playing her part as if it were as natural as breathing, which made her think that she really could become a professional actress someday.

"Bang!" said Keltan.

"Bang!" said Kreg.

"Bang!" said Lizzy.

269

Tunnel Vision

With Kreg in the lead they made their way through the narrow passageway. Lizzy was determined to be brave. The light she summoned floated just above her walking stick. The walls seemed to squeeze in on her, making her feel claustrophobic. They reached the main tunnel, which was much wider and loftier than the little slit of a passage they had just passed through. The first time Lizzy spoke, she was surprised at how the tunnel amplified her voice. It reminded her of the time her family visited Meramac Caverns in Missouri. After that she only spoke in a whisper.

"The castle is this way," said Kreg, turning right.

"What's down the other way?" asked Lizzy.

"It goes to the vaults under Saint Tyndall's," explained Keltan, "and it's not very far. Most of the tunnel is from here to the castle."

Lizzy's senses were heightened. The dank, musky air was so still and heavy that it made her skin cold and clammy. She was unnerved by the lingering echoes of their footsteps and the magnified plops of dripping water that fell from the vaulted stone ceiling. She slipped on a slick, wet stone and reached to the wall for support. Her hand landed on a patch of slimy moss, which caused her to recoil in disgust and sent shivers down her spine. After that, she paid much closer attention to where she was stepping.

"Check this out," said Kreg. He led Lizzy into an alcove and showed her the large stone basin that was half filled with stagnant water. The stone walls reflected in the black, mirrored surface of the pool. Keltan pumped the handle and a gush of water splashed into the basin. Lizzy peered over the edge. The ripples distorted her reflection and she immediately shrieked and jumped back.

"What's the matter?" asked Kreg

"She's in the water! I saw her in the water!"

"Who?" asked the boys.

Lizzy was obviously shaken, and she finally whispered, "Calixta!"

The boys' hearts raced as they peered into the basin. The ripples had dissipated and the surface had become smooth as glass. They saw their own images staring back at them.

"It's just a reflection," said Kreg, but Lizzy's outburst made him doubt. Kids at school had once told them that Calixta could fly through the dark on a breeze and sneak into rooms through a keyhole. His insides were twirling with fear but he tried not to show it.

Lizzy hesitantly peered into the pool again. Kreg was right—it was just a reflection. She looked at herself with a prolonged curiosity and imagined herself to be a real sorceress.

"Let's go," insisted Kreg. "There's not a lot of time."

The boys were both spooked. They had stolen their way into the tunnel on several occasions, but this was the first time that they wanted to hurry and get out. They quickly made their way to the door at the lower level of the castle.

The boys pointed out the corridor that led to the main level of the castle. Then they drew her attention to a small set of stairs located in an archway on the far side of the room.

"Those stairs spiral up into the tower," Kreg whispered. "You can see most of the outside statues from up there."

"I'm not sure if I want to see them now," said Lizzy. Her nerves were starting to get the best of her.

"They're just statues," said Keltan. "They don't move; they can't hurt you."

Even though Lizzy was hesitant, she still followed Kreg up the spiraling stairs and climbed the tower. As they neared the top, Lizzy heard a low, muffled sound. It stopped her in her tracks.

"What's that?"

"It's them," said Kreg, "...the stones. Their mouths are sealed shut so the only thing they can do is groan. I don't know if they can see or hear, but all of them make that sound."

At the top of the stairs was another arched doorway that emptied into a circular room. Directly across from the doorway was an open window. The moon's dull gray light flowed through the window, casting long, grim shadows across the floor. Over the years, dirt, leaves, and other bits of refuse had filtered through the window and formed little piles of debris on the floor. Lizzy raised her staff so that the light would allow them to see more clearly.

A thick layer of dust blanketed the upholstered furniture. Surfaces that were once polished and shined were now dull and caked with layers of grit. There was a writing desk on one side of the room and a small chest sat under the window. A broken lamp was lying on the floor near a divan.

Near the center of the room were the statues of a man and a woman. Their stance indicated that they had been moving toward the stairs when the curse fell upon them. They had typical features like noses and ears—and depressions for eyes—but they were not intricate or refined. The lady was trim and her hair was long and curly. The man was taller. He had a sturdy figure and was dressed in a regal and stately manner. He was holding the woman's arm as if he had been trying to guide her to safety.

Lizzy had imagined something much scarier, but the statues were not scary at all. They looked similar to the life-sized statue of her ancestor, Malcolm McHale, that stood in Glasford Park. But then, one of the statues groaned again, and the ominous sound frightened Lizzy. She stepped back into the arched doorway.

Kreg tried to reassure her. "Like I said, they can't move...so they can't hurt you."

Lizzy slowly eased back into the room.

Keltan added, "We've been here when they groaned at the same time...all of them...these...*and* the ones outside. It was the creepiest thing ever."

Kreg walked right up to the statue of the lady and gently touched her cheek.

"You should touch her," he suggested.

Lizzy was shocked. "I'm not going to touch her."

"Maybe it helps them," Kreg suggested. "Maybe they can feel it."

"I'm *not* going to touch them," she reemphasized.

"So, have you ever looked at any of the cinebits from that day?" asked Kreg.

"No," said Lizzy, "I haven't."

"You can find them on your sPeaksee, if you search hard enough."

Lizzy was trying not to show her ignorance. She of course didn't have a sPeaksee and didn't know how they worked. She wouldn't know how to do a search on it even if she had one in her hand.

"I wanted to see if I could figure out who these two were," said Kreg. "The old cinebits captured everything, and there's tons of them from different angles. Right before Calixta announced the curse,

Corinna appeared in the window and called out to her mother. You can't see her very well, but you can hear her, and you can see her being pulled back inside. It was right at that moment that everyone started freezing in place. So this *has* to be Corinna and Bartlett."

A wave of panic washed over Lizzy. There were too many things racing through her mind all at once. Although she still doubted being the princess, the facts kept adding up. If she were the princess, then standing in front of her, trapped in stone, were her parents. It was all too surreal. Blood drained from her face and her stomach churned with nausea. She needed fresh air so she ran over to the window, climbed on the chest, and stuck her head outside. In an instant, several grackles that had been perched on the ledge, took off in the direction of Brackleton Park. The sight of them terrified her. As she gasped for fresh air Lizzy's head began to buzz and everything went black.

Kreg managed to catch her as she slumped onto the chest. Her walking stick fell to the floor and the light went out.

"Elisabeth!" cried Kreg. He jostled her and patted her face. "Elisabeth, wake up!"

"Is she dead?" asked Keltan.

"No, she's not dead. She just fainted," replied Kreg. "Elisabeth, wake up!" Lizzy began to mumble and slowly opened her eyes.

The room was dark, making it hard for her to focus. The moonlight filtered through the window, but it didn't help much.

"What happened?" she mumbled. The boys managed to get her up, and she sat on the chest.

Kreg knelt in front of her. "I think it was all too much for you. I'm sorry. Are you okay?"

"I think so," she replied, "but it's dark."

"Make another light?" ask Keltan.

Lizzy wasn't sure if she could. She guessed that since she had done it once, that she could do it again. Keltan instinctively handed her the walking stick, thinking it might help. Lizzy stood up and steadied herself.

"Light! Alamah!"

Nothing happened. There was no light—not even the briefest flash or spark. She tried again.

"Light! Alamah!"

Nothing.

"What's the matter?" asked Kreg.

Lizzy was asking herself the same question. "I don't know. It's just not working. Maybe I'm just too scared to focus."

They heard the soft rustle of fluttering wings at the window. The velvet black shape of a large bird appeared and perched on the sill, carving an inky silhouette into the starry night sky. They all stepped backward from the window and moved deeper into the darkness.

"Try again," said the shadow.

"Try what?" asked Kreg. "Who are you?"

"Not you...the girl. Try again. Conjure a light."

Lizzy was petrified. She knew who it was. "You're Omen, aren't you? You're Calixta's raven."

"I am," said Omen calmly. "I had a nice chat with your furry friend a while ago. He's beating himself up because he lost you in the crowd. How lucky I am to find you. I suspect that he will be very happy to know where you are."

"What did you do to him? Where is he?"

Kreg and Keltan stood by, trying to comprehend what was going on.

"I didn't do anything; we just chatted. He said something about coming with you...and riding on a goose, and he mentioned something about the Tunnel of Stars. Does that make any sense to you?"

Lizzy's fear morphed into anger. "What did you do with Mc-Doogle?" She was furious. In addition, the darkness had become a complication. So she screamed, "Light! Alamah!" and stabbed her stick onto the floor.

A blinding light flashed and Lizzy's orb returned—only this time it was much brighter.

"Now, isn't that better?" said Omen.

"What did you do with McDoogle?" Lizzy's voice was strong and commanding.

"I didn't do anything with him. I gave him directions because he was lost, but not before he confessed that you are the princess—the one we are looking for."

The boy's jaws dropped in utter amazement as they tried to comprehend what they were hearing.

"You really shouldn't have come to Castlehill," said Omen. "It's forbidden for anyone to be inside these walls."

"We just came to see the statues," Kreg blurted out. "We're not hurting anything."

"Yes, yes, yes, of course...but perhaps you'll agree, it is not a good place for children, especially at night and especially tonight of all nights."

"Maybe," jabbed Lizzy, "but now that I've seen them, I know how evil, mean, and horrible she is."

"And just who is it that you think is so evil, mean, and horrible?" asked Calixta.

The three children turned simultaneously and saw her blocking their exit. Her dark, red robe hung heavily over her shoulders and clung to her thin frame. Her hair was white, wild, and tangled. Long, thick scars cascaded down her cheek and glistened from the illuminated orb that floated above her staff. Her eye patch sunk into her face. Her other eye widened and blazed with delight as it scanned Lizzy from top to bottom.

"You dear child, you are the perfect vision of what I imagined."

Kreg bolted toward Calixta. She raised her hand, palm first. Without touching him, she easily pushed him away and he fell to the floor. Keltan charged at her as well, and with a flip of her wrist, she tossed him to the wall.

"That's enough of that," she insisted. "Stay where you are, or I'll bind you and make sure you don't bother me. I'm not interested in you."

The boys didn't move again. Lizzy didn't move either. She was trapped, scared, confused, and angry all at the same time.

"I saw her at Future Falls with Igree and Gretta," confirmed Omen. "I also saw her earlier in the park. She's the one you are looking for."

"Well...that *is* a relief, and so wonderfully convenient," said Calixta. "We won't have to go very far. The Ravenclaw Staff is just outside. Shall we get this over with?" Lizzy didn't respond.

Omen knew Calixta's *modus operandi* and offered his advice. "Wouldn't you prefer an audience? The crowds will come tomorrow, especially if I go tell the mages that you have her. You've waited all this time...and remember, tomorrow is her birthday. It's also Midwinter's Eve. Just think of the gift that she will deliver to them if she restores Castlehill on such an important day."

Calixta hesitated as she mulled over the option in her mind and envisioned the triumphant scene that would take place. "You're right, Omen. Go tell the mages that I have her."

She then stepped out of the doorway and into the room, gesturing for the boys to leave. "Go home, you fools. Tell everyone you know that I have the princess. Invite them to come to the courtyard at seven bells tomorrow."

The boys flew through the door and down the stairs as fast as they could. Omen shot into the night sky.

Calixta sat down on the dusty divan and patted her hand on the spot beside her, beckoning Lizzy to join her. Puffs of dust exploded into the air.

"I guess it's just the two of us now. Come...sit. Let's get acquainted, shall we?"

The Girl Who Would Be Queen

Calixta was digging in a patch of bitterschrooms next to the Rose Wall in Kings Park when Beatrice called out, "Come see this beautiful flower! I've never noticed it before."

Calixta was preoccupied with her search and continued prodding through a pile of decaying leaves.

"Did you hear me, Calixta? Will you come look? I don't know what this blue flower is."

"The blue one? With five tapered petals? If that's what you're asking about, it's a phladelia," Calixta called out, without even going to look.

Beatrice counted the petals, "One, two, three, four, five." She mumbled to herself, "Of course she knows...she knows everything."

Beatrice was envious of Calixta's ability to comprehend and retain information. They were the same age, took the same classes, had the same professors, and studied from the same books. They maintained the highest marks in the class, but Calixta was always *primo perfecto*.

Last year, during frosh year, Beatrice got the highest score on a Mental Dominance Over Elements test. But it happened only once. So far, during their sophic year, Beatrice held the second position on all scores. Calixta was a sponge when it came to learning, especially when it came to anything with respect to mysticism and magusology. In that regard, Calixta was very much like her father.

"If you brew the petals with a viper's tail, it will heal lungblight," added Calixta.

Beatrice put her hands on her hips and gazed in Calixta's direction. She wasn't sure how to respond. A chill went through her bones and a knot formed in her stomach. She couldn't ignore the comment—not this time. There had been too many similar comments in recent months.

"Wouldn't the use of a snake's tail be a violation of *The Accepted Laws*?"

Beatrice was referring to *The Accepted Laws and Principles of Mysticism and Magic*, a series of volumes that outlined all protocols, permissions, violations, and punishments for anything that fell under the umbrella of the mage guild. Anyone who studied or practiced sorcery, witchcraft, simple magic, telepathy, therianthropy, and any other of the mage disciplines were required to abide by *The Accepted Laws* or face the consequences outlined therein.

Calixta kept rooting around the bitterschroom patch in an attempt to ignore the question, but Beatrice persisted.

"Wouldn't using a snake's tail be considered animal mutilation?"

It was a bold question and they both knew what it implied. The use of dark arts had been banned for ages because they required the death or mutilation of a living being. The ancient tomes and scrolls that contained this forbidden knowledge were kept locked away in the iron vaults of the mage guild library and guarded at all times. The punishment for using the dark arts was severe.

Having received no response, Beatrice walked over to the bitterschroom patch. "So...how do you know about that potion?" Beatrice was insistent.

Calixta picked up her basket, shrugged, and then laughed. "Oh, I just made it up. I was being silly."

"You know you shouldn't joke about such things, Calixta."

"I'm thirsty," she replied, redirecting the conversation. "Let's go inside and brew some cardamom tea!"

They walked through Kings Park in the direction of their dormitory. Calixta stopped next to a young drangia bush that had just started to flower. She reached out, touched one of the fragrant clusters of tiny pink flowers, and pulled it close. She inhaled deeply and the sweet perfume filled her nostrils. She sank as she let out a long sigh.

"What's the matter?" asked Beatrice.

"This was my mother's favorite flower. We would always take some from the garden and set them around the castle. I just miss her, that's all."

"I miss her too," said Beatrice.

She was unsure of what she should say and hoped that she didn't have to say anything. Beatrice didn't need her cousin to remind her just how much her mother loved drangia blossoms. When Oris died last year, the Grace of the Moon Oratory was overflowing with them. Cedric's grief had caused him to lose control during the eulogy and he went into a rage, knocking over several of the arrangements, shattering vases, sending glass shards sailing across the marble floors, and leaving a sea of drangias in his wake. The fragrance was so dense in the oratory hall that Beatrice hadn't been able to stomach the smell of them ever since.

Calixta lingered for a moment, admiring the blossoms and absorbing the fragrance that wafted in the air. Beatrice took a few steps back, trying to avoid their scent. Calixta wiped her eyes and took a deep breath.

"Are you sure you're alright?"

Calixta nodded.

"Do you want to cut some?" suggested Beatrice, hoping that she would say no.

"Yes, let's do! These are young. They will continue to flower for a long time."

Beatrice pulled a pair of small garden snips from the inside pocket of her cloak, collected four of the larger drangia clusters, and added them to her basket. The bell in the clock tower began ringing the top of the hour.

"It's five bells," said Beatrice. "We've got an hour before we have to be in the dining hall. Let's go brew that tea."

They went to Beatrice's room and hung their red cloaks on the hooks by the door. Beatrice placed the drangia flowers in a vase and set them on the window sill. She opened the window, hoping that it would draw some of the drangia fragrance outside.

"I much prefer the outside air...don't you?" asked Beatrice.

"Yes," said Calixta, "when it's not too cold."

Beatrice set her mortar and pestle on the table and began crushing the cardamom pods. She loved how the spicy scent exploded into the air while she was grinding them. She considered it a bonus that they partially masked the obnoxious fragrance from the drangias.

Calixta filled the kettle with water. Each dorm room had a small fireplace that could be used during cold weather—which wasn't very often. Most students used the fireplaces to make tea. The main fireplace burned wood, but off to the side there was a small, raised metal grate that could hold a kettle or a small pot. Under the grate was a gas burner. Calixta turned the knob and the gas hissed.

She snapped her fingers and shouted, "Spark! Alamah!"

The burner ignited and Calixta adjusted the flame. Conjuring a spark was simple magic. The spark spell was part of the standard curriculum that was taught in practical magic class during the fifth year of primaries. It wasn't much harder than making a light, which they had learned to do during fourth year. Calixta took every opportunity to use what she had learned—and after all, snapping her fingers was far more convenient than striking a match.

"When you are queen, you could issue an edict making drangias the official royal flower. I don't think there is such a thing...yet," said Beatrice, "but *you* could change that!"

The water came to a roaring boil and the kettle rattled and whistled. "What a great idea," beamed Calixta. "Drangias, the royal flower of Ailear! That has a nice ring to it. And when I do, I'll remember to give you credit for the idea."

The girls laughed and spent the next few minutes creating a long list of other proclamations for Calixta to issue once she became queen.

There was a knock at the door. It was their headmaster, Mr. Caldwell. Behind him stood two civic guards. It was highly unusual for a headmaster to enter the dormitories, much less with guards. Beatrice could tell they were there on serious business.

"What's wrong?" asked Beatrice. "What's happened?"

"Is Calixta here with you?" asked Mr. Caldwell.

Calixta appeared behind Beatrice, "Yes, I'm here. What is it?"

"You both need to go with them...please," said Mr. Caldwell.

"Why? What's wrong?" asked Calixta, "And where are the royal guards? Why wouldn't *they* be here for us?"

"It's a civic matter. Please, come. I don't know the full details, and I don't have the authority to tell you what little I know. But the guards need to get you both to safety. They will take you to someone who can explain."

"Has someone died?" asked Beatrice.

"No, nobody has died," said the headmaster. "Please...get your cloaks and go with the guards."

The street in front of Mage Guild Hall was filled with authorities. Calixta and Beatrice were escorted to the courthouse. Once inside they were taken to separate rooms for interrogation. Calixta called out to Beatrice as she was being ushered into a room down the way.

"Beatrice! I'm scared!"

Beatrice paused at the doorway and called back, "Don't be scared. I'm sure this is for our own protection, like Mr. Caldwell said. Let's see what this is all about and we will meet afterwards."

"Okay, I'll see you soon."

The girls were visited by a group of magistrates who explained the situation. Once they had been thoroughly briefed, they were taken to separate quarters. It would be years before they saw each other again.

King Cedric had been arrested and charged on numerous counts of using dark arts. At the trial, the prosecution presented an abundance of evidence. They easily proved that the king had killed several creatures, and that he had mutilated even more, in his attempt to bring Oris back from the dead. His desire to formulate a spell of resurrection had become an obsession born from love and grief. Nothing he tried worked.

He had not been the only one to grieve Oris's death. The entire kingdom mourned her passing. They had loved her as their queen, but for many citizens, she would always be remembered as an Ice Angel.

At the trial, King Cedric took the stand and admitted his guilt. Even so, the defense argued that it was a case of temporary insanity—hoping to ease the sentence. It didn't help. The jury found him guilty on all charges. The king was remorseful, and he was totally broken when the verdict was read. He held his head in his hands as the judge sentenced him to a life of exile on the Isle of Ni'Tar. He was forced to instantly abdicate the throne.

He was allowed to speak to the gallery. In a tearful message, he shared his thoughts.

"I once saved a baby robin," he said. "I was no more than five years old. I remember holding the lifeless creature in my hand and willing it to come back. I was praised for having done so. That was a long time ago. My desperation and arrogance has brought me to this moment. I've let you all down...I've let myself down...I've let my beloved Oris down...I couldn't bring her back."

The thought of her sent him to his knees, and he wept. It took a moment for him to regain his composure.

"I will never be able to forgive myself. I selfishly *took* life believing that I could *give* life...that I could bring Oris *back* to life, and in doing so, I sealed my own fate. The result of my actions will no doubt have far-reaching repercussions. And while I am deeply sorry for disappointing the citizens of Ailear, I am most sorry for how my actions will affect my beautiful daughter, Calixta."

He embraced Calixta for the last time. She sobbed on his shoulder. The bailiff took him away.

On the same day as Cedric's sentencing, a quiet ceremony was held in the senate chamber. Gethric was crowned king of Ailear, and Genevra became queen consort. Beatrice, who had not been in attendance at the trial, stood silently by and smiled. She felt satisfied bearing witness to her father's private coronation and knew that a public celebration would soon follow.

To Tell the Truth

Lizzy had no intention of getting near Calixta, much less sitting beside her. Their two lights created eerie and suspenseful shadows in the room. Calixta had leaned her staff against the wall next to the divan. Lizzy maintained a tight grip on hers. She slowly took several paces backward, but the additional separation didn't provide any extra comfort. She was petrified and trapped. She darted her eyes to the door that led to the stairs. Instinctively, she wanted to run. She knew she was fast, but she was also aware that her injured ankle might hinder her from being fast enough. She recalled how easily Calixta had managed to fend off Kreg and Keltan and suspected she would fare no better. Still, she scanned the room searching for a way to distract Calixta that might give her a chance to escape.

"Come, come now, my dear child," Calixta said calmly, reading her mind. "There's really no point in you being stubborn or trying to leave. I have no intention of hurting you. You are very important to me, and you are about to become the most famous person in the history of Ailear."

Calixta's voice was aged and raspy. Lizzy was surprised that it didn't sound sinister or threatening. Even so, she refrained from acknowledging Calixta's comment. She once again cut her eyes toward the door. Calixta extended her index finger, making a deliberate "come hither" gesture. Lizzy didn't budge, but it didn't matter. The request was not intended for her. It was the door that obeyed Calixta's bidding. The hinge began emitting a rusty, ratchety creak, and the door slammed shut. Lizzy heard the lock click into place. She wanted to scream, but she knew that no matter what sort of commotion she made, there wasn't a living soul close enough who would be able to hear her cries and come to her rescue.

"You really should make yourself comfortable, Princess. It's going to be a long night."

Lizzy had become accustomed to being called princess, but she cringed when Calixta said it. It dawned on her that if she weren't the real Princess of Ailear, then she *wouldn't* become Calixta's captive. The thought gave her courage to speak up.

"I'm not a princess!" Lizzy shouted abruptly. "I'm Lizzy Albright from Overland Park, Kansas, and I shouldn't be here. I'm here by mistake—or maybe I'm just dreaming. But no matter what, I'm not who you think I am. I'm *not* a princess."

"Lizzy is it? Lizzy Albright? Well then, Lizzy, why don't you sit down and tell me all about it?"

Lizzy didn't budge. She looked around the room. Abandoned bird nests were tucked in behind wall sconces. Cobwebs clung to the ceiling and swayed with the slightest breeze. The furniture remained untouched and unmoved. A cushioned chair was pushed up against the writing table. Its feet were carved with claws clutching an orb that reminded Lizzy of the Chippendale chairs in Granny's dining room. The thought suddenly made her homesick and she sank into the chair—not out of obedience, but rather because she felt there was nothing to do but surrender.

Calixta sat quietly and gave Lizzy time to collect her thoughts. A smothering silence permeated the air, and an invisible barrier of defiance seethed within Lizzy's soul. The two statues let out an agonizing groan that caused her stomach to sink.

"She shouldn't have betrayed me! Beatrice...*Queen Bea*! She's the one to blame for this, not me," said Calixta in defense. "I was used, manipulated, and betrayed for more years than I would like to remember.

I'm not sorry for my actions. I was treated like a rat—put in a cage and lowered into a well. I was forced to fend for myself and left to escape using whatever means I could. The choices I've made were necessary for my survival."

Lizzy grew more sullen, clenched her jaw, and refused to respond to what she was being told. She wasn't buying Calixta's "poor me" scenario. Calixta stood up, slowly paced the floor, and continued her defense.

"If Beatrice had not broken her promise, this would have never happened. Did anyone bother to tell you that she tricked me? I'm curious to know what you've been told."

Calixta came closer and stopped near the statues. The angle of light cut across her face and emphasized the scars on her cheek. Her eye patch and wild white hair made her look more horrendous than Lizzy had imagined. When Lizzy put an eye patch on Fluffs and pretended he was a pirate, it was a wonderful, imaginative experience. But nothing about this situation was wonderful, and she felt certain that this moment was not coming from her imagination.

"I'm sure you know that I am the one responsible for the curse at Castlehill." Calixta caressed the face of the female statue. The statue moaned in response.

"Don't touch her!" exploded Lizzy. She was stunned at her own reaction, but she couldn't stop. Lizzy leapt up and threw her walking stick at Calixta. Calixta waved her hand and redirected the stick, sending it to the other side of the room. It crashed into the wall and Lizzy's light vanished.

"You're a horrible, evil witch! You murdered Ravol and stole his claw. You practice black magic and you imprisoned the queen in stone. You're worse than the Wicked Witch of the West...and I hope you melt!"

"Sit down!" Calixta commanded. Lizzy had no intention of sitting down again. Calixta raised her hand and, without touching her, pushed Lizzy back into the chair.

"No!" said Lizzy. "Let me go!" Lizzy wriggled and squirmed, but a force unlike anything she had ever experienced was keeping her in place.

"Evil witch? Murderer? Is that what you believe? I'm not surprised. But you should know by now: things are not always as they seem!"

The phrase caught Lizzy by surprise. Gretta had used those same words before, and she had been right. Things were not always as they seemed.

"I know what people think of me. I know the stories they tell. Do you even know why I'm an outcast? Do you think this is the life that I dreamed of when I was the princess of Ailear? I longed for the day when I would be queen. I would have ruled with kindness and generosity."

Lizzy couldn't comprehend what Calixta was saying. She replayed the words *princess* and *queen* in her head. All she knew was that Beatrice was the queen.

"I don't believe you," jabbed Lizzy. "You're lying."

"It doesn't matter what you believe. It's true. I was the princess and I should have become queen. My father, Cedric, was the king of Ailear."

Lizzy's mind raced to the portrait of the master mages in Igree's parlor. She reflected on the story that Igree told her of how Cedric's grief had led him to a place of darkness, and that his actions started the chain of events that brought about the current situation. She remembered the poster of the Ice Angels and began putting the pieces together.

"If King Cedric was your father, that means your mother was... Oris. Your mother was Oris, one of the Ice Angels."

Calixta was surprised that Lizzy knew that particular detail.

"Yes, she was."

Lizzy was still on edge about being Calixta's captive, but the story she had been told now seemed like a puzzle with several missing pieces.

Calixta had no motivation to hide anything from Lizzy. She wanted Lizzy to know everything.

"Since you know about the Ice Angels, I'll start there. After all, it was at one of the Ice Angels performances that my mother and her sister, Genevra, forged a relationship with the twins."

"Twins? What twins?" asked Lizzy.

"You don't know about the twins? Cedric, my father, and Gethric, Beatrice's father, were the royal twins. They fell in love with the Biggleston sisters, Oris and Genevra, two of the Ice Angels."

This was news to Lizzy. She had not been told anything about Gethric and Genevra, and she was surprised to learn that two of the Ice Angels were sisters.

Lizzy couldn't restrain her curiosity. "Was the third Ice Angel their sister too?"

"No," said Calixta. "Miona was their friend."

Lizzy repeated the name Miona in her head.

"The four were wed in an unprecedented double wedding ceremony, complete with matching wedding rings."

Calixta extended her hand, touched the ring with her thumb and showed Lizzy the simple gold band with a small heart-shaped top.

"This ring is the most precious treasure I have left from my mother. I still miss her."

Lizzy studied the ring, but maintained a safe distance from Calixta.

"Three years after the wedding, Beatrice and I were born. I'm the oldest, by three weeks. We were known as the inseparable cousins. Both of our families lived in Castlehill, so we were rarely apart from each other. We played together, ate together, shared a room together, and started mage school together.

"We were only three years old when King Eoseph died. He was my grandfather. That's when my father, being the eldest, was crowned king. I was the princess, the heir to the throne. I would someday be queen—a fact that Beatrice never let me forget. She thought it was exciting and would make up various queenly things for me to do when we played in the garden."

As Calixta revealed more facts, she noticed that Lizzy would respond with slight changes in body language or subtle facial expressions, indicating that she was piecing the story together.

"Does any of this surprise you, Princess?" Hearing Calixta once again call her princess made Lizzy uneasy, but she didn't react. She was determined to appear unaffected by Calixta's story.

"I wonder what else was conveniently left out. Do you know how my mother died?"

Lizzy shook her head.

"I was fifteen years old, in my frosh year at mage school. She fell and hit her head on a rock. Beatrice was with her. They were out harvesting toadshrooms at the far end of the castle gardens when she slipped on a moss-covered stone and fell. The blow to her head rendered her unconscious. Beatrice ran for help, but by the time help arrived, she was dead."

The two sat in silence for a few moments. Lizzy was curious to know what it was that Cedric had done. She finally found the courage to ask.

"What did your father do?"

Calixta walked over to the window and looked at the stars. She felt anger and sadness at the same time, but she restrained herself from lashing out.

"He loved my mother. That's what he did wrong. He loved her so much that he couldn't fathom his life without her. She was gone too soon. He was a gifted master mage and he tried to save her. And yes, he turned to the dark arts. He wanted to bring my mother back to life. He was convicted and sentenced to a life in exile. The parliamentary chamber crowned Gethric king of Ailear, and Beatrice became heir to the throne. My father was carted away and he died—alone—on the Isle of Ni'Tar. There were false accusations and rumors being published about me. I was only sixteen. I began receiving threats and I feared for my life. The hate that was spewed at me became more than I could bear, so I fled, and I have lived a life of seclusion in Valendale Forest ever since."

Lizzy tried to assimilate this new information. In some regards, she pitied Calixta, but it didn't change the fact that she was to blame for the curse. And although Calixta defended her father's actions, she knew that he must have harmed *someone* because the dark arts required mutilation or death. Lizzy was hesitant to speak up, but she also wanted to know the whole story.

"I didn't know you and Beatrice were cousins. But I know she broke her promise, and I know you sought revenge and put the curse on Castlehill. I also know that you think I'm the princess, and that your intention is to take me away, but I'm telling you again, I'm not."

Calixta raised her eyebrow. "I'm fairly certain you are the princess, and you are no doubt very clever by trying to make me believe you are not. But that truth will be determined soon enough. What else do you know?"

Lizzy hesitated. She knew the accusation would stir a pot of trouble, but she wanted confirmation. "Like I said before, I know you killed Ravol...the high mage! And that makes you a murderer! You used his claw to make the staff for the curse."

"You weren't there!" exclaimed Calixta. "You only know what you've been told: circumstantial evidence, speculation, and even worse—lies. I *was* there. I know what happened. I know the truth, and I have these scars to remind me."

Calixta pulled off her eye patch and ran her fingers down her cheek, making sure Lizzy saw the full extent of her disfiguration. Her eyelids displayed scars from where they had been stitched shut. The skin sank into her eye socket, creating a void of blackness. Lizzy was repulsed by the sight, but she couldn't force herself to look away.

"It's not pretty, is it? I don't like it either, but I'm lucky to be alive. Yes, I was angry. Yes, Beatrice betrayed me and broke her promise. I created my own world and my own life. I left her alone. She sought me for help, and we swore a promise in blood. Even that didn't stop her from double-crossing me. I have no pity for her. She knew her actions would have serious repercussions. She is the one responsible for the curse on Castlehill.

"You can choose to believe me, or not, but I have been forced to do things that I would have never chosen to do. I was banished to a life of darkness because of Beatrice and my reputation became dark and heinous. There isn't a court anywhere in the realm that would believe what I am about to tell you. But for all of the things I *have* done, I assure you...I did *not* murder Ravol.

"I broke into mage hall and followed a secret corridor that I had discovered when I was a student there. It led to a hidden door located in the atrium near the entrance to the vaults. I was surprised to discover there were no guards. I managed to gain entry with no problem. The lock turned easily at my command.

"I worked my way to the deepest recesses of the library and silently paged through volumes of curses. I came across the Curse of the Groaning Stones. It *didn't* require a life sacrifice, but it *did* require a hand, or a claw, in order to hold an enchanted orb. The curse was adequate for me to reap my revenge. Nobody had to die. I stole the page and tucked it into the pocket of my cloak.

"As I was leaving, I heard a soft thud that sounded like a book being dropped onto a table. I made my way toward the sound and peered through a gap in the books. Can you guess who I saw? Who do you think was sitting at the desk, transcribing pages of forbidden spells and curses?"

Lizzy suspected that she knew the answer, but she only shrugged.

"Ravol. Yes, it was Ravol, the high mage himself. He seemed comfortable and confident, as if he were following one of his normal routines. It appeared to me that this was not his first visit to the vaults. He must have managed to transcribe many forbidden curses on previous occasions. He most likely bribed the guards and sent them away during his visits.

"Even though I had been quiet as death, he still sensed my presence and caught me watching him. I ran back into the atrium, but he flew and was on me in an instant, sinking his talons into my neck. He threatened to kill me. I tried to fend him off, but he held on to my hair. I finally managed to get free, but in the process, a clump of my hair remained in his claw.

"He cast a spell of confinement that bound my feet, causing me to fall to the floor. His talons sliced deeply into my face, releasing a river of blood. He stabbed his beak into my eye and then plucked it out.

"I covered my head, and using all of my strength, I summoned the *Force of a Canon* and flung him across the room. He hit the wall with such intensity that his skull shattered. He died instantly, but I didn't murder him. I killed him in self defense. I needed a claw, and his was convenient. That, Princess, is how it happened."

Lizzy was silent. She didn't know what to think or what to do. She was still scared, yet she didn't feel threatened. She felt conflicted from hearing different stories. She even began to wonder if Calixta was the horrible sorceress that she had been led to believe. They sat in silence for a long while. Lizzy had no intention of sleeping. It was going to be a very long night.

A Slight Change of Plans

Omen flew to Mage Guild Hall to deliver the news to the council.

"What's your name? State your business," demanded one of the two sentinels on duty.

"My name is Omen. I need to speak with the high mage. It's urgent."

"Baron is in council. He cannot be disturbed," snarled the badger.

Omen puffed his chest, shook his shaggy throat feathers, and advanced closer to the guards. The badger's hair bristled. The wolf snarled and lifted his upper lip. His white fangs glinted in the lamplight. Both guards braced themselves and prepared for an altercation.

"That's close enough," said the badger. "If you come any closer you'll be sorry you did."

"You *must* interrupt him. It's extremely urgent. Tell him that I am here with a message from Calixta. He won't refuse to see me."

Omen's mention of Calixta captured their attention. The badger looked to the wolf, who gave a slight, approving nod. "Wait here!" commanded the guard.

The badger disappeared through the massive doors of the main entrance. He returned and escorted Omen to the rotunda where Baron was waiting for him. Baron asked the guard for privacy, so the badger went back to his post.

Omen's message was brief. Baron didn't respond immediately. He paced in a circle around Omen—collecting his thoughts. He finally stopped and let out a long sigh.

"So...that's how it will be," said Baron. "Tomorrow evening then... the mages will be there. No doubt everyone will be there. Go on, be on your way. I'm sure Calixta has plenty for you to do."

Before returning to the council chambers, Baron called Igree.

Abandoned motorbies were still clogging the streets, so Igree had gone to the apothecary on foot. He was out of breath when he answered the call. "I'm almost there. I'm less than a block away."

"It's no use," said Baron. "Calixta has her...she has the princess in the castle tower."

"What? How in the seven heavens did Calixta get to her?"

"I just now learned about it from Omen...come on back...we need you here," urged Baron. "I have to tell the council."

The chamber erupted when Baron made the announcement. "Order!" shouted Baron, demanding their attention. "We will have order in this chamber!" As the ruckus subsided, he offered reassurance.

"It's not what we wanted, but the plan will still work. The princess will remain safe."

McDoogle pulled back his ears. "What dae ye mean remain safe? She's no safe. She's been captured by that evil witch! Tell me how tae get tae the tower and I'll go fetch her masel!"

"As brave as you are, I highly advise against it," said Baron. "No matter how hard you try, you are not likely to succeed—none of us would succeed. Calixta is well protected. The princess may be frightened, but I assure you she is safe. Our plan was to escort her to the courtyard. Now it will be Calixta who will bring her to the Ravenclaw Staff. Nothing else has changed. It may not be what we planned, but it will be okay. We *will* get the princess back...of that I am certain."

"I dinnae ken how ye're so sure. Just how do ye expect to accomplish this when yer plans have already gone astray?" barked McDoogle. "Maybe ye should start tellin' me how ye're goin' going to get the lass oot o' the mess ye've put her in."

Gretta, who had been silently mulling over the situation, spoke up. "Mr. McDoogle, the high court has already found Calixta guilty. Due to the extraordinary and unprecedented circumstances, they made an exception and tried her case without her being present. They used evidence from numerous recorded cinebits where Calixta, by her own admission, confessed to using the dark arts. She was sentenced to exile for life.

"However, as you know, she is protected by Omen and her army of grackles. It has been impossible to apprehend her. The master mages testified that even if she were captured and sent into exile, the grackles would come to her aid and she would certainly find a way to escape.

"After much consideration, the judge granted the master mages permission to seek an enchanted sort of imprisonment for Calixta... one from which she could not escape. If we found a spell that he deemed to be acceptable and reliable, he would allow us to use it, as long as it was not a spell that required the use of the dark arts. Igree was unanimously selected to take the lead in researching the ancient spells...specifically those for confinement and imprisonment...to find one that could be adapted so that it wouldn't require a sacrifice."

Gretta drew McDoogle's attention and pointed to a portrait that hung near the main entrance to the council chambers. McDoogle had not noticed it before—but it was Gertie, Gretta's mother. Under the portrait was a plaque that was engraved with the words *Gertie Flutterfield, Mage Guild Librarian*.

"My mother began overseeing our guild's library long before I came along. Being the librarian, she was selected to supervise the project. She placed extra guards at the doors to the vault to assure her protection and to make certain that no books or scrolls left the library. Igree spent hundreds of days tediously pouring through volumes of books and scrolls looking for a spell that he could adapt in order to bring Calixta to justice.

"One day, while Igree was busy researching, my mother noticed a book that was not in the section where it belonged. She pointed it out to Igree. When Igree began looking through the volume, he discovered that a page was missing. It had been torn from the section that contained the Curse of the Groaning Stones—a spell of imprisonment."

Gretta paused and looked to Baron, who nodded, giving her permission to continue.

"Igree realized that the subsequent page contained a critical part for reversing the curse. We know that the Curse of the Groaning Stones cannot be reversed using only the portion that Calixta stole."

McDoogle was trying to make sense of the information. "So ye're just goin' to give the page to the witch?"

Baron interjected, "Essentially...yes. This is our chance to finally get close to Calixta. There's never been an opportunity like this until now. She won't know it, but she will be walking into a trap."

"What sort of a trap?" asked McDoogle.

"Igree found a spell and has adapted it to meet the senate's approval," said Gretta. "Even though it's never been tried before, we all feel confident that it will work—and Calixta will be imprisoned. Better than that...the princess will be free. She will also be able to break the curse and restore Castlehill."

The explanation didn't put McDoogle's concerns to rest. He turned and addressed the assembly. "I dinnae ken why someone else couldna dae the job. Ye keep sayin' she's the only one who can reverse the curse. I am in a room fou o' powerful wizards and magicians who can summon light, shoot rockets from yer feathers, and enchant stones with a magic so grand that naebody can recognize ye. Goodness knows whut other tomfoolery ye have up yer sleeves. So why can't ye save the castle on yer own and leave the lass oot o' it?"

Baron shuffled through several files. "This might help you to understand," replied Baron. Baron left the bench carrying a document and laid it down for McDoogle to read.

"Some spells are simple and some are complex. All spells are carefully worded. The slightest alteration can cause the spell to fail, or go wrong. But when a spell is properly stated, it is fixed...set in stone, as it were. No one can change it. Calixta's curse on Castlehill was perfect. She altered it to make sure she would get what she wanted—the child. This is a transcript of the curse. We have translated it from the original archaic language. We have studied the curse carefully for all these years. There is no loophole that we can find. We had one choice...to find the princess and bring her here."

McDoogle took a moment to study the document.

> *Dwellen a Carlington*
> > House of Carlington
> *An ara castila vara*
> > And all who keep inside
> *Ve ara vasha. Ve ara vasha.*
> > You are cursed. You are cursed.
> *Ver dermisa an ver sangrati*
> > Your flesh and blood
> *Lan darnsor*
> > Will harden
> *An ve curna ti granatita.*
> > And you will turn to stone.
> *Alamah! Alamah!*
> > I command it! I command it!

Ve am visio, no ve am vociliea.
  You will not see, nor will you speak.
Ve lan bahah, an ve lan ohshah.
  You will moan, and you will groan.
Alamah! Alamah!
  I command it! I command it!

Im solion am vasha destranta.
  Only I can break the curse.
Be mi im tonse im fentosum authoriznia
  By my right, I relinquish that power
An transtum ti babitor o Corinna.
  And give it to the child of Corinna.
Urgentorum luna dun
  This must be done before the moon sets
Supra montanus tenta entersun av babitor.
  Over the mountain on the tenth birthday of the child.
Ravin pedtron cradiltun luminor vitor
  The raven claw will hold the orb of life
An solion babitor am disambilora et.
  And only the rightful child can reverse it.
Alamah! Alamah!
  I command it! I command it!

McDoogle reread the ending several times and then quietly repeated it out loud, "And only the rightful child can remove it." They were telling the truth. The turbulence that had been boiling inside of him began to subside. He realized there was nothing else to do but to trust the mages. He sighed and looked at Baron.

"Ye better not muck it up! I'll have yer hide," McDoogle said sharply. "Whut can I do to help?"

"I would like you to be next to me for the processional of mages tomorrow evening," said Baron. "We will make our way from here to the courtyard at Castlehill. You'll be as close to the princess as possible. Seeing you there will no doubt be a comfort to her. You will give her courage."

Baron addressed the mages, "May I remind everyone that the constables will be in attendance. You are all aware that Queen Beatrice is considered an accomplice with regard to the forbidden potion that Calixta made. The court is withholding judgement, but should the spell be successfully reversed, the queen will be taken into custody and questioned."

The room filled with rumbles and murmurs. Some of the mages approved of the senate's course of action, but others disapproved. Regardless, the issue was not for the mages to decide. It was a civic matter and the senate had the authority to interrogate the queen. They were determined to learn the whole truth. It was time to put an end to the tumultuous and troublesome years that had plagued the kingdom since Oris's death.

Baron adjourned the council and urged them to get plenty of rest. It was already the early morning hours of Midwinter's Eve. Today was destined to become one of the most memorable days in the history of Ailear.

Midwinter's Eve

A fter the council adjourned, Baron contacted the city officials and told them about the situation. He recommended
that they put more safeguards in place than they had originally planned. Throughout the rest of the night, the remaining abandoned motorbies were towed away or pushed to the curb. Many roads
were closed to traffic and barricades were set in place to help control
the masses that were expected to flock to Imperial Plaza to witness
the spectacle. Unconfirmed rumors about Calixta and the princess
began to spread like a brushfire. Even though no official announcement had been made, many Ansans—primarily those who were obsessed with the curse—rushed to the plaza in order to secure the best
vantage point.

A steady, soft, persistent rain began just before dawn. Late in
the morning, a powerful cloudburst sent a deluge that inundated the
drainage system, forcing the runoff onto sidewalks and turning the
streets into rushing streams. Low-lying areas turned into shallow lakes.
The incessant drizzle had kept most inhabitants indoors—waiting for
news. At noon they finally received the confirmation that they had
anticipated, but it didn't come from the authorities. It was a message
from Calixta stating that she had the princess and she would be at
Imperial Plaza at seven bells that evening.

Prayers were sent heavenward and stargrass pots were lit. The
air in the streets was thick with the sweet smell of incense. Ansans
pulled on their galoshes, donned their rain cloaks, and began flowing
en force to Castlehill. Every available civic guard was stationed in a
strategic location in an attempt to prevent another stampede. During
the late afternoon, the sky thickened, and a heavy blanket of ominous

clouds smothered the city, plunging Ansa into a dismal, premature, and eerie twilight.

At six bells the procession of mages exited Mage Guild Hall. They passed through the eastern gate of Barleywick Quarter and made their way to the plaza. Baron and Igree led the procession. McDoogle trotted beside them. Gretta, Gertie, and Molly followed next. Orlin circled overhead keeping watch for any suspicious activity. The mage guild sentinels flanked the procession.

All the mages had activated a spell of deflection to keep themselves dry. The barrier floated above them and acted like an invisible umbrella. Raindrops bounced off the unseen surface—dancing and splashing in every direction before falling to the ground a short distance away. The mages filed into Imperial Plaza and took their places along the perimeter inside the barricade. Citizens shuffled through the streets and steadily pressed their way toward Castlehill.

A large contingent of well-guarded senators and justices arrived. They were ushered to the VIP seating area that had been designated for government officials. Several priests, prioresses, and other high-ranking clerics filed down Saint Murphy Blvd., swinging heavy pots of stargrass and chanting a series of monotonous prayers as they made their way to the plaza. The clerics stationed themselves opposite the mages inside the barricade.

By half past six bells, the rain had stopped and the clouds began to dissipate. A muted, golden glow illuminated the city as the late evening sun filtered through the haze that remained in the sky.

A faint high-pitched chattering echoed in the distance. The shrieks intensified as the grackles made their approach. The crowd raised their sPeaksees and began capturing cinebits of the scene. Hordes of the black birds perched on the roofs, ramparts, ledges, turrets, and window sills. Throngs of grackles infiltrated the trees and a large swarm stirred the air high above Castlehill.

At the top of the hour, the bells from the satinaries throughout Ansa began clanging. A cacophony of clattering tones lasted for over a minute before the last bell to toll faded into silence. The crowd grew still.

A gravelly caw ricocheted off the castle walls. The crowd looked on as Omen made several vast sweeping circles above Castlehill. He rocketed toward the plaza and skimmed just above the heads of the crowd. After a few more magnificent displays, he finally came to rest on top of the gate not far from the stone statue of Queen Beatrice.

A loud crack shattered the silence, startling the crowd. It was followed by a series of laborious creaks and scrapes as the reluctant rusty chains and the stubborn dry gears of the portcullis were magically forced into action after a decade of tranquil repose. Everyone watched in suspense as the massive gate slowly began its ascent. It howled under the agonizing stress and heaved a tenebrious sigh when it reached the apex and came to rest.

All eyes were transfixed on the gate. A gust of bitter wind surged through the plaza. A dull explosion erupted from inside the wall. A cloud of dense red smoke burst through the gate and billowed into the plaza. The smoke began to dispense, unveiling the sorceress and her captive.

Calixta coaxed Lizzy through the entrance. Rumblings rippled through the crowd. They were seeing the princess for the first time. Lizzy remained reluctant to comply with Calixta's instructions and her defiance was evident. Still, she didn't fully resist. Earlier in the day she had reasoned with herself that somehow Gretta, Igree, and the other mages would make sure that she would be rescued. She didn't know what the mages had conspired to do, but she knew they had a plan—and for now, she had faith that their objective would succeed. She was exhausted. She had not had a wink of sleep since leaving Deep

Glen. As Calixta nudged her toward the staff, it became apparent that she was weary and suffering from fatigue.

The mages watched Calixta's dramatic entrance with intense interest. McDoogle was about to run to Lizzy when Igree quickly caught his eye. With one stern glance, McDoogle was reminded of his agreement. He had promised Igree that he wouldn't interfere no matter how difficult it might be.

"Leave it to us," Igree said quietly. "Be strong. Please don't attempt to intervene."

McDoogle looked at Lizzy and was overwhelmed with concern and compassion. He restrained himself but secretly swore, if the plan started to go wrong, he would do whatever he felt necessary to protect her.

Lizzy was astonished as she gazed across the sea of onlookers. There was something threatening about the sheer volume of living beings in such close proximity that added to her anxiety. Yesterday, when the crowd pushed in around her, her fear was more claustrophobic in nature. She had been cloistered in the crowd, but she had not been fully aware of the mass that had streamed to Brackleton Park. Today was a different story. Her stomach sank and she almost panicked when she realized that all eyes were focused on her.

Lizzy's heart leapt when she saw the assembly of mages. She spotted the large bear and assumed that it was Baron—the high mage. His height gave him a foreboding and frightful presence, but she saw an underlying softness in his face that helped her understand why Gretta had spoken so fondly of him. His flowing black and purple cloak wafted in the breeze.

Then Lizzy saw McDoogle sitting next to Igree. She wanted to run to him, but she knew any attempt to escape would be futile. Gretta managed to catch Lizzy's eye. She nodded, giving a comforting and encouraging look that bolstered Lizzy's confidence.

Calixta ushered the princess to the Ravenclaw Staff. Lizzy found herself mesmerized by the colorful, ever-changing arcs that were being emitted by the globe. She had never seen anything like it. It was beautiful, but she dreaded the idea of touching it for fear that she would be electrocuted.

Then she saw Ravol's claw clinching the orb. It repulsed her and reminded her of the two conflicting stories about his death, and she wondered whether or not she would ever learn the truth. Lizzy's stomach was spinning with a whirlwind of emotions, but she was determined not to express anything other than stubbornness and courage.

The accounts that Calixta had told Lizzy about her life were persuasive, and there were times in the tower when Lizzy had felt compassion for Calixta. But regardless of what Lizzy was led to believe, the fact remained that if she were the princess, Calixta would take her. That thought alone gave her the will to fight. She would do what she was asked, and she wagered her life on whatever scheme that the mages were about to unveil.

Calixta raised her staff and the crowd instantly fell silent. "Here she is," Calixta shouted. "I present to you the princess of Ailear!"

The crowd wasn't sure how to react. Ailearians were excited to see their princess, but they were also appalled and angry knowing that she was now Calixta's prisoner. There was a spattering of awkward clapping, but for the most part, a spirit of heaviness and uncertainty hung in the air.

Calixta was not pleased with the response. "What's wrong with you imbeciles? I've presented to you the missing princess, and soon you'll once again have your queen. Never in the history of this kingdom has there been such a cause for celebration...so celebrate!" she demanded.

She then stabbed her staff into the ground and the grackles began chattering. The crowd, out of fear of being attacked, made a feeble attempt to appease Calixta by raising half-hearted cheers and delivering an anemic, but obedient applause.

Calixta removed the stolen page from her cloak and raised it for all to see. "You are here to witness the princess restore your precious Castlehill. As the rightful heir, she is the only one who can turn the stones back into living flesh." The crowd murmured and watched with great anticipation. Calixta handed the page to Lizzy.

Baron took a few steps forward and interrupted. "You are going to need this!" he said, holding up the ancient book. It was cracked and brittle from age—and secured with twine.

Calixta was angry that Baron had interrupted. "Silence! Do you take me for a fool? Stand back and don't interrupt us again."

"I'm trying to help," persisted Baron. "We all want Castlehill to be restored, but I'm telling you...you are not going to succeed without this book."

Calixta looked at Baron and seethed. "What sort of trick are you up to? I have *this*!" She snatched the page from Lizzy and once again held it up for all to see.

"Yes, you have that, but it's incomplete," said Baron. "We found the book, and we found where you ripped out the page. You failed to notice that there was more. The spell won't be broken if the princess doesn't read it all."

Calixta suspected that the mages were up to some trick, but she began to question her certainty. She studied the page briefly. It looked complete. Knowing the extent of the archives, she also doubted that they had found the volume with the missing page.

"I don't believe you!" she shouted.

"I will prove it," said Baron, taking a few more steps forward.

"Don't come any closer," said Calixta, raising her staff.

Baron stood his ground. "See for yourself. That page will match the tear in this book, and then you will see that there is more to the spell than you thought. If the princess doesn't read everything, then the curse will fail, and *you* will be the one responsible for the deaths of everyone inside Castlehill."

Calixta was suspicious, but she had to know the truth. "Give the book to Omen," she instructed. Omen flew to Baron, retrieved the book, and carried it to Calixta.

Baron called out, "There is a placeholder where the page is missing." As Calixta examined the book, Baron gave Lizzy a reassuring nod. Lizzy sensed that whatever was transpiring was going as planned. She gave him an appreciative smile.

It had been ten years, but Calixta recognized the book. She momentarily drifted back to the night when she encountered Ravol. She touched the patch over her eye and ran her finger down the scars on her face. She untied the twine and let it fall to the ground.

"It will fit," Baron said with assurance.

"I'll be the judge of that," snapped Calixta. She thumbed the pages, found the placeholder, and focused her attention to the torn remnant along the spine. She slid the torn edge of her page into place and it matched perfectly.

As soon as the page was in position, Molly sent up a feather that exploded, startling everyone, including Calixta who looked up to see what it was. At that very moment, Baron shouted, "Shut! Alamah!" The book slammed shut, trapping the page inside, and startling Calixta who had not had time to realize that there was no additional information about the groaning stones on the facing page. She shot a disbelieving glance at Baron. He immediately shouted, "Vanish! Alamah!" and the book disappeared. The trick had been successful.

Calixta was furious. "You idiot! Do you think I care whether or not the curse is broken? All I want is the child!" Calixta grabbed Lizzy and pulled her close. "You can seal the fate of Castlehill as you wish, but this one is mine no matter what happens!"

"You can't keep her," said Baron.

"I can and I will! She's mine now. I'm taking her. *You* are now responsible for the fate of everyone inside Castlehill."

"How do you know she's the princess?" asked Baron. "How do you know *she* is the child who was promised to you? You can't take just any child. The only way to prove it is for her to break the curse."

"Of course she's the princess. That goose brought her here," she said, pointing to Gretta.

Lizzy felt the tension building, but she remained hopeful. She wondered if she would receive any guidance and was prepared to act quickly if she was instructed to do so.

While Calixta was pointing to Gretta, Baron shouted, "Twine to Vines! Alamah!"

The twine on the ground instantly turned into a vine. It began sending roots into the ground and began snaking its way around Calixta's ankles. She was not quick enough to escape. The vine twisted around her calves and constrained her legs.

Baron shouted. "Run, Princess, Run!" Lizzy wrestled free from Calixta's grasp and instinctively ran to McDoogle. The crowd was surprised with the unexpected turn of events and they cheered when Lizzy escaped. Baron ran to Calixta and wrenched her staff from her grasp. He tossed it far out of her reach.

Calixta was outraged. "What are you doing, you fool? I'll bring death to you all!" She extended her arm toward the staff and shouted, "Come to me! Alamah!" As she gave the command, she lost her balance, and the spell missed its target.

Lizzy perceived what Calixta was attempting to do and shouted to McDoogle. "Quick, McDoo...fetch it!" Without hesitation McDoogle lunged forward and retrieved the staff. He delivered it to Igree who then passed it on to the other mages for safekeeping.

The vine multiplied and continued an upward ascent— wrapping around Calixta's torso and securing her arms.

Calixta didn't have an ounce of concern for her predicament. She was annoyed and felt her confinement was nothing more than a temporary inconvenience. She called out to her grackles. "Attack! Kill them all!"

An almost deafening chatter arose from the grackles, but they didn't obey the command. They remained in place. Calixta was outraged by their disobedience.

"Fly!" she commanded. But the grackles didn't fly.

Omen shot into the air and glided over the crowd.

"Omen, send your army to attack!" she insisted.

Omen continued circling above the plaza—ignoring Calixta's orders. Finally, he glided down and landed on the ground in front of her.

"It seems you've been lax and have failed to notice that we are no longer under your enchantment. We have been free from your spell of servitude for many months."

Calixta couldn't comprehend what Omen was saying.

Omen added, "You killed my father!"

Calixta was speechless. She reached into the recesses of her mind trying to retrieve information that would help her to comprehend what was transpiring.

Calixta finally muttered, "Your father?"

Omen moved closer. "You killed my father...Ravol." Calixta reeled from the news. She never knew that Omen was the son of the high mage.

The raven continued. "I left my family when I was a young, bull-headed, and disobedient juvenile. You swayed me and placed me under your spell during my darkest hour. You imprisoned me and used me. I lived many years full of regret and despair. I couldn't break free. But with Baron's help, I did. You no longer have any power over me. You thought I was here to protect you. Quite the contrary. I am here to avenge my father's death." Omen turned and addressed the crowd.

"I am Omen, from the house of Blackstorm, son of Ravol, the former high mage. I speak for the grackles. We owe our lives to Baron from the house of Bron, the reigning high mage of Ailear. We are indebted to him for the guidance he gave that set us free from Calixta's oppression. We will forever be at his service."

A tremendous clattering arose from the grackles along with an uproarious burst from the crowd. Omen took flight and shouted, "Grackles, the time has come. The deed is done. You are free to go wherever you wish!"

The birds launched from their perches and shot into the air. The sky churned with a fluttering blackness. The grackle's joyous chatter was met with thunderous applause from below. They filtered off into every direction. In a matter of minutes, the skies were clear over Ansa—the grackles were gone.

Omen flew down, landed, and took a position near the mages. They were stunned. None of them had been aware that Baron had secretly helped Omen and the grackles break free from Calixta's spell.

Shouts and celebrations continued as the crowd watched on. Nobody was more overjoyed than Lizzy. All the worry and fear she had felt up to that moment vanished. She would never become Calixta's prisoner.

Baron nodded to the chief justice, who stood, silenced the crowd, and addressed Calixta.

"Calixta, from the house of Carlington, by your own confession, for using the forbidden dark arts to create a fertility potion, for using the forbidden dark arts to confine and endanger the lives of all those who dwell in Castlehill, and for the murder of the high mage of Ailear, Ravol, from the house of Blackstorm, you are hereby sentenced to life—confined to this place as a living reminder to all that good expels evil, that light repels darkness, and that love dispels hate. Your sentence is immediate. Do you have any final words?"

Calixta was completely constrained by the vines. She struggled to break free but soon realized that her efforts were futile, and she finally stopped resisting.

"Take me away. Curse me. Be done with me!" she seethed. "But I'm not the root of your problem. I'm not sorry for my actions. I've done my part. The rest will be revealed in time." Calixta fell silent and never spoke again.

Igree came forward, faced Calixta, spread his leathery wings, and began the chant.

Henceforth shall this mortal be
A Forever Tree for all to see
Roots pushed deep into the ground
Branches thrust upward, heaven bound
Eternal life is planted here
Bright and silver, year to year
May this soul search day by day
Why thus the price she had to pay
Alamah! Alamah!

Igree and Baron stepped back. The vines tightly embraced Calixta as she began her transformation. Her feet sank into the ground, growing roots that mingled with those of the vine. Her body became a trunk that rose skyward. Her skin turned into rough, gray bark. Branches stretched out, dividing and forking into glorious, perfectly shaped limbs. An abundance of buds emerged—popping open and revealing shiny, silvery leaves that flashed and danced in the light of the rising full moon.

The citizens of Ansa were transfixed at the sight. There wasn't a breath to be heard. Calixta was gone and a hypnotic, mesmerizing, towering silver tree now stood in the plaza. Those who gathered would never have imagined that it would turn out this way. They were in shock as they tried to absorb their disbelief and amazement.

Baron turned to Gretta and said, "Appear! Alamah!" She had been protecting the invisible book and it reappeared. Baron opened it and removed the page.

"This was our plan, Princess. We needed to capture Calixta and make sure that you were safe before letting you read the spell. Do you feel comfortable now? Will you read this? You are the only one who can restore Castlehill." Lizzy noticed that his voice was confident and insistent, but at the same time, it was soft and reassuring.

Lizzy was nervous, but she didn't feel reluctant. She felt the worst of her ordeal was over. She had come this far and knew what had to be done.

"I'll do it," she said quietly.

Baron handed Lizzy the page.

"Don't I need the next page too?" She asked. Although Baron had insisted there was a second part to read, Lizzy wasn't yet aware that there was just the one page.

"No," Baron assured her, "that's all you will need. The second page was just the ruse that we used to trick Calixta."

All eyes were on Lizzy as she made her way to the Ravenclaw Staff. She took a deep breath and found the courage to grasp it. She didn't feel a shock, which was a relief. She looked at the page and then glanced to Baron with a perplexed expression. She looked back down to the page, turned white, and began to tremble.

"What's wrong?" asked Baron.

"I..." Lizzy's voice faltered. "I...I can't read this. I don't know any of these words."

Baron felt dumb. Of course she wouldn't know how to read the archaic language. To her, it must look like gibberish. He was trying to sort out the best way to proceed when a voice called out from the tower window.

"Don't let her do it! Please...don't. She will kill them all!"

315

Expect the Unexpected

The woman's cry caught everyone's attention. At first, Baron suspected that an onlooker was being disrespectful, but when he realized that the voice came from the tower, he knew it wasn't a prank. The crowd had reacted with surprise as well. Castlehill had been off limits and secured for nearly ten years. It didn't seem possible that anyone could have managed to breach the castle and reach the tower.

The cry came again. "Please...don't let her read it. We are coming down. Please...wait!"

The woman disappeared from the window. The crowd stirred with curiosity. Soon two figures emerged from the portcullis. Most of the crowd had no idea who they were. But there were some—including Baron, Igree, and most of the mages—who recognized them immediately. Lizzy knew them by name. It was Aloris and Marten, the proprietors of the Hyssop and Sage. They hastily made their way to Baron.

"What do you want? What's the problem?" Baron asked the couple.

"She's not the princess!" Aloris insisted.

Baron was perplexed—as was everyone else. He was aware that Lizzy had been at the apothecary prior to being abducted, but even so, he was baffled as to how they could make such a claim.

"How would *you* know whether or not she's the princess?" asked Baron.

"I assure you, she's not," replied Marten.

"What evidence do you have?"

Aloris gazed upon the imposing silver tree, shivered, and took a deep breath.

"I can do this," she said under her breath. "She's no longer a threat."

The couple turned and faced the crowd. They slowly removed their pendants. As if on cue, the spectators drew a collective gasp. Aloris and Marten had faded. Standing in their places were Princess Corinna—the beloved *Darling of Ailear*—and Prince Bartlett. They were not stones; they were very much alive. Although ten years had passed, they were easily recognizable. Gasps, whispers, and questions reverberated through the crowd. A few onlookers rejoiced, but for the most part, the situation was so incomprehensible that nobody knew exactly how to react. There were some who thought that the curse might have already been broken, but when they looked to the fortress wall, they saw the familiar statues, including the figure of Queen Beatrice. The crowd began to reverently bow to the royal couple—many knelt, others cried tears of joy.

Baron was equally surprised, and so was Lizzy. She watched the transformation with amazement. She let her eyes fall to the pendant that Corinna was holding. Now that she knew it held some form of magic, she was even more suspicious of it. She felt certain that it was the same pendant that Gorva was wearing in Igree's portrait. Lizzy gave Baron a dumbfounded and questioning glance. He gently patted her reassuringly on the shoulder, but he didn't offer an explanation.

Baron bowed his head and said, "Your Highness, I'm at your service."

"Please...no. I mean...thank you," replied Corinna, "but it is we who are at *your* service. You have allowed us this opportunity to come forward."

Corinna raised her hand and silenced the assembly. "Good citizens of Ailear, I know this will come as a surprise. Prince Bartlett and I were spared from the curse. Many of you will know us as the proprietors of the Hyssop and Sage. These are pendants of deception and they provided our disguise." Corinna held them up for all to see and then handed them to Bartlett, who slipped them into his pocket.

"You were told that Gracella had taken our baby through the Tunnel of Stars to a safe place far away, but that was not true. My child never left the kingdom."

Rumblings rippled through the crowd. Even the mages, clerics, and politicians broke decorum and began talking with each other as they reacted to this revelation.

"My mother withheld her secret from me for years. She didn't tell me about the agreement until I was already expecting a child. As you can imagine, I was horrified and angry that she had promised my first-born child to Calixta. She assured me that she never planned on fulfilling her promise and took a risk, hoping that it wouldn't be required. She swore to me that it would never happen.

"An intricate plan was wrought and instigated. It was a plot to deceive everyone. Ten years ago today, a pink banner was unfurled from the tower. The citizens of the kingdom were the first to be deceived. For you see, I didn't give birth to a daughter. I gave birth to a son...a prince. He's the rightful heir to the throne. His name is Kreg."

The citizens reacted to the surprising news and it caused a multitude of thoughts to race through Lizzy's mind. "Kreg?" she thought. She had enjoyed meeting both Kreg and Keltan. She liked the boys, and she had admired Kreg's intricate carvings. But the boys had led her through the tunnel, which made her wonder if they had deliberately set her up to be captured. It also dawned on her that if Kreg is the prince, then she isn't the princess, and she wasn't born in Ailear. She had a family in Kansas. She had been right all along: this whole ordeal was a mistake.

Corinna went on to explain that a few months before the baby was born, Gorva died. The royal family had quietly acquired the Hyssop and Sage and built a secret tunnel that connected Castlehill to the apothecary. She and Bartlett started new lives as the proprietors. The pendants allowed them to live their lives incognito, and nobody ever made the connection. The tunnel allowed them direct access to Castlehill anytime they wanted to visit—or to escape.

Bartlett noticed that Corinna was trying to hold back her emotions. He took her hand, pulled her close, and continued the story on her behalf.

"The queen lied to Calixta about the child's whereabouts, and we braced ourselves for retaliation. As you might expect, nobody was prepared for the horrific curse that was about to befall Castlehill. On the day Calixta arrived, I took Corinna and Kreg and fled to the apothecary. Euna and Nelson disguised themselves to look like us so that Calixta would believe that we were inside the castle. We were gone and safely situated before she arrived."

This news put another piece of the puzzle in place for Lizzy. She had wondered about the two statues in the tower. She had believed what everyone else believed, that they were the royal couple, but now she realized they must be Euna and Nelson.

The moon was full, magnificent, and bright, but it failed to stop the blackness of night from devouring the remnants of twilight. The street lamps surrounding the plaza were inadequate to sufficiently illuminate the courtyard. Only a few of the stone statues were visible. Most of them had completely fallen into shadow. The orb on the Ravenclaw Staff emitted a swirling iridescence and was a reminder that time was running out. Igree conjured a gigantic ball of light and sent it skyward so that it floated high above the castle. It drenched the entire area with the soft, bluish light of dawn.

Baron approached the royal couple. "Is your son here? Will he restore Castlehill?"

Corinna hesitated before answering. She looked once more at the silver tree. The leaves appeared to shiver with excitement and the rustling sound they made seemed to applaud her resolve. She knew what must be done. Kreg was no longer in danger, but there would still be repercussions. A knot formed in her stomach.

"The boys are at home," she replied. "We forbid them to come; it was too dangerous. They don't know anything. They don't know the truth about who they are."

"We do now."

Corinna and Bartlett spun around and saw both Kreg and Keltan walking toward them. Corinna dropped to her knees and the boys ran into her arms.

"Please don't be angry," begged Kreg. "We couldn't resist the temptation to be here."

Corinna squeezed the boys tightly. "I'm not angry, but do you now understand why we didn't want you to be here?"

Both boys nodded. Kreg turned to Lizzy. "I'm really sorry that we took you to the tower. I didn't think anything bad would happen. I didn't know you were the one Calixta was looking for. I thought you were a novice mage."

Lizzy glanced at her red cloak. She realized that there was nothing about her that would make anyone in Ansa think any differently. "It's okay. I'm fine...and I'm also relieved. I kept trying to tell everyone that I *wasn't* a princess."

Even as she said it, Lizzy felt a twinge of disappointment. Her dad had often called her a princess. She liked to pretend to be a princess. Since arriving in Ailear she had almost convinced herself that she was a princess. She decided that being a real princess was far too much trouble and that she much preferred being a pretend princess, and from now on she would make sure she did just that.

"Would you like to go stand with McDoogle?" asked Baron.

Lizzy didn't hesitate. She looked at Baron, smiled from ear to ear, and ran to McDoogle.

He was so excited that he ran in circles until Lizzy knelt down and gave him a hug. He then licked her face and barked. "Why McDoo! You barked! I haven't heard you bark in days."

"Aye, Lass, it's purely ma nature. I'm glad I havenae forgotten how to do it."

"I understand, McDoo! Let's promise each other to be true to ourselves no matter what."

"Is that a promise that we have tae swear in blood?" asked McDoogle slyly.

"I think a regular promise is good enough. I think that a promise is a promise, no matter what." Lizzy looked at Gretta and gave her a wink. Molly was bouncing back and forth on her feet, trying to contain her excitement and praying she would not disrupt this historic moment by accidentally setting off one of her feathers.

Baron handed the page to Kreg. "Can you read this?" Kreg looked at the writing. It was familiar. Corinna and Bartlett had made sure both boys learned the ancient language. They were expected to help prepare medicines and many of the recipes used archaic words.

"I can," replied Kreg softly.

His head drooped. It was obvious that he was reluctant. Ansa was the only home he knew. He had seen the Ravenclaw Staff on many occasions. It was a familiar fixture in the Imperial Plaza and stood as a constant reminder of the oppressive curse that plagued the castle. He had a general idea of what was supposed to transpire, but he had never suspected that he would be required to play the leading role in the restoration.

He had just learned the truth about himself and his family. Now he was being thrust into the spotlight as the prince who must save the kingdom. Normally, he was extremely confident for his age. His courage in difficult situations rarely wavered. But this moment had taken him by surprise and he wasn't prepared for the pressure that was being put upon him.

Bartlett sensed his apprehension. "You've been charged with a huge responsibility. You didn't ask for it, nor do you deserve it. Unfortunately, you are the only one who can do this. For the sake of those who are innocently imprisoned here, I urge you to help them. You are likely to be the future king of Ailear. Your decision will undoubtedly make a big impact on how you will be perceived as a ruler someday."

Kreg knew his father was trying to be helpful, but the speech made him feel pressed even harder. He scanned the crowd. Everyone was looking at him. When he saw Lizzy, it dawned on him that she had faced her situation bravely, stepping away only because she couldn't read the words. Her courage bolstered him and gave him the fortitude to approach the staff. He overcame his fear and gripped the staff firmly. As he cautiously read the words, it began to vibrate and emit a dull humming sound. His voice was timid at first, but he gained confidence. Soon it resounded with a forceful authority that demanded obedience. When he finished reading, Kreg let go of the staff. The humming ceased, the light faded, the arcs disappeared, and the orb went dark. Everyone watched and waited, but nothing seemed to happen.

Kreg turned to Baron. "Do you think I made a mistake?"

"I'm confident that you didn't."

The entire plaza trembled with anticipation. Silence blanketed the crowd. The suspense was so thick that it appeared the world had stopped breathing. The tension was almost unbearable, but nobody said a word.

Suddenly the orb flickered and flashed. It exploded into a radiant and blinding light. Kreg and the others stepped away and shielded their eyes. There was a loud bang and the orb cracked, spewing bolts of energy in every direction. Each ray that was sent forth sought a target. Several arcs shot up to the fortress wall and connected with the statues. Some of them soared into the windows of the castle, enveloping everyone who was imprisoned there.

The spectacle dazzled the onlookers. It was more resplendent than a royal fireworks display. Everyone turned their attention to the statue of Queen Beatrice. Spine-chilling groans resounded from the statues as they started shedding their stone casings. Their glazed eyes began to clear and soon each statue was gasping for air. Queen Beatrice drew a breath and then sent forth a shriek that terrified the crowd. Her head turned from left to right, and then it nodded up and down. She bent her torso and rolled her shoulders. Soon her arms reached out and she stretched her fingers to their full extent. Then she crumpled to her knees.

Burris, the captain, along with the other guards, reacted to the transformation in a similar manner. With each breath, they regained strength. Several witnesses pointed to the two figures who appeared in the tower window. Beatrice stood, steadied herself, and looked down into the plaza. She was overcome with joy at the sight of Corinna. Her body was rejuvenated and her fortitude was restored. She entered the watchtower, descended the stairs, rushed to Corinna, and embraced her. Corinna did not reciprocate. Instead, she held her mother's shoulders and pushed her away. She managed to keep her at arm's length and coldly stared into her eyes. Bartlett pulled both boys back and guarded them.

Beatrice was perplexed. "My dearest Corinna, what's the matter? Are you not happy to see me?"

Corinna considered her options one last time before finally shouting, "Guards!" Almost instantly two guards appeared and took Beatrice into custody.

"What is this? What are you doing? Let me go!"

Bartlett reached into his coat pocket, produced a book, and gave it to Corinna. She held it up for all to see. Beatrice immediately recognized it and stiffened. "No! No, you can't have that! Give that to me!"

Corinna spiked back, "But I *do* have it...and I have *read* it...I've read *all* of it...many times! It's time for everyone to learn the truth about their queen."

Beatrice wailed in defiance and fought against the guards to no avail.

Corinna had discovered a depth of courage that she never knew she had—and began to speak with venomous authority. "This is my mother's *Book of Secrets*. I discovered it inside the castle when I was searching for answers. It reveals many things and answers many questions. Allow me to read to you just a few of the passages before I turn it over to the authorities. Corinna opened the book to one of the pages she had marked.

"On the 24th of Murth, 3318. My mother and Calixta were only fourteen years old. It was the last year of their primaries. Here's what my mother wrote:"

> *Once again Calixta was* primo perfecto *in the class. She's smart, but she's not that smart. I must find a way to get rid of her. She won't be princess for long; I will make sure of that! Someday, I will be queen.*

The crowd whistled and roared in disgust. Beatrice's anger had boiled to overflowing. She spat on the ground. "I will curse you if you read any more."

Corinna continued. "A year later, in 3319. The cousins were fifteen years old. They were frosh year students. On the 3rd of Eloindil, she wrote:"

> *I've done it. I've gotten rid of Aunt Oris. I used a large rock, but I managed to make it look like she tripped, fell, and dashed her head on the stone path. I tossed the rock over the edge of the cliff and watched it crash into the sea. Everyone is boohooing about it. Everyone but me!*

"In her next entry, she added:"

> *Uncle Cedric may be a king, but he's a pushover. He's wallowing in self-loathing and despair. That's perfect, and it's only been two days since I did away with her. I'm confident he will do anything to bring her back—if he wants to. I plan to make sure he wants to.*

"She continues documenting her diabolical scheme. Listen to this:"

> *I persuaded the king to keep Aunt Oris in one of the cold chambers in the bowels of Castlehill, where he would be the only one to have access to her. Last night, I managed to sneak into the forbidden vaults at the mage guild. The guards are exceptionally inept. Anyone could break in if they wanted to. I was able to smuggle out a book of resurrection spells and put it in the king's room. I have no doubt he will use it.*

Corinna thumbed to another page.

Today is a wonderful day! The birds are singing. Early this morning I sat under the old chester tree listening to the ruckus as the civic guards arrested the king. They found the book and evidence that he had killed two bats and cut the lips off of several toads. I wonder how they found out about it...(giggle).

"And this is what followed:"

I suspect there will be an inquiry and that both Calixta and I will be questioned. I must remember to be as kind and thoughtful as possible. The drangias in the garden are starting to bloom. The stench is toxic to my soul, but she loves them. I must make sure she notices them.

The crowd was furious to hear about Beatrice's vile deceptions. They were further sickened to learn that it all started at such an early age. They felt betrayed. They shouted obscenities at her. Some hurled rocks in her direction. The guards escorted her through the portcullis and lowered the gate. They were not about to let an angry mob get to her. However, they did not leave the area. Beatrice was forced to stay and listen.

"There are many more passages that are equally disgusting. They will be revealed in court. But there is one more that you must hear. It was written on the 16th of Musica in 3362. This was written just a few months before my son Kreg was born."

I visited Gorva today. For someone who is supposed to be the best physician in the city, she certainly never managed to do anything good for me. We had a cheerful meeting and we raised a glass to celebrate her many long years of great success. The poison worked fast. Gorva didn't suffer long. I took her pendant. When I removed it, I was shocked. She was a hideous sight to behold. I never knew her skin had scale blight. I do need one more pendant for Bartlett. I'm certain that Gracella has the skills to make one.

*Now I can purchase the old apothecary and make sure that
Corinna and the baby are safely tucked away, far from Calixta's nasty greed. Corinna won't suspect a thing, and a
tunnel is the perfect way for me to see my grandchild. I wish
I could do away with Bartlett, but I feel Corinna will need
him. When the time comes, I'm certain that Calixta will
come for me, but what can she do...really? Will she send her
little band of grackles to peck out my eyes?*

The diary entries that Corinna presented were absolutely appall-
ing. Lizzy was pleased to know that she had been right about Gorva's
pendant. But she found it hard to comprehend that anyone could be
so evil and manipulative. Beatrice's conniving personality made Lizzy
feel sorry for Calixta. She began to believe that the stories Calixta told
in the tower were most likely true. And if it is true that Calixta killed
Ravol in self defense, Lizzy might very well be the only one who knew
the truth—though she couldn't prove anything. Omen was a hero. How
could she possibly tell him that his father had drifted to the dark side?
One thing seemed to be certain: Beatrice is a murderess.

The chief justice stood and bellowed. "Take her away...confine the
queen. We've heard and seen enough! What we have learned is despicable,
but we also have reasons to rejoice. Calixta has been subdued, Castlehill
has been restored, and our prince has been revealed. Raise your voices and
celebrate. Today is his birthday. Hail, Prince Kreg!"

The multitude erupted in joyous celebration. Molly could no longer contain her excitement and three of her largest feathers shot into
the air where they exploded and sent a cloud of sparkles floating down
over the crowd. A cleric stood and shouted, "The prophecy has come
true! It was a boy...a king...and he was born on Midwinter's Eve, just
like the prophecy foretold."

*And on the eve of the glorious feast day, the moon in its
fullness will rise.*

It will usher the arrival of a king who will possess the light, and at whose command all darkness shall flee.

Hardened hearts will sing again, and the celestial queen will shower her grace o'er all the land.

Then shall it be, that the Forever Tree will burst forth with such a perpetual radiance that the eyes of those who gaze upon her shining leaves will be opened to the truth; that good expels evil, that light repels darkness, and love dispels hate.

Lizzy
Albright

CHAPTER THIRTY-NINE

Underneath the Forever Tree

Ansa had never experienced such an eventful Midwinter's Eve. Some of the citizens dispersed to their homes to prepare for the feast day, but many stayed near Imperial Plaza, celebrating and reveling because Ailear was starting a new chapter and the cloud of despair that had enveloped it for so long seemed to have lifted. A renewed spirit of hope wafted on the breeze.

Guards encircled the perimeter of the plaza to protect the royal family and the others: those who had assembled to recap the evening's events and to congratulate each other on the success of all that had transpired—even though it had not turned out as expected. Baron met with Corinna, Bartlett, and their sons, while Lizzy gathered with McDoogle, Igree, Omen, and the geese.

Igree heaved a great sigh. "I promised to keep you safe, Princess... and then I lost you. I'm sorry that you had to fend for yourself. I felt hopeless because the situation was out of my control. I couldn't be more proud of how you handled yourself."

Lizzy smiled and rolled her eyes. "Please, call me Lizzy. I'm done with the idea of being a princess and I'm begging all of you to set that notion aside too. I've come to realize that being a princess is far too much trouble."

Everyone laughed.

"And you didn't let me down. You all gave me courage. Each time I felt afraid, I reminded myself that you were looking out for me, that you had a plan, and that somehow I was going to be okay. It also taught me that I can manage some difficult things on my own—even when I'm afraid."

McDoogle chimed in. "Aye, Lass, ye are brave. I dinnea ken how ye've put up wi' aw the tomfoolery. Ye're braver than I am, that's for sure. I'll be bustin' me buttons bragging to everyone aboot ye once we get back home."

"Thank you, McDoo." Lizzy smiled and hugged McDoogle tightly. She didn't let go right away. "Home," she said. "I do want to go home."

Molly stepped forward and began spilling all of her thoughts. "I know you don't think you are a princess, but you will always be a princess to me. With your curly red hair and spattering of freckles... well, you're more adorable than any princess I could ever imagine. When I was a little gosling, I often imagined that I was a princess, but then I looked in the mirror and realized that a silly goose like me could never be a princess. It didn't matter. I decided that anyone could be a princess if she used her imagination. So I..."

"Molly!" Gertie interrupted and looked over the top of her eyeglasses. Molly got the message.

"Well...I'll just pretend that you are a princess and leave it at that. I will never forget you."

"And I will never forget you either, Molly. Every time I watch the fireworks on the Fourth of July, I'll be thinking of you and your exploding feathers."

"Oh, that's wonderful! That makes me so happy. What's the Fourth of July? Is that a feast day or something more like a traffle festival? Is there food? Because I love special occasions. You know...when you make special dishes..."

"Molly!" Gertie scolded.

Omen met with McDoogle and the two of them recounted their meeting in the alley. Omen apologized for his behavior. McDoogle understood the importance of keeping the plan secret and didn't hold a grudge against Omen—especially when he realized that Omen had essentially been looking after Lizzy on his behalf. The two of them discovered they were truly kindred spirits.

A voice called out, "Please tell them to let me pass." It was Gabby. Baron heard her plea and motioned for the guards to let her through.

Seeing Gabby reminded Lizzy of the adorable tiny houses at Fiddler's Cove. That was the morning that she learned a valuable truth—that not everything was as it seemed. In fact, it seemed to Lizzy that weeks had passed since she had breakfast in Gabby's parlor, but in reality, it had happened just three days ago.

Gabby approached Lizzy. "Princess, how can we ever repay you for sparing Castlehill from a horrible fate?"

"But I didn't save anyone, and I'm *not* a princess. It was Kreg who reversed the curse."

"But in a way, you *did* save us. If you were not here, Corinna would not have brought her son forward. She wouldn't have wanted to risk losing him. We all thought that you were the heir. We believed that you were the princess. That's why we brought you here. So in that regard, your part in this was just as important as Prince Kreg's. The fact that you were here allowed everything else to transpire the way it did. You are a true heroine."

Lizzy blushed. "Thank you, Gabby...and thank you for teaching me about traffles. They were wonderful."

"But not as wonderful as mine," Igree interjected, stretching out his leathery wings. "My traffles are prizewinning delights."

Lizzy laughed, "I'll have to leave that for you to decide. I liked them both. I can be stubborn when I want to, so don't make me choose one over the other."

The mood was relaxed and comfortable. The reminiscing brought great peace and reassurance to everyone. Baron and the royal family made their way over to the group and overheard the end of Lizzy's story, where she was recounting how frightened she was when she came face to face with Violet.

Baron chuckled. "I hope you are no longer afraid of bears."

Lizzy shook her head and smiled. "Not any more—at least not here in Ailear."

"The mages are all embarrassed and very sorry," said Baron. "We mistook you for someone you weren't. We owe you the kingdom for not being angry about it."

"Angry? How could I possibly be angry?" She looked at Kreg. "Why, this is the most *bang* thing that has ever happened to me. Nobody will believe me when I tell them...and I most certainly *will* tell them!"

"Bang!" said Kreg.

"Yeah, bang!" said Keltan.

Corinna and Bartlett approached Lizzy. Lizzy instinctively bowed. She raised her head and for the first time noticed Corinna's regal and stately appearance. Her countenance reflected the same caring and healing spirit that Lizzy had experienced at the Hyssop and Sage when Aloris had wrapped her ankle. Bartlett exuded the same warmth and compassion that Marten had displayed. It seemed logical. After all, they were one and the same.

Corinna and Bartlett both knelt down in front of Lizzy. Corinna took Lizzy's hand. "Baron has told us of your journey and your bravery. On behalf of the kingdom of Aliear, and the royal house of Carlington, we have a small token to give you in appreciation for your part in the restoration of Castlehill."

Bartlett joined his hand with the other two and said, "We could never repay you for your willingness to help. You were mistakenly put in great danger. We know you want to go home, but you can't go empty handed."

Bartlett reached into his pocket and produced the red pendant that Corinna had worn—and that Gorva had worn before her.

"I saw you admiring it when I was tending to your ankle," admitted Corinna.

Lizzy couldn't believe it. The pendant was a treasure beyond anything she could have ever hoped for.

"Keep it safe," urged Igree. "People won't recognize you when you are wearing it...unless you want them to."

Lizzy held the pendant and studied it. She noted small nuances and details that she had not seen before. She ran her finger over the notch where it appeared to have been chipped. It looked very old, which made her wonder how many others had worn it before Gorva. She imagined that it had a long history and that it would have many stories to tell, if only it could talk.

"It's beautiful! Thank you so much. I promise to take very good care of it." Lizzy wanted to put it on, but she knew it wasn't a toy and that it should only be used when necessary. She dropped the pendant into the pocket of her cloak and patted it to make sure that it was safely tucked inside. Her lack of sleep was quickly beginning to catch up with her. She tried to stifle a yawn and squinched her eyes.

"Oh goodness, look at you," said Gretta. "You're exhausted. You must get some rest. We'll put you in a nice comfortable bed at mage hall. First thing tomorrow we will have tea and traffles and see to it that you get back home. How does that sound?"

Lizzy eyes grew heavier. The thought of home warmed her heart. They were gathered not far from the Rose Wall that surrounded Barleywick Quarter. But there was still a crowd of Ansans reveling in the streets. Gretta knew it would be safest and quickest if she flew Lizzy to mage hall.

"Do you think you can manage to get on my back? I'll fly you there and we'll have you in bed quick as a snap."

The thought of flying with Gretta made Lizzy smile from ear to ear. She tried to answer with a nod, but when she did, her chin didn't come back up. She fell asleep on her feet. Baron managed to catch her just as she was beginning to slump to the ground.

"McDoogle, shall I fly you as well?" asked Omen. McDoogle almost accepted, but suddenly he remembered his vision at Future Falls and his promise to Lizzy that he would never fly on the back of a black bird no matter what.

"Nay, Mr. Omen, nay…but thank ye kindly. I cannae accept yer offer, but I dae appreciate yer consideration. I hae nae doot the lass and I will be wheechin away with Miss Gretta soon enough and I fear that's all ma nerves can stand."

"I hope we will meet again," said Omen.

"Aye," said McDoogle. "It would be a pleasure."

The feast moon was steadily trekking through the night sky and her moonbeams gently bathed Ailear with a lustrous glow. The sweet scent of stargrass wafted through the streets and filtered heavenward, carrying the fervent prayers of gratitude that had been offered to the guardian spirits of the celestial realm. The leaves on the Forever Tree quaked and glistened with silvery radiance. Many Ansans were captivated by it and found it difficult to look away. Omen flew up and perched on one of the higher branches. It was later said that he was heard praying, but others perceived that he was making peace with

Calixta—and perhaps laying his past to rest so that he might face the future with no regrets.

Lizzy was lost in a dream—walking through a vast field of orange jumping jacks with a colony of blue butterflies dancing about her head. Baron gently nestled her between Gretta's wings. He softly caressed her cheek with his paw.

Lizzy
Albright

CHAPTER FORTY

Not Everything Is as It Seems

Tap, tap, tap.

Tap, tap, tap.

Lizzy's sleep was interrupted by an annoying and persistent sound. She rolled over and pulled the covers up over her head. She wasn't ready to wake up. She suddenly sensed a faint, familiar smell.

Tap, tap, tap.

"The traffles must be ready," she thought.

"Woof!" McDoogle suddenly barked from the foot of the bed, which caused Lizzy to jolt upright.

"McDoo! You scared me! Is Gretta here? Is it time to go?"

Lizzy rubbed her eyes. "Where am I?" she wondered.

It took her a few seconds to realize that she was in bed—at Granny's house. She saw the wisps of snow that had drifted into each window pane. From what she could tell it was very wintery outside, and that meant it was a White Christmas—the first one she could remember. But then she realized that it was possible she was confused, and that it might not be Christmas at all.

She remained warmly nestled under Granny's quilt. She pulled it up under her chin and looked at the blocks, trying to remember their names—only this time, the blocks took on different meanings.

"Baron? Violet?" she asked, touching the Bear Paw block. It no longer seemed scary.

She found the Honey Bee block. "Queen Beatrice? Oh no!" she exclaimed with disdain, and quickly moved on to the others.

"Scottie Dog...that's you, McDoo!" she giggled. The quilt was bringing back memories, even though she knew those memories were just part of a dream. It had felt so real. Lizzy ran her finger over the triangular patches that chased each other around the border.

Tap, tap, tap.

"Flying geese? Oh, McDoo...It's Gretta! She must be here!" McDoogle wagged his tail and barked with excitement. Lizzy jumped out of bed. As soon as her feet hit the floor she felt a slight pain in her ankle.

"Ouch! That's odd," she thought. "I surely couldn't have injured my ankle if it was only a dream." The ache was nothing more than an annoyance, but she felt it just the same.

Lizzy rushed to the attic and McDoogle followed at her heels. She climbed the stairs and swung open the door. She expected the room to be filled with snow—but it wasn't. The windows were shut. The red cloak was hanging neatly on the hat rack where she had left it. "The pendant!" she thought. Lizzy reached into the pocket—but it was empty. She felt heartbroken.

She climbed on the cedar chest and used her palm to wipe frost from the window panes. Ice had built up on the outside so she wasn't able to see as clearly as she had hoped. Along the eave was a piece of gutter that had come loose. A gust of wind caught it and she heard the familiar...

Tap, tap, tap.

Tap, tap, tap.

"Gretta? Is that you?" Lizzy's hope faded when she saw the gutter clacking against the house. Her heart sank with disappointment.

She looked at McDoogle. "What about you, McDoo? Do you remember going with me through the Tunnel of Stars?"

"Woof," McDoogle reacted.

"Can you tell me anything? What do you remember?"

McDoogle danced around excitedly and let out another "Woof!"

"I mean, can you really tell me? You know...with people talk?"

"Woof, woof!" was all that Lizzy got in reply. She hopped down off the cedar chest and sat on the floor. McDoogle wriggled into her lap and licked her face.

"Elisabeth?" Granny called out from the bottom of the attic stairs. "Are you up there?"

"Yes," Lizzy replied dejectedly. "I'm here."

Granny entered the attic and saw Lizzy looking melancholy, cradling McDoogle, and rocking from side to side. "Why, what's the matter, child?"

"It's...well...I really don't want to talk about it. Nobody would believe me anyway."

"My dear Elisabeth! What would possibly make you think that? How about a little faith? Tell me all about it." Granny took a seat on the divan. Lizzy let out a sigh and bit her upper lip. If there were anyone who would believe her, it would be Granny. So she decided to give it a try.

"Well, a goose named Gretta came to the attic window and took McDoogle and me on a ride through the Tunnel of Stars. People had tricycles that flew...only they were much bigger. There was a witch who had cursed everyone in the castle and they thought I was their princess. They believed that I was the only one who could fix their problem.

"The witch had a huge flock of really mean grackles. There was also a queen who was the witch's cousin. The queen was really bad...a horrible person...but nobody knew that at first. As it turned out, the witch wasn't as bad as everyone thought she was. As a matter of fact, nobody knew that...except me...because she captured me."

"She captured you?" Granny asked excitedly. "That must have been *very* frightening!"

"It was! She captured me in the castle tower!" Lizzy became more and more animated as she went on.

"Baron—he's a bear—tricked the witch and she was tangled by a vine. Then Igree—he's half kangaroo and half bat—turned her into a silver tree."

"Half kangaroo?...And half bat?"

"Yes, he was...he *really* was! And he wore goggles!"

"Oh my! That must have been a sight to see!"

"He was so bang! That means cool. And he had a funny way of making tea! Then there was Molly. She's another goose who liked to talk so much that it was hard for her to stop. She had feathers that shot up into the air and exploded. They were like bottle rockets that we get at the firework stand."

"Exploding feathers? Why, I never knew there was such a thing!"

"Me neither! But listen to this: the *real* princess gave me a magical red pendant. If I wear it, people won't know who I am. But I think I lost it. I put it in the pocket of the red cloak you gave me and now it's not there."

"Well, maybe we can look for it after while," suggested Granny. "But first, how about we go down for breakfast? We've warmed up

Pearline's Southwestern Surprise breakfast casserole and Doug is helping Nellie make those famous homemade buttermilk waffles."

Waffles on Christmas was a McHale family tradition. Doug loved using the waffle iron and he had become an expert at making perfect, toasty, golden-brown waffles.

Lizzy sniffed the air. "That's it!" she cried. "I knew that smell was familiar. Waffles smell like traffles!"

Granny raised her eyebrows and then gestured for Lizzy to go first. Lizzy descended the attic stairs, stopped at the banister, and looked down into the stairwell. She was elated to see that the globe on the pedestal was working. From now on she would imagine that it was a magical orb that emitted colorful swirling energy.

Granny shut the attic door. "What did you say? Traffles? What are traffles?" As they made their way to the ground floor, Lizzy explained all about traffles and Granny listened patiently.

They walked past the solarium and Lizzy froze in the doorway. The aluminum Christmas tree had caught her eye. It was reflecting the colorful lights of the rotating wheel. The sight of it reminded her of moonbeams shimmering on the Forever Tree. She decided not to mention anything about that to Granny—at least for now.

As they walked past the dining room, Mrs. Albright called out, "Merry Christmas, Lizzy!" Everyone shared in the Christmas greeting.

"You slept in a bit later than we expected," said Mr. Albright. "It's Christmas Day! Have you looked outside? We've got a white Christmas!"

"I saw it from the attic," replied Lizzy. "It's beautiful."

"You're usually the first one up on Christmas morning. Did you have visions of sugar plums dancing in your head?" asked Mr. Albright.

Her father knew her very well. She was always the first one up on Christmas Day—not only because she was eager to open her presents, but because December twenty-fifth was also Granny's birthday, and Lizzy knew what it was like to have a birthday on a holiday. For the past several years, Lizzy would wake up early, get orange juice from the kitchen, and take it to Granny in her room. Lizzy would also hide Granny's birthday present under her bed the night before so that she could give it to her first thing the next morning. Of course, Granny knew the gift was there, but she always acted surprised when Lizzy presented it to her.

"Oh, Granny! It's your birthday...Happy birthday! I'm sorry I didn't wake you—and that you had to come up and find me." Lizzy was disappointed in herself.

Granny gave a warm chuckle, "Elisabeth, I wasn't concerned about my birthday. Having the family here is the best gift I could ever receive. It's a birthday present *and* a Christmas gift rolled into one. I noticed that you hadn't come down yet, so I thought I would go up and check on you. I'm glad I did. I liked hearing about your adventure." Granny gave Lizzy a wink, which also made her feel better. Lizzy ran to the kitchen and poured a glass of orange juice. She could at least keep *that* part of her tradition alive.

"Happy birthday, Esther," said Mr. Albright. Everyone followed his example and offered an array of birthday greetings.

Nellie brought in two more plates of waffles that were piping hot, drenched in maple syrup, and swimming in melted butter. Lizzy decided that from now on she would call them traffles—even if nobody ever understood why.

"Hurry up, Lizzy. We want to open our presents," insisted Doug.

"Yeah," said Allen. "I wanna see the look on your face when you open the jigsaw puzzle."

341

"Allen!" Lizzy shouted. "Mom! Dad! Make him stop telling what all the presents are!"

Mr. Albright caught Allen's eye and scolded him with a stern *don't-do-that-again* expression.

Lizzy left the table and ran to Granny's room to retrieve the gift from under the bed. She returned beaming with pride. With the help of her mother, she had picked out a gold locket and chain. She asked the jeweler to engrave an elaborate "E" on the front. It was something she and Granny shared in namesake. Inside were two pictures, one of Granny and one of Lizzy.

"Oh, Elisabeth, it's wonderful! I'll treasure it forever!" Lizzy fastened it around Granny's neck. As she did, she was reminded of the photo in Igree's parlor, with Gorva wearing the red pendant necklace.

After breakfast the family retreated to the parlor and the excitement of opening all the presents began. They ate toffees, butterscotch, and cinnamon disks. Lizzy even found the bowl of ribbon candy. Allen had been correct on a few of his guesses, but there were several that he had failed to get right. They all teased him, but he was good-natured and took their jesting in stride.

"It's been a wonderful morning," admitted Granny. "I'm so glad we can share these memories together." The kids played with their gifts and they all enjoyed reminiscing about past Christmases.

Granny interrupted. "Lizzy, I think there's a small gift hiding back behind the tree stand that must have been overlooked."

Lizzy looked under the tree. "I don't see it."

"From my angle there seems to be a small package wrapped in gold and tied with a red ribbon."

Lizzy crawled under the tree and sure enough it was there. She looked at the label. It read "To Elisabeth." This gift didn't have to say who it was from. Granny was the only one who called her Elisabeth.

"Well, go on. Open it!" urged Granny.

Lizzy carefully untied the bow and removed the wrapping, revealing a small white cardboard box with a lid. Inside was a black velvet jewelry box. Lizzy opened it. Her eyes widened. She was astonished. Lying on a tiny white satin pillow was a red stone pendant necklace. It seemed to be an antique. It had a small chip where a piece had broken off. The chain was slightly tarnished. Lizzy was at a loss for words.

"That pendant has been in the McHale family for years. I understand it was brought over from Scotland when the McHales immigrated, but I can't confirm it. I know it must be very old. I think that's a Celtic design on the bail. It was given to me by my mother when I turned eighteen. I thought I had lost it, but after you went to bed last night, I went back to the attic to tidy up. I saw the red cloak and something told me to check the pockets. This was tucked inside and must have been there for years. I'm not even sure how it got there."

Lizzy was still silent and spellbound. It seemed impossible. She was baffled as to how she could *dream* of such a thing if she had never *seen* such a thing?

"Maggie, my first inclination when I found it last night was to give it to you. But if you don't mind, it somehow feels right that I give it to Lizzy. I hope that doesn't bother you."

"Why no, Mother. I think that's a lovely gesture and she will treasure it forever," replied Mrs. Albright. "What do you think about it, Lizzy?"

Lizzy looked at Granny. "I don't know what to say except thank you. It's the most beautiful thing I've ever seen. I'm just really surprised, that's all."

"The best gifts are almost always surprises," replied Granny.

"I know," said Lizzy. "But it's an extra surprise because it's exactly like the pendant in my dream."

Mr. and Mrs. Albright didn't know anything about a dream, but they were curious, and therefore continued to listen with great interest.

"When I was there, I kept telling myself that it was just a dream. It helped me to manage the times when I was reluctant or afraid, but most of the time it felt wonderful. I guess I really wanted it to be real. Now that I'm back, I know it was only a dream. I'm just not sure how I could have possibly dreamed about this pendant."

"My dearest Elisabeth," Granny said firmly, "I would hope that by now you have learned that things are not always as they seem!" Granny gave her a wink.

Lizzy blinked her eyes. She couldn't believe that Granny had said those words. She paused for a moment and then bolted out of the parlor. She ran past the globe and took the stairs two at a time. McDoogle ran after her—barking the entire way.

She flew up the attic steps, raced across the room, and climbed on top of the cedar chest. She was determined to see outside. She attempted to open the window—but the latch wouldn't budge.

She said to herself, "It's not stuck. It will open."

She took a breath, closed her eyes, and tried it again.

The biting winter air rushed through the opening—catching Lizzy by surprise and causing her to shiver. She peered onto the overhang that was just below the attic window. Her heart leapt and she gasped.

"McDoogle, come look!"

McDoogle jumped up onto the cedar chest, raised up on to the window sill, and barked.

Lizzy pulled him close and giggled.

"I knew it!"

They both gazed in wonderment at the set of goose tracks that were imprinted in the snow.

THE END

GLOSSARY
& SCOTTISH BROGUE

GLOSSARY

bail	Device, usually metal, that attaches to a stone pendant to accommodate the chain
cacophony	Chaotic indiscernible mixture of sounds
cantilevered	Projecting out and over
cloistered	Closed in, sheltered
coalesced	Assembled together
coiffure	Fancy hairdo
effervescence	Bubbly, lively, appealing personality
escarpment	Long cliff or steep slope rising up from the surrounding area
gobsmacked	Surprised, shocked, speechless
indomitable	Impossible to subdue or overcome
iridescent	Luminous rainbow of color
lintel	Horizontal support above a door
luminescence	Glow or emission of light
magusology	Study of magic
modus operandi	One's particular way of doing things
nom de guerre	Fake name, an alias (French, pronounced nam di ger)
niggled	Persistently bothered
pediment	Triangular section that forms the gable of a roof
petits fours	Small, frosted, bite-sized cakes (French, pronounced pe-te-for)
portcullis	Iron grate that covers a gate, typically a castle gate
primo perfecto	Top of the class
rampart	Protective walkway on top of a fortress wall

repose	State of rest
sentinel	Guard, watchman
telepathy	Communication without speaking, as in reading someone's thoughts
tenacious	Never giving up
tenebrious	Dark and gloomy
therianthropy	Ability to change shape, like a werewolf
tomfoolery	Foolish behavior

SCOTTISH BROGUE

aye	Yes
bùrn	Small river or stream
drookit	Drenched; soaked
dinnae ken hoo	Don't know how
fou o'	Full of
git ye oot	Get you out
haunless	Awkward, clumsy, incompetent
hing on	Hang on
ken	Know
loch	Lake
ma	My
masel	Myself
michty me	Goodness me
mingin	Smelly
ony mair	Anymore
rin awa	Run away
tae	To

TOPICS FOR DISCUSSION

Spoiler Alert!

**This section contains information that readers might
not want to know prior to finishing the novel.**

The Sixties The Kansas portion of this story is set in 1964. For
older readers, those references are purposefully nostalgic. For younger
readers they provide a snapshot into the past. If you are an older reader
who lived during the sixties, what aspects of the story were you able to
relate to? Did other things come to mind that were not mentioned? If
you are a younger reader, what did you learn about the sixties? What
surprised you about how life must have been back then? This is a great
cross-generational topic for discussion.

Foreshadowing Make a list of things from Lizzy's life in Kansas
that similarly appeared in her adventure. Are there any characters from
Kansas that were represented in some way in the kingdom of Ailear?

Colors There are many references to color throughout the book.
What single color is most referenced in the story?

There are times in the story when colors shift and change. How many
instances can you find where this happened? How are those things
alike? How are they different? What underlying message might
changing color represent?

The Forever Tree The Forever Tree can be a topic of discussion
for several reasons. Some of these may be obvious, and others may require deeper examination in order to glean additional insight. Discuss
the Forever Tree and the various aspects about it that come to mind.

Lizzy's Transfiguration   Describe Lizzy when we first meet her. What lessons does she learn and how do they change her? How does she overcome obstacles and how does she manage her fears? How does Lizzy change as the story progresses—both mentally and physically?

How Did You See It?   The book is riddled with visual descriptions in an attempt to captivate the imagination of the reader. Discuss the visual imagery in the book. Here are a few suggestions: Lizzy's bedroom; the outside Christmas display; Granny's mansion; the attic and Lizzy's leap of faith; Fergus and the wardrobe; the "style" of life in Ansa; Fiddler's Cove; Valendale Forest; Deep Glen; Future Falls; the castle tunnel; Sourbelly Sink; and Calixta arrives to curse Castlehill.

Justice For All   A global theme throughout the book is choices/actions and their consequences. This could be as simple as Lizzy's brothers playing a prank or a lifetime of deception and deceit. Discuss various choices/actions and the repercussions that came about as a result of those choices/actions. In each situation, did justice prevail?

Reality vs. Fantasy   Some things must be left up to the reader to decide. Did Lizzy have a dream or did she really go on an adventure? Discuss both options. What is your personal conclusion?

Ailear and Ansa   Both of these names were not casually selected. Are you able to determine why?

Granny's 1930 Sampler Quilt Not all of the blocks in Granny's 1930 Sampler Quilt are featured in this story. Even so, study the reference chart and see how many can you find that were included in the story. Some are obvious—and some are subtle.

The concept for this novel came about from Kat Bowser's idea that the names of traditional quilt blocks could ignite the imagination of a child. The sampler quilt in our story was designed by Ricky Tims. In addition, Ricky designed all of the vintage fabrics used to make the quilt. The fabrics (printed by Benartex) are available for purchase as are a pattern book and a kit to make the quilt. The quilt (and story) is intended to inspire a new generation to learn about quilts. Learn more about the quilt and other related items at www.lizzyalbright.com.

Lizzy's Ancestry and the McHale Mansion There is history to be learned regarding the Civil War, the rise of the railroads, the discovery of oil, and the addition of new states as the United States grew. Learn about the development of towns and cities due to the Westward Expansion. The Great Depression is a worthwhile topic to explore as well.

Inside the McHale Mansion are paintings by Sir Edwin Henry Landseer, china with images of paintings by Currier and Ives, and Chippendale furniture. Consider researching these subjects. Fun fact: The china described for Christmas Eve dinner really exists.

Traditions There are a few traditions that appear in the story. Are there any you were not familiar with? Are there any that you might consider adopting for yourself?

Fill in the Blanks

1. If Kreg and Keltan were not supposed to know about the small passageway that led from the hideout to the main tunnel, what do you think transpired at the Hyssop and Sage when the boys returned—and Lizzy was missing?

2. If the real heir, the infant Kreg, never left Ailear, why was the mage council so dedicated in their search to find the princess in Overland—beyond the Tunnel of Stars?

3. Kreg and Keltan are surely getting an education. The reader could assume it's not at the mage hall since they don't recognize Lizzy. What are the other options?

4. Why did Gretta select Lizzy out of all the other possibilities in Overland Park?

5. Have fun discussing the pendant in both Ailear and Cordelia. Did it really make the journey? Is it really magic?

6. Gracella did not fly through the Tunnel of Stars, so what do you suppose was her "mission" immediately after Corinna had her baby?